Praise for Gene Wolfe ar

"Gene Wolfe is as good a writer as there i
a musical contemporary attempting to te
Mozart."

—*Chicago Sun-Times*

"Sentence by sentence, Mr. Wolfe writes as well as anyone in science fiction today."

—*The New York Times*

"**Most Underrated Science Fiction Writer**: *The Book of the New Sun*, a tetralogy of couth, intelligence, and suavity that is also written in VistaVision and Dolby sound. Imagine a *Star Wars*–style space opera penned by G. K. Chesterton in the throes of a religious conversion. Wolfe has continued in full diapason ever since, and a crossover success is long overdue."

—*American Heritage*

"For anyone who loves a complex science fiction that reads like the best fantasy, or just a good adventure story, Gene Wolfe is a gift to be treasured."

—*SF Site*

"The stage is set for what Wolfe does best: an adventure occupying hundreds of pages quite compellingly, thanks to sea and land monsters, androids, a beautiful sea siren, and the shadowy natives of Blue. Despite his yarn's vast, sometimes confusing scope, Wolfe never sacrifices the telling intimate detail. Highly recommended."

—*Booklist*

"As always, Wolfe's prose is masterful and his main characters are well developed."

—*Publishers Weekly*

"The best novel Wolfe has written in over a decade, and the opening part of possibly the finest work he has ever undertaken."

—*Locus*

"Disturbingly fascinating."

—*SF Age*

"Gene Wolfe, it is easy to infer, is one of literature's gentle giants. He has always got something interesting to say, and a fatherly way of saying it, and the stories well up from inside a house-large heart, or so it seems. . . .

"Quite apart from being a beautiful, compelling read, which deals with the challenge of writing itself, *On Blue's Waters* is a fixed stare at the complexities of apostlehood."

—*Interzone*

By Gene Wolfe from Tom Doherty Associates

The Book of the New Sun

Shadow & Claw

(comprising *The Shadow of the Torturer* and *The Claw of the Conciliator*)

Sword & Citadel

(comprising *The Sword of the Lictor* and *The Citadel of the Autarch*)

The Book of the Long Sun

Litany of the Long Sun

(comprising *Nightside of the Long Sun* and *Lake of the Long Sun*)

Epiphany of the Long Sun*

(comprising *Caldé of the Long Sun* and *Exodus from the Long Sun*)

The Book of the Short Sun

On Blue's Waters

In Green's Jungles

*Return of the Whorl**

Novels

The Fifth Head of Cerberus

The Devil in a Forest

Peace

Free Live Free

The Urth of the New Sun

Soldier of the Mist

Soldier of Arete

There Are Doors

Castleview

Pandora by Holly Hollander

Novellas

The Death of Doctor Island

Seven American Nights

Collections

Endangered Species

Storeys from the Old Hotel

Castle of Days

The Island of Doctor Death and Other Stories and Other Stories

Strange Travelers

*forthcoming

On Blue's Waters

VOLUME ONE OF THE
BOOK OF THE SHORT SUN

Gene Wolfe

TOR®

A Tom Doherty Associates Book
NEW YORK

This is a work of fiction. All the characters and events portrayed in this novel are either fictitious or are used fictitiously.

ON BLUE'S WATERS

This book is printed on acid-free paper.

Edited by David G. Hartwell

A Tor Book
Published by Tom Doherty Associates, LLC
175 Fifth Avenue
New York, NY 10010

www.tor.com

Tor® is a registered trademark of Tom Doherty Associates, LLC.

Design by Lisa Pifher

Library of Congress Cataloging-in-Publication Data

Wolfe, Gene.
On Blue's water's / Gene Wolfe.
p. cm.—(Volume one of the Book of the short sun)
ISBN 0-312-86614-3 (hc)
ISBN 0-312-87257-7 (pbk)
ISBN 978-0-312-87257-1
I. Title. II. Series: Wolfe, Gene. Book of the short sun ; v. 1.
PS3573.O524O46 1999
813'.54—dc21 99-26659
CIP

Printed in the United States of America

P1

Respectfully dedicated to
Roy and Matt

Proper Names in the Text

Many of the persons and places mentioned in this book first appeared in *The Book of the Long Sun,* to which the reader is referred. In the following list, the most significant names are given in CAPITALS, less significant names in lower case.

Alubukhara, a concubine.
Auk, a Vironese burglar.
BABBIE, a tame hus.
Bahar, one of the RAJAN's ministers.
Barsat, a woodcutter.
Beled, a coastal town on Blue settled by people from Trivigaunte.
Blazingstar, a New Vironese merchant.
Blood, a crime lord, now dead.
BLUE, the better of the two habitable planets of the SHORT SUN System.
Book of Silk, HORN and NETTLE's great literary work, also called *The Book of the Long Sun.*
Brother, a small boy living with his sister in a forest northwest of GAON.
Bush, a tavern in PAJAROCU.
Chandi, a concubine.
Chenille, the woman who accompanied *Auk* to GREEN.
Choora, a long, straight, single-edged knife favored by the RAJAN.
Chota, a nickname given EVENSONG by her fellow concubines.
Trooper *Darjan,* a Gaonese boy.
Dorp, a coastal town.
Echidna, a major goddess, the mother of the gods of the LONG SUN WHORL.
Eschar, a New Vironese merchant.
EVENSONG, the concubine given the RAJAN OF GAON by the MAN OF HAN.

Gadwall, a New Vironese smith.
GAON, a troubled inland town on BLUE.
Geier, one of travelers assembled in PAJAROCU.
Gelada, a convict murdered by *Auk* long ago.
GREEN, the worse of the habitable planets of the SHORT SUN System.
Gyrfalcon, a New Vironese merchant.
Corporal *Hammerstone,* a soldier in the army of VIRON.
HAN, a populous town south of GAON.
HARI MAU, the citizen who brought the RAJAN to GAON.
He-bring-skin, a citizen of PAJAROCU.
He-hold-fire, the captain of PAJAROCU's lander.
He-pen-sheep, a hunter.
He-sing-spell, one of *He-hold-fire's* subordinates.
He-take-bow, one of *He-hold-fire's* subordinates.
Hephaestus, a minor god of the LONG SUN WHORL.
Hide, one of HORN's twin sons.
Hierax, a major god of the LONG SUN WHORL, the god of death.
Hoof, one of HORN's twin sons.
Hoop, one of the RAJAN's scribes.
Aunt *Hop,* one of NETTLE's sisters.
HORN, a New Vironese paper-maker, the protagonist.
Hyacinth, SILK's beautiful wife.
Jahlee, an inhuma rescued by the RAJAN and EVENSONG.
Kilhari, a hunter of GAON.
KRAIT, the inhumu adopted by HORN.
Kypris, the goddess of love in the LONG SUN WHORL.
Lake Limna, a large lake south of VIRON.
Lal, a small boy of GAON, *Mehman's* grandson.
LIZARD, an island north of NEW VIRON, the site of HORN's mill.
LONG SUN WHORL, the interior of the WHORL.
Mahawat, the RAJAN's elephant driver.
Main, the eastern continent.
Mamelta, the sleeper rescued by SILK, now dead.

MAN OF HAN, the ruler of HAN.
Maytera *MARBLE*, the former sibyl who accompanied the colonists to BLUE and resumed her vocation there, a chem.
MARROW, a New Vironese merchant.
Mehman, the RAJAN's head gardener.
General *Mint*, the heroine of VIRON's revolution, also known as Maytera Mint.
Molybdenum, a name assumed by Maytera MARBLE.
Mota, a citizen of GAON.
The *Mother*, a monstrous sea-goddess of BLUE.
Moti, a concubine.
MUCOR, a young woman possessing paranormal powers.
NADI, a river flowing past GAON.
Namak, an officer in the horde of GAON.
Nauvan, an advocate.
NEIGHBORS, BLUE's sentient native race.
NETTLE, HORN's wife.
NEW VIRON, the town on BLUE founded by colonists from VIRON.
Olivine, a young chem of VIRON.
OREB, a tame night chough.
OUTSIDER, the only god trusted by SILK.
PAJAROCU, a phantom town on BLUE's western continent.
Pas, a major god, the father of the gods in the LONG SUN WHORL.
Pehla, the RAJAN's principal concubine.
Pig, a mercenary of the LONG SUN WHORL.
Patera *Pike*, Patera SILK's predecessor.
Quadrifons, an aspect of the OUTSIDER in the LONG SUN WHORL.
Patera *Quetzal*, the inhumu who became Prolocutor of VIRON.
The *RAJAN OF GAON*, the narrator.
Rajya Mantri, the RAJAN's principal minister.
Ram, a citizen of GAON.
The *Rani*, the ruler of *Trivigaunte*.
Patera *Remora*, the head of the Chapter in NEW VIRON.

Maytera *Rose,* an elderly sibyl, now dead.

Roti, a citizen of GAON.

General *Saba,* an officer in the horde of *Trivigaunte.*

Sciathan, the Flier who accompanied SILK, HORN, and others to Mainframe.

Scleroderma, a friend of Maytera MARBLE's, now dead.

Scylla, a major goddess of the LONG SUN WHORL, the patroness of VIRON.

SEAWRACK, a one-armed maiden.

Shadelow, HORN's name for the western continent.

She-pick-berry, He-pen-sheep's wife.

SHORT SUN, the star orbited by the *WHORL.*

Patera *SILK,* the caldé of Viron at the time the colonists boarded their landers, also called Caldé SILK.

SINEW, HORN and NETTLE's eldest son.

Sister, a small girl living with her brother in a forest northwest of GAON.

Generalissimo *Siyuf,* the commander of the *Rani's* horde.

Skany, an inland town some distance from GAON.

Somvar, an advocate.

Captain *Strik,* a master mariner of *Dorp.*

Sun Street, a wide diagonal avenue in VIRON.

Tail, the southern end of LIZARD Island.

Tamarind, a fishmonger's widow.

Tartaros, a major god of the LONG SUN WHORL, the god of darkness and commerce, and the patron of thieves.

Thelxiepeia, a major goddess of the LONG SUN WHORL, the goddess of learning, trickery, and magic.

Three Rivers, an inland town near NEW VIRON.

Tor, a rocky peak on LIZARD Island.

Trivigaunte, a desert city well south of VIRON.

Toter, Strik's son.

Tuz, one of the travelers assembled in PAJAROCU.

Urbasecundus, a foreign town not far from NEW VIRON.

Vanished Gods, the gods of the NEIGHBORS.

Vanished People, the NEIGHBORS.

VIRON, the city of the LONG SUN WHORL in which SILK, HORN, NETTLE, and many others were born, also called *Old Viron*.

Vulpes, an advocate of the LONG SUN WHORL.

West Foot, the westernmost peninsula of LIZARD Island.

The WHORL, the generation ship from which the colonists came.

Wichote, a riverine village on BLUE's eastern continent.

Captain *WIJZER*, a master mariner of *Dorp*.

Yksin, the traveler who robbed and deserted SINEW.

Zeehra, the daughter of the RAJAN's head gardener.

To Every Town:

Like you we left friends and family and the light of the Long Sun for this new whorl we share with you. We would greet our brothers at home if we could.

We have long wished to do this. Is it not so for you?

He-hold-fire, a man of our town, has labored many seasons where our lander lifts high its head above our trees. The gray man speaks to He-hold-fire and to us, and it is his word that he will fly once again.

Soon he will rise upon fire and fly like the eagle.

We might clasp it to our bellies. That is not the way of hunters, and there are many beds of hide. Send a man to come with us. Send a woman, if it is your custom.

One alone from each town of this new whorl, whether he or she.

With us the one you send will return to our old home among the stars.

Send soon. Send one only. We will not delay.

Speak our word to others.

The Men Of
PAJAROCU

On Blue's Waters

1

Horn's Book

It is worthless, this old pen case I brought from Viron. It is nothing. You might go around the market all day and never find a single spirit who would trade you a fresh egg for it. Yet it holds . . .

Enough.

Yes, enough. I am sick of fancies.

At present it holds two quills, for I have taken the third one out. Two were in it when I found it in the ashes of our shop. The third, with which I am writing, was dropped by Oreb not so long ago. I picked it up, put it in this pen case, and forgot both Oreb and his feather.

It also holds a knife for pointing pens and the small bottle of black ink (more than half full) into which I dip mine. See how much darker my writing has become.

It is facts I need—facts I starve for. To Green with fancies!

My name is Horn.

This is such a pen case as students use in Viron, the city in which I was born, and no doubt in many others—a case of black leather glued over pressboard; it has a brass hinge with a steel spring, and a little brass clamp to keep it shut. We sold them in our shop and asked six cardbits; but my father would accept four if the purchaser bargained awhile, and such purchasers always did.

Three, if they bought something else, a quire of writing paper, say.

The leather is badly scuffed. More facts later, when I have more time. Rajya Mantri wants to lecture me.

★

★ ★

Reviewing what I wrote yesterday, I see that I have begun without plan or foresight, and in fact without the least notion of what I was trying to do or why I was trying to do it. That is how I have begun everything in life. Perhaps I need to begin before I can think clearly about the task. The chief thing is to begin, after all—after which the chief thing is to finish. I have finished worse than I began, for the most part.

It is all in the pen case. You have to take out the ink and string it together into the right shapes. That is all.

If I had not picked up this old pen case where my father's shop once stood, it is possible that I might still be searching for Silk.

For the phantom who has eluded me on three whorls.

Silk may be here on Blue already, after all. I have dispatched letters to Han and some other towns, and we will see. It is convenient, I find, to have messengers at one's beck and call.

So I am searching here, although I am the only person here in Gaon who could not tell you where to find him. Searching does not necessarily imply movement. Thinking it does, or rather assuming it without thought, may have been my first and worst mistake.

Thus I continue to search, true to my oath. I question travelers, and I write new letters subtracting some facts and adding others, composing flatteries and threats I hope will bring this town and that to my assistance; no doubt my scribe thinks I am penning another such letter at this moment, a letter that he, poor fellow, will have to copy out with broad, fair flourishes upon sheepskins scraped thin.

We need a paper mill here, and it is the only thing that I am competent to do.

I wish Oreb were here.

Now that I know what I mean to do, I can begin. But not at the beginning. To begin at the beginning would consume far too much time and paper, to say nothing of ink. I am going to begin, when I do, just a day or two before the moment at which I put to sea in the sloop.

Tomorrow then, when I have had time to decide how best to tell the convoluted tale of my long, vain search for Patera Silk—for Silk my ideal, who was the augur of our manteion in the Sun Street Quarter of Our Sacred City of Viron in the belly of the *Whorl.*

When I was young.

★

★ ★

The mainshaft had split—I remember that. I was taking it out of the journals when one of the twins ran in. I believe it was Hide. "A boat's coming! A big boat's coming!"

I told him that they probably wanted to buy a few bales, and that his mother could sell it to them as well as I could.

"Sinew's here, too."

Just to get rid of Hide, I told him to tell his mother about it. When he had gone, I got my needler from its hiding place and stuck it in my waistband under my greasy tunic.

Sinew was stamping up and down the beach, lovely shells of purple, rose, and purest white snapping beneath his boots. He looked surly when he saw me, so I told him to bring the good telescope out of the sloop. He would have defied me if he had possessed the courage. For half a minute we stood eye to eye; then he turned and went. I thought he was leaving, that he would put out for the mainland in his coracle and stay there for a week or a month, which to tell the truth I wanted much more than my telescope.

The boat they came in was indeed large. I know I counted at least a dozen sails. It carried a couple of jibs, three sails on each of its big masts, and staysails. I had never seen a boat big enough to set staysails between its masts before, so I am sure of those.

Sinew came back with the telescope. I asked whether he wanted the first look, and he sneered at me. It was always a mistake to try to treat him with any courtesy in those days, and I could have kicked myself for it. I put the telescope to my eye, wondering what Sinew was doing the second I could no longer watch him.

It was a good instrument, made in Dorp they said, where they are good sailors and grind good lenses. (We were good sailors in New Viron, too—or thought we were—but did not grind lenses at all.) Through it I could see the faces at the gunwale, all looking toward Tail Bay, for which their boat was plainly making. Its hull was white above and black below—I recall that, too. Here on Blue the sea is silver where it is not so dark a blue that it seems it might dye cloth, not at all like Lake Limna at home where the waves were nearly always green.

I had become used to Blue's blue and silver sea long ago, of course. Perhaps I only think of it now because we are so far from it here in Gaon; but it seems to me, as I sit here to write at this beautifully inlaid table the Gaonese have provided for me, that I saw it then through the glass as though it were new, that there was some magic carried in the big black and white boat that made Blue new to me again. Perhaps there was, for boats are magic—living things that ordinary men like me can shape from wood and iron.

"Probably pirates," Sinew snarled.

I took my eye from the telescope and saw that he had his long, steel-hilted hunting knife out and was testing its edge with his thumb. Sinew could never sharpen a knife properly (Nettle did it for him in those days), although he pretended he could; but for a moment before I returned to my study of the boat, I wondered whether he would not stab me and try to join them if pirates in fact came again. Then I put my eye back to the telescope, and saw that the faces at the gunwale included a woman's, and that one of the men was old Patera Remora. I should make it clear here that he and Marrow were the only ones I knew well.

There were five besides Gyrfalcon's sailors, who had been brought along to work the boat. Perhaps I ought to list all five now and describe them, since Nettle may want to show this to others. You would do everything much better, darling, I know, working in the descriptions cleverly as you did when we wrote *The Book of Silk*; but it is a skill I have never possessed to the same degree.

No doubt you remember them better than I, as well.

Gyrfalcon is fat, with busy eyes, a noble face, and a mop of sinknut-brown hair just starting to turn gray. It was his boat, and he let us know that the moment that he came ashore. Do you remember?

Eschar is tall and stooped, with a long, sad face, slow to speak until his passions are roused. He was on our lander, of course, just as Marrow and Remora were.

The woman came later, perhaps on Gyrfalcon's lander. Her name is Blazingstar. She has humor, as you do, a rare thing in a woman. I know you liked her, and so did I. She talked about her farms, so she must own at least two in addition to her trading company.

Marrow is large and solid, not so fat as he was at home, but balder even than I was then. When we were children, he owned a greengrocery as well as his fruit stall in the market. He still deals in vegetables and fruits mostly, I believe. I have never known him to cheat anyone, and he can be generous; but I would like to meet the man who can best him in a bargain. Marrow was the only one of the five who helped me after I was robbed in New Viron.

His Cognizance Patera Remora is of course the head of the Vironese Faith—quite tall but not muscular, with lank gray hair he wears too long. He was at one time coadjutor in Old Viron (as we say it here). A good and a kind man, not as shrewd as he believes, prone to be too careful.

They were too many for our little house. Hoof and Hide and I made a rude table on the beach, laying planks across boxes and barrels and bales of paper. Sinew carried out all the chairs, I brought the high and low stools I use in the mill, and you spread the planks with cloths and set what little cheer we had before our uninvited guests. And so we managed to entertain all five, and even Gyrfalcon's sailors, with some show of decency.

Marrow rapped the makeshift table, calling us to order. Our sons and the sailors were sitting on the beach, nudging one another, whispering, and tossing shells and pebbles into the silver waves. I would have sent them all away if I could. It did not seem to be my place to do so, and Marrow let them stay.

"First let me thank you both for your hospitality," he began. "You owe us no favors, since we have come to ask you for a big one—"

Gyrfalcon interrupted, saying, "To grant you a privilege." From the way he spoke, I felt sure that they had argued about this already.

Marrow shrugged. "I should have begun by explaining who we are. You know our names now, and even though you live so far from town, it's likely that you also know we're its five richest citizens."

Remora cleared his throat. "Not, um, so. No—ah—intent to, um, contradict, but not, er, I."

"Your Chapter's got more gelt than any of us," Eschar remarked dryly.

"Not mine, hey? Custodian—um—solely." The sweet salt wind ruffled his hair, making him look at once foolish and blessed.

Blazingstar spoke first to you, Nettle; then to me. "We are the five people who have jockeyed most successfully for money and power, that's all. We wanted them, we five, and we got them. Now here we are, begging you two to keep us from cutting our own throats."

"Not, um—"

"He'll deny it," she told us, "but it's the gods' own truth just the same. Our money belongs to us, mine to me, Gyrfalcon's to him, and so on. Patera here is going to insist that his isn't really his, that it belongs to the Chapter and he only takes care of it."

"Brava! Quite—um—ah . . . Precisely the case."

"But he's got it, and as Eschar said he's probably got more than any of us. He's got bravos, too, buckos to break heads for him whenever he wants."

Stubbornly, Remora shook his own. "There are many men of—ah—high heart amongst the faithful. That I, um, concede. However, we—ah—none—"

"He doesn't have to pay his," Blazingstar explained. "We pay ours."

Eschar asked Remora, "If it isn't so, what are you doing here?"

Marrow rapped the table again. "That's who we are. Do you understand now?"

You looked at me then, Nettle darling, inviting me to speak; but all I could think of to say was. "I don't think so."

Marrow said, "You don't know why we're here, naturally. We haven't told you. That will come soon enough."

Gyrfalcon snapped, "New Viron needs a caldé. Anybody can see it."

You nodded then, Nettle darling. "It's become a terrible place."

"Exactly. We came here to escape the Sun Street Quarter, didn't we? The Sun Street Quarter and the Orilla." Gyrfalcon chuckled. "But we carried them with us."

"It isn't just crime," Blazingstar declared, "though there's much too much of that. The wells are polluted and there's filth everywhere."

Gyrfalcon chuckled again. "Just like home."

"Worse. Filth and flies. Rats. It isn't just that the people want a caldé, though they do. *We* do. We're businesspeople at base, all of us. Traders and merchants. Sharpers, if you like."

"I must—ah," Remora began.

"All right, all except His Cognizance, who never hedges the truth even a finger's width. Or so he says." Blazingstar gave Remora a scornful smile. "But the rest of us need to carry on our businesses, and it's become almost impossible to do that in New Viron."

Marrow added, "And getting worse."

"Getting worse. Exactly."

You asked, "Can't one of you be caldé?"

Gyrfalcon laughed aloud at that; he has a good, booming laugh. "Suppose one of us became caldé tomorrow. How about old Marrow there? He wants it."

"I feel sure it would be a wonderful improvement."

Marrow thanked you. "For you and your family it would be, Nettle. What do think it would be for them?" He glanced around at Gyrfalcon, Remora, Eschar, and Blazingstar.

"An improvement, too, I think."

"Not a bit of it." Marrow had rapped the table before; now he struck it with his fist, rattling our mugs and plates. "I would take everything I could get. I would do my best to ruin them, and if you ask me I would succeed." He smiled, and glanced around at the woman and the three men I had believed were his friends. "They know it well, my dear. And, Nettle, they would do the same to me."

Eschar told you, "We need Caldé Silk here. I was the first to suggest it."

"He's still in the *Whorl*, isn't he? And . . . I don't like to say this."

"Then I will." Blazingstar reached across the table we had made to cover your hand with her own. "He may be dead. I left sixteen years ago, and by this time it's certainly possible."

"Hem!" Remora cleared his throat. "Theocracy, hey? I have suggested it, but they will, er, won't. Not if—ah—me. But, um, Patera Silk, eh? Yes. Yes, to that. Third party. Still an augur, eh?

Indelible—ah—consecration. So, um. Modified? A mitigated theocracy. We, um, two in concert. I concur."

Gryfalcon summed up, "It's that or we fight, and a fight would destroy the town, and all of us, too, in all probability. Show them the letter, Marrow."

★

★ ★

Hari Mau and I have formalized the court. Up until now, it seems, litigants have simply done whatever they could to come before the rajan (as their ruler was called at home) and made their cases. Witnesses were or were not called, and so forth. We have set up a system—tentative, of course, but it *is* a system—in a situation in which any system at all will surely be an improvement. Unless they choose otherwise, Nauvan will represent all the plaintiffs, and Somvar all the defendants. It will be their duty to see that evidence, witnesses, and so forth are present when I hear the case. In criminal cases, I will assign one or the other to prosecute, depending.

I feel like Vulpes.

They will have to be paid, of course; but demanding fees from both parties should encourage them to come to agreement, so that may work out well. Besides, there will be fines. I wish I knew more about our Vironese law—these people don't seem to have had any.

Back to it.

I swore an oath, administered by Remora, with my left hand upon the Chrasmologic Writings and my right extended to the Short Sun. That is the part I wish very fervently that I could forget. I cannot recall the exact words—in all honesty, I am tormented more than enough as it is—but I cannot forget what I swore to do, and not one day passes without my conscience reminding me that I have not done it.

No more letters. What farce!

Gyrfalcon offered to take me to New Viron. While thanking him, I declined for three reasons that I might as well list here to show where my mind was when I left Lizard.

The first was that I wanted to speak to my family privately, and that I did not want to subject them—to subject you, Nettle darling, particularly—to the pressure Marrow, Blazingstar, and Gyrfalcon himself would undoubtedly have brought to bear.

I waited until supper, then longer so that we could dispose of the questions and gossip our five visitors had provoked. As I was carving the roast Sinew had supplied, he asked what had been said when you and I, Remora, and the others, had walked to the tip of the tail.

"You heard us earlier," I told him, and continued to carve. "You know what they wanted."

"I wasn't paying much attention."

You sighed then, Nettle, and I recalled your listening at the door when Silk conferred with the two councilors. I leaped to the conclusion that you had listened while I talked privately with Marrow and the others, and I was ready for you to explain everything to our sons when you said, "They want us to stop writing. Isn't that really it?"

I thought it so ludicrously wrong that I could have laughed aloud. When I denied it, you said, "I was sure that was what it really was. I still am. You look so gloomy now, Horn, and you're always such a cheerful person."

I have never thought myself one.

Hoof said, "They wanted to get paper on credit. Things are bad in town. Daisy just got back, and she says it's really terrible."

And Hide, "Did you give them credit, Father?"

"No," I told him, "but I would have."

"Those cardcases." Sinew sneered. "You'd have had to."

"You're wrong," I told him, and pointed the carving knife at him. "That's what I have to make clear from the beginning. I don't have to do what they want. They threatened me, or at least Gyrfalcon did. I ought to say he tried to, since I didn't feel threatened.

He could bring some pressure to bear on us, perhaps. But in less than a year I'd have him eating out of my hand."

Sinew snorted.

"You think I couldn't? You think it because I've always been gentle with you for your mother's sake. It wasn't like that in my family, believe me. Or in hers either. If you find yourself begging me before shadelow tomorrow," to emphasize my point, I struck the table with the handle of the knife, "will you admit you were wrong? Are you man enough for that?"

He looked surly and said nothing. He is the oldest of our sons, and although I loved him, I did not like him. Not then, although things were different on Green.

Nor did he like me, I feel certain. (Nettle knows these things, naturally.)

She murmured, "This is worse than anything that they said to us."

Hoof asked, "What did they say, anyhow?"

Hide seconded him, as Hide often did. "What did they want, Mother?"

It was then, I feel certain, that I passed the slice I had been cutting to you, darling. I remember what it looked like, which I find very odd tonight. I must have known that something enormously significant was happening, and associated it with our haunch of greenbuck. "In a way," I told you, "you're quite right. It was our book that brought them, though they were very careful not to say it until I got them in a corner. You, Hoof, are right too. Things are getting harder and hungrier for everybody every year. Why do you think that is?"

He shrugged. The twins are handsome, and to my eyes take after your mother more than either one of us, though I know you pretend to think they look like me. "Bad weather and bad crops. Their seed's giving out."

Hide said, "That thin one talked about that. I thought it was kind of interesting."

I gave Sinew, who had always eaten like a fire in good times and bad, a thick slice with plenty of gristle. "Why is the seed yielding a poorer crop each year?"

"Why are you asking me? I didn't say it was."

"What difference does it make whether you asked or not? It happens to be true, and you being older than your brothers ought to be wiser. You think you are, so prove it. Why is the seed weakening? Or were you too busy throwing stones at the waves to listen?"

Hoof began, "I still want to know—"

"What those five people wanted. We're talking about it."

Sinew said slowly, "The good seed is the seed from the landers. That's what everybody says. When the farmers save seed, it isn't as nearly as good. The maize is worse than the others, but none of it's quite as good."

You nodded, Nettle darling. "That's one of the things they said. I knew it already, and I'm sure your father did, too, but Eschar and Blazingstar lectured us about it anyway. Let's talk about maize, for the present. It's the most important, and the clearest example. Back home we had ever so many kinds. Do you remember, Horn?"

I nodded, smiling.

"At least four kinds of yellow maize that I can remember, and it wasn't something I paid much attention to. Then there were black, red, and blue, and several sorts of white. Have any of you boys ever seen maize that wasn't yellow?"

No one replied.

I had cut more slices while you spoke; I gave them to Hoof and Hide, saying, "I never saw any at home to equal the first crop we got on our farm. Ears a cubit long, packed with big kernels. The ears from the next planting weren't any longer than my hand."

You said, "I've been seeing those here lately, in the market and the village gardens."

"Yes, and here's something I hadn't known—something they explained to us. You get the best maize by crossing two strains. Some crosses are better than others, as you'd expect; but the best ones will yield a lot more than either of the original two, fight off blight, and need less water."

I sat down and began to cut up the meat I had just given myself. It was clear from their expressions that neither Hoof nor Hide had understood.

You said, "Like crossing red and black maize. Isn't that right, Horn?"

"Exactly. But according to what we were told, all those good qualities disappear in a year. The crop after the first is liable to be worse than either of the strains you crossed, in fact, and it's always worse than the parent strain, the one from the crossing."

Sinew muttered, "It doesn't come from a pure strain at all. It comes from the good crop, and the good crop was good but it wasn't pure." He tilted his chair until its back struck the wall, something that always annoyed me. "The god that stocked the landers put all that mixed seed in them, didn't he? No pure strains, so we can't make new mixes ourselves."

"Pas," you told him. "Pas prepared the landers for us out of his infinite wisdom. You may not credit him, but Pas is a very great god."

"Back on the Long Sun Whorl, maybe." Sinew shrugged. "Not here."

Hoof said, "All those gods you talk about, they're only back there. Scylla and her sisters."

Your smile was sad then, Nettle darling—it hurt me to see it. "Yet they are beautiful and true," you told him, "as real as my parents and your father's father, who are not here either."

"That's right," I told Hoof, "but what you said wasn't. You implied that Pas was a god only in the Long Sun Whorl." Secretly I agreed with him, although I did not want to say so.

Sinew came to his brother's defense, surprising and pleasing me. "Well, Pas isn't much of a god here, no matter what the old Prolocutor in town says."

"I agree. The point that you're both forgetting . . . I'm not sure how I can explain. We call this whorl Blue, and call our sun here the Short Sun."

"Sure."

"At home, we called the whorl our ancestors came from the

Short Sun Whorl. Your mother will remember that, I'm sure, and I remember talking with Patera Silk about all the wisdom and science that we left behind there."

You said, "We put that in our book."

"Yes, we certainly did."

Hide had been waiting for a chance. "I don't see what any of this has to do with maize."

"It has everything to do with it. I was about to say that when Pas stocked the landers it was on that earlier Short Sun Whorl. He was a god there, you see, and I think probably the greatest. Since he was, he's capable of becoming a god here, too, although he hasn't done it, or at least hasn't let us know he's done it yet."

No one contradicted me.

"One evening, when I was being punished for making fun of Patera Silk, he and I talked about the science of the Short Sun Whorl. The wrapping that healed his ankle had been made there. We couldn't make it, we didn't know how. Glasses and the Sacred Windows, and so many other wonderful things we had at home, we had only because they had been made on the Short Sun Whorl and put into ours by Pas. Chems, for example—living people of metal and sun-fire."

At that, Sinew's chair came down with a thump; but he said nothing.

I ate, and cut another slice for myself. "You used your bow when you killed this greenbuck for us," I said.

He nodded.

"I'm going to offer a prayer. If any of you want to join in, you'll be welcome. If you prefer to continue eating, that's a matter between you and the god."

Hide began, "Father, I—"

I was already making the sign of addition over my plate. I bowed my head and closed my eyes, imploring the Outsider, whom Silk had honored above all the other gods, to help me act wisely.

When I opened them and began to eat again, Hoof said, "You jumped from maize to all the other things you and Mother had in the *Whorl*."

At the same moment, Hide said, "You promised you'd tell us what those people wanted."

You motioned them to silence, telling Hide, "Your brother knows, I think. What was it, Sinew?"

Sinew shook his head.

Hoof asked him, "Why did he say about your bow?"

"He meant they had better things," Sinew grunted. "Slug guns and needlers. But they're making slug guns now in town. Father's still got his needler. You've seen it. He let me hold it one time."

"I am going to give it to you," I told him. "Tonight or tomorrow, perhaps."

Sinew stared, then shook his head again.

Hoof said, "If we could make those here, we'd have a lot more to eat, I bet."

"The new slug guns aren't nearly as good as the old ones," Sinew told him, "but they're still too expensive for us, and conjunction's coming. It's only a couple years now. You sprats don't remember the last one."

Hide said, "A whole bunch of inhumi came and killed lots of people."

Hoof added, "If we had more needlers and a new slug gun, we could fight them better."

You—I am nearly certain it was you, Nettle darling—said, "The slug gun we've got is just about worn out."

No one spoke after that; the boys ate, and I made a show of eating, although I have never been less hungry than I was then. When a minute and more had passed, Sinew asked, "Why you?"

"Because I built our mill, and because I knew Patera Silk better than almost anyone else in New Viron did."

Shaking his head, Sinew bent over his plate again.

"What's that got to do with anything?" Hide wanted to know.

"A great deal, I'm sure," you told him, Nettle. "May I, Horn? I think I've followed everything."

I suppose I said that you could, or indicated it by some gesture.

"We need new seed, Hide. More than that, we need pure strains that we can cross for ourselves. I imagine it would be possible to develop pure strains from what we have, and it may be that someone's trying to, but it will take a long time. Before the next conjunction—"

Sinew interrupted you, as he invariably did. "We can't even make needles, and they're just little slivers of metal. Most of the slug guns people have can't be used because there aren't any more cartridges for them. Everybody's worried about next conjunction. I think we'll get by like we did before, but what about the one after that? Bows and spears, that's all we'll have. Anybody planning to be dead before then?" When none of us spoke, he added, "Me neither."

I said, "We lost one whole level of knowledge when we left the Short Sun Whorl and went aboard the *Whorl.* We lived in there for about three hundred years, if the scholars are right, but we never got that knowledge back. Now we're losing another level, as Sinew says."

He made me a mocking bow.

"If it were just the weapons, that would be bad enough, but there are other problems I haven't mentioned."

You said, "We brought knowledge, even if it isn't enough. People from other cities have landed all over this whorl. If all of us pooled what we know . . . ?"

I nodded. (It seemed to me that I scarcely looked at her; yet I can see her face, scrubbed and serious, as I write.) "It might be, as you say. But to pool it we'd have to have glasses, when we don't even have a Window for our Grand Manteion."

Hide put in, "Amberjack says that old Prolocutor's trying to build a Sacred Window."

"Trying," Sinew sneered.

I ignored it. "Or if we cannot make glasses, wings like the Fliers', or vessels like the Trivigaunti airship."

But now, darling, I have been reconstructing our suppertime conversation for several hours, exactly as you and I used to try to reconstruct Silk's when we were writing our book. The work has rekindled many tender memories of those days; but you recall this conversation better than I, I feel sure, and you can fill in the rest for yourself. I am going to bed.

★

★ ★

Three days in which I have had no chance to write in this sketchy half-book I have begun without Nettle's help. I suppose it is no loss; she will never read it. Or if she does, she will have me at her side, and this account will be superfluous. Yet she may show it to others, as I said. Are not the people of our town entitled to know what became of the emissary they sent for Silk? Why and how he failed? Pig's blindness, and all the rest? I will proceed, if I do, upon the assumption that it will be read by strangers and perhaps even copied and recopied as our own book—the book that ultimately brought me here—has been.

Our house and our mill stand on Lizard Island, as I should explain. Lizard Island is called by that name because we, seeing it from the lander, at once noted its resemblance to that animal; and not (as some now suppose) because it was first settled by a man named Lizard. No such person exists.

The head is more or less coffin-shaped. All four legs are extended, and their rocky toes splayed. The sandspit that forms the tail curves out to sea, then north, to shelter Tail Bay, which is where we keep our logs. A lengthy ridge of granite gives the lizard a spine. Its highest peak, near the tail, is called the Tor. The spring that turns our mill originates there, giving us a long and very useful fall. Our house is set back some distance from the sea, but the mill stands with its feet in the bay to make it easier to hook and drag out logs.

Let me see. What else?

The Lizard's head looks to the north. Our mill and our house are on the weather side of the island, their site dictated by the stream. On the lee side is a fishing village that is also called Lizard;

it consists of six houses, those of our nearest neighbors. Lizard Island lies well north of New Viron, a day's sail in good weather.

That night, as I walked along the shingle, I recalled the whole island as I had glimpsed it from the lander twenty years before. How small it had appeared then, and how beautiful! A green and black lizard motionless upon the blue and silver sea. It came to me then, with a force that seemed to snatch away my heart, that if only we could build an airship like General Saba's I might see it so again.

And be again, if only for an instant, young. What would I not give to be the boy I was once more, with a young Nettle at my side?

Time for court. More this evening, I hope.

★

★ ★

A difficult case, and I must settle each case that comes before me on the basis of custom and common sense, having no knowledge of the law and no law books—not that Vironese law would have any force here.

I was leading up to my departure, and how Sinew came out to speak with me as I walked back up the Tail, leaping from one floating log to the next with energy and dexterity that I could only envy. When he reached me, panting, he asked whether I was still thinking of going. I told him that I no longer had to think about whether I would go—that I had been thinking of how to go and what to take with me, and when to leave.

He grinned, and actually rubbed his hands together like a shopkeeper. "I thought you would! I was thinking it over in bed. You know how you do? All of a sudden I saw it didn't make sense to wonder, even. You'd already decided, you were just trying to make it easy for Mom and me. Want to know how I knew?"

"Because you saw me take the oath. So did everyone else, I imagine." Promises meant very little to Sinew, as I had reason to know; but I supposed that he understood how seriously I take mine.

"You know I've read your book?"

I told him I knew he said he had.

"When you and Mom were coming here, you were only doing it because Silk had told you to. But when he didn't go, you went anyway. I remembered that, and as soon as I did, I knew you were really leaving."

"This isn't the same thing at all."

"Yes, it is. You were supposed to come here because some god wanted it, that boss god in the Long Sun Whorl. The old Prolocutor and that witchy lady want you to bring him here, and that's really it, not the maize or even needlers. You're just the same here as you were up there, just exactly like Mom is."

I shook my head. "The principal thing is to find Silk and get him to govern New Viron, assuming that he's still alive. The maize, and the kinds of skills necessary to make glasses and needlers, as well as many other things, are very important, though not central. As for bringing Great Pas, no one so much as mentioned it. If anyone had, he would have been laughed at. It would be much more sensible to talk about bringing back Lake Limna."

"But that's what it comes down to." Still grinning, Sinew stepped closer, so close I could feel his breath on my face. "Silk got made a part of this Pas, didn't he? That girlfriend of Pas's invited him to."

"I don't know that, and neither do you."

"Well, he went off with the flying man and wouldn't let you tag along. That's what you and Mom said."

I shrugged. "That's what we wrote, because it was all we knew. I don't know anything more now than I did when we wrote it."

"Of course he did! You know he did. Who wouldn't? So if you bring him, we'll have a boss who's the partner of this very powerful god up there. You say you couldn't bring a god back, and naturally you couldn't. But if this god Pas really is a god he could come here anytime or go anyplace else."

I said nothing.

"You know I'm right. Are you taking the sloop? We'll have to build another one if you do. The old boat never was big enough."

"Yes," I said.

"See, you're going. I knew you were. What are you going to say at breakfast? Raise your hands?"

I sighed, having only a moment before definitely deciding to take the sloop. "I had intended to ask each of you individually what I ought to do, beginning with Hide and ending with your mother. I hoped that all of you would have concluded by that time that I must go as I promised, as I have, no matter how badly I'm needed here." I turned away with a feeling of relief, and resumed my walk along the Tail.

He loped beside me like an ill-bred dog. "What if she said you had to stay?"

"She wouldn't, and I was hoping that none of you would. But if any of you did, I was going to explain myself again to that person and try to persuade him. I say 'him' because it would surely be Hide or Hoof or you. Not Nettle."

I saw his pleasure by starlight. "I like it. Mom can go live with Aunt Hop. Me and the sprats can take care of things here."

"Your mother will stay right here to take care of things, including you. You'll have to run the mill and make any repairs. She'll handle most of the buying and selling, I imagine, if you and she are wise."

For a moment I thought that he would object violently, but he did not.

"You know the machinery and the process," I told him, "or at least you've had ample opportunity to learn them. The bleach we've got should last you six months or more, if you're careful, and I hope to be back before then. Don't waste it. Be careful about extending credit, too, and doubly careful about refusing to extend it. Never buy a log you haven't seen, or rags that you haven't handled." I laughed, pretending a warmth of feeling that I did not feel. "It cost me a lot to learn that, but I'm giving it to you for nothing."

"Father . . . ?"

"If there's anything you need to know about the mill or the

various papers we make, ask me now. There won't be time in the morning."

Together we walked back to the tip of the Tail, where I had given my oath, until we stood at last at the place where soil and stone vanished altogether and the last of the coarse seagroats with them, and there was only sand and shells, with here and there a stick of driftwood cast up by the unresting waves. At last I took out my needler and offered it to him, telling him that there were only fifty-three needles left in it, and that he would be wise not to waste any.

He would not accept it. "You'll need it yourself, Father, traveling to—to . . ."

"Pajarocu. It's a town, but nobody seems to know where it is. Inland, perhaps, though I hope not. They say that they've refitted a lander there so they can cross the abyss to the *Whorl* again, and they've invited New Viron to send a passenger."

"You."

"I knew Silk better than anybody else." Honesty compelled me to add, "Except for Maytera Marble, Magnesia as she's called now." I offered him my needler again.

"Keep it, I said. You'll need it."

"And Maytera Marble is unable to make the journey, they say. She was already very old when we came, twenty years ago." For a few seconds I tried to frame an argument; then I recalled that no argument of mine had ever changed his mind, and said, "If you don't take this now, I'm going to throw it into the sea."

I cocked my arm as though to make good my threat, and he was on me like a snow cat, clawing for the needler. I let him take it, stood up, and brushed off sand. "When it isn't on my person, I've kept it in the mill. Since you boys never go in there unless you're made to, it seemed safe. It has been. You might want to do the same thing. You wouldn't want Hoof and Hide to get hold of it."

He frowned. "That's good. I will."

I could have shown him how a needler is loaded and fired, but experience had taught me that trying to teach him anything only made him resentful. Instead, I said, "I may need it, as you say. But I may not, and I'd much rather know that you and your mother and brothers are safe. Besides, a traveler with a weapon like that might be killed for it, as soon as anyone knew he had it."

Sinew nodded thoughtfully.

"Conjunction in two years. You remember the last one, the storms and the tides. Any logs you've got in here then will be a danger to you. And of course there will be—" I searched for a word. "Strangers. Visitors. Very plausible ones, sometimes."

The reality of conjunction seemed to dawn upon him then. "Don't go, Father!"

"I must. Not just because I've sworn to; I wouldn't be the first man to break his oath. And certainly not because of Marrow and the others—I'd hurt them far more than they hurt me before it was over—but because I couldn't live with myself if I didn't. You and your mother can run the mill as well as I could, and nobody else would have anything like as good a chance of persuading Silk to join us. At supper tonight we agreed that we were sinking into savagery here on Blue, that we'd soon be fighting off the inhumi with the bows and spears we use for hunting now. You may be confident that we could survive as savages and even regain what we lost, eventually. No doubt—"

The stubborn head shake I had come to know so well.

"I don't think so either. There were people here before, or something very like people. They had a civilization higher than ours, but something wiped them out. If it wasn't the inhumi, what was it?"

"That's another thing I wanted to talk to you about." There was a pause, perhaps while Sinew collected his thoughts, perhaps only while he moistened his mouth. "You're trying to bring Pas, all the gods from the Long Sun."

"No," I said.

He ignored it, or did not hear it. "That's good, because gods could help us if they would. But they had gods of their own, the Vanished People who were here first. They might help us, too. There's a place on Main, way up on Howling Mountain a little before the trees stop. I found it almost a year ago. Maybe I should have told you."

★

★ ★

I see that I said I had three reasons for not accompanying our five visitors as they proposed. The first (as I indicated) was that I wanted to take leave of my family, and get them to agree to my going, insofar as possible. Nettle would agree because she loved me and Sinew because he hated me, I felt sure; and with their support I had hoped to persuade the twins that it was necessary.

The second was that I wanted to sail my own boat in search of Pajarocu, and not the boat Marrow had offered to let me have, however good it might be. I did not intend to disparage his offer, as he may have thought; it was a generous one, and one that would have resulted in a serious loss if I had accepted it. He showed me that boat, the *Sealily,* when I spoke with him in town, and I would guess that it was nearly as fast as my own, and rather more capacious and seaworthy.

"I'd never been on the water till we came down here," Marrow told me, "and I haven't been but twice now. If you'd come by the shop or my booth and told me someday I'd be having boats built for me, I'd have thought you was cracked. I thought Auk the Prophet was cracked when I talked to him up there, and it would have been the same with anybody who said someday I'd want boats. You didn't put that in your book, about Auk. That I'd thought he was cracked as old eggs. But I did."

I told Marrow that Auk was, that he had fractured his skull in the tunnels.

"Used to see him at sacrifice," Marrow said, leaning heavily on his big carved stick. "Old Patera Pike's manteion. The wife and I used to go now and then because he traded with us, him and the sibyls. Maytera Rose that was, and young Maytera Mint, only they sent Maytera Marble to do their buying. Shrike wouldn't go, just sent his wife. They traded with him anyhow because she went all the time. Gone now, both of 'em. I guess you remember Pike's manteion?"

I did. I do. The plain shiprock walls, and the painted statue of Lord Pas (from which the paint was peeling) will remain with me until the day I die, always somewhat colored by the wonder I felt as a small boy at seeing a black cock struggling in the old man's hands after he had cut its throat, its wings beating frantically, beating as if they might live after all, live somehow somewhere, if only they could spray the whole place with blood before they failed.

My own bird has flown. Only this lone black feather remains with me, fluttering above this sheet (a sheet that for all I know or all that anyone here knows may have been made in my own mill) spraying the whorl of Blue with the black ink that has done so much good and so much harm. If it had not been for our book, Marrow and the rest would have chosen someone else, beyond argument. As it was, our book—*The Book of Silk,* or as others would have it, *The Book of the Long Sun*—spread over this whorl more rapidly than Nettle and I had dared hope. Silk—

"Silk has become an almost mythic figure," I began to write. The truth is that he has become a mythic figure. I hear rumors of altars and sacrifices. Disciples who have never seen him promulgate his teachings. If it had not been for our book, Hari Mau and the rest would have chosen someone else, or no one.

★

★ ★

Heretofore I have written whatever crossed my mind, I fear. In the future, I will attempt to provide you (whoever you may be) with a connected narrative. Let me say at the outset, however, what readers I hope for.

First of all for Nettle, my wife, whom I have loved from boyhood and will always love.

Second, my sons Hoof and Hide. Should he see it, Sinew will read no further, I suppose, than he must to learn that I am its author; and then, unless he is greatly changed, he will burn it. Burning *The Book of Horn* will smell foul, but if it is to burn, no whiff has yet reached me. Sinew is on Green in any event, and is unlikely to see it. (For so many years I feared that he would try to murder me, but in the end it was I who would have murdered him. He may burn my book if he chooses.)

Third, our descendants, the sons and daughters of our sons and their children. If a dozen generations have passed, be assured that you are one; after a dozen generations it cannot be otherwise.

★

★ ★

How difficult it is to touch the spirits of these people, although I doubt that they are worse than others. Two farmers quarreled over a strip of land. I rode out with them and saw it, and it is of no value save for cutting firewood, and of little for that. Each said he had claimed it since landing, and each said his claim was undisputed until a few months ago. I had each tell me the price he would charge the other to lease it for ten years, then awarded it to the one who would charge the least, and ordered him to lease it, there and then, for the price he had specified. Since the leaseholder's price had been more than twice as much, he was getting a great bargain, and I told him so. He did not appear to agree.

This is a stopgap at best, however. The whole situation regarding the ownership of land is confused or worse. It must be reformed, and a rational system as secure from corruption as we can make it set in place.

That I intend to do. My principles: that possession long unchallenged need only be recorded, but that unused property is the property of the town. Now to begin.

I have already given more than I should of our conversation at supper. I will say nothing more about it, although when I close my eyes and lean back in this chair it seems that I smell the brown rolls, fresh from the oven, see the honey dyeing with dark gold its earthenware dish, and taste a vanished summer in the wine. I cut our meat that night, and ate as I had for years, yet if I had known then what I know now—if I had let my imagination carry me forward beyond the next few days—I would have clasped my wife to me, embracing her until it was time to go.

She will have found another husband by this time, I hope. A good man. She was always a sensible woman. (Which is, now that I come to think of it, what His Cognizance the inhumu used to say of Molybdenum.) I wish both well, and wish him better luck with Hoof and Hide than I had with Sinew.

He was my right hand in the lander, as well as on Green, and he threw me his knife. I see I have not yet written of that.

Before I left he begged me not to go, exactly as I had predicted at dinner. He was shocked, I believe, that I was going to leave that night while Nettle and the twins slept; and to confess the truth, so was I. I had not intended to go until morning.

Have I said how closely Sinew resembled me? Perhaps not. There was something devilish about it. The twins, with their large eyes and too-regular features, resemble Nettle's mother, or so I have always thought, while Nettle herself resembles her father. But Sinew looks as I did when we left Main and built the mill. We lived in a tent on the beach in those days, and he was only a squalling toddler, although he had already taken her from me to a certain extent. The twins had not been born, or even thought of.

I left that night, not so much when Sinew and I had finished talking as when I was tired of his talking to me. I took little with me; even then I was not under the illusion that I would be welcomed back to the whorl I had left, or provided with any sort of transport. If I had known then how long it would be before I set foot in the whorl in which I was born, I would have taken more, perhaps, although so much was stolen as it was, and I was able to bring precious little beyond my two knives from Pajarocu, and nothing at all from Green, not even Seawrack's ring.

I brought two changes of clothing, and a warm blanket.

A copy of our book, which I meant to read during calms and the like, not so much to relearn the facts we had set down as to gently persuade my memory to dwell upon our conversations, and the conversations I had with Nettle, Moly, and others about him. You that read will not credit it, but I do not believe I have forgotten anything that Nettle and I put into our book, or that I ever will.

Three bales of our best white paper to trade, and some other valuables I hoped might be exchanged for food.

I had been afraid that Sinew would wake up the rest of the family, that he would wake Nettle, particularly, and that seeing her I would lack the resolution to go. He did not, but stood upon our little floating wharf and waved (which rather surprised me) and then, when the distance seemed too great to throw anything and score a hit, flung something that missed my head by half a cubit and dropped rattling into the boat.

That, too, surprised me; but nothing could have been more like him than to try to hurt me in some way when I could not defend myself; and it soon occurred to me that he could have drawn my needler and killed me. It was my humiliation he intended; however much he may have wanted to kill me, he would not have dared to shoot. A stone or a shell (I thought) had served his purpose better.

When I had rounded the Tail and could safely tie the sheet, I groped in the bilgewater to find out what his missile had been; there I found his hunting knife, next to his bow his most prized possession, still in the turtle-skin sheath he had made for it. In his own mind at least he had squared accounts, I felt sure; it is onerous to be indebted to someone you hate.

There would be no point in describing my trip down the coast to New Viron in detail. It had been foolhardy of me to leave when I did, but no harm came of it. Until shadeup, I kept the sloop under short sail and dozed at her tiller, not yet having confidence enough to tie it in position and lie down, as I was later to do almost routinely, though from time to time I toyed with the notion of furling both sails and snatching a few hours of real sleep. Mostly I looked at the stars, just as I had before Sinew joined me on the Tail. The Long Sun Whorl in which Nettle and I were born was only a faint gleam when it could be seen at all. For that faint speck I was bound (as I imagined then) in a lander that had somehow been repaired and resurrected. I could not help thinking how much more I would have liked to sail there. Before shadeup, the Long Sun Whorl would touch the sea in the southwest; why should I not sail to meet it? It was an attractive idea, and when I was sleepy enough seemed almost possible.

Once some monstrous, luminous creature four or five times the size of the sloop glided beneath it, for there are fish in the sea that could swallow the great fish that swallowed Silk's poor friend Mamelta, as everyone knows; but although the loss of boats that fail to return is conventionally laid to them, I think carelessness and weather are the true culprits in almost every instance. I do not deny that they can sink boats much bigger than my old sloop, or that they occasionally do.

At one moment it was night. At the next, day.

That was how it seemed to me. I had slept, leaning on the tiller, and not wakened until the light of our Short Sun struck me full in the face.

There were bottles of water (mixed with a little wine to keep it sweet) in one of the chests, and a box of sand for a fire aft of the mast. I baited a hook with a morsel of dried meat and fished for my breakfast, which was my lunch by the time I caught it. If I had not hung Sinew's hunting knife on my belt, I would have split and gutted it with the worn little pocketknife that came with me from Old Viron. As it was, I used his, vaguely conscious that he might ask if it had been helpful someday and wanting to tell him that it had been; gestures like that had become a habit, however futile. It was a good knife, made here on Blue by Gadwall the smith from a single bar of steel which supplied the blade, the stubby guard, and the grip. I remember noticing how sharp it was, and realizing that the bulbous pommel might be almost as useful for pounding as the blade for cutting. I have Hyacinth's azoth now (locked away and well hidden); but I would almost rather have Sinew's knife back, if he would give it a second time.

Here in landlocked Gaon, people would think it queer that we who came from a city so remote from any sea that we had scarcely heard rumors of them should build our new town on the coast. But Viron had been a lakeshore city in the beginning, and it was Lake Limna that left Viron, and not Viron that had left the lake. When we landed here, it seemed natural to us to direct our lander to the shore of our bay, since we thought the water we saw was potable and might be used for irrigation. We were disappointed, of course. But the sea has given us food in abundance—much more, I believe, than even a large lake could have supplied. Even more important, it has been better than the best road for us, letting us move ourselves and our goods faster and better than pack mules or wagons ever could. Gaon is greatly blessed by its cold, clear River Nadi; but I do not believe New Viron would exchange the sea for it.

When Nettle and I decided to build our mill, after trying farming without much success, it was obvious that we would have to have a location to which logs could be floated. We tramped up and down the coast in search of a suitable spot until at last it occurred to me that we would never find it as long as we searched by land for a place to which logs could be floated by sea. That was when I built our first boat, a sort of pointed box with one ludicrously short mast and a tendency to drift off to leeward that would have been quite funny if it had not been so serious. Eventually Tamarind, whose husband had been a fishmonger and knew something of fishermen and their boats in consequence, showed me how to rig a leeboard that could be dropped when necessary and pulled up for shallows. After that, with a taller mast stepped farther forward, we used that boxy little boat for years.

From it, we first landed on Lizard. There was a fishing village there already (if four very modest cottages make a village) at the back of East Bay, which was far from the best part of the island to our way of thinking. We claimed the Tor and everything west of it, with the Prolocutor's support; and since nobody else wanted it, we made our claim good. The land is sparse and sandy (except for our garden, where the soil has been improved with kitchen waste); but there is the Tor with its spring, which gives us water to drink and turns our mill, and Tail Bay, more than half enclosed by the Tail, to which the woodcutters bring the logs we need.

I can see everything as I write. I believe that I could draw a good map of it on this paper now, showing where the house and mill stand, the Tor, the West Foot, and the rest of it; but what good would such a map be? No matter how accurate, it could not take me there.

It has been a good place for us, with plenty of space for barking and chipping the logs we haul out with block and tackle, although it is somewhat dangerous because it is so remote. I must not forget that the twins are older now. Between birth and twenty, a year is an immensity.

★

★ ★

Not long after I finished my fish, the sun was squarely overhead. I have never become completely accustomed to a sun that moves across the sky. We speak here of the Long Sun we left and this Short Sun to which we have come; but it seems to me that the difference implied by the change of shape is small, while the difference between this sun which moves and that one which does not is profound. At home, that part of the sun that was directly overhead always appeared brightest; to east and west it was less bright, and the farther you looked the dimmer it became. At noon, the sun here does not look very different; but the Long Sun is fixed, and seems to speak of the immortality of the human spirit. This Short Sun is well named; it speaks daily of the transitory nature of all it sees, drawing for us the pattern of human life, fair at first and growing ever stronger so that we cannot help believing it will continue as it began; but losing strength from the moment it is strongest.

What good are its ascension and domination, when all its heat cannot halt its immutable decline? Augurs here (such augurs as there are) still prattle of an immortal spirit in every human being. No doctrine could be less convincing. Like certain seeds from the landers, it was grown beneath another sun and can scarcely cling to existence in the light of this one. I preach it like the rest, convincing no one less than myself.

When I left home, I had promised myself that by noon I would tie up at the wharf in New Viron, having supposed, or hoped at least, that the west wind would last. It had been weakening since midmorning, and while I washed my fork and little, red-brown plate, it died away altogether. I lay down in the shade beneath the foredeck and slept.

Less than two hours had passed, I believe, when I woke. The shadow of the mainsail was slightly larger and had moved a trifle; otherwise everything was the same. For half a minute, the sloop rose a hand's breadth upon the oily water, and for the next half minute descended again. Halfway to the horizon, one of the snake-necked seabirds skimmed the water hunting fish, a creature capable of soaring almost to the stars that rarely rose higher than a donkey's ears.

It was only then, after I had truly slept, that the full weight of my decision fell upon me. The leaders (self-appointed, you may be sure) who had come to speak to us had believed (or had pretended to believe) that my absence from my family, and the house and mill that Nettle and I had built together, would be merely temporary, like a trip to Three Rivers. I would discover the location of Pajarocu without difficulty, board a lander just as we had boarded the one that had brought us there and revisit the Long Sun Whorl, find Silk (again without difficulty), easily persuade him to accompany me, procure samples of maize and other seeds, learn all I could about the manufacture of this and that—or still better, find someone skilled who would come with us—and return home. They had spoken of it as something that might with a little good luck be accomplished in a few months. On the sloop that day I realized that I might as well have volunteered to fly to Green by flapping my arms and wipe out every inhumu there. One would be no more difficult than the other.

The enormity of the oath I had taken so lightly back on the Tail had not yet sunk in, and would not until Babbie and I were sailing alone, north along the coast. If I had been able to reach New Viron, I would have gone to Marrow and the rest and declared that I had changed my mind, gone back to the sloop, and gone back to Lizard at once. But I could no more give up my errand than I could continue it. The reefs and rocks of the mainland waited immobile to my left. The horizon ducked away from my eyes to starboard. Nothing moved except the white bird, which flew back and forth with a slow, sad motion that seemed so weary that every time two wings rose I felt that it was about to fall into the sea, and the Short Sun, which crept down to the empty horizon as remorselessly as every man creeps toward his grave.

2

BECALMED

To do nothing is a talent, one I have not got. I have known a few people who possessed it to a superlative degree, as one of my scribes here does. They can, if they wish, sit or even stand for hours without occupation and without thought. Their eyes are open and they see the whorl before them, but see it only as the eyes of potatoes do.

Seriously, it is perceived but means nothing to the owner of the eyes. Silk said once that we are like a man who can see only shadows, and thinks the shadow of an ox the ox and a man's shadow the man. These people reverse that. They see the man, but see him as a shadow cast by the leaves of a bough stirred by the wind. Or at least they see him like that unless he shouts at them or strikes them.

I have never struck the scribe I mentioned (his name is Hoop), although I have been severely tempted. I have shouted at him once or twice, or asked what he was writing before the ink dried upon his pen. But I have never asked him how he does nothing, or how I can learn to do it in case I find myself alone again in a boat upon a windless sea. I should.

There are always half a dozen little jobs waiting on a boat like the sloop. The standing rigging should be tightened here and there, simple though it is. It might be well to rake the mast a bit more—or a bit less. There is not much water in the bilge, but what there is can be removed with a little satisfying labor. The harpoon and its coil of line, carelessly stowed by Hide two days ago, can be stowed more neatly, so that they occupy a trifle less space. One by one I found them and did them all, and searched diligently for more, and took out the few belongings I had packed, and refolded and repacked them all, except for our book.

And settled down to read, searching out Silk's trip to Lake Limna with Chenille and reading about the poster they saw there and how he separated from Chenille, who had drawn his picture in colored chalks as soon as he was gone—all in my wife's neat and almost clerkly hand.

How long and how diligently she had labored to produce copy after copy, until she had done six altogether and several persons were clamoring for more, and several others were copying the ones she had produced earlier (and producing with the wildest abandonment both abridgments and annotated editions in which their annotations were not always clearly distinguished, and sometimes were not distinguished at all). Then she—you, my own darling—although she had already labored for the better part of a year to satisfy what must have seemed a mere whim to her (as indeed it sometimes has to me), began, and toiled over, and at last completed that seventh fair copy, which she proudly presented to me.

I had been tempted to leave it at home. Not because I did not love it—I did, and almost certainly loved it too much; no man is so secure in his sanity that he can afford to lavish on a mere inanimate object the passionate affection that every good man at some time feels for another person. Loving it as I did, I had known I was carrying it into deadly danger when I resolved to take it to the Long Sun Whorl and present it to Silk. So it proved; I nearly lost it at once, and it did not remain with me long. I can only say that I knew the risk from the beginning, resolved with open eyes to run it, and am very glad I did.

So it has proved, and where is the Nettle who shall produce copy after copy of this, of this record of my travels and dangers and lucky escapes that I have begun, this *Book of Horn*? But you must surely think that in all this I have left my earlier self and our motionless sloop far behind.

I have not, because it was then, reading in the sloop by the light of the declining sun, that the thought of printing struck me with full force. I had read (I believe) that Silk had come upon a stone carved with a picture of Scylla, and I moved by imperceptible mental stages from the carving of that stone to the cutting into fine stone of pictures for books, as artists sometimes did at home, and from there to cutting whole pages as the pictures are cut, pages that might then be duplicated again and again, and from that to the memory of a visit to a printing shop with my father, who had supplied its owners with certain papers and inks, not all of which had proved completely satisfactory.

I ought to say here that Nettle and I had discussed the possibility of printing long before I wrote the incident in which Silk stopped to pray before the Scylla-marked stone. We had discussed it, but both of us had quickly concluded that it would be far easier to create the two or three copies we then envisioned by hand than to build the equipment necessary to print them and learn the process. Having thus sensibly concluded that printing was beyond our grasp, we abandoned all thought of it.

Now I, having seen the eagerness with which Nettle's copies were bought, thought of printing again—but in a whole new light: I knew beyond doubt that we could sell as many as twenty or thirty in the course of a year, if only we had them.

Furthermore, we might also print the much shorter account of our departure from Old Viron that Scleroderma had completed before death claimed her. A grandson had her manuscript, and allowed others to copy it. Surely he would allow Nettle to copy it as well, and from her copy we might print and sell a dozen at least. In addition, there was a man in Urbasecundus who was said to have produced a similar book, although I had never seen it. We had paper, and the modest skills and tools required to sew folded sheets into a book and to bind the book between thin slats of runnerwood. We needed nothing but printing to create a new and profitable use for the paper we made and sold already.

Nor was that all. Printing tens of thousands of words would surely require hundreds of reusable letters, and perhaps a thousand or more. In the shop I had visited with my father, they had made their letters by pouring molten metal into metal molds. (This reminded me of Chenille's description of the way in which the heads of taluses are made, and I found and reread it.) The metal, which I recalled seeing a woman heat in an iron ladle held in a charcoal fire, had appeared to be pure silver when it was poured; but my father had said that it was mostly lead.

That in turn reminded me of a conversation a week earlier with Sinew, who delighted in discussing weapons of every kind and was prone to pontificate about them. I had urged that needlers were better suited to conditions here than slug guns, if only because the projectile fired was a simple, slender cylinder, not greatly different from a short piece of wire. We owned a slug gun as well, the one with which Nettle had fired on the pirates, and although the gun itself was considerably simpler than a needler, every shot required a separate casing and a multitude of other parts that could be used only once: a dot of special chemical in a tiny copper cup, an explosive to propel the slug, the slug itself, and a disk of stiff paper, heavily waxed, with which to seal the casing—this last (I said) being the only item on the entire list that we ourselves could supply.

Sinew had disagreed. "Some man in town gave Gadwall a couple of needles and told him to make him some iron ones. He did, too. He cut them out of a thin rod he had and rolled them between red-hot plates and polished them. He showed them to me, and the real needles. His looked like the real thing. I couldn't tell them apart. But when you put them in a needler, they wouldn't shoot. Gadwall said you could have dropped in that many straws and done every bit as well."

I started to object, but Sinew interrupted.

"Slug guns are different. We're already making slug guns that work. In that book you and Mother wrote, you have one of the soldiers tell somebody his slugs are made of some stuff I never heard of."

I agreed. "Yes, depleted uranium. That was what Silk said he said."

"Well, I don't know what that is. But I know the slugs they make in town are lead. You know about the silver mine they found up in the mountains?"

"I know everybody's talking about one. I haven't been there, but it sounds very promising."

"Yeah." He was silent for a moment, and I could see the dream of finding such a mine himself in his eyes. "We need a lot of things, and we've got to have things to trade for them, stuff that doesn't take up a lot of room on the boat and won't spoil. Silver should be perfect. The miners already swap it for whatever they need, like mining tools and powder, and the goldsmiths are making it into rings and stuff so it will bring more. Or you can just swap a little silver bar for twenty times that much iron. It's better than the paper, all the traders want it."

"Are you saying that silver can be used in the slug gun cartridges in place of depleted uranium? Or that iron can? Iron would be cheaper, naturally."

He had shaken his head. "There's lead in the silver ore. It's heavier than silver, so the two are pretty easy to separate. So we've not only got silver here we've got lead, too, and that works great. You can't trade it, not now anyway, because it's heavy and nobody wants it much. But it's a metal you can feed to slug guns, and we've got it."

Lead could be cast into type, even cut into type by hand if the casting proved difficult, and lead was available and cheap. We would not need to start with thousands of movable pieces and print a book. Most people who wanted our paper wanted it for writing letters. We could—we would!—offer them decorated papers. Marrow could have a picture of a vegetable marrow on his paper if he liked, in green or yellow ink. Men named for birds, as Auk had been and Gyrfalcon and Gadwall were, could have a picture of the appropriate bird. Nettle drew very skillfully and had taught Hoof and Hide to draw almost as well as she did. Most women were named for flowers, and flowers were easy to draw (Nettle sometimes sketched them for amusement) and should be easy to print.

I was so excited by the prospect that I would have paced up and down if the size of the sloop had permitted it. As it was, I climbed out on the bowsprit and waved my cap to the empty, rolling sea and the dim and distant land. If the trolling bird was impressed, he showed no signs of it.

Returning to our book (in which I had lost my place) I read as before, often carried away by thoughts of printing and the wonderful possibilities it offered, until I chanced on a passage that caught me up short, the one in which Silk brings the Peace of Pas to the talus he has killed in the tunnels. Many prayers and blessings were already falling into disuse; but Nettle had told me of a woman she knew who had written dozens on sheets of our paper and hung them on the walls in her house to preserve them. Others might do the same, and no doubt some already had; but by printing, such things could not only be saved but disseminated.

Even that was not all. His Cognizance Patera Remora, with whom I hoped to speak again when I reached the town, had a copy of the Chrasmologic Writings he had brought from Viron—it was the book upon which I had sworn my oath. That would give us a third text much longer than the first two; and by printing and selling selections from it, we would not only perpetuate and preserve what foreigners here call the Vironese Faith but propagate it.

It was a thought that gave me pause. If, as so many of us thought, the gods we had known in the *Whorl* were not to be found here, the Vironese Faith was a lie undeserving of my credence, or anyone's. For the ten thousandth time I wished with all my heart that Silk had come with us.

★

★ ★

I have found a kind of paint that will stick to the lens of my glasses. It may be no great relief to those to whom I speak—they swear it is not—but it is to me. Returning to this airy bedroom tonight, I admired my reflection like a girl.

When I wrote last, it was about my wish that Silk had come with us, as he had intended to do. How I wish now that I could have brought him with me to Gaon! But I was describing that terrible night on the sloop.

If I slept, Silk might appear in dream, or so I supposed, and unravel the knot of faith for me; if I continued to read, something he had said (first set down in our book by my own hand and now forgotten) might solve everything; but I was no longer sleepy, and the Short Sun was so low already that reading would soon be impossible. I baited my hook and threw it out, and sat in the stern, pondering.

It might well be that Pas and Echidna, and Scylla and her siblings, were gods only in the Long Sun Whorl. That, I felt fairly confident, had been Silk's opinion; but Silk's opinion had been expressed before our lander left the *Whorl.* It was at least possible that we had somehow brought them with us, as Remora alleged. He was certainly correct in one sense: people who had revered those gods through half a lifetime, as so many had, had carried them to Blue in their hearts.

What was it Sinew had said?

That if Pas were truly a god he could come here whenever he wished, or go anywhere. If Silk was right, and Pas did not leave the Long Sun Whorl, it could only be because he did not want to. Or (Pas had been murdered with apparent success by his wife and children, after all) because he was somehow prevented by the other gods. The same might be said of Echidna, Scylla, and the rest—but if they restrained Pas, who restrained them? It might easily be that the gods were in fact present, remaining unknown to us because we lacked the Sacred Windows through which they had spoken at home.

There was one at least whom even Silk had expected to find here. The Outsider was so called, in part at least, because he was to be found outside the whorl as well as in it. Presumably he was here, although there was no more evidence to suggest it than there was for presence of the other gods. I had prayed to him occasionally ever since we had landed, in imitation of Silk, although less and less often as I found my prayers unavailing as the years wore on, maintaining the custom of prayer at family meals because I hoped it might promote the moral development of my sons.

Hope.

That is the trouble with all prayer. Because we hope, we find success where success is not to be found. How easy it would be for me to write here that Sinew would have been worse without the empty ritual of those prayers! It may be true; but try to find an honest man anywhere who would willingly say that Sinew's moral development ever benefited from anything.

He was brave on Green, at least, and loyal for a time.

★

★ ★

As for the gods that Sinew proposed on the night that I left Lizard, the original gods of this whorl of Blue, I asked myself then how much power they can have possessed, and whether they would not have saved at least a few of their worshippers if they could. I know better now, of course.

When I reached New Viron I asked Remora about it, and to my surprise he took the question very seriously, his long face growing longer still while he tried again and again to push back the lank hair that persisted in falling over his high forehead to obstruct his vision. "The—ah—um," he said, and managed to load those noises with sacred dignity. "Ah—ah—er."

"If the gods don't want to be worshipped, there's no reason for them to be swayed by our prayers and sacrifices," I argued. "Therefore, they do, if you will allow that they sometimes answer prayers, as I know you will, Your Cognizance. Granting that, they ought—"

"Hum—ha!" It had been intended as an interruption, and I stopped talking.

"Logic, hey? Yes, um, logic. You said logic like a god. In your book, hey? You had Silk say it."

It had been an idea Silk had once expressed to me, and I thought it might well have occurred to him when he climbed the insurgents' barricade; but I did not trouble Remora with all that.

"Your god, um, logic, betrays you."

I told him I did not see how.

"Ah—multiplely. In diverse ways, eh? To, ah, begin. There are many—yes, many—here who, er, do not. They offer no sacrifices. Nor do they attend sacrifice, hey? Never come to the manteion. I, um, inquire when it is, um, not unwelcome, concerning private prayer and—ah—special devotions. No. None. I—ah—credit it, for the most part."

I nodded. "So would I, Your Cognizance."

"Not worshippers, eh? Numbers, ah, fluctuate. Well known in the Chapter back home, eh? Much piety sometimes. In, er, time of test. Trial, hey? Floods might be—ah—instanced. Fires. Plagues. Wars. Or after a theophany, hey? At others, but little." He lifted his hand and let it fall. "Up and down, eh? You follow me?"

I nodded again.

"Suppose it dropped to, er, nought. Zero. Not a single spirit, eh? Not a one. Never here, long as I live. Um—no. But suppose. No worshippers. Might not these—ah—foreign deities which you, um, suggest take the occasion to, ah, scourge?"

"It doesn't seem likely," I objected

"Hum? I beg to differ. Likely enough. Only too, ah, likely, I should say. Let us continue. You, er, we assume they are—um—deceased. These Vanished People, eh? The whorl is—ah—commodious? Voluminous? Extensive. You agree?"

"I suppose it is."

"Capital. We progress. There is another, um, factor. No skylands, eh? Only, ah, stars there, as they are called. Whorl at home bent upwards, hey? Revealed itself to, ah, the eyes. This the, er, contrary. Reverse. Bent down. You, um, arrived via water?"

"Yes," I said, and I told him what had happened on the sloop.

"Indeed, indeed! Capital! One prayer, eh? Only one, and, er, small faith, as you confess. Concede. See what one small prayer can do." He rocked gleefully, his blue-veined fingers gripping the armrests of his chair.

I said forcefully that if the leatherskin had come in answer to my prayer I would just as soon as the Outsider had ignored it.

"Ingratitude. Rampant everywhere." Remora shook his head. "But we—ah—digress. Yes, digress. You came by, um, sea. This is established. You must have observed that most of this—ah—fo-reign whorl. Concealed. Not like home, eh? You conceive that its former—um—population dead, eh? Extinct. Everyone does, even,er, myself. Ask how I know, and I am—ah—constrained to respond that I do not. I, um, assume it. You—ah—similarly? Synonymously, eh?"

I nodded, wondering how to ask him what I most desired to know.

Now I must ready myself to cut the throat of a stonebuck for Echidna, and prepare my homily.

★

★ ★

I see that I have mentioned my prayer on the sloop without saying anything substantive about it.

The truth is that I grew frightened. The Short Sun was setting without the least hint of a breeze, and the fishing line I had put out had caught nothing. With the water and food I had brought, I could spend one more day sitting in an idle boat with some comfort, but after that the matter would become serious. I had been thinking about the gods, as I have indicated already. I decided to venture a prayer. After all, if the gods I addressed did not hear it, was that my fault or theirs? The only question was which I should address, and I soon found that I could make convincing arguments for three.

First, Pas. He was the greatest of all, and it seemed that Silk might have influence with him. Silk had been my staunch friend, as well as my teacher.

An even better case might be made for Scylla. I had come from her sacred city, where I was born; and I was trying to reach New Viron, which is her town as well, at least nominally. Besides which, she is the goddess of water, and I was on the water and would soon be in need of drinking water.

Last the Outsider, whose case was nearly as good. Of the three, he seemed most apt to hear my prayer. No god, perhaps, had much reason to think well of me; but he had more than any other. Also, he had been Silk's favorite, and when Silk did not say that he trusted no god at all (which to tell the truth he frequently did) he said that the Outsider was the only god he trusted.

To be safe, I decided to address all three jointly. I knelt, and found myself tongue-tied. How could I address those three as a group? Pas might or might not be Silk, in part at least. Sinew had been quite correct about that. From what Auk and Chenille had told Nettle and me, Pas's daughter Scylla was willful, violent, and vindictive. If ever a goddess seemed apt to resent being put in second place, it was she.

The Outsider seemed to me at that time as faceless and mysterious as the god or gods of the ancient inhabitants of this whorl we call Blue. He was, moreover, the god of outcasts and outlaws, of the broken and discarded. I considered myself neither an outcast nor an outlaw; and far from being discarded, I was about to undertake a mission of utmost importance for my town. Such being the case, what could I find to say to him? That I had no claim on his benevolence, but hoped for his help without one?

In the end, I prayed to whatever god might hear, stressing the helplessness and hopelessness we settlers felt, who had left our manteions and their Sacred Windows behind us, with so much else that we held dear, in obedience to Pas. A wind from the west, north, or east would be of greatest service to me, I told the hypothetical god.

I had to go to New Viron, and eventually reach Pajarocu—a town quite unknown to me—before its lander lifted off. The feeblest breeze would be more than welcome, if only it would move my boat.

Had I ended my prayer there, I might have saved myself an infinity of fear and dismay; but I did not. Out of my heart I spoke of my loneliness and of the feelings of isolation that had swept over me as I waited half a day and more for a change in weather. Then I promised to learn all that I could about the Outsider and the gods of this whorl, to honor Pas and Scylla most highly if I ever returned to the whorl in which I was born, and to do anything in my power to bring them both here if they were not here already. I also (but this was to myself) solemnly swore to buy sweeps when I got to New Viron; and I recited every prayer that I could recall.

All this, as you may imagine, occupied quite some time. When I lifted my head at last, it was already shadelow, with only the smallest crescent of the Short Sun visible above the western horizon. Day was passing; but something else had gone before it, or so I felt. For what must have been half a dozen minutes, I watched the Short Sun set and looked about me, hoping to learn what it had been. The sloop seemed unchanged, with only a trifle more water in its bilge than there had been after I had bailed it. The sky was darker, and its few clouds ruddy in place of white, but that was only to be expected. The dim and distant shore of Main (I thought of it as distant, at least) was nearly black now, but otherwise the same.

At length it came to me: the trolling seabird had vanished. I had complained, most probably to no god at all, of loneliness. I had begged for company. And the only living thing in sight had been taken away. Here was proof of the cruelty of the gods, or of their absence from the whorl to which their king and father had consigned us.

Thinking of it I began to laugh, but was interrupted by a loud plop as my fishing float was jerked beneath the silvery surface. I reached for the line. It broke and vanished before I could touch it, leaving me with two slack cubits or so tied to a belaying pin. I was still staring down at the water when the sloop rocked so violently that I was almost thrown overboard.

The horror of it will never leave me entirely. Looking behind me, I saw great, coarse claws, each as thick as the handle of our ax, scrabbling for hold on the port gunwale and rowling its wood like so many gouges. A moment later the head appeared and shot toward me, the clash of its three jaws like the slamming of double doors. I threw myself backward to escape it, and fell into the sea.

I nearly drowned. Not because of the roughness of the water—there was none—nor because of the weight of tunic, trousers, and boots; but out of sheer panic. The leatherskin would release its hold on the sloop, swim under it, and kill me in a second or two; it seemed completely certain, and paralyzed by terror as I was, I was unable to conceive of an escape and equally unable to ready myself for death. Surely, these were the longest moments of my life.

Sea and air were still, and at last it came to me that the noises I heard resulted from the leatherskin's continued efforts to climb aboard. It was not swimming swiftly and silently beneath the hull as I had feared, but struggling with idiotic ferocity to go straight to the place in which it had last seen me.

I am a strong swimmer, and I considered the possibility of swimming ashore. I knew it was a league or more away, because it had been almost out of sight when I stood in the waist of the sloop; but the sea was calm and warm, and if I paced myself carefully I might succeed.

An instant more, and I realized that I would have no chance whatever. The leatherskin would follow me over the starboard gunwale, and once it was back in the water was certain to hear my splashings and track me down. However slender it might be, my only chance was to reclaim the sloop the moment that the leatherskin returned to the sea.

By the time I had understood that, I had managed to kick off my boots. Diving so as to make less noise, I swam to the bow, surfaced, and risked grasping the bowsprit Sinew and I had added when it had become apparent that our new sloop would benefit from more foresail.

The sloop was still rocking violently; it was clear that the leatherskin had not given up its struggle to clamber aboard. I waited, trying very hard to breathe without gasping, and heard, and felt, the impact as its great inflexible body crashed to the bottom of the sloop, which sank under its weight until the freeboard was a scant hand.

I pulled myself up, and risked a look.

It was a sight I shall never forget. The leatherskin, one of the largest I have seen, stood with six massive legs and half its weight on the starboard gunwale, over which silver water cascaded. Its long, corded neck was stretched toward the last fleck of the vanishing Short Sun, its mouth so wide agape that every spike of its thousand fangs stabbed outward. Before I could have drawn breath, it had tumbled over the side and back into the oily sea.

The bowsprit was jerked up as if by the mighty hand, and I with it, although I nearly lost my grip. When it plunged down again to strike the sea (for the foundering sloop was pitching as though in a gale) I was able to throw myself onto the foredeck.

By the time I had scrambled to my feet, the leatherskin had heard me and turned back, its head above the surface and its ponderous bulk moving so rapidly below that the sea swirled and frothed above it. Floundering knee-deep, I got the harpoon I had re-stowed that afternoon; and when the leatherskin's huge claws gripped the starboard gunwale and its hideous jaws had snapped shut upon the barbed head, I rammed the harpoon so deep that its fangs actually tore the skin of my right hand. It fell back into the water, its head dripping bloody foam, and was lost to my sight, the harpoon line hissing after it as it sounded.

I was afraid that it might snatch the boat under, and bailed frantically, telling myself again and again that I must cut the line, which was tied to a ringbolt in the keel. I groped for it, terrified that a loop of the uncoiling line would catch my wrist or my ankle. But although I would have sworn an hour before that I could put my hand on that ringbolt in the dark, I would not find it.

The leatherskin surfaced thirty cubits from the bow, snorting blood and water. In less than a minute, the sloop was jerked along behind it, listing fearfully and making more speed than it ever had under sail. I lunged forward (I had been too far aft searching for the ringbolt) to cut the line, but before I could, the leatherskin had done the job for me. The line went slack.

By that time the first stars were out. I ought to have finished bailing and recoiled the line, I suppose, and no doubt done other things as well—gotten out our little tin lantern and lit it.

But I did not. I sat in the stern instead, where I was accustomed to sit, with my trembling hands resting on the tiller; and tried to catch my breath, and felt the hammering of my heart, and tasted the sweet-salt tang of the sea. Spat, and spat again, too tired and shaken to get up and break out a fresh bottle of water.

Green rose larger and brighter than any star, a flying whorl of visible width, where the stars are but twinkling points of light. I watched it climb above the dim white cliffs and swaying incense willows, and wondered whether Silk had seen it, at the bottom of the grave in his dream (where it would have been a fit ornament) and forgotten it when he awakened—or perhaps had only forgotten to tell me about it. Even if it had been there, he would not have known what a horror he saw.

After an hour or more had passed, it occurred to me that if the leatherskin had arrived a few minutes later it would almost certainly have killed me. By the last rays of the Short Sun I had scarcely escaped it.

In the dark . . .

The thought re-energized me, although I cannot explain why it should. I lit the lantern and ran it up the mast, found the bailer and resumed work, wearily scooping up water as black as ink and flinging it over the side. When I was a boy, we had pumps to raise the water from our wells; none but very backward country people and the poorest of the poor dropped buckets down their wells and hauled them up again; I thought as I worked how much easier a similar device would make it to empty a boat half filled with water, and resolved to build one when I could, and thought about how such a thing might be constructed—a tube of copper or waxwood, with a plunger that would first draw the water up, and then, the positions of the valves being reversed by the motion of the handle, force it out another opening and back into the sea.

I longed for paper, pen, and ink. There was plenty of paper in the cargo chests, but I would not have dared to open them for fear it would get wet; and I had no ink and nothing with which to make my drawings, anyway.

Bailing is easy at first, when the water is high. It grows more difficult (as I suppose everyone knows) as it progresses. When my own bailer was scraping wood, I heard a soft and almost stealthy sound that seemed to have returned from the distant past, a whisper of sound that I associated with some similar labor long, long ago, with youth, and with the acrid smell of yellow dust. I left off bailing, straightened up to rest my back, listened, and heard, in addition to that remembered and practically inaudible rustling sigh, the faint creaking of the mast.

The swell was running a trifle higher now, I thought, and rocking us; but the sloop felt as steady under my feet as any floor. The faint rustling returned, perhaps minutely louder, and this time I knew it for what it was—or rather, for what it had been: the sound my father made turning over the pages of his ledger while I swept the floor of his shop. Day was done, palaestra was over, and the shop was about to close. Time to enter the sales, so many few of this and many fewer of that, which would have to be reordered at the end of the month or perhaps at the end of the year. Time to tote up the bits in the cash box and calculate that the total would not quite cover the cost of dinner tonight for Horn (who was helping around the shop so very unwillingly), the rest of the sprats, and the wife.

I spoke aloud to no one, saying, "Time to close," and went aft to where the pages of Silk's book were turning themselves, page after water-spotted page, upon one of the chests, in the faintest possible breeze.

Time to close.

So it was, and I thought about that then, I believe for the first time ever. My boyhood was over and done with long ago, and my young manhood was behind me. I had married because it had seemed natural for Nettle and me to marry as we had planned from childhood. We would not willingly separate as long as we both lived, no matter how much distance might separate us; and if she should die before me, I would not marry again. Life and chance had given us three sons; we would have liked a daughter as well, a daughter certainly, or even two; but it was too late for that now, perhaps. Or if not too late, it would be when I returned from the Long Sun Whorl.

Time to close, to tote up accounts.

That, as I realized sitting alone upon the quiet sea, had been the chief reason I had so readily accepted the task those five people had come to persuade me to undertake. How surprised they had been! They had brought food, tents, and trunks full of clothing, expecting to spend a week or more on Lizard; but in my books Silk was an account that had never been closed, one so large that it dwarfed all others. At fifteen, I had thought him the greatest of great men. At thirty-five, only a little taller, thick-bodied and nearly bald, I thought him a great man still.

I closed the book, and secured it in the cubby under the foredeck.

He would meet us at the lander, he had said, if he could; he had not met us there. Latecomers such as Blazingstar had reported that he was still caldé when they had left Viron; but even their information was years out of date. There had been Trivigaunti troopers in the tunnels, and it seemed probable to me then (I mean then, on the sloop) that they had captured him when he had tried to rejoin us. If so, it seemed likely that Generalissimo Siyuf would soon have restored him as caldé, subject to her orders. That would account for the latecomer's reports, and in that case he might be governing Viron still, with every decision he made dictated by some cruel and arrogant Trivigaunti general.

Yet there were half a dozen other possibilities. No more settlers had reached us from Old Viron for years now, and Silk might have died aboard a lander that had failed to reach either whorl; everyone knew that not all the landers that left the *Whorl* landed safely on Blue or Green.

Equally, he might have been killed on Siyuf's orders at a later date, or been deposed by her or some other Trivigaunti; in which case he might be living in exile.

With or without Hyacinth, he might have boarded a lander that took him to Green, and if he had he was presumably dead. Equally, he might have landed on some part of Blue remote from us. (This still seems possible to me, as I wrote when I began this straggling history.) Before they left Lizard, I had brought up the possibility with Marrow and the rest, and they had agreed that it could not be discounted entirely. Here I am in a part of Blue a very considerable distance from New Viron, and hear nothing of Silk; but that means nothing. If he were a hundred leagues east of Gaon and me—or on Shadelow—it would explain everything.

I may find him yet. Perseverance and prayer! All is not lost until I give up the search.

★

★ ★

Very busy the last few days, busy until I was at length forced to put off all the others who desired to speak with me or desired to do it again, telling them that I required rest and prayer (which was true enough) and that my subordinates would hear their protestations, weigh their proofs, and decide matters. And telling my subordinates in turn that I trusted their judgment (which is not entirely false) and would support their decisions as long as they played no favorites and took no bribes.

Having said all that, and made it clear that I meant it, I retreated to this pleasant room and shut and barred the door. Here I sit, surrounded by a reverent hush, having prayed and read this rambling account of the beginning of my adventures through, and prayed again. All with intervals of pacing up and down, slamming my fist into my palm, and providing food and fresh water against the return of the pet who is no longer on his perch.

I am stunned to find this account as worthless as it is. It tells me nothing about myself (or Nettle, or the boys, or even Patera Silk) that I did not know already. It contains no plans for returning home, the very thing I should be thinking about most intently. Yet under these circumstances what plans can there be?

I must free myself from these handsome, generous, feckless people upon some pretense, and somehow procure a swift horse. Conceivably some other beast, although I would think a horse would be best. I must escape with cards enough—or the new rectangles of gold we use for cards sometimes here—to enable me to buy a small but seaworthy vessel when I reach the coast. After that, it will be in the hands of the Outsider and the weather gods of Blue—of the monstrous goddess whom Seawrack called the Mother, perhaps.

There is my plan, then. Under these circumstances, how can I plan anything more? The terrible aspect is that these people need someone like me very badly, and I am in a sense responsible for my own abduction.

As well as for them. They have made me their ruler, in name and very nearly in fact, and I have accepted the office. I, who have only a single wife for whom I long, now have no less than fifteen more—all young enough to be my daughters. Fifteen graceful and charming girls whom I sometimes permit as a very special favor to sing and play for me while I sit dreaming of home.

No, not of Old Viron, though I have been calling Old Viron "home" all my life. Dreaming of the house of logs at the foot of the Tor we built when we were young, of the flapping tent of scraped and greased greenbuck skins upon the beach, and of eager explanations of papermaking made to Nettle and—sometimes—to the wind. Dreaming of Lizard, the rushing water and thumping hammers of my mill, the measured clanking of the big gear, the crawl of the laden wire cloth, and the golden glory of the Short

Sun sinking into the sea beyond a Tail Bay crammed with prime softwood.

Once I planned to print our paper as well as make it. But I have written about that. What would be or could be the use of setting it down again?

3

The Sibyl and the Sorceress

The Marrow I had known as a boy had been portly in the best sense, a fat man whose bulk promised strength and gave him a certain air of command. He was no longer steady on his legs, and limped along (as Silk once had) with the help of a stick; his face was lined, and such hair as remained to him was white. Yet I could tell him quite truthfully that he had scarcely changed since we had fought the Trivigauntis in the tunnels together. He was fat still, though somewhat less energetic than he had once been; and the air of command had become a settled fact.

He was the same man.

"I don't need to talk to you," he said. "I know you, Horn, and know you'll do your best. That's all I need to know. But maybe you need to talk to me. If there's anything I can tell you, I will. If there's anything you need, I'll supply it if I can, or get somebody to."

I told him that I had come largely to buy provisions and get directions, that I had wanted to leave most of the food we had with my family; and I reminded him that he had promised to try to locate someone who had been to Pajarocu and could provide firsthand information regarding the best routes.

"Food's no problem." He waved it away. "I'll give you a barrel of apples, some dried stuff, cornmeal, and leavening powder." He paused, looking thoughtful. "A ham, too. A case of wine and a cask of pickled pork."

I doubted that I would need that much, and I told him so.

"Better to have it and not need it than need it and not have it. How was the voyage down?"

I shrugged. "I lost my harpoon."

"I'll get you another one, but it may take a day or two."

With thoughts of the leatherskin still fresh in my mind, I asked whether he could lend me a slug gun, adding that I could not afford to buy one.

His bushy eyebrows rose. "Not a needler? You had one in the old days. Still got it?"

I shook my head.

"I'll get you one." He leaned back, sucking his teeth. "It may take longer, I don't know. If worst comes to worst, I'll give you mine. I doubt that I'll ever need it again."

"I'd prefer a slug gun. I've heard that someone here is making them now, and making cartridges for them."

He rose with the help of his stick, saying, "I've got a couple in the next room. I'll show them to you."

It was a far larger house than ours, though not, I believe, so solidly built. The room to which he led me held cabinets, several well-made chairs, and a big table covered with papers. I bent to look at them.

He saw me, and picked up a sheet. "Your stuff. Just about all of it is. The traders have it sometimes, mostly off a lander if you ask me. They're surprised to find out we're making our own here in New Viron." He chuckled. "*We* means you, this time. I tell them we can make slug guns and mean Gyrfalcon, and we can make paper and mean you."

He handed me the sheet and took out a key. "We can do a couple of other things that mean a lot more. We can make a paper mill, and make a lathe and a milling machine for metal that are good enough to let us copy a slug gun. But I don't tell them that. We want sales, not competitors."

I protested that he made no profit when I sold my paper.

He smiled. "Sometimes you sell it to me."

"Yes, and I'm extremely grateful to you. You're a good customer."

"Then I sell it to them, some of it. I don't make anything when Gyrfalcon sells his slug guns either, or not directly. But it brings money here, and sooner or later I get my share. So do others. You did your own woodworking, didn't you, building your mill?"

I had, and said so.

"What about the metal stuff? Did you do that, too?"

"Others made those for us. They had to extend us credit, but we repaid them some time ago."

The key turned in the lock, and the door of a cabinet swung open. "Then you could make the paper Gyrfalcon and his workmen used when they drew out the parts for this slug gun. One hand scratches the other, Horn."

"I thought you said they copied the parts of a slug gun someone brought from home."

"Oh, they did. But it's better to measure once and draw it up than to keep on measuring. I won't ask you to tell me which of these was made back in the old place and which here. You could do it pretty easily, and so could any other man who had his wits about him. I want you to take them both in your hands, though. Look them over, and tell me if you think one ought to shoot better than the other, and why."

I did, opening the action of each first to assure myself that it was unloaded. "The new one's a little stiff," I said. "The old one's smoother and a fraction lighter. But I don't see why they shouldn't shoot equally well."

"They do. They're both mine, and I'll consider it an honor to give either one to you, if you want it." Marrow paused, his face grave. "The town ought to pay you. We can't, or not nearly enough to make you want to go for the money. The question is, is New Viron going to be richer in a few years, or poorer? And I don't know. But that's all it is, not the rubbish about morals and so forth that the old Prolocutor goes on about. We need Silk for the same reason we need better corn, and we're asking you to bring him here to us for nothing."

I picked up the newly made slug gun, and told Marrow that I would need a sling of some kind for it.

"Aren't you going to argue it with me? Your Caldé Silk would have, if you ask me."

"No," I told him. "If the parents are poor enough, the children starve. That would be enough for Silk, and it's enough for me."

"Well, you've the right of it. If they're poor enough, the parents do, too. That boy of yours would tell me people can hunt, but you think about filling every belly here, year in and year out, by hunting. They'd have to scatter out, and when they were, every family'd have to hunt for itself. No more paper and no more books, no carpentry because they'd be moving camp every few days and tables and so on's too heavy to carry. Pretty soon they wouldn't even have pack saddles."

I said it would not matter, since those who owned horses or mules would eat them after a year or two, and he nodded gloomily and dropped into a chair. "You like that gun?"

"Yes. Very much."

"It's yours. Take it out to your boat when you go back. Take that green box on the bottom shelf, too. It's cartridges from a lander and never been opened. Our new ones work, but they're not as good."

I said that I would prefer new cartridges nevertheless, and he indicated a wooden box that held fifty. I told him about the paper I had on the sloop, and offered it to him to offset—in part, at least—the cost of the slug gun and the food he had promised me.

He shook his head. "I'm giving you the gun and the rest of it. The cartridges and harpoon, and the apples and wine and the other stuff. It's the least I can do. But if you'll let me have that paper, I'll give whatever I get for it to your wife. Would you like me to do that? Or I can hold the money for you, until you get back."

"Give it to Nettle, please. I left her with little enough, and she and Sinew are going to have to buy rags and more wood soon."

He regarded me from under his brows. "You took your own boat, too, when I was going to let you have one of mine."

"Sinew will build a new one, I'm sure. He'll have to, and I believe it will be good that he has something to do besides run our mill, something he can watch grow under his hands. That will be important, at first particularly."

"You're deeper than you look. Your book shows it."

I said that I hoped I was deep enough, and asked whether he had found anyone who had actually been to Pajarocu.

"Not yet, but there's a new trader in the harbor every few days. You want to wait?"

"For a day or two, at least. I think it would be worth that to have firsthand information."

"Want to see their letter again? There's nothing there to tell where it is, not to me, anyhow. But you might see something there I missed, and you hardly looked at it back on your island."

"I own only the southern part, the southern third or so. No, I don't want to read it again, or at least not now. Can you have somebody copy the entire thing for me, in a clearer hand? I'd like to have a copy to take with me."

"No trouble. My clerk can do it." Again, he looked at me narrowly. "Why does my clerk bother you?"

"It shouldn't."

"I know that. What I want to know is why it does."

"When we were in the tunnels and on the lander, and for years after we landed, I thought . . ." Words failed me, and I turned away.

"You figured we'd all be free and independent here? Like you?"

Reluctantly, I nodded.

"You got a farm, you and your girl. Your wife. You couldn't make a go of it. Couldn't raise enough to feed yourselves, even."

This is too painful. There is pain enough in the whorl already. Why should I inflict more on myself?

★

★ ★

On Green, I met a man who could not see the inhumi. They were there, but his mind would not accept them. You might say that his sight recoiled in horror from them. In just the same way, my own interior sight refuses to focus upon matters I find agonizing. In Ermine's I dreamed that I had killed Silk. Is it possible that I actually tried once, firing Nettle's needler at him when he disappeared into the mist? Or that I did not really give him mine?

(I should have told Sinew that the needler I was leaving with him had been his mother's. It was the one she had taken from General Saba and given to me outside the entrance to the tunnels, and I have never seen a better one. Later, of course, I did.)

More pain, but this I must put down. For my own sake, I intend to make it as brief as possible—just a paragraph or two, if I can.

When I returned to the sloop, I found that I had been robbed, my cargo chests broken into and my paper gone, with much cordage and a few other things that I had brought from Lizard.

Before I had left to go to Marrow's, I had asked the owner of the boat tied up beside mine, a man I had attended palaestra with, to watch the sloop for me. He had promised he would. Now I went to speak to him. He could not meet my eyes, and I knew that it was he himself who had robbed me. I fought him and beat him, but I did not get my paper back.

After that, bruised and bleeding, I sought help from Gyrfalcon, Blazingstar, and Eschar, but received none. Eschar was away on one of his boats. Gyrfalcon and Blazingstar were both too busy to see me.

Or so I was told by their clerks.

I received a little help from Calf, who swore that it was all he could give, and none at all from my other brothers; in the end I had to go back to Marrow, explain the situation, and beg to borrow three cards. He agreed, took my bond for the amount plus eight percent, then tore it up as I watched. I owe him a great deal more than the three cards and this too-brief acknowledgment.

When I had refitted I put out, sailing south along the coast, looking for something that had been described to me as a rock with a haystack on it.

While I had talked with Marrow before I was robbed, I had considered how I could learn something that His Cognizance had been unwilling to tell me when we had conferred the day I made port. Eventually I realized that Marrow was more than acute enough to see through any sleight of mine; the only course open to me was to ask him outright, which I did.

"The girl's still alive," he said, stroking his chin, "but I haven't seen or heard tell of the old sibyl in quite a time."

"Neither have I," I told him, "but I should have. She was here in town, and I was out on Lizard, mostly, and it always seemed possible I would run across her someday when I brought paper to the market." Full of self-recriminations I added, "I suppose I imagined that she would live forever, that she would always be here if I wanted her."

Marrow nodded. "Boys think like that."

"You're right. Mine do, at least. When you're so young that things have changed very little during your lifetime, you suppose that they never will. It's entirely natural, but it is a bad mistake and wrong even in the moral sense more often than not."

I waited for his comment, but he made none.

"So now . . . Well, I'm going to look for Silk, and he's far away if he's alive at all. And it seems even more wrong for me to leave without having seen Maggie. She's no longer a sibyl, by the way."

"Yes, she is." Marrow was almost apologetic. "Our Prolocutor's made her one again."

"He didn't tell me that." (In point of fact, he had flatly refused to tell me anything about her.) "Did you know I talked to him?"

Marrow nodded.

"That was what I wanted to learn, or the principal thing. I

wanted to find out what happened to her and Mucor, but he wouldn't tell me or even say why he wouldn't. You must know where they are, and he concedes that they're still alive."

"I've heard talk from the people I do business with, that's all. I don't keep track of everybody, no matter what people may think." Marrow folded both hands on his stick, and regarded me for a long moment before he spoke again. "I doubt I know as much as he does, but she wanted to help out here, teaching the children like she used to. That was why he made her a sibyl again, and she used to mop and dust and cook for him. Only he wouldn't let the crazy girl in the house."

I smiled to myself. It would not have been easy to keep Mucor out.

"There was some trouble about her anyhow. About the crazy granddaughter."

He waited for me to speak, so I nodded. Mucor had often thrown food and dishes at Nettle and me when we had cared for her.

"They said she made other people crazy, too. I don't believe it and never did, but that's what they said. One day they were gone. If you ask me, the old Prolocutor gave them a shove. He's never admitted it that I've heard of, but I think probably he did. Maybe he gave them a little help moving, too. This is," Marrow rolled his eyes toward the ceiling, "five years ago. About that. Could be six."

He rocked back and forth in his big, solidly built chair, one hand on his stick and the other on the finale of the chair arm, where its grip had given the waxed wood a smoother finish as well as a darker tone. "I didn't put my nose in it, but somebody told me he'd found them a farm way out. To tell you the truth I thought some wild animal'd get the mad girl, the granddaughter, and Maytera'd come back."

I said, "I take it that didn't happen. I'm glad."

"That's right, you knew them both. I'd forgot. I went to the palaestra in my time, just like you, so I knew Maytera, too, way back then. I never did understand how she could have a granddaughter at all. Adopted, is what everybody says."

Clearly, Marrow had not read as much of our book as he pretended; I tried to make my nod noncommittal. "Are they still on the farm His Cognizance found for them? I'd like to see them while I'm here."

Once more, Marrow regarded me narrowly. "Island, just like you. I'm surprised you don't know."

When I did not comment, he added. "Just a rock, really. House looks like a haystack. That's what they say. Up in the air to keep the hay dry, you know how the farmers do, and made of sticks."

It seemed too bizarre to credit. I asked whether he had seen it himself, and he shook his head. "Driftwood I guess it is, really. Way down south. It'll take you all day, even with a good wind."

★

★ ★

I slept aboard the sloop, as you may imagine, and so was able to get under way at shadeup. There is no better breakfast than one eaten on a boat with a breeze strong enough to make her heel a trifle. Most of Marrow's promised provisions had arrived before I finished refitting, and I had purchased a few things in addition; I dined on ham, fresh bread and butter, and apples, drank water mixed with wine, and told myself with perfect truth that I had never eaten a better meal.

He had been surprised that I knew nothing of Maytera Marble (as she was again, apparently) and Mucor, although they lived on an island two days' sail from mine. The truth, I thought, might well be that I did know something. Boats that put into Tail Bay to trade for paper had spoken sometimes of a witch to the south, a lean hag who camped upon a naked rock and would tell fortunes or compounded charms for food or cloth. When I had heard those tales, it had not occurred to me that this witch might be Mucor. I reviewed them as I sailed that day, and found various reasons to think she was—but several more to think that she was not. In the end, I decided to leave the matter open.

Evening came, and I still had not caught sight of the house of sticks that Marrow had described. I was afraid I might pass it in the dark, so I furled my sails and made a sea anchor, and spent the night upon the open water, very grateful for the calm, warm weather.

It was about midmorning of the second day out when I caught sight of the hut, not (as I had supposed it would be) near shore to port, but a half league and more to starboard upon a sheer black rock so lonely that it did not appear to be a separated part of the mainland at all, but the last standing fragment of some earlier continent, a land devoured by the sea not long after the Outsider built this whorl.

Rubbish, surely. Still, I have never been in any other place that felt quite so lonely, unless Seawrack sang.

★

★ ★

Three days since I wrote that last. Not because I have been too busy (although I have been busy) and not because I did not wish to write, but because there was no more ink. Ink, it seems, is not made here, or I should say was not. It was an article of trade that you bought in the market when it appeared there if you wanted it, and hoarded against the coming shortage. It had not appeared in the market for a long time, my clerks had very little and most other people—people who wrote, that is to say, or kept accounts—none. Nettle and I had made our own, being unable to find any in New Viron, and I saw no reason why ink should not be made here.

Several trials were needed; but guided as I was by past experience, we soon had this very satisfactory ink. Glue is made here by boiling bones, hoofs, and horns, as I suppose it must be everywhere. We mixed it with the oil pressed from flax seed and soot, and then (it was this that we had to learn) boiled everything again with a little water. It dries a trifle faster, I believe, than the ink you and I made with sap, and so may be a step nearer the inks my father compounded in the back of our shop. At any rate it is a good dark black and satisfactory in every other way, as you see.

My father, Smoothbone, made colored inks as well. There is no reason we should not have them, too. It is clearly just a matter of finding the right colored powders to put in instead of soot. I have a bright young man looking into that. My clerks say that they have never seen colored inks in our market here, or in this big pink and blue house we call my palace for that matter. I imagine they would trade very well—which means, I suppose, that I am starting to think like Marrow. Since our positions are somewhat similar, that is not surprising.

Here I am tempted to write about the market in New Viron, and compare it, perhaps, to the one here; but I will save that for some other opening of the pen case.

Now back to the sloop.

There was a tiny inlet on the southeast side of Mucor's Rock that gave excellent shelter. I tied up there and climbed the steep path to the top carrying a side of bacon and a sack of cornmeal. She did not recognize me, as far as I could judge. To set down the truth, I did not know her either until I looked into her eyes, the same dead, dull eyes that I recalled. The witch had been described to me as being very thin. She was, but not as thin as she had been in the Caldé's Palace and on the lander afterward—not as thin as the truly skeletal young woman I recalled.

She was said to be tall, too. The truth is that she is not, although her thinness and erect carriage, and her short, ragged skirt, combine to make her appear so.

The Mucor I had known would never have spoken to me first. This one whom I had heard called the witch and the sorceress did, but seemed at first to be recalling an almost forgotten language as she licked her cracked lips. "What . . . Do . . . You . . . Want . . . ?"

I said, "I must speak with you, Mucor." I showed her the bacon, then patted the sack of cornmeal I was carrying on my shoulder. "I brought you these, thinking you might need them. I hope you like them."

Without another word, she turned and went into the hut, which was larger than I had expected. When I saw that its rough door remained open, I followed her.

The only light came through the open doorway and a god-gate in the middle of the conical roof. For half a minute, perhaps, I stood just inside the door, blinking. A motionless figure in black sat with its back to me, facing the ashes of a small fire that had burned itself out in a circle of blackened stones some time before. Its aged hands clasped a long peeled stick of some light-colored wood. Mucor stood beside it, one hand upon its shoulder, regarding me silently. Beyond them, on the other side of the circle of stones, something stirred; in that near darkness, I heard rather than saw it.

Pointing at the figure in black, I asked, "Is that Maytera Marble?" and her head pivoted until it seemed to regard a place somewhat to my left. The metal face thus revealed was the smooth oval that I recalled so well, yet it appeared somehow misshapen, as if it were diseased.

After a pause that I considered much too long, Mucor said, "This is my grandmother. She knows the future."

I put down my sack and laid the bacon on it. "Then she should be able to tell me a great many things I want to know. First I have a question for you, however. Do you know who I am?"

"Horn."

"Yes, I am. Do you remember Nettle?"

Mucor only stared.

"Nettle and I used to bring you your food sometimes when you lived in the Caldé's Palace." She did not reply, so I added, "Silk's palace."

Maytera Marble whispered, "Horn? Horn?"

"Yes," I said, and went to her and knelt before her. "It's me, Maytera."

"You're a good, good boy to come to see us, Horn."

"Thank you." I found it hard to speak, impossible when I looked at her. "Thank you, Maytera. Maytera, I said I used to take your granddaughter's food up for you. I want you to know that

I've brought her some now. It's only bacon and a sack of cornmeal, but there's more food on my boat. She can have anything there she wants. Or that you want for her. What about apples? I have a barrel of them, good ones."

Slowly her metal head bobbed up and down. "The apples. Bring us three apples."

"I'll be right back," I told her.

Mucor's hand scarcely moved, but it brought me to a halt as I went through the doorway. "You will eat with us?"

"Certainly," I said, "if you can spare the food."

"There is a flat rock. Down there. You stepped on it."

At first I supposed that she intended one of the flat stones that made up the floor of their hut; then I recalled the stone she meant and nodded. "When I tied up the sloop. Is that the one?"

"There will be fish on it. Bring them up, too."

I told her that I would be happy to, and discovered that it was easy as well as pleasant to step out of that hut and into the sunlight.

The steep path from the more or less level top of the island to the little inlet in which I had moored gave me a good view of it (and indeed of the entire inlet) at one point, and there were no fish on the rock she had indicated. I continued my descent, however, thinking I would bring up the apples with something else in lieu of the fish. When I reached the rock, three fish flopped and struggled there so vigorously that it seemed certain that all three were about to escape. I dove for them and caught two, but the third slipped from between my fingers and vanished with a splash.

A moment afterward, it leaped from the water and back onto the rock, where I was able to catch it. I dropped all three into an empty sack I happened to have on board, and hung it in the water while I got three apples from Marrow's barrel and tied them up in a scrap of sailcloth. As an afterthought, I put a small bottle of cooking oil into one pocket, and a bottle of drinking water into another.

When I returned to the hut, there was a fire blazing in the circle of stones. After giving Maytera Marble the apples, I filleted the fish with Sinew's hunting knife, and Mucor and I cooked them in a most satisfactory fashion by impaling fillets wrapped in bacon on sticks of driftwood. I also mixed some of the cornmeal with my oil (I had forgotten to bring salt), made cakes, and put them into the ashes at the edge of the fire to bake.

"How is dear Nettle?" Maytera Marble asked.

I said that she had been well when I left her; and I went on to explain that I had been chosen to return to the Long Sun Whorl and bring Silk here, and that I was about to set out for a foreign town called Pajarocu where there was said to be a lander capable of making the return trip, as none of ours were. I went into considerably more detail than I have here, and she and Mucor listened to all of it in silence.

When I had finished, I said, "You will have guessed already how you can help me, if you will. Mucor, will you locate Silk for me, and tell me where he is?"

There was no reply.

When no one had spoken for some time, I raked one of the cornmeal cakes out of the fire and ate it. Maytera Marble asked what I was eating; that was the first time, I believe, that I realized she had gone blind, although I should have known it an hour before.

I said, "One of the little cakes I made, Maytera. I'll give your granddaughter one, if she'll eat it."

"Give me one," Maytera Marble said; and I raked out another cake and put it into her hand.

"Here is an apple for you." She rubbed it against her torn and dirty habit, and groped for me. I thanked her and accepted it.

"Will you put this one in my granddaughter's lap, please, Horn? She can eat it after she's found Patera for you."

I took the second apple, and did as she asked.

She whistled shrilly then, startling me; at the sound, a young hus emerged from the shadows on the other side of the fire, at once greedy and wary. "Babbie, come here!" she called, and whistled again. "Here, Babbie!"

It advanced, the thick, short claws some people call hooves loud on the stone floor, its attention divided between me and the food Maytera Marble held out to it. I found its fierce eyes disconcerting, although I felt reasonably sure it would not charge. After hesitating for some while, it accepted the food, the apple in one stubby-toed forepaw and the cornmeal cake in its mouth, giving me a better look than I wanted at the sharp yellow tusks that were only just beginning to separate its lips.

As it retreated on seven legs to the other side of the fire, Maytera Marble said, "Isn't Babbie cute? The captain of some foreign boat gave him to my granddaughter."

I may have made some suitable reply, although I am afraid I only grunted like a hus.

"It's practically like having a child with us," Maytera Marble declared. "One of those children one's heart goes out to, because the gods have refrained from providing it with an acute intellect, for their own good and holy reasons. Babbie tries so very hard to please us and make us happy. You simply can't imagine."

That was perfectly true.

"The captain was afraid that ill-intentioned persons might land here and fall upon us while we slept. It's active mostly at night. From what I have been given to understand, they all are, just like that bird dear Patera Silk had."

I said that while I had never hunted hus, according to what my son had told me, that was correct.

"So dear little Babbie's always active for me." She sighed, the weary *hish* of a mop cleaning a floor of tiles. "Because it's always night for me." Another sigh. "I know that it must be the gods' will for me, and I try to accept it. But I've never wanted to see again quite as much as I do today with you come to visit us, Horn."

I tried to express my sympathy, embarrassing both myself and her.

"No. No, it's all right. The gods' will for me, I'm sure. And yet—and yet . . ." Her old woman's hands clasped the white stick as if to break it, then let it fall to wrestle each other in her lap.

I said that in my opinion there were evil gods as well as benevolent ones, and recounted my experience the week before with the leatherskin, ending by saying, "I had prayed for company, Maytera, and for a wind, to whatever gods might hear me. I got both, but I don't believe the same god can have sent both."

"I—you know that I've become a sibyl again, Horn? You must because you've been calling me Maytera."

I explained that Marrow had told me.

"With my husband and I separated, and no doubt separated permanently—well, you understand, I'm sure."

I said I did.

"We had begun a child, a daughter." She sighed again. "It was hard, dreadfully hard, to find parts, or even things we could make them from. We never got far with her, and I don't suppose she'll ever be born unless my husband takes a new wife, poor little thing."

I tried to be sympathetic.

"So there wasn't any reason not to. I couldn't have my own child anymore, the child that had been my dream for all those empty years. Since I could not, I thought it might be nice to teach bio children like you again, the way I used to when I was younger. The ordinances of the Chapter let married women become sibyls, His Cognizance said, under special circumstances like mine, provided that the Prolocutor consents. He did, and I took the oath all over again. Very few of us have ever taken it more than once."

I nodded, I believe. I was paying more attention to Mucor, who sat silently with the apple untouched in her lap.

"Are you listening, Horn?"

"Yes," I said. "Yes, of course."

"I taught there in New Viron for a good many years. And I kept house for His Cognizance, which was a very great honor. People are so intolerant, though."

"Some are, at least."

"The Chapter has fought that intolerance for as long as I've been alive, and it has achieved a great deal. But I doubt that intolerance will ever be rooted out altogether."

I agreed.

"There are children, Horn, who are very much like little Babbie. Not verbal, but capable of love, and very grateful for whatever love they may receive. You would think every heart would go out to them, but many don't."

I asked her then about Mucor, saying that I had not realized it would take her so long to find Silk.

"She has to travel all the way to the whorl in which we used to live, Horn. It's a very long way, and even though her spirit flies so fast, it must fly over every bit of it. When she arrives, she'll have to look for him, and when she finds him, she'll have to return to us."

I explained that it was quite possible that Silk was here on Blue, or even on Green.

Maytera Marble shook her head, saying that only made things worse. "Poor little Babbie's quite upset. He always is, every time she goes away. He understands simple things, but you can't explain something like that to him."

Privately, I wished that someone would explain it to me.

"He's really her pet. Aren't you, Babbie?" Her hands, the thin old-woman hands she had taken from Maytera Rose's body, groped for the hus, although he was far beyond her reach. "He loves her, and I really think that she loves him, just as she loves me. But it's hard, very hard for them both here, because of the water."

For a moment I thought she meant the sea; then I said, "I assumed you had a spring here, Maytera."

She shook her head. "Only rainwater from the rocks. It makes little pools and so on, here and there, you know. My dear granddaughter says there are deep crevices, too, where it lingers for a long time. I've had no experience with thirst, myself. Oh, ordinary thirst in hot weather. But not severe thirst. I'm told it's terrible."

I explained that a spring high up on the Tor gave us the stream that turned my mill, and acknowledged that I had never been thirsty as she meant it either.

"He must have water. Babbie must, just as she must. If it doesn't rain soon . . ." She shook her head.

Much too late, I remembered that the uncomfortably large object in my pocket was a bottle of water. I gave it to her, and told her what it was. She thanked me effusively; and I told her there were many more on my boat, and promised to leave a dozen with her.

"You could go down and get them now, couldn't you, Horn? While my granddaughter's still away."

There had been a pathetic eagerness in Maytera Marble's voice; and when I remembered that the water would not be of the smallest value to her, I was deeply touched. I said that I did not want to miss anything that Mucor said when she came back.

"She will be gone a long, long time, Horn." This in her old classroom tone. "I doubt that she's even reached our old whorl yet. There's plenty of time for you to go down and get it, and I wish you would."

Stubbornly, I shook my head; and after that, we sat in silence except for a few inconsequential remarks for an hour or more.

At last I stood and told Maytera Marble that I would bring up some water bottles, and made her promise to tell me exactly what Mucor said if she spoke.

It had been morning when I arrived, but the Short Sun was already past the zenith when I left the hut. I discovered that I was tired, although I told myself firmly that I had done very little that day. Slowly, I descended the path again, which was in fact far too steep and dangerous for anyone to go up or down it with much celerity.

At the observation point I have already mentioned, I stopped for a time and studied the flat stone on which I had found our fish. It was sunlit now, although it had been in shadow when I had failed to see them; I told myself that they had certainly been there whether I had seen them or not, then recalled their vigorous leaps. If in fact they had been there when I had looked down at the sloop, they would certainly have escaped before I reached them.

As I continued my descent to the inlet and my sloop, I realized that it actually made no difference whether they had been there when I looked or not. They had certainly not been present when I had tied up. Even if I had somehow failed to see them, I would have kicked them or stepped on them.

Mucor had been in my sight continuously from the time I had encountered her outside her hut, and Maytera Marble from the time I had gone in. Who, then, had left us the fish?

I rinsed the sack that had held the fish, put half a dozen water bottles into it, and spent some time peering down into the calm, clear water of the inlet, without seeing anything worth describing here. One fish had regained the water, as the other two surely would have if I had not caught them in time. It had been forced to leap back onto the rock almost immediately.

By what?

I could not imagine, and I saw nothing.

Maytera Marble was waiting for me outside the hut. I asked whether Mucor had returned, and she shook her head.

"I have the water right here, Maytera." I swung the sack enough to make the bottles clink. "I'll put them anywhere you want them."

"That's very, very good of you. My granddaughter will be extremely grateful, I'm sure."

I ventured to say that they could as easily live on the mainland in some remote spot, and that although I felt sure their life there would be hard, they could at least have all the fresh water they wanted.

"We did. Didn't I tell you? His Cognizance gave us a place like that. We—I—still own it, I suppose."

I asked whether their neighbors had driven them away, and she shook her head. "We didn't have any. There were woods and rocks and things on the land side, and the sea the other way. I used to look at it. There was a big tree there that had fallen down but wouldn't quite lay flat. Do you know what I mean, Horn?"

"Yes," I said. "Certainly."

"I used to walk up the trunk until I stood quite high in the air, and look out over the sea from there, looking for boats, or just looking at the weather we were about to get. It was a waste of time, but I enjoyed it."

I tried to say that I did not think she had been wasting her time, but succeeded only in sounding foolish.

"Thank you, Horn. Thank you. That's very nice of you. Look at the sea, Horn, while you can. Look at it for me, if you won't do it for yourself."

I promised I would, and did so as I spoke. The rock offered a fine view in every direction.

"It wasn't good soil," Maytera Marble continued. "It was too sandy. I grew a few things there, though. Enough to feed my granddaughter, and a little bit over that I took to town and sold, or gave the palaestra. I had a little vegetable patch in the garden at our manteion. Do you remember? Vegetables and herbs."

I had forgotten it, but her words brought back the memory very vividly.

"Patera had tomatoes and berry brambles, but I had onions and chives, marjoram and rosemary, and red and yellow peppers. All sorts of things. Little red radishes in spring, and lettuces all summer. I tried to grow the same things on our farm, and succeeded with most of them. But my granddaughter would swim out here and stay for days and days. It worried me."

Looking east to the mainland, I said, "It would worry me, too. It's a very long swim, and she can't be strong."

"I built a little boat, then. I had to, so I could come out here and get her. I found a hollow log and scraped out all the rotten wood, and made ends for it. They were just big wooden plugs, really, but they kept the water from running in. Sometimes she would not go, and I'd have to stay out here with her till she would. That was why I built this little house. Then a storm came, a terrible one. I thought it was going to blow our little house away. It didn't, but it broke my boat. I can't swim, Horn."

She looked up as she said it in such a way that sunshine struck her face, and I saw that her faceplate was gone. The lumps and furrows that had seemed deformities were a host of mechanisms her faceplate had hidden when I had known her earlier. Trying to ignore them, I said, "I can take you both back to the mainland in my sloop, Maytera. Nettle and I built it to carry our paper to the market in town, and it will carry the three of us easily."

She shook her head. "She wouldn't go, Horn, and I won't leave her out here alone. I only wish—but I don't worry about falling off anymore. I tap on the stone with my stick, you see." She demonstrated, rapping the rock between us. "A man who came to consult my granddaughter made it for me, so now I can always find the edge."

"That's good."

"It is. Yes, it is. I was feeling blue when you came, Horn. I feel blue at times, and sometimes it lasts days and days."

Her free hand groped for me, and I stepped nearer so that she could put it on my shoulder.

"How tall you've grown! Why, you've taken me out of myself, just by coming to see us. Not that I should ever be blue anyway. I had good eyes for hundreds and hundreds of years. Most people don't get to see things for anything like that long. Look at all the children who die before they're grown! Dead at fifteen or twelve or ten, Horn, and I could name a dead child for you for every year between fifteen and birth."

When she spoke again, the voice was Maytera Rose's. "My other eyes. I had them less than a hundred years, and Marble ought to have taken them when she took my hands and so many other things. Taken the good one, I mean, for one was blind.

"But I didn't. I left her eyes, because I never realized my own were wearing out. Her processor, yes. I took that, but not her eye. Horn?"

"Yes, I'm still here, Maytera. Is there some way I can help you?"

"You already have, by bringing us those nice bottles of water for my granddaughter and her pet. That was very, very fine of you, and I will never forget it. But you're going home, Horn? Isn't that what you said? Going back to—to the whorl we used to live in?"

I told her that I was going to try to go wherever Silk was and bring him to New Viron, which was what I had sworn to do; and that I thought he was probably in Old Viron, in which case I was going to go there if the people of Pajarocu would allow me on their lander.

"Then I want to ask a very great favor. Will you do me a very great favor, Horn, if you can?" Her free hand left my shoulder and went to her own face. "My faceplate is gone. I took it off myself, Horn, and put it away somewhere. Have I told you?"

I shook my head, forgetting for a moment that she could not see it.

"We were here on this rock, my granddaughter and I, after the storm, and one of my eyes just went out. I told myself that it was all right, that the other one would probably last for years and years yet, and I could take good care of my poor granddaughter with one eye as well as I had with two."

She sounded so despondent that I said, "We don't have to talk about it if you don't want to."

"I do. I must. It was only four days, Horn. Four days after my left eye failed, my right eye failed, too. I took them out and reversed them, because I knew there was a chance that one might work then, but it didn't help. That was when I took my faceplate off, because I felt somehow that it was in the way, that I was trying to look through it. And I couldn't have. It's solid metal, aluminum I think. They all are."

Not knowing what else to say, I said, "Yes."

"It didn't help, but I've left it off ever since. My poor granddaughter doesn't complain, and I'm more comfortable without it for some reason."

As she spoke, she had plucked her right eye from its socket.

"Here, Horn. Take it, please. It's a bad part, and not of the least use to me anymore."

Reluctantly, I let her put it into my hand, which she closed around it for me with her own slender fleshlike fingers.

"If I were to tell you what it is, the part number and all that, it would be of very little use to you. But with the actual part, you might be able to find another one, and you'll recognize it if you come across one."

I resolved then to make every effort to find two (at which I have failed also) and told her so.

"Thank you, Horn. I know you will. You were always such a good boy. Sometimes it's very hard to bear, but I shouldn't feel blue. I really shouldn't. The gods have given me a—a consolation prize, I suppose you'd call it. I can see into the future now, just as my dear sib Maytera Mint could. Did I tell you?"

I believe I must have said that I had always assumed she could prophesy, as all sibyls could.

"I wasn't any good at it, because I couldn't ever see the pictures. I knew the things everybody knows, what an enlarged heart means, and all those commonplace indicants. But I couldn't see things in the entrails the way my dear sib could, and Patera, too. Now I can. Isn't that strange? Now that I'm blind, I have interior vision. I can't see the entrails till I touch them. But when I do, I see the pictures."

Silk, I knew, had prophesied in that way; but I also knew that he had not had great faith in such prophesies. He had been both fascinated by and skeptical of the entire procedure. Bearing all that in mind, I asked whether she would be willing to prophesy for me, provided I could supply a good big fish for a victim.

"Why, yes, Horn. I'm very flattered."

She paused, thinking. "We must have another fire for your sacrifice, however. A fire here outside. I built a little altar of stones, too. It's what I use when the men who come in boats want me to do it."

She began to walk slowly, searching left and right with the white wand she carried; and for a moment I saw her, and the rock itself and Mucor, as strangers must have—as the "men in boats" she talked about no doubt saw them: a place and two women so uncanny that I was amazed that anybody had the courage to consult them.

There is no point in recounting here how I caught a fish and carried it up that steep and weary path in a bucket, or how we built a small fire for it on the altar, lighting it from the one inside, before which Mucor sat motionless while the young hus munched her apple.

I loaned Maytera the long hunting knife Sinew had given me, and held my fish steady for her. She cut its throat neatly (not through the gills as one commonly kills fish, but as if it had been a rabbit); turning, she raised her thin arms to the point at which the Sacred Window would have stood, had we possessed one, and uttered the ancient formula.

(Or perhaps I should say that the empty northern sky was her Window. Is not the sky the only Sacred Window we have here, in which we strive to trace the will of gods who may not yet have deserted us?)

"Accept, all you gods, the sacrifice of this fine shambass. And speak to us, we beg, of the times that are to come. What are we to do? Your lightest word will be treasured. Should you, however, choose otherwise . . ."

As she pronounced these words, I was beset by a sensation so extraordinary that I hesitate to write about it, knowing that I will not be believed.

No, my dearest wife, not even by you.

I saw nothing and heard nothing, yet it seemed to me that the face of the Outsider had appeared, filling the whole sky and indeed overflowing it, a face too large to be seen—that I was seeing him in the only way that a human being can see him, which is to say in the way that a flea sees a man. Call it nonsense if you like; I have often called it nonsense myself. But is it really so impossible that the god of lonely, outcast things should have favored those two, exiled as they were to their sea-girt, naked rock? Who was, who could be, more broken, exiled, and despairing than Maytera Marble? Whether or not there was truth in the presence that I sensed then, I fell to my knees.

Turning back to the altar and me, Maytera Marble laid my fish open with a single swift cut that made me fear for my thumb. I took back the knife, and her old-woman's fingers probed the abdominal cavity in a way that left me feeling they had eyes in their tips I could not see.

"One side's for the giver, that's you, Horn, and the augur. That's me. The other's for the congregation and the city. I don't suppose—"

Abruptly she fell silent, half crouching with her head thrown back, her blind eye and empty, aching socket staring at nothing, or perhaps at the declining sun.

"I see long journeys, fear, hunger and cold, and feverish heat. Then darkness. Then more darkness and a great wind. Wealth and command. I see you, Horn, riding upon a beast with three horns."

(She actually said this.)

"Darkness also for me. Darkness and love, darkness until I look up and see very far, and then there will be light and love."

After that she was silent for what seemed to me a very long time. My knees hurt, and with my free hand I tried to brush away the small stones that gouged them.

"The city searches the sky for a sign, but no sign shall it have but the sign from the fish's belly."

Now I must get to bed, and there is really nothing more to record. Although Maytera urged me to spend the night in their hut, I slept on the sloop, very tired but troubled all night by dreams in which I sailed on and on, braving storm after storm, without ever sighting land.

★

★ ★

It is very late. My palace is asleep, but I cannot sleep. Earlier I was yawning over this account. If I write a little bit more, perhaps it will make me sleepy again.

Darling, you will want to know about Maytera's prophecy, and what Mucor said when at last she returned to us from her search for Silk.

You will also want to know the solution to the mystery of the fish. About that, I can really tell nothing. I have certain suspicions, but no evidence to back them up.

Let me say this. An island—our own island of Lizard, for instance—is in fact a sort of mountain thrust out of the sea, as all good sailors know. If the sea were to recede, we would discover that our mill is really situated not at the foot of the Tor but on a mountaintop. An island, that is to say, exists not only in the air but in the water that is beneath the air. I have reason to suspect that there were four of us, not three, on the island I have named Mucor's Rock. (I do not include Babbie.) Mucor, I believe, communicated with that fourth person by means you understand no better—and no worse—than I do. You will recall how she appeared to Silk and others, in the tunnels, on the airship, and even in Silk's own bedroom. This may have been something of the same kind.

Maytera's prophecy regarding me was entirely accurate. You may object that save for the part about the beast with three horns—which I will treat separately in a moment—it was very general. So it was; but it was correct as well, as I have said. I did indeed journey long, endure hunger, thirst, cold and heat, and terrible darkness of which you shall read before this record closes—assuming that I will someday finish it for you. Here in Gaon, I have great wealth at my command and my orders are obeyed without question.

On Green I rode a three-horned beast, as Maytera foresaw. Indeed, I was riding it at the time I was wounded fatally. But I shall say no more about that. It would only disturb us both.

As for Mucor's report, I am yawning again already. I will leave that anticlimax for another day.

4

THE TALE OF THE PAJAROCU

The next morning I found Mucor and Maytera Marble enjoying the sunshine in front of their hut. At the sound of my steps, Maytera blessed me as she used to bless our class at the beginning of each day at the palaestra, recommending us to the god of the day. Mucor, to my astonishment, actually said, "Good morning."

"Good morning," I replied. "You're back. I'm very glad to have you back with us, Mucor. Happier than I can say. Did you find Silk?"

She nodded.

"Where is he?"

"Sit down." She and Maytera Marble were sitting upon one sun-warmed stone, she cross-legged and Maytera with hands clasped over her shins.

I sat on another. "But you found him? He's still alive? Please tell me. I've got to know."

"Once I found him, I stayed with Silk a long while. We talked three times."

"That's wonderful!" He was alive, clearly, and at that moment I could have jumped up and danced.

"He asked me not to tell you where he is. It will be very dangerous for you to try to go where he is. If you find him, it will be dangerous for him, and for Hyacinth as well." This was said without any expression, as Mucor always spoke; but it seemed to me that there was a spark of concern in her eyes, which were usually so empty.

"I have to, Mucor. We need him, and I have given my word that I will try."

She shook her head, sending her wild black hair flying. "I told Silk what you told me, that the people here want him to come and lead them. He said that if he were their leader he would only tell them to lead themselves, telling every man and every woman to do what he or she knows should be done. Those words are his."

"But we need the favor of the gods!"

Maytera remarked quietly, "You knew once whom the good gods favor, Horn. I taught you that while you were still very small. Have you forgotten it?"

I sat thinking for a few seconds. At last I said, "Mucor, you told Silk what I told you when I came."

She nodded. Her eyes were dull once more, and fixed upon something far away.

"This is my fault, because I didn't explain the situation as fully as I should have. It's actually my fault twice. My fault for not explaining, and my fault that certain people in New Viron want Silk to be their caldé. The same thing is true, I'm told, in Three Rivers and some other towns, and that's my fault, too. My wife and I wrote our book, and it has been more widely read, and much more often copied, than we had ever dreamed it would be."

"What about the women troopers from Trivigaunte?" Maytera inquired.

"No. Though their men may feel differently. But they want him in Urbasecundus, and in other towns even farther from here. I said my wife and I wrote that book, and it sounds as if I'm trying to divide the blame. I'm not; our book would never have been written if I had not been determined to write it before I died. Nettle saw how hard it was and offered her help, which I gladly accepted. But the fault is mine alone."

I waited for Mucor to speak, which was nearly always a mistake.

"Maybe it was a foolish thing to do, though I didn't think so at the time. It was to be a book about Silk, Silk's Book, and mostly it was. But you're in it, both of you, and so are General Mint and Maytera Rose. Maybe I should have said all three of you are in there."

"Really?" Maytera asked.

"Yes. So too are your son Blood, and His Cognizance, and the inhumu that we called His Cognizance Patera Quetzal back in Old Viron. And Corporal Hammerstone, and Patera Incus. Do you remember Patera Incus?"

"Yes, Horn. Yes, I do. My husband thought the whorl of him." I had been away from her for too long to tell whether she was smiling or frowning.

"But it was mostly about Patera Silk," I continued, "and I tried to show how good and wise he was, and how he made mistakes sometimes but was never too proud to acknowledge that he'd been wrong. Most of all, how he never gave up, how he kept working for peace with the Ayuntamiento and peace with Trivigaunte, no matter how badly things were going or how impossible any peace seemed. I believed that a book like that would help everyone who read it, not just now or next year, but long after Nettle and I were gone. Nettle thought so, too, and wanted to help create a gift that we could give our children's children, and their children."

Maytera's hand groped toward me. "You're a good boy, Horn. Too lively and fond of mischief, but good at heart. I always said so, even when I had to take my switch to you."

I thanked her. "There was something else, Maytera. I felt he deserved it, deserved a book telling everyone what he had done, and I felt sure that if I didn't write down all the things I knew about him, nobody would."

Maytera said, "He deserved your tribute, dear."

And Mucor, "He does."

"So I tried. It was a lot of work for me and even more for Nettle, because she had to copy what I'd written over and over. But when we were finished and I read it as somebody who hadn't known him would, I realized I hadn't done him justice, that he had been greater than I had been able to show. Ever since it began to be read, people have been telling us that we exaggerated, that he couldn't have been as great and good a man as my wife and I said he was. We've always known that all the error was on the other side."

Maytera Marble sniffed. One of the parts she had taken when Maytera Rose died had been that sniff, so expressive of skepticism and contempt. "You think you've got to go because they'd never have known about young Patera Silk if you and that girl hadn't written about him."

"Yes, I do."

"That was how I used to treat Maggie, our maid. Every time she did some little favor for me, I made it her task, and added to it. Oh, I knew it was wicked, but I did it just the same."

Hoping to bring her to herself again, I said, "Did you really, Maytera Marble?"

She nodded, and something in the movement of her head told me that it was still Maytera Rose who gave her assent. "I said to myself that if she was ninny enough to let me impose on her like that, she deserved everything she got. I was right, too. Both ways. . . . Horn?"

"Yes, Maytera. I'm still here. What is it?"

"You don't owe my granddaughter and me any more favors. You've been very, very generous with us, and the only help that my granddaughter's been able to give you has been to tell you to help yourself. Now I need to ask you for another favor, one that I want almost as much as I want a new eye—"

"I'll get two if I can, Maytera."

"You're going to go anyway? In spite of what Patera Silk said?"

I was, of course, because I had to. I temporized by saying that there were many other things in the Long Sun Whorl that were needed in New Viron.

"We must be realistic, Horn. Are you realistic?"

I said that I tried to be.

"You may not be able to find a new eye for me, much less two. I—I understand that. So do you, I feel sure."

I nodded and said, "I also understand that because we told

everyone about Silk, I'm the one who must go back for him when he's needed so badly here. When I got to New Viron I asked Marrow for a copy of a certain letter he had shown me. Do you remember Marrow, Maytera?"

Her old woman's fingers smoothed her dirty black skirt over her thin metal thighs. "I used to go to his shop twice a week."

"He's not a bad man, Maytera. In fact, he's a very good man as men are judged in New Viron today. He has been a good and generous friend to me ever since I agreed to go back and get Silk. But when his clerk came in to copy that letter, he wore a chain."

She said nothing, and I was afraid she had not understood me. I said, "I don't mean jewelry, a gold or silver chain around his neck. His hands were chained. There were iron bands around each wrist, and the chain ran between them."

She said nothing. Neither did Mucor.

"They make those chains short enough that a man wearing one can't fire a slug gun properly. He can't work the slide to put a fresh round into the chamber without letting go of the part that his right hand holds."

"You needn't explain any more, Horn. Not about the gun or the chains, I mean."

I did anyway. I had lived on Lizard too long, perhaps, seeing few people other than you yourself, Nettle darling, and our sons. I said, "I watched him write, copying it out for me, and I couldn't help seeing how careful he was to keep it back, keep it from smearing his ink. It wasn't a big chain, Maytera. It wasn't a heavy chain at all, just a little, light chain with seven little links. The men who unload boats wear much heavier ones. He probably thinks that he's being treated kindly, and in a way he is."

"I quite understand, Horn. You don't have to tell us any more."

"Once—this is two or three years ago—I talked to a man in town who was boasting about how beautiful a girl he had was. He even offered to take me to his house so that I could see her."

"Did you go?"

I had but I denied it, one of those lies we tell without knowing why. "I asked him if the chain didn't get in the way when they made love, and he said no, he made her hold her hands over her head."

"Is this about Silk? Yes, I suppose it is." Maytera was silent for a moment. "Like Marl. Marl was a friend of mine back home. Like the clerk, except that he didn't have to wear a chain. All right, I understand why you think you must bring Silk here. In your place, I suppose I would, too."

"Even though he doesn't want to? He wanted very badly to go with us when we left. You must remember that, Maytera—how much he wanted to go with us, how eager he was. He hated all the evil he saw in the *Whorl*, and he must have hoped that people would be better in a new place."

She said nothing.

"A lot are. Many of us are. That's what I ought to say, because I'm one of them. We're not as good as he would want us to be, but we're better than we were in a lot of ways. Just thinking about starting fresh in a new place made Auk better, and if he and Chenille landed here—"

Mucor said distinctly, "On Green."

"They landed on Green?" I turned to her eagerly. "Have you talked to them there?"

My question hung in the air, whispered by the waves at the feet of the cliffs.

At last I shrugged, and went back to Maytera Marble. "Even if they landed on Green, Maytera, they may be better people than the Auk and Chenille we knew, better people than they ever were at home."

"What I started out to say, Horn, is that even if you cannot bring back a new eye for me, you could still make me very, very happy."

I assured her that I would do anything I could for her.

"We agree that it will be difficult for you to find a new eye. This is worse, or anyway I'm afraid it may be. But if you should see my husband, see Hammerstone . . ."

I waited.

"If he's still alive, if you should run across him, I'd like you to tell him where I am and how very deeply I regret tricking him into marriage as I did. Tell him, please, that I wouldn't have come here, or brought my granddaughter here, if I had been able to face him. Ask him to pray for me, please. Will you do that for me, Horn? Ask him to pray for me?"

Naturally I promised that I would.

"He didn't pray at all when I was with him, when we were . . . It pained me. It gave me pain, and yet I knew that he was being open and honest with me. It was I, the one who prayed, who lied and lied too. I know that must seem illogical, yet it was so."

Here I tried to say something comforting, I believe. I am no longer certain what it was.

"Now I'm blind, Horn. I am punished, and not too severe a punishment, either. Are you going to tell him that I'm blind now, Horn?"

I said I certainly would, because I would try to enlist Hammerstone's help in finding new eyes for her.

"And where we are now, my granddaughter and I? Will you tell him about this rock in the sea?"

"I'll probably have to, Maytera. I'm sure he'll want to know."

She was silent for a minute or two, nor did Mucor speak again. I stood up to gauge the force and direction of the wind. The western horizon showed no indications of bad weather, only the clearest of calm blue skies.

"Horn?"

"Yes, Maytera. If Mucor won't tell me anything more, and won't tell Patera Silk that I'm going to come for him whether he wants me to or not, I ought to leave."

"Only a moment more, Horn. Can't you spare me a moment or two? Horn, you knew him. Do you think that my husband—that Hammerstone might try to come here and kill me? Is he capable of that? Was he?"

"Absolutely not." Privately I thought it likely that he would come, or try to, although not to do her harm.

"It might be better if he did." Her voice had been growing

weaker as she spoke; it was so faint when she said that that I could scarcely hear her over the distant murmur of the waves. "I still try to pretend that I'm taking care of my granddaughter, as I did when we were on our little farm, and in the town. But she's taking care of me, really. That is the truth—"

Mucor interrupted, startling me. "I do not."

I said, "You don't require much taking care of, Maytera, and your granddaughter wouldn't have the bottles of water I brought for her if you hadn't told me she needed them. You were taking care of her then."

For seconds that dragged on and on, Maytera was silent; when I was on the point of leaving, she said, "Horn, may I touch your face? I've been wanting to, the whole time you've been here."

"If it will make you happy to do it, it will make me happy, too," I told her.

She rose, and Mucor rose with her; I stood close to Maytera Marble and let her hands discover my face for themselves.

"You're older now."

"Yes, Maytera. Older and fatter and losing my hair. Do you remember how bald my father was?"

"It's still the same dear face, though it pains me to—to have it changed at all. Horn, it's not at all likely that you'll be able to find new eyes for me, or find my husband, either. We both know that. Even so, you can make me happy if you will. Will you promise to come back here after you have tried? Even if you have no eye to give me, and no word of my husband? And leave me a copy of your book, so that I can hear, sometimes, about Patera Silk and Patera Pike, and the old days at our manteion?"

It was on the tip of my tongue to say that our book would be of no use to her, but it occurred to me that the seamen who came to consult Mucor might be induced to read passages to her. I said something to that effect, and she said, "Mucor can read it to me, if she will."

Surprised yet again, I asked, "Can you read, Mucor?"

"A little." She seemed almost on the point of smiling. "Grandmother taught me."

"She would have, naturally." I was ready to kick myself for not having anticipated something so obvious.

Maytera Marble said, "If she doesn't know a word, she can spell it out to me so I can tell her."

The love in her voice touched me; for the space of a breath, I considered what you would want me to do, Nettle; but I know you too well to have much doubt. "You want me to bring you a copy of our book, when I return from the Long Sun Whorl, Maytera? From the *Whorl*?"

Very humbly she said, "If it's not too much trouble, Horn." Her hands had left my face to clutch each other. "It—I would appreciate it very much."

"You won't have to wait. I have a copy in my boat. I'll be back in a few minutes."

I had not gone ten steps when I heard the tapping of her stick behind me. I told her that she did not have to come, that I would bring the book up to her.

"No. No, I want to, Horn. I can't ask you to make that climb again, and—and . . ."

She was afraid that I might sail away without having given it to her. Perhaps I should have been angry that she had so little confidence in my promise; but the truth was, as I realized even then, that she wanted the book so badly that she could not bear to run even the slightest risk, and waiting for me to return with it would have been agony. I took her free hand, and we descended the precipitous path together.

When we had reached the flat rock upon which the fish had so mysteriously appeared, she asked me about the sloop, how long it was, how wide, how one managed the sails and so on and so forth, all of it, I believe, to postpone the delicious instant when she would actually hold the book in her own hands, pushing the moment back again and again.

I gave her each measurement she asked for, and explained the rudiments of sailing as well as I could, how one trims the sails depending on the angle of the wind to the course, how to navigate by the sun and the stars, how the management of a laden boat differs from that of an empty one, and other matters; and while I was descanting upon all this Mucor appeared, standing upon an outcrop halfway up the cliff so small that it had escaped my notice up to then. I waved to her and she waved in return, but she did not speak.

At last I went aboard, retrieved our book from the cubby, and standing in the stern with one foot on the gunwale presented it to Maytera Marble, a present from both its authors.

It seems foolish now to write that her face, a face composed of hundreds of tiny mechanisms, glowed with happiness. Yet it did. "Horn! Oh, Horn! This—this is the answer to so many, many prayers!"

I smiled, although she could not see it. "All of them yours, I'm sure, Maytera. A good many people have taken the trouble to read it, though."

"It's so thick! So heavy!" Reverently she opened it, turning pages to feel the paper. "Are they written on both sides, Horn?"

"Yes, they are, Maytera. And my wife's handwriting is quite small."

She nodded solemnly. "I remember dear little Nettle's hand. She had a very good hand, Horn, even when she was just a child. A neat little hand. It may give my granddaughter trouble at first, but she'll soon be reading it like print, I feel sure."

I said that I was, too, and prepared to cast off.

"We're all in here, Horn? Dear old Maytera Rose, Maytera Mint, and my granddaughter and I? And Patera, and Patera Pike, and you children in the palaestra?"

"There's a great deal about Patera Silk," I told her, "but only a little, really, about Patera Pike. I'm afraid most of the other students at the palaestra aren't even mentioned, but Nettle and I pop up pretty frequently."

I was on the point of saying good-bye, but now that the moment for it had come I found myself every bit as reluctant as she was. "Do you remember how I followed you to the gate of Blood's villa? How I wanted to come in with you, but you wouldn't let me?"

"You were a good, brave boy. I couldn't risk your life like that, Horn."

"It's in there," I said, and cast off. "I'm leaving now. Remember me in your prayers."

"I will. Oh, I will!"

I sighed, and put one of my new sweeps into the water with a plop that she surely heard.

"Good-bye, Horn." She clutched our book to her chest. "You will come back someday? Please?"

"When I've got eyes for you," I told her, and pushed off. The little inlet was so sheltered by its cliffs that there was scarcely any wind; I had to scull the sloop to its mouth before the mainsail began to draw.

I was trimming it when I heard Mucor's long, shrill whistle and looked up. She was pointing at the sloop and me, her left arm stiffly extended; and because the outcrop on which she stood was a good deal higher than the top of the mast, her rag of gown and long, coarse, black hair were whipped by the wind. Whenever I think of her now, that is the image I recall first: poised upon the outcrop she has reached by the almost invisible crevice behind her, her arm stretched forth and her face the face of General Mint restrained by some subordinate, ordering forward troops she would rather have led in person.

Mucor might, as I have tried to say here, have commanded ten thousand spectral troopers; but at the time I could not see even one. Then some slight sound from the top of the rock reached my ears, and I realized that her gesture had misled me. Like any actual general, she was not pointing to whatever forces she commanded, but to their objective.

At the top of the cliff, I saw a small dark figure that seemed almost a cluster of boys, or two men upon their hands and knees. It vanished, then reappeared as it made a flying leap from the top of the cliff. For a moment I thought its target was the sloop, and that it would strike it and die. It sent up a waterspout five cubits from the tip of the bowsprit, however, and vanished as if it had sunk like a stone.

Back in the inlet, Maytera Marble was shouting, her voice audible but unintelligible, echoing and re-echoing from cliff to cliff. Mucor waved, but disappeared into the crevice too quickly for me to wave in return. Earlier I wrote that she is not tall, but that was misleading. Majesty is not a mere matter of a hand or two over the eight. In twenty years, I myself had matured and even aged; yet subconsciously I had supposed that Mucor was still the preternatural adolescent I remembered.

★

★ ★

Nearly noon, although I am writing by lamplight. Gusts that would lay the sloop on her beam ends rock my cracker-box palace, whistling through every lattice and shutter. Green was bigger than a man's thumb last night when it rose over the willow in the garden, and I was reminded that my people here call it the Devils' Lantern. Seeing it, I thought only of the inhumi, and not of the storms and the tides, which I in my folly imagined would mean nothing to us in this inland place. I needed a good lesson, and I am getting it, and the whole unhappy town of Gaon with me. Between gusts, I hear my elephant trumpeting in his stall.

No quantity of preaching or teaching will make the people wholly safe from the inhumi's sleights and subterfuges. No one knows that better than I. But preaching and teaching may do something, may even save a few lives, and so they are worth doing. It may be at least as valuable, however, to encourage the farmers to plant crops that will not be beaten flat by the storms—yams for example. This is surely the first storm, and not the last.

I see that when I described my departure from Mucor's Rock I never actually mentioned that Babbie came on board, his black snout and little red eyes breaking water just aft of the rudder, and his stubby forepaws clutching the gunwale beside me in a way that reminded me unpleasantly of the leatherskin. Hus can swim like rainbow-frogs, as Sinew and everyone else who has ever hunted them attests, and certainly Babbie could.

Only the leatherskin could have been a less welcome boarder. I ordered him to return to Mucor, and he crouched in the bow and defied me. I grappled with him then, and tried to drop him over the side, but he was as heavy as a stone, and clung to me with all his legs so tightly that the two of us might have been hewn from a single block of flesh; and when, after a long tussle, I was able to tear him loose and push him out of the sloop, he swam under the keel and climbed back on board in far less time than it had taken me to throw him off.

After that, I sat by the tiller frowning at him, while he squatted like a spider on the other side of the mast, glaring at me through close-set crimson eyes that seemed only slightly bigger than the heads of pins. When I ate that night, I flung him a loaf of bread and a couple of apples, reflecting that if I fed him he might be somewhat less likely to charge when my back was to him.

I could have broken out the slug gun, loaded it, and shot him. Or at least, I supposed at the time that I could have, though in point of fact Babbie could have killed me long before I got the first cartridge in the chamber. I am no longer quite sure why I did not, although there were certainly some compelling arguments against it. The first, which I could not help giving considerable weight, was that I might well hole the sloop. If I missed, the slug would undoubtedly smash through her planking, unless the new cartridges were vastly inferior to those made beneath the Long Sun. Hus are notorious for their tough hides and massive bones; and yet it was quite possible that a slug fired at close range might penetrate this small hus and a plank, too.

Hus are difficult to kill as well, and almost always charge if a hunter's first shot merely wounds them. A fast second shot is often necessary, and although one or two dogs would be enough to track one down, most hunters recommend taking eight or ten to impede the charge. I had none, and the distance would be too short for me to have any hope of getting off a second shot.

There was also a chance at least that this particular hus would be of value to me. A tame hus might always be sold, and while I had him he would, presumably, guard the sloop in my absence. Recalling my old fellow pupil, and the shame I had felt at being forced to borrow three cards from Marrow, I could almost wish that Babbie had been with me earlier.

But the most serious reason was that I would be destroying the gift Mucor had sent me as a gesture of good will. Mucor, whose spirit might be watching us invisibly for all I knew (or could know) would surely take that amiss, and if Silk were to change his mind and choose to reveal his whereabouts once he learned that I was determined to search him out, only Mucor could bring me that information. When I had turned this last reason over in my mind for a few minutes, I acutely regretted having thrown Babbie overboard.

Half joking, I told him, "We may never be friends, Babbie, but we need not be enemies either. You try to be a good beast, and I'll try to be a good master to you."

He continued to glare; and his glare said very plainly, You hate me so I hate you.

I filled my washbowl with fresh water then, and gave it to him.

★

★ ★

An inhuma was caught last night, and today I was forced to watch as she was buried alive. There is no trial for these monsters, and understandably so—we burn them in New Viron—but I could not help wishing it were otherwise; I would like to have granted her a death less horrible. As things are, I had to preside over the customary means of extermination. One of the big, flat paving stones was lifted in the marketplace and set aside, and her grave dug where it had lain. Into that grave she was forced, though she pled and fought. Five men with long poles pinned her there until a cartload of gravel could be dumped on top of her. Dirt was shoveled on top of the gravel, and at last the stone was returned to its place and a symbol, too awful to describe, was cut into it so that no one will dig there again.

These people, like people everywhere here, seem to fear that an inhumu may live on even with its head severed. That is not the case, of course; but I cannot help wondering how the superstition originated and became so widespread. Certainly the inhumi have no bones as we understand them. Possibly their skeletons are cartilage, as those of some sea-creatures are. On Green, Geier maintained that the inhumi are akin to slugs and leeches. No one, I believe, took him seriously; yet it is certain that once dead they decay very quickly, though they are difficult to kill and can survive for weeks and even months without the blood that is their only food.

But I can continue this little lecture best by returning to my narrative.

Back in New Viron, Marrow had been told of a trader named Wijzer who knew the way to Pajarocu. We found him on his boat (which was four times the length of mine, and five times the width) and Marrow invited him to his house.

"If what I know a good supper it will buy . . ." He shrugged "Or you want to see me eat."

We assured him that it had never occurred to us that he might be an inhumu.

"Strangers you don't know, I think. Before Pajarocu with a hundred you must speak. Sharp you better be. Sharp they are, those inhumi. Sharp always."

Marrow grunted agreement.

"Many in Pajarocu I meet. Some I killed. Them you cannot drown. That you know?"

I said I had heard it, but that I did not know whether it was true.

"True it is." Wijzer paused to inspect a load of melons, then looked around and pointed. "You, Marrow. Your house that way it is? A house bigger than all the rest it is? The whole town you steer?"

Marrow leaned upon his stick. "The town doesn't always think so."

"Him sending you are." Wijzer pointed to me. "To go he wants?"

"Yes," I told him. "I want to because it is my duty."

"Careful be. Careful you must be." He made off through the hay market, pushing others out of his way and leading us as if he knew the route to Marrow's better than either one of us; he was a big man, not so much tall as broad, with a big, square, sun-reddened face and muscular, short-fingered hands whose backs were thick with reddish hair.

"He's rough," Marrow whispered, "but don't let that make you think he's honest. He may send you wrong."

The set of Wijzer's shoulders told me he had overheard, so I said, "I'm a good judge of men, Councilor, and I think that this one can be trusted." At the word *councilor*, Marrow's eyes went wide.

His cook had prepared a good, plain dinner for us. There were seven or eight vegetable dishes variously prepared (most of Marrow's wealth came from trading fruits and vegetables still), a big pork roast with baked apples, hot breads with a bowl of butter, and so forth. Wijzer pitched into the meat and wine. "No cheese, Marrow? Councilor Marrow? So said it is? Like a judge you are? No one this to me tells, or before more polite I am."

"A few people call me that." Marrow leaned back in his carved chair, toying with his wine glass. "But it has no legal force, and I don't even make my servants do it."

"This man Horn, he does. Him I hear. Why him you send it is?"

Marrow shook his head. "We're sending him because he's best qualified to go, and because he will. If you're asking if I trust him, I do. Absolutely."

"I'm going because I want Silk here more than anybody," I told Wijzer.

"Ahh?" His fork, laden with a great gobbet of pork, paused halfway to his mouth.

Marrow's look suggested that I hold my tongue.

"So. Silk. Why you want so far to go I wondered. A long sail for you Pajarocu is. Long even for me from Dorp it is, where nearer I am." The pork attained its ultimate destination.

"Do you know about Silk?"

He shrugged. "Stories there are. Some I hear. Someone a big book he has. Things he said, but maybe not all true they are. A good man, just the same he is. In Pajarocu Silk is, you think? Why? Him I did not see."

"We don't believe he's in Pajarocu," I said, "either one of us. I believe that he's probably still in Viron, the city we left to come here. But Councilor Marrow got a letter from Pajarocu not long ago, a very important letter. I asked him to have a copy made for me, and he did. I think you ought to read it."

I got out the letter and handed it to Wijzer, but he only tapped it, still folded, against the edge of the table. "This city, this Viron. From there you come. A councilor it steers. Not so it is?"

Marrow shook his head. "Under our Charter, the caldé decided things in Viron. We didn't always follow our Charter, but that's what it said. The Ayuntamiento was under him, and it was composed of councilors. When Horn and I left, Silk was caldé, and he told us to go. People from other landers who came later than we did say he was still caldé when they left, and urged them to risk the trip."

Wijzer gestured with the folded letter. "One of these councilors you were, Marrow?"

Marrow shook his head again.

"Nothing you were. When this Silk comes, nothing again you will be. Why him do you want, if nothing you were?"

I began to protest, but Marrow said, "That's right. I was nothing."

Wijzer swallowed half his wine. "So here Silk you bring, where people who have never him seen him love. Caldé here he will be, and a council like before he will want. A councilor then you are that real is."

"It could happen." Marrow shrugged. "But it probably won't.

Do you seriously think that's why we're sending Horn here to fetch Silk?"

"Enough for me it is."

"Who governs your own town? You?"

"Dorp? No. My boat I govern. For me, enough she is."

Marrow buttered a roll while we waited for him to speak again. "You may know winds and landmarks, but you don't know men. Not as well as you think you do."

"Anybody that can say." Wijzer helped himself to another salsify fritter.

"You're right. Anybody can say it. Even Caldé Silk could, because it's true." Marrow picked up his wine glass and put it down with a bang. "I'm one of five who try to steer New Viron. Horn can tell you about that, if you want to hear it. I'm not always obeyed, none of us are. But I try, and our people know I want what's best for the town. You say Caldé Silk will want a new Ayuntamiento if he comes here. He may not, he had a lot of trouble with our councilors back home."

Wijzer continued to eat, watching Marrow's face.

"If he doesn't, I'll be nothing again. All right, I'll see to my turnips, and if Silk ever asks my help, he'll get it. If he wants an Ayuntamiento, he may want me to be on it. That will be all right, too. If he asks my help, I may bargain for a seat. Or I may not. It'll depend on what help he wants and how badly it's needed. I won't ask if all this satisfies you."

"Good that is. Not you ask."

"I say I won't ask, because I'm not asking your help for my own sake. I'm asking for everybody in my town, and everybody on this inside-out whorl Pas packed us off to. If that's not exact enough for you, I'm asking for Horn here. He's going off alone to a place that neither one of us have ever been to, because there's a chance we can get Silk to come here."

Marrow pointed to me with his fork. "Look at him. There he sits, and inside of a week he may drown. He has a wife and three boys. If you know something that might help him, this is your chance to tell him. If you don't and he dies, maybe I'll be the only one who blames you. One old man in a foreign town, that's nothing. But maybe you'll blame yourself. Think about it."

Wijzer turned to me. "This wife, a beautiful young girl she is?"

I shook my head and explained that you are my own age.

"Me?" He indicated himself, a broad thumb to his chest. "A beautiful young girl I got. In Dorp she is."

"You must miss her, I'm sure."

Marrow started to speak, but Wijzer stopped him with an upraised hand. "Did I say I wouldn't tell? No!" He belched. "This I will, I have said. A trader that his word keeps I am. Who and why to know I wish. My right that is. But who you are I see, Marrow, and why it is they here to you listen."

He unfolded the letter and rattled it between his fingers. "Good paper. Where this do you get?"

Again, Marrow pointed to me.

I said, "I made it. That's what I do."

"The papermaker you are?"

I nodded.

"Not a sailor." Wijzer frowned. "Why a sailor does he not send?"

Marrow said, "He's a sailor, too. He's going instead of somebody else because getting to Pajarocu won't gain us anything unless he can persuade Silk to come back with him. He's the only one, or almost the only one, who may be able to."

Wijzer grunted, his eyes on the letter.

I said, "There are two other people who might have as much influence with Caldé Silk, or more. Do you want to hear about them?"

"If you want, I will listen."

"Both are women. Maytera Marble might, but she's old and blind, and believes that she's taking care of the granddaughter who cares for her. Would you want me to step aside so they could send her?"

Wijzer made a rude noise. "Not as far as Beled she would get."

"You're right. The other is Nettle, my wife. She's a fine sailor, she's strong for a woman, and she's got more sense than any two men I know. If I had not offered to go, they were going to ask her, and I feel sure she would have gone."

Wijzer chuckled. "And you at home to sit and cook! No, you must go. That I see."

"I want to go," I told him. "I want to see Silk again, and talk to him, more than anything else in the whorl. I know Nettle feels the same way, and if I succeed, she'll get to see him and talk to him too. You said Maytera Marble wouldn't get as far as Beled. Beled's the town where the Trivigauntis settled, isn't it?"

Marrow said, "That's right."

"It's that way? North?"

Wijzer nodded absently. "Here of this He-hold-fire I read. Back to the *Whorl* he will make his lander go. How it is, this he can do? Other men this cannot do."

"I have no idea," I said. "Perhaps I can find out when I get to Pajarocu."

"Horn's good with machinery," Marrow told Wijzer. "He built the mill that made that paper."

"In a box it you make?" Wijzer's hands indicated the size.

"No. In a continuous strip, until we're out of slurry."

"Good! A lander here you got? A lander everybody's got."

Marrow said, "We have some, but they're just shells. The one Horn and I came in . . ." He made a wry face. "For the first few years, everybody took everything they wanted. Wire, metal, anything. I did it myself."

"Dorp, too."

"I used to hope that another would land. That was before the fourth came. I had a plan, and men to carry it out. We would arrive before the last colonist left, and seize control. Search them as they got out, and make them put back the cards they'd taken, any wiring, any other parts. We did, and it took off again."

Wijzer laughed.

"They—Pas—doesn't want anyone to go back. You probably know it. So unless a lander's disabled before it unloads, it goes back to the *Whorl* so it can bring more people here."

"A good one at Mura they got," Wijzer remarked pensively. "This I hear. Only nobody near they will allow."

"If I had succeeded," Marrow told him, "I wouldn't have let anyone near ours either."

"Dorp, too. Our judges there, but none they got." Wijzer refolded the letter and handed it back to me. "Pajarocu to go, a sharp watch you must keep, young fellow. The legend already you know? About the pajarocu bird?"

I smiled; no one had called me young in a long time. "I'll try, and if you know the legend, I'd like to hear it."

He cleared his throat and poured himself another glass of wine. "The Maker everything he made. Like a man a boat builds it was. All the animals, the grass, trees, Pas and his old wife, everything. About the Maker you know?"

I nodded and said that we called him the Outsider.

"A good name for him that is. Outside him we keep, into our hearts we don't let him come.

"When everything he's got made, he got to paint. First the water. Easy it is. Then the ground, all the rocks. A little harder it gets. Then sky and trees. Grass harder than you think it is, the little brush he had got to use, and paint so when the wind blows the color changes, and different colors for different kinds. Then dogs and greenbucks, all the different animals. Birds and flowers going to be tough they are. This he knows. So for the last them he leaves."

I nodded. Marrow was yawning.

"While the other stuff painting he is, the pajarocu with the big owl up north they got makes friends. Well, that big owl the first bird the Maker paints he is, because so quick it he can do. White for feathers, eyes, legs, and everything. But that owl not much fun he is, so the snake-eater bird next he calls. At the owl the pajarocu bird looks, and all over white he is. Does it hurt the pajarocu wants to know. That big owl, he never laughs. To have a game he wants, so he says yes. A lot it hurts, he says, but over quick it is.

"So the pajarocu, over to look he goes. The Maker the snake-killer bird painting is, and two dozen colors using he is. Red for the tail, brown for wings, blue and white in front, yellow around the mouth and the chin, everything he's got using he is. So the pajarocu hides. When the Maker finished is, the pajarocu nobody can find. Because he has never been painted and nobody him can see, it is."

Marrow chuckled.

"So the Maker for the owl and the snake-eater bird calls, and them for the pajarocu to look he tells. The owl at night can look, and the snake-eater bird when light it gets. But him they never see, so him they never find. All the time the owl around the night he flies, and cu, cu he says. Never the snake-eater bird talks, till somewhere where the pajarocu might be he comes. Then Pajarocu?"

I said, "That's a good story, but if I understand you, you're telling me that even with your directions I may have a lot of trouble finding Pajarocu."

Wijzer nodded solemnly. "Not a place that wants to be found it is. Traders to steal will come back, they think. If close you get, wrong their friends to you will tell."

Marrow, who had eaten nearly as much as Wijzer, said, "They have invited us to send someone, one man or one woman to fly back to the Long Sun Whorl and return to this one. You've seen their letter, and that's an accurate copy. How do you explain it?"

"They it maybe can explain. Them ask. Everything this young fellow to tell I want, so that careful he will be. Afraid you are that so much I will tell that not he will go?"

Marrow said, "No," and I reaffirmed that I was going.

"You a question I ask." Wijzer swirled what little wine remained in his glass, staring into it as though he could read the future in its spiral. "One man back can go, your letter says. This fellow Silk to bring here you want. Two you will be."

I nodded. "Marrow and our other leaders and I talked about that. A great many people know about Patera Silk now. When he identifies himself, we believe they'll let him come aboard their lander."

When Wijzer only stared at me, I added, "We hope that they will, at least."

"You hope." Wijzer snorted.

Marrow said, "We do. Our own lander held more than five hundred. I doubt that they'll get two hundred from other towns with their invitation, but suppose they do. Or let's say they get a hundred, and to that they add four hundred of their own people. The lander reaches the Long Sun Whorl safely, and the hundred scatter, every man looking for his own city."

Wijzer frowned. "It you must finish."

"When the time to return comes, do you think a hundred will reassemble at the lander?"

Wijzer shook his head. "No. Not a hundred there will be."

Marrow made a little sound expressive of satisfaction. "Then why not let Silk take one of the empty seats?"

"Because none there may be. Not a hundred I said. Two hundred, maybe. When about this town that you got I ask, what they say it is? You know? The first it was. The first lander from the *Whorl* came, and here landed. True it is?"

"No," I told him. "Another lander left some time before ours, with a group led by a man called Auk. They were also from Viron. Have you ever heard of them?"

Wijzer shook his head. "Someplace else they landed, maybe."

"On Green," I said, "or so I've been told. There was also another lander that left at the same time ours did. One lander wouldn't hold all of us, and we had cards enough to restore two, so we took two. It came here with us, but we've never learned what became of Auk's."

Wijzer leaned toward me, his elbows on the table and his big, square face ruddy with sun, wind, and wine. "You listen. Here twenty years now you been. For me, nine it is. Back up there," he pointed to the ceiling, "where the Long Sun they got, what like it is, not you know. What like it was when away I went. Everybody out Pas wants. Storms, and a week all nights he gives. Even me, out he drives. Everybody! The landers up there that they got? No good! No good! You the cards had, this you said. Enough back you put, and it flies. Right that is?"

I nodded.

Wijzer directed his attention to Marrow. "Landers here you got, you say. But the wires pulled out are, seats, too. Cards, pipes, glass, all that. Again to fly, not you can them make. Those landers up there? How it goes with them, you think? First of all you went, so the best ones you took. The one I ride, like what it is, you think? Forty-eight seats for us left. Forty-eight for six hundred and thirty-four. That I never forget. Up we fly, and fifteen dead we got. No food but what we bring. No water. Pipes, taps, what you sit on every day, all gone they are. When here we get, how our lander smells you think? Babies all sick. Everybody sick or dead they are. Terrible it is. Terrible! So why go? Because we got to."

He looked back to me and pointed a short, thick finger. "Not everybody comes back, you think. So more seats there are. Maybe not everybody comes. But the ones . . . Family up there you got?"

"My father, if he's still alive. An uncle and two aunts, and some cousins. They may have left by this time."

"Or not, maybe. Friends?"

"Yes. A few."

"Father. Uncle. Aunt. Friend. Cousin. Care I don't. Father we say. On his knees he gets. He cries. What then will you do? About that you got to think. Ever of you they beg? Your father, to you down on his knees before he has got? Crying? Of you begging?"

"No," I said. "He never did."

"Twenty years. A very young man then you are. Maybe a boy when you go, yes?"

I nodded again.

"At your father you looked, your father you saw. A man not like you he was. The same for me it is when a boy I am. No more! This time your own face you see, but old you are. Not strong like twenty years ago. Weak now he is. Crying, begging. Tears down his cheeks running. Horn, Horn! Me you got to take! My own flesh you are!"

Wijzer was silent for a moment, watching my face. "No extra seats there will be. No. Not one even."

Marrow grunted again, and I said, "I understand what you mean. It could be very difficult."

Wijzer leaned back and drank what remained of his wine. "To Pajarocu you go? Still?"

"Yes."

"Stubborn like me you are. For you a good voyage I wish. Something to draw on you got, Marrow?"

Marrow called his clerk, and had him bring paper, a quill, and a bottle of ink.

"Look. Main this is." Carefully, Wijzer drew a wavering line down the paper. "We on Main here. Islands we got." He sketched in several. "North the Lizard it is." He began to draw it, a tiny blot of ink upon the vastness of the sea. "The Lizard you know?"

I told him I lived there.

"Good that is. Home for another good dinner you can stop." Wijzer looked at me slyly, and I realized with something of a start that he had bright blue eyes like Silk's.

"No," I said, and found it not as hard to say as I expected. "I doubt that I'll stop there at all, unless I find that I need something I neglected to bring."

Marrow grunted his approval.

"Better you don't. Rocks there is. But those you must know." Wijzer added towns up the coast. "Too many islands to draw, but there these rocks and the big sandbar you I must show. Both very bad they are. Maybe them you see, maybe nothing." He gave me another sly glance. "Nothing you see, me anyhow you believe. Yes?"

"Yes," I said. "I know how easy it is to stave a boat on a rock that can't be seen."

Wijzer nodded to himself. "Coming Green is. The sea to go up and down it makes. The tide in Dorp we say. About the tide you know?"

"Yes," I repeated.

"How more water Green makes, then not so much, I will not tell. Not till someone to me it explains. But so it is. About this tide you must think always, because bigger and bigger it gets while you go. Never it you forget. A safe anchorage you got, but in an hour, two hours, not safe it is."

I nodded.

"Also all these towns that to you I show. At all these towns, even Wijzer would not put in. But maybe something there is you need. Which ones crazy is, I will not show. All crazy they are. Me you understand? Crazy like this one you got they are. Only all different, too."

"Differing laws and customs. I know what you mean."

"So if nothing you need, past best to go it is. Now these two up here . . ." He drew circles around them and blew on the ink. "Where you cross they are. Because over here . . ." Another wavering line, receding to the south and showing much less detail. "Another Main you got. Maybe a name it's got. I don't know."

"Shadelow, the western continent," I proposed.

"Maybe. Or maybe just a big island it is. Wijzer, not smart enough you to tell he is. An island, maybe, but big it is. This coast? Better well out you stand."

"I'm sure you're right."

"Two or three towns." He sketched them in, adding their names in a careful script. "What down for you I put, what I them call it is. Maybe something else you say. Maybe something else they do. Here the big river runs." Meticulously he blacked it in. "It you got to see, so sharp you got to look. What too big not to see is, what nobody sees it is."

I told him that I had been thinking the same thing not long before.

"A wise saying it is. Everyplace wise fellows the same things say. This you know?"

"I suppose that they must, although I'd never thought about it."

"Wise always the same it is. About men, women, children. About boats, food, horses, dogs, everything. Always the same. No birds in the old nest, wise fellows say, and the good cock out of the old bag. A thief, the thief's tracks sees. The meat from the gods it is, the cooks from devils. All those things in towns all over they say. You young fellows laugh, but us old fellows know. The lookout, the little thing always he sees. Almost always, because to see it sharp he must look. The big thing, too big to look out sharp for it is, and nobody it sees."

Dipping his quill for what might have been the tenth time, he divided the river. "The big stream to starboard it is. Yes? Little to port. The little one fast it runs. Hard to sail up. Yes? Just the same, the way you go it is." He drew an arrow upon the unknown land beside it, and began to sketch in trees beside it.

After a moment I nodded and said, "Yes. I will."

Wijzer stopped drawing trees and divided the smaller stream. "Same here, the little one you take. A little boat you got?"

"Much smaller than yours," I told him. "It's small enough for me to handle alone easily."

"That's good. Good! For a good, strong blow you must wait. You see? Then up here you can sail. Close to the shore, you got to stay. Careful always you must be, and the legend not forget. A good watch keep. Here sometimes Pajarocu is." He added a dot of ink and began lettering the word beside it: PAJAROCU.

"Did you say it was there only sometimes?" I asked.

Wijzer shrugged. "Not a town like this town of yours it is. You will see, if there you get. Sometimes here it is, sometimes over there. If I tell, you would not me believe. That you coming are they know, maybe it they move. Or another reason. Or no reason. Not like my Dorp, Pajarocu is." He pointed to Dorp, a cluster of tiny houses on his map. "Not like any other town Pajarocu is."

Marrow was leaning far over the table to look at it. "That river is practically due west of here."

Wijzer's face lost all expression, and he laid aside his quill.

"Couldn't Horn save time by sailing west from here?"

"That some fellows do, maybe," Wijzer told him. "Sometimes all right they go. Sometimes not. What here I draw, what Wijzer does it is."

"But you want to trade from town to town," Marrow objected. "Horn won't be doing that."

I said, "If I were to do as you suggest, sailing due west from here, I would eventually strike the coast of this big island or second continent that Wijzer has very kindly mapped for us. But when I did, I wouldn't know whether to turn south or north, unless the river mouth was in view."

Reluctantly, Marrow nodded.

"With the greatest respect to Captain Wijzer, a map like this one, drawn freehand, could easily be in error by, oh, fifty leagues or more. Suppose that I decided it was accurate, and sailed north. It might easily take me a week to sail fifty leagues, tacking up the coast. Suppose that at the end of that week I turned back to search south. And that the river mouth was five leagues beyond the point at which I turned back. How long would it take me to locate it?"

Wijzer smiled; and Marrow said reluctantly, "I see what you mean. It's just that they're going to leave as soon as their lander's ready, and it's nearly ready now. You read that letter. Anybody who hasn't arrived before they go will be left behind."

"I realize that there's no time to waste," I told him, "but sometimes it's best to make haste slowly." Privately I reflected that I might have the best of both plans by sailing north for a hundred leagues or so, then turning west well south of the place where Wijzer had advised me to.

And I resolved to do it.

5

The Thing on the Green Plain

How long ago it seems! So much has happened since then, although at times I almost feel that it happened to someone else.

Yet I remember Wijzer clearly. What if he were to walk into court tomorrow? He would ask whether I ever reached Pajarocu, and what could I say? "Yes, but . . ."

Let me make one thing clear before I go further. I did not trust Wijzer completely. He seemed a trader not greatly different from dozens of others who sail up and down our coast, having begun, perhaps, with a cargo of iron kitchenware and exchanged it for copper ingots, and exchanged the ingots for paper and timber in New Viron, always in search of a cargo that will bring immense profit when it is sold in their home port. I was afraid that Wijzer might be lying to make himself seem more widely traveled than he was, or even that he might not want Silk brought here for reasons of his own. In all this I wronged him, as I now know. He had been to Pajarocu, and he advised me to the best of his ability.

★

★ ★

Some people have accused Nettle and me of penning a work of fiction; and even though that is a slander, we did present certain imagined conversations when we knew roughly what had been said and what had been decided—that among Generalissimo Oosik, General Mint, Councilor Potto, and Generalissimo Siyuf, for example. We knew how each of the four talked, and what the upshot of their talk had been, and ventured to supply details to show each at his or her most characteristic.

If this were a similar work, instead of the unvarnished, straightforward account that I intend, I would simply explain why I doubted Wijzer, and leave the reader in suspense as to whether those doubts were justified. It is not. Because it is not, I want to say here plainly that except for some slight exaggerations of coastal features and the omission of many small islands (notably that terrible island on which I fell into the pit) his map was remarkably accurate, at least regarding the areas through which I traveled in my long search for the elusive Pajarocu, called a town.

Before I returned to my boat that evening, I bought a tightly fitted little box of oily desertwood and a stick of sealing wax; once back on board, I studied the map with care, then put it into the box with my copy of the letter, melting the wax in the flame of my lantern and dripping it over every joint, a process that Babbie watched with more interest than I would have expected any beast save Oreb to show.

He was there still, although I had half expected to find him gone when I came back. It was the first time that I left him on the boat alone.

With the robbery still fresh in my memory, it was almost pleasant to have him. Although my boat had never been pillaged before on the few occasions when I had left it tied to a pier with no one on board, I had known that others had been, and that some had lost their boats. To confess the truth, when I returned to mine that first night I had been happy to find the damage and losses no worse than they were. Normally we had taken Sinew or (more often) the twins, so as to have someone to watch the sloop while Nettle and

I traded our paper for items we needed but could not grow or make for ourselves, or for spirits, food, and clothing we could trade with the loggers.

"We'll be going for a sail in the morning," I told Babbie. "If you want to go ashore, now's the time." He only grunted and retreated to the foredeck, his expression (as stubborn as Wijzer's own) saying You won't sail off without *me*.

Naturally it had occurred to me that I might put out that very night, but I was tired and there was scarcely a breath of wind; in all probability it would have meant a good deal of work for nothing.

It might also have altered the course of events radically, if the wind had picked up enough for me to pass the Lizard while it was still dark.

Who can say?

★

★ ★

It is very late, yet I feel I must write a little tonight, must continue this narrative I have not touched for three days or abandon it altogether. How odd to come to it by lamplight and read that I went to sleep instead of putting out from New Viron. I was so confident then that the lander at Pajarocu would fly as soon as it was ready, that it would return to the *Whorl* as promised, and that I would be on it if only I arrived in time. I was a child, and Marrow and the rest (whom I thought men and women as I thought myself a man grown), were only older children who risked far less.

The storms are worse. There was a bad one today, though it is nearly spent as my clock's hands close. Almost all our date palms are gone, they say, and we will miss them terribly. I must remember to find out how long a seedling must grow before it bears. Twelve years? Let us hope it is not as long as that. The people are apprehensive, even the troopers of my bodyguard. Tonight I gathered some around me while the storm raged outside.

"A few of you seem to think that since the inhumi cross the abyss at conjunction they must leave before conjunction is past," I said. "Why should they, when there are so many of us here, so much blood for them? I tell you that though some who have tarried here for years will leave as the whorls conjoin, returning to Green to breed, most will remain. Do you doubt me?"

They were shamefaced, and did not reply.

"There were many here last year, or so you tell me. And many the year before. Are you in greater danger from them now? Surely not! More will come, but we will be on guard against them; and they, being less experienced, will be a lesser threat to us. Will you sleep at your posts when the first is caught and interred alive in the market? The second? The third? I hope not. Nor should you relax when this conjunction is over, as it soon will be."

Brave words, and they served a dress rehearsal for the speeches I must give in the next few months.

Would it be effective for us to dig up one of the recent inhumations and release him to warn the others? The thought recurs.

If the inhumas' eggs hatched in our climate, would not our human kind become extinct? What tricks Nature plays! If they are natural creatures at all.

But they surely are. Natural creatures native to Green. Why would the Neighbors create something so malign?

★

★ ★

Last night I intended to continue my narrative, but failed to advance it by even a finger's width. I will do better this afternoon.

I sailed at shadeup, as I had planned. Much to my surprise, Marrow came down to see me off and present me with two parting gifts, small square heavy boxes. The wind was in the southeast, and a very good wind it was for me, so we shook hands and he embraced me and called me his son, and I untied the mooring lines and raised the mainsail.

Just as Mucor had waited until I was well under way and could not easily return her gift before presenting me with Babbie, and as Sinew had waited before throwing me his precious knife, so Marrow waited before presenting me with his third and final gift. It was his stick, which he flung aboard in imitation of Sinew (I had told him about it) when I was well away from the pier. I shouted thanks, and I believe I picked it up and flourished it, too, though I could not help thinking about Blood's giving Patera Silk his lion-headed stick.

Was I wrong to think of it? Marrow has his bad side, I am sure; and I am perfectly certain he would be the first to admit it. Blood, who was Maytera Rose's son, had his good side, too. Silk always insisted on it, and I have not the least doubt that Silk, who was nearly always right, was right about that as well. The head of a large enterprise—even a criminal enterprise—cannot be wholly bad. If he were, his subordinates could not trust him. Orchid signed the paper he gave her without reading it, and accepted the money he gave her to buy the yellow house, knowing that he would extort as much money from her and her women as he could—but knowing, too, that he would not destroy her.

Marrow's stick, as I ought to have said somewhat sooner, was of a heavy wood so dark as to be nearly black, and had a silver band below the knob with his name on it. I do not believe that he meant to give it to me until the moment arrived, and I liked him and it all the better for it. I showed Babbie that I had something to beat him with now, and as a joke ordered him to put up the jib; but he only glared, and I hauled it up myself. Sometime after that I saw him fingering the halyard, and was amazed.

A little after noon, as I recall, we passed Lizard. Course due north, wind moderate and west by south. I had promised myself that I would stand far out, and I did, and likewise that I would not peer ashore in the hope of catching sight of Nettle or the twins. That promise, as I quickly discovered, was worth very little. I stared, and stood upon the gunwale, and stared some more, and waved. All of it was to no purpose, since I saw no one.

Did anyone see me? The answer must surely be yes. Sinew did, and launched our old boat, which he must have spent the days since my departure in repairing and refitting. I did not see him or it, and nothing that he had said before I left had suggested he might do anything of the kind.

Marrow's other gifts proved to be a small box of silver jewelry with which to trade, and an even smaller box of silver bars. These last I hid with great care, promising myself that I would not trade them unless I was forced to. I would (as I then thought) find somebody at Pajarocu who would watch the sloop for me while I went for Silk. When the lander returned, Silk and I could sail back to New Viron in it; and I would have the silver bars for my trouble, and to help him if their help were required.

Wijzer had cautioned me against stopping at every port I came to, but his advice had been unnecessary. I was acutely conscious that putting in anywhere would cost me at least a day and might easily cost two or three, and resolved to sail north until resupply was urgent, put in at the nearest town, and turn west. That plan held only until I passed the first. Thereafter it always seemed that something was needed (water particularly) or advisable, and we put in at almost every town along the way. As Babbie came to trust me, the nocturnal nature of all hus asserted itself, so that he drowsed by day but woke at shadelow—a most useful arrangement even when we were not in port. The wind was so steady and so reliably out of the west or the southwest that I generally lashed the tiller and let the sloop sail herself under jib and reefed mainsail. Before I lay down each night, I instructed Babbie to wake me if anything unusual occurred; like Marrow he grunted his assent, but he never actually woke me, to the best of my memory. I have forgotten how many towns we put in at altogether. Five or six in six weeks' sailing would be about right, I believe.

★

★ ★

A visitor has presented me with a great rarity, a little book called *The Healing Beds* printed more than a hundred years ago in the *Whorl*. It is a treatise on gardening, with special emphasis on herbs, the work of a physician; but although it is pleasant to page through it, studying its quaint hand-colored illustrations and reading snatches of text, it is not of that book I intend to write today, but of its effect on this one.

It has made me acutely aware that this book of mine, which I have intended for my wife and sons, may very well be read long after they—and I—are gone. Even Hoof and Horn [sic], who must just be entering young manhood now, will someday be as old as Marrow and Patera Remora. There is argument about the length of the year here, and how well it agrees with the year we knew in the Long Sun Whorl, but the difference must be slight if there is any; in fifty years, Horn and Hide [sic] may well be dead. In a hundred, their sons and daughters will be gone too. These words, which I pen with so little thought—or hope—or expectation—may possibly endure long beyond that, endure for two centuries or even three, valued increasingly and so preserved with greater care as the whorl they describe fades into history.

Sobering thoughts.

[Needless to say, we are making the greatest efforts to preserve this record, both by the care we take in printing and conserving individual copies and by disseminating it.—Hoof and Hide, Daisy and Vadsig.]

I wish that one of the first people to settle the Long Sun Whorl had left us a record of it. Perhaps one did, a record preserved now in some skyland city far from Viron. That book, or a copy of it, may have been brought here already if it exists, as I sincerely hope it does.

Many in and around our town were very happy to have Scleroderma's short account of our departure, and overjoyed to have the one that Nettle and I wrote. It sounds boastful, I know; but it is true. They gave us cards, and even exchanged things they themselves had made or grown—things that had cost them many days of hard work—for a single copy. Yet to the best of my knowledge (and I believe I would surely have heard) none of them began an account of the founding of New Viron, the land raffle, and the rest of it. After considering this at some length, I have decided to salt this account of mine with facts that Nettle and my sons already know, but that may be of interest or value to future generations. Even today, who here in Gaon would know of the high wall that surrounds Patera Remora's manteion and manse, for example, if I failed to mention it?

When I recall our sail up the coast, which seemed so idyllic as far as I have yet described it, I am struck by the speed with which so many new towns have sprung up here on Blue. The people on each lander have tended to settle near the place where they landed, since their lander could not be moved again once they had pillaged it, and it still constituted an essential source of supplies. In addition to which, they had no horses or boats, and would have had to walk to their new destination. Thus we built New Viron within an hour's walk of the lander in which we arrived, and I am sure the people on other landers acted much as we did, save for those who landed too near us and have been forced into servitude by their captors; like us, they would have had little choice.

We were lucky, perhaps. There was no lake or river where we settled to provide fresh water, but there were a couple of well-diggers among us, and a ten-cubit well there provided better and purer water in abundance. To the west we have a fine harbor and a sea full of fish, and on the lower slopes of the eastern mountains, more timber than a hundred cities the size of Viron could ever need. The mountains themselves are already providing us with iron, silver and lead, as I believe I have mentioned before.

Most cannot have been so fortunate. Gaon has little access to the sea; ten leagues from where I sit, the River Nadi reaches us from the Highlands of Han in a succession of rapids and falls we call the Cataracts. Downstream are the Lesser Cataracts, then tropical forests and swamps, as well as a seemingly endless string of foreign towns, many of them hostile to us and some hostile to everyone. In theory, it might be possible to sail from here to the sea; but no one has ever done so, and it seems likely no one ever will.

Still, we have fresh water and fish from our river, timber, three kinds of useful cane, reeds for matting and the like, and a rich, black, alluvial soil that yields two generous crops per year. Even quite near town, the jungle swarms with game, and there are wild fruits for the picking. It seemed a poor place to me when I arrived, but no one needs warm and solid houses with big stone fireplaces here. Metals are imported and costly, which in the long run may prove the gods' blessing.

The gods (I should say) are very naturally those we knew in the *Whorl*. Echidna gets more sacrifices than all the rest together, but is generally shown as a loving mother holding the blind Tartaros on her lap while her other children swarm around her vying for her attention. A snake or two peeps from her hair, and her image in the temple has a snake coiled around each ankle. (Our people are not in the least afraid of snakes, as I ought to have explained. They seem to think them almost supernatural, if not actually minor gods, and set out bowls of milk laced with palm wine for them. Even a mother-goddess with a roving collection of pet snakes seems entirely normal. I have not been told of a single case of snakebite while I have been here.)

★

★ ★

In my last session I intended to write about the settling of Blue, but I see that I wandered from the topic to describe this town of Gaon.

I nearly wrote "this city," but Gaon is nothing like the size of Viron or the foreign cities I saw from General Saba's airship. Viron had more than half a million people. While I have no way of knowing exactly how many we have in Gaon, I doubt that there are a tenth that many.

The pirate boat came from no town, but from a little freshwater inlet where drooping limbs had concealed it from me until it put out. I shall never forget how it looked then, so black against the warm green of the trees and the cool blue and silver sea. Hull and masts and yards had all been painted black, and its sails were so dark a brown that they were nearly black, too. When I think back upon it here at my bedroom writing table, now that I am no longer afraid of it, I realize that its owners must have expected someone to hunt it, and wanted it to vanish from sight the moment the sun went down. It was half the sloops' beam, or a trifle less, and must have been more than twice our length, with two masts carrying three-cornered sails so big that a good gust should have laid it over at once. There were eight or nine on board, I think, mostly women.

One in the bow shouted for me to haul down. I got out the slug gun Marrow had given me instead, loaded it, and put extra cartridges in my pocket.

"Haul down!" she shouted again, and I asked what she wanted. Her answer was a shot.

I put the slug gun to my shoulder. I have seldom fired one, but I tried very hard then to recall everything that I had ever heard about them—Sinew's advice, and that of a hundred others—how to hold the slug gun and aim, and how to shoot well and swiftly. I still recall my trepidation as I pushed off the safety catch, laid the front sight on the pirate boat, and squeezed the trigger.

The report was an angry thunder, and the slug gun seemed to convulse in my hands, nearly knocking me off my feet; but my first shot was as ineffectual as theirs, as well as I could judge. Before I could fire a second time, Babbie was beside me gnashing his tusks.

The sound of the shot had awakened my intelligence as well as Babbie, however; I put down my slug gun and turned the sloop into the wind until we were sailing as near it as I dared, and trimmed sail while trying my best to ignore the shots aimed at me.

When I looked back at the long black craft pursuing us, I saw that I had been right. She could not hold our course, which was nearly straight out to sea.

The sloop was pitching violently, and dipping her bowsprit into the waves that had been lifting her by the stern when the wind was quartering. I returned to the slug gun nonetheless, and after two or three more shots learned to fire at the highest point of each pitch, just before the stern dropped from under me. Before I had to reload, I had the satisfaction of seeing the woman who had been shooting at me tumble headlong into the sea.

"We're going to Pajarocu!" I told Babbie while I reloaded my gun with the cartridges from my pockets, and he nodded to show that he had understood.

My intuition had outrun my reason. But as I fired again, I realized it had been right. With one of their comrades dead, the crew of the black boat would certainly try to keep us in sight until shadelow, and during the night to position themselves between the mainland and us, assuming that we were bound to some northern port and would turn northeast as soon as we believed we were no longer observed. If we did, and they were lucky, they would have us in sight at shadeup.

"The sea will be much wider at this point, if Wijzer's map is right," I explained to Babbie, "and I'm sure it would be dangerous even for a boat much larger than ours, with more people on it and ample supplies. But it won't be nearly as dangerous as going back and falling in with that black boat again, and if we get across it will be much faster." I nearly added that if he did not like the idea he was free to jump out and swim. He nodded so trustingly that I was ashamed of the impulse.

Perhaps I should be ashamed of having killed the woman who fell from the black boat instead. It is a terrible thing to take the life of another human being, and I had killed no one since Nettle and I (with Marrow, Scleroderma, and many others) had fought Generalissimo Siyuf's troopers in the tunnels long ago. It is indeed a terrible thing—to reason and to conscience. It is not always felt as a terrible thing, however. I felt more concern for my own life than for hers at the time, and would gleefully have sent the black boat to the bottom if it had been within my power.

The wind died away toward shadelow, but by then we were well out of sight of both the black boat and the coast. I tied the tiller and lay down with the slug gun beside me, resolved to wake up in an hour or two and have a long and careful look at the sea and the weather before I slept again; but when Babbie woke me, grunting and tapping my cheek and lips with the horn-tipped toes of his forelegs, the first light was already in the sky.

I sat up rubbing my eyes, knowing that I was on the sloop, but believing for a few seconds at least that we were bound for New Viron. The wind had picked up considerably (which I thought at the time had been the reason that Babbie had felt it necessary to wake me); but the hard chop of the previous day had been tamed to quick swells that rolled the sloop gently and smoothly, our masthead bowing deeply and politely to starboard, then to port, and then to starboard again, as if it were the honored center of some stately dance.

This was of some importance, because I glimpsed what appeared to be a low island to port. In a calmer sea, I would have climbed the mast for a better look at it, but my weight would have amplified the roll, and if it amplified it to the point that we shipped water the sloop would founder. I stood upon one of the cargo chests instead, a very slight improvement on the foredeck.

"If it's an island," I told Babbie, "we might be able to get water and information there, but we're not so badly off for water yet, and we'd be a lot more likely to find ourselves in trouble."

He had leaped to the top of another chest, though he was not sure enough of his balance to rear on four hind legs there, as he often did when he could brace a foreleg on the gunwale. He nodded sagely.

"I'm going to put out more sail to steady her," I told him. "Then she won't roll so much."

I shook out the mainsail and trimmed it, and went forward to break out the triangular gaff-topsail. There were traces of blood on the half-deck there, dark, clotting blood in a crevice where it had survived Babbie's tongue. What remained was so slight that I doubt that I would have noticed it without the bright morning sun, and the fact that the surface of the foredeck was scarcely two hands' width from my face as I pulled the gaff-topsail out. On hand and knees on the foredeck, I looked for more blood and found traces of it everywhere—on the deck, on the bow, on the butt of the bowsprit, and even on the forestay.

My first thought was that Babbie had caught a seabird and eaten it; but there should have been feathers in that case, a few blood-smeared feathers at least, and there were none. "Not a bird," I told him. "Not a fish, either. A fish might jump on board, but there would be scales. Or anyway I'd think there would be. What was it?"

He listened attentively; and I sensed that he understood, though he gave no sign of it.

When the topsail was up, I went to the tiller, steering us a bit wider of the low island I had sighted. There was weed in the water, as there often was off Lizard, long streamers of more or less green leaf kept afloat by bladders about the size of garden peas. Like everyone else who lived near the sea, we had collected this weed on the beach and dried it for tinder; it occurred to me that we had very little left, as well as very little firewood. Tinder without firewood would be useless, but if I kept an eye out, I might snag a few sticks of driftwood as well. I collected a good big wad of seaweed and spread it over the waxed canvas covers of the cargo chests, tossing the tiny crabs that clung to the strands back into the water. Others skittered about the boat and swam in the bilges until Babbie caught and ate them, crushing their shells between his teeth with unmistakable relish and swallowing shell and all.

Watching him, I realized that I had gone astray when I had supposed that he had eaten the creature whose blood I had found on the half-deck. It could not have been small, and he would have had to have eaten it entirely, skin, bones, and all. Yet he was clearly hungry. I threw him an apple, and ate one myself after listening to his quick, loud crunchings and munchings. By that time I had heard what Babbie did to bones more than once, and I felt quite sure that the noise he would have made while devouring an animal of any size would certainly have awakened me.

What had happened, almost certainly, was that something had climbed aboard at the bow, perhaps grasping the bowsprit in some way, as I had when I had climbed back on board after escaping the leatherskin. Babbie had charged and wounded it, and it had fallen back into the sea. The clatter of Babbie's trotters would not have awakened me because I had become accustomed to hearing him move about the boat while I slept. He had licked up all the blood he could find, just as he later licked up the clotted blood I extracted from the crevices between the planks with the point of Sinew's knife.

Something had fallen back into the sea, bleeding and badly injured. What had it been? For a moment I thought of the woman I had shot, swimming league upon league after our boat, intent upon revenge. If I were spinning a fireside tale for children here, no doubt it would be so; but I am recounting sober fact, and I knew that any such thing was utterly impossible. The woman I had shot was dead, in all probability; and if she was not dead, it was because she had been rescued by the black boat from which she had fallen.

Had it really come out of the sea at all? The inhumi could fly, and though they possessed no blood of their own, they could and did bleed profusely with the blood of others when they had recently fed, as the inhumu we had called Patera Quetzal had in the tunnels. Babbie would almost certainly attack an inhumu at sight, I decided. But could he have thus caught and bested one? A big male hus might have, but Babbie was no more than half grown.

What, then, had come out of the sea? Another leatherskin? Even a small one would have killed or injured any hus bold enough to attack it, I felt sure; and Babbie seemed quite unhurt. I resolved to nap during the afternoon and stand watch with him after shadelow.

The sloop was no longer rolling as it had been, and by that time was heeling rather less than it had when I had first set the topsail. I shinnied up the mast (something I had not done in some time, and found more difficult than I remembered) and had a look around. The island I had seen to port was distant but plainly visible, a level green plain hardly higher than the sea, dotted here and there with bushes and small, swaying trees.

Looking to starboard, I thought that I could make out another, similar, island there. "If those are parts of the same landmass, we may have found our western continent a lot sooner than we expected," I told Babbie; but I knew it could not be true.

The weed in the water became thicker and thicker as the day wore on; but there was no driftwood.

★

★ ★

Once, when Seawrack and I were on the riverbank, I felt that there were three of us. Half a dozen speculations raced through my mind, of which the most obvious and convincing were that Mucor was accompanying us without revealing the fact, or that Krait had left the sloop and was shadowing us for some purpose of his own. The most fantastic—I am embarrassed at having to set it down here and confess that at the time I actually came close to giving it serious credence—was that the shaman whose help we had tried to enlist the previous night had put an invisible devil upon our track, something he had boasted of having done to others. After an hour or more of this uneasiness, I realized that the third person I sensed was merely Babbie, whom I had by a species of mental misstep ceased to consider an animal.

The shaman may have had something to do with that after all, because the western peoples do not make our distinction between the human and the bestial. The shearbear is a person, certainly, and an important one, and Babbie was counted as a sort of son to us, an adopted son or foster child. When I learned this, I smiled to think that it made Krait his brother, and made him Krait's.

So it was that day, as I dozed in the shade of the foredeck. Another sailor sailed with me, and I felt that I could rest as long as the sea remained calm. If a hand on the tiller was needed, he would provide it, and if it was advisable to take another reef in the mainsail, he would take it.

When I woke, I found that the sun was touching the horizon. The wind had died away to a breath, and the jib, which I was nearly sure I had struck before lying down, had been set again. I let out the last reef in the mainsail (which I had, I thought, double reefed) and trimmed, explaining to Babbie everything that I was doing and why I was doing it as I worked. If he understood any of it, he said nothing.

"You can turn in now, if you want," I told him, and much to my surprise he lay down under the little foredeck just as I had, though he was up and about again in less than an hour. After that, we stood watch together.

There was nothing much to watch, or at any rate that was how it seemed at the time. The weed was thicker than ever, so that I felt it was actively resisting our passage and had to be pushed aside by the bow like floating ice. I was nodding at the tiller when Babbie began grunting with excitement and with a running leap plunged over the side.

As I have said, he was a faster and a stronger swimmer than any man I have ever known, his multitude of short, powerful limbs being well adapted to it. For ten minutes if not more I watched him swim away, noticing the faint green glow of his wake; then his small, dark head was lost among the gentle swells. After so many days of increasingly less surly companionship, it was a strange and forlorn feeling to find myself alone in the sloop again.

In half an hour he was back, still swimming strongly but not making anything like the progress he had earlier because he was pushing a small tree ahead of him, roots and all. I had hoped to snare driftwood in the form of a broken timber or a few floating sticks; now it seemed that all the gods had chosen to help me at once.

It was too big to bring on board. I lashed it alongside until I could lop off as many branches as would fill our little woodbox. Sinew's hunting knife was large and heavy enough to chop with after a fashion, although barely. A hatchet (with a pang of nostalgia I recalled the one that Silk had used to repair the roof of our manteion, the hatchet he had left behind at Blood's) would have been a good deal better. I resolved to add one to the sloop's equipment at the first opportunity; but however wise, it was a resolution that did me no good while I was leaning over the gunwale to hack away at those springy branches, which were still full of sap and decked with green leaves.

"I hope you weren't hoping for a fire tonight," I remarked to Babbie. "This stuff's going to have to dry for days before it will burn."

He chewed a twig philosophically.

"For a moment there I thought I saw somebody." It sounded so silly that I was ashamed to voice the thought, even though there was no one but my little hus to hear it. "A face, very pale, down under the water. It was probably a fish, really, or just a piece of waterlogged wood."

Babbie appeared skeptical, so I added, "Some trees have white bark. They're not all brown or black." Sensing that he still doubted me, I said, "Or green. Some are white. You must have lived in the mountains before somebody caught you, so you must surely have seen snowbirch, and you probably know that underneath the bark of a lot of trees, the wood is whitish or yellow. A log that had been in the water for a long time—"

I broke off my foolish argument because something had begun to sing. It was not Seawrack's song (which torments me for hours at a time even now), but the Mother's, a song without words, or at any rate without words that I could understand. "Listen," I ordered Babbie; but his ears, which usually lay flat against his skull, were up and spread like sails, so that his head appeared twice its normal size.

There is a musical instrument, one that is in fact little more than a toy, that we in Viron used to call Molpe's dulcimer. Strings are arranged in a certain way and drawn tight above a chamber of thin wood that swells the sound when they are strummed by the wind. Horn made several for his young siblings before we went into the tunnels; when I made them, I dreamed of making a better one someday, one constructed with all the knowledge and care that a great craftsman would bring to the task, a fitting tribute to Molpe. I have never built it, as you will have guessed already. I have the craft now, perhaps; but I have never had the musical knowledge the task would require, and I never will.

If I had built it, it might have sounded something like that, because I would have made it sound as much like a human voice as I could; and if I were the great craftsman I once dreamed of becoming, I would have come very near—and yet not near enough.

That is how it was with the Mother's voice. It was lovely and uncanny, like Molpe's dulcimer; and although it was not in truth very remote as well as I could judge, there was that in it that sounded very far away indeed. I have since thought that the distance was perhaps of time, that we heard a song on that warm, calm evening that was not merely hundreds but thousands of years old, sung as it had been sung when the Short Sun of Blue was yet young, and floating to us across that lonely sea with a pain of loss and longing that my poor words cannot express.

No, not even if I could whisper them aloud to you of the future, and certainly not as I am constrained to speak to you now with Oreb's laboring black wingfeather.

Nor with a quill from any other bird that ever flew.

★

★ ★

Nothing more happened that night, or at least nothing more worth recounting in detail. Certainly Babbie and I listened for hours, and when I think back upon that time it seems to me that we must have listened half the night. Sometime before dawn it ceased, not fading away but simply ending, as if the singer had come to the conclusion of her song and stopped. The light airs that had been moving us ever more slowly through the weed died out altogether at about the same time, leaving the sloop turning lazily this way and that without enough way to make her answer the helm. I sat up with Babbie until shadeup, as I had planned, then stretched myself out for most of the morning under the foredeck. Babbie slept too (or so I would guess), but slept so lightly that the sloop could hardly have been said to have been unwatched.

When I woke, I saw that we were much nearer the low green island than I had imagined. If we got a good wind, I decided, we would sail on in search of Pajarocu; but if Molpe permitted us only the light and vagrant airs I more than half expected, I would steer for the island, and tie up there until we had sailing weather.

It was noon before we reached it, pushed along at times by faint breezes that never lasted long, and handicapped almost as often by others. I jumped from the sloop to make her fast, and found myself on a moist and resilient turf that was not grass, and that stretched its bright green carpet not merely to the edge of the salt sea, but beyond the edge, extending some considerable distance underneath the water, where it had been crushed and torn by our prow. Nowhere was there a tree, a stump, or a stone—or anything else that I could tie the sloop to. I sharpened a couple of sticks of the green firewood we had gotten the day before, drove them deeply into the soft turf with a third, and moored to them.

While I was sharpening my stakes and pounding them in, I argued with myself about Babbie. He was clearly eager to get off the sloop after having been confined there for several weeks, and though I had planned to leave him to guard it, I could see for a league at least in every direction, and could see nothing for him to protect it from. Determined to be prudent no matter how great the temptation, I sternly ordered him to stay where he was, fetched my slug gun, and set off by myself, walking inland for a half hour or so. Finding no fresh water and seeing nothing save a few distant trees of no great size, I returned to the sloop and pulled up my stakes (which was alarmingly easy), and sailed along that strange shore until midafternoon.

Sailed, I just wrote, and I will not cross it out. But I might almost have said we drifted. In three or four hours, we may have traveled half a league, although I doubt it. "At this rate we'll die of thirst ten years before we sight the western land," I told Babbie, and tied up again at a point where the green plain seemed slightly more variegated, having hills and dales of the size loved by children, and a tree or bush here and there. I moored the sloop as before, but when I left it this time I let Babbie come with me.

It puzzled me that an island so richly green should be so desolate, too. I do not mean that I did not know what that bright green carpet was. I pulled up some and tasted it; and when I did, and saw it in my hand, a little, weak, torn thing and not the vast spongy expanse over which Babbie and I wandered, I knew it for the green scum I had often seen washed ashore after storms, too salty for cattle, or even goats or any other such animal.

And yet it seemed irrational that so vast a quantity of vegetable matter should go to waste. Pas, who built the *Whorl*, would have arranged things better, I felt, little knowing that I would soon encounter one of the gods of this whorl of Blue that we call ours in spite of the fact that it existed whole ages before we did, and that it has been only a scant generation since we came to it.

For an hour or more we walked inland, and then, just as I was about to turn back and call for Babbie (who ranged ahead of me, and sometimes ranged so far that he would be lost to sight for several minutes), I saw the silvery sheen of water between two of the gentle, diminutive hills.

At first I thought that I had reached the farther side of the island, and hurried ahead to see if it were true; but as we came nearer, I saw more hills beyond the water, and realized that we had found a little tarn, captive rain nestling between hills for the same reason that similar pools are found in the mountains here, or among the mountains inland of New Viron; then I trotted faster still, hoping that it might be fresh enough to drink.

Before I reached it, I knew that it was not, because Babbie had plunged his muzzle into it and quickly withdrawn it in disgust. I was determined to test it for myself, however, and stubbornly continued to walk, impelled by a vague notion that we human beings might be more tolerant of salt than hus, or failing that, that I might be thirstier than Babbie. Common sense should have sent me back to the sloop; if it had, I would almost certainly have lost Babbie then and there. As it was, we both came very near death.

When I bent to taste the water, I saw something huge move in its depths, as though a great sheet of the green scum had been torn free and was drifting and undulating near the bottom of the tarn. I dipped up a handful of water, and had just brought it toward my mouth when I realized that the undulating thing I had seen was in fact rushing toward me.

I may have shouted a warning to Babbie—I cannot be sure. I know that I backed away hurriedly, brought up the slug gun, and cycled the action to put a cartridge in the chamber.

The thing erupted from the water and seemed almost to fly toward us. I fired, and it sank at once into the shallows. I was left with a not very clear impression of something at once huge and flat. Of black and white, and great staring yellow eyes.

Babbie was clearly terrified. All his bristles stood straight up, making him barrel-sized, humpbacked, and as spiny as a bur. His gait, which was always apt to be lively, had become an eight-legged dance, and he gnashed his tusks without ceasing. Although he had retreated from the tarn until his thrashing tail whisked my knees, he interposed himself between the unknown thing we both feared and me. I was badly frightened, too; and in spite of the assurance I gave myself again and again that I was not as terrified as Babbie, it was he who was trying to protect me.

I must have looked over my shoulder a hundred times as we left the place, seeing nothing. When we reached the crest of the rounded ridge that would shield the surface of the water from our view once we had crossed, I stopped and turned around for a better view. An appallingly vivid memory of what I saw then has remained with me beyond even death.

For the great, flat creature I had shot at, and had by that time convinced myself that I had killed, was rising from the shallows. It lifted itself tentatively at first, looming above, and then subsiding into, the water. In a few seconds it rose again and left the tarn altogether, running very fast over the soft green vegetation as a bat runs, using its wide leathern wings as legs. It was black above and white beneath, oddly flattened as I have said, and larger than the carpet in the reception hall of the Caldé's Palace. I fired once as it dashed toward us, and had pumped a fresh cartridge into the chamber before it bowled me over. The wings that wrapped me then were as rough as files, but rippled like flags as they propelled me toward the gaping, white-lipped mouth.

It was Babbie who saved me, charging that monstrous flatfish (or whatever it was) and laying open the tough skin of one wing. I got my arm free then, and was able to draw Sinew's knife, which I plunged into the creature again and again until it was covered with its own blood.

Here I would like very much to write that I killed it with Sinew's knife; the truth is that I do not know. A slug is a formidable projectile, so much so that a single shot will often fell a horse or a fourhorn, as I have seen, and when we examined the carcass of the creature from the tarn I found that both my shots had struck it within a hand of its head. I cannot doubt that both did a good deal of damage, although the first clearly did not do enough to prevent the thing's pursuing us when it had recovered from the initial shock.

Babbie's efforts must be considered, too. Certainly the wounds he inflicted on it in the space of five or ten seconds would have killed half a dozen men.

Yet, in my heart of hearts, I believe that it was Sinew's long hunting knife, that in stabbing frantically at the only parts of the creature I could reach I struck some vital organ by chance. I believe that was what happened, I say. I cannot be sure.

Afterward I examined the knife with care and found that I had dulled its edge somewhat when I had cut the wood, although not nearly as much as I had feared. Since I have not described it in detail until now, I believe, I shall do so here. The blade was a hand and two fingers in length, two fingers wide, and very thick and strong at the back. It was a single-edged knife made for skinning and cutting up game, not a dagger, and had been forged (both blade and grip) from a single billet of steel by a smith in New Viron, who had followed a sketch that my son Sinew had made for him. The minor god Hephaestus, who in Old Viron we reckoned the patron of all who worked with fire, stood invisible behind Gadwall as he worked, I feel certain. I have heard men speak of better blades, but I have never met with one.

★

★ ★

I got a bad fright today. I was to sacrifice an elephant in the temple, this at the urging of the priests, who seem to feel that a large and valuable animal will provide better omens than a sheep or goat. Seeing me await it with the sacred sword in my hand, the elephant appeared to understand what we had intended, and broke free from its weeping trainer, trumpeting and flailing its trunks like muscular whips. I stood as still as any statue when it charged, knowing that to move would be to die. It knocked me down and did a great deal of damage before it could be brought under control again, and I find that I am being hailed as a man of superhuman courage; but I trembled and wept like a little child when I was alone.

So it was after the devil-fish was dead. Perhaps I would have behaved better if another human being had been present, but as it was, my hands shook so violently that I found it very difficult to sheath Sinew's knife. We like to think (or at any rate I always have) that our arms and legs will not betray us; but in moments like that we learn just how wrong we are. My hands trembled, my knees had lost their strength, and tears I could scarcely blink back threatened to wash the devil-fish's blood from my face. I tried to joke with Babbie then, to make light of what had happened to us; my teeth chattered so badly, however, that he thought I was angry and stood well clear of me, lagging behind so as to keep me under observation for safety's sake.

The most logical thing to do would have been to return to the tarn and wash there. The thought filled me with horror, and I promised myself instead that I would wash in the sea; and so I was covered with blood when we returned to the sloop and found Seawrack waiting on board. It is a testament to her courage that she did not scream at the sight and leap back into the water.

As for me, I was ready to believe that fear and the fight with the monstrous bat-fish had destroyed my reason. To see her as I saw her then, naked except for her gold and the waist-length mantle of her hair (which was gold too in places, but in others green), you must imagine first the days and nights at sea and the hours-long walk across that featureless green plain, where it seemed that no one and nothing lived in the whole whorl but Babbie and me.

6

Seawrack

Ambassadors from a distant town arrived today. It is called Skany, or at least that is as close as I can come to the name. Its ambassadors are three gray-bearded men, dignified and grave but not humorless, who rode mules and were accompanied by thirty or forty armed servants on foot. They had been told that Silk was here, "ruling Gaon," and wished to invite me to rule Skany as well.

I explained that I did not rule (for I am in reality no more than an advisor to the people here) and that I could not and would not take responsibility for two towns so widely separated.

They then placed several problems before me, saying that these were cases that had arisen in Skany during the past year, and asked me to judge each and explain the principles on which I made my decisions. In one, both parties might well have been telling the truth as they saw it. It could not possibly be decided by someone who could not question them both, and question witnesses as well, and I said so.

I will set it down here.

The people of Skany had been able to leave the Long Sun Whorl only because a wealthy man of their native city had supplied several hundred cards and other valuable parts to repair a lander for them. He did so on the condition that he would be permitted to claim a very extensive tract of land, whose size was agreed upon in advance, to be selected by him. (He was, I believe, one of the three ambassadors, although at no time did they allude to it.) This was done.

This man now desires to marry a young woman, hardly more than a girl, whom he had employed as a servant previously. The bride (as I shall call her) is entirely willing. The difficulty is that a certain poor woman has come forward to claim the bride-price, saying that she is the bride's mother. The bride herself denies this, saying that her father was left behind in the Long Sun Whorl, and that her mother was a woman (whom she names) who perished when their lander took flight. Perhaps I should say here that it is their custom for the groom or his family to buy the bride from her parents; but that when the bride is orphaned she is bought from herself—that is to say, she receives her own bride-price, which becomes her property.

All this brought Seawrack and the gold she wore to mind vividly; yet her case was in certain respects the very reverse of this one. I had intended to write a great deal about her tonight in any event, and I will do so. The reversals should be obvious enough.

Her pale gold hair was long, as I have said, and in places dyed a misted green by some microscopic sea-plant that had taken refuge there. I am tempted to say that it was her hair that impelled me to name her as I did, but it would not be entirely true; the truth is that her name, which was no word of the Common Tongue, baffled me, and that *Seawrack* was near to it in sound and seemed to suit her very well.

Her face was beautiful, strong, and foreign. By that last, I mean that I had never before seen anyone with her sharp chin, very high cheekbones, and tilted eyes. Her skin was as white as foam in those days, which made her lips a blazing scarlet and her midnight-blue eyes darker than the night. I noticed her nakedness first, as I suppose any man would, and then the length of her legs and the womanly contours of her body, and only then the gold she wore. It was not until she released her hold on the backstay and waved, very shyly and tentatively, with her left hand that I realized that her right arm had been amputated just below the shoulder.

"Hello?" Her voice was just above the threshold of audibility. And again: "Hello?"

That word is one of the most ordinary, and I remember that when I was a small boy Maytera Marble used to ridicule people who used it, saying that we ought to bless those whom we greet in the name of the god of the day.

Or if we were too self-conscious for that, to say *good morning, good afternoon, good evening,* or *good day.* But I shall never forget seeing Seawrack as she stood in my old sloop, the way in which she waved to me (she was terrified of Babbie, as I quickly discovered), and the delicious music of her voice when she whispered, "Hello?"

As for what I replied, I may have said, "Good afternoon," or "Hello!" or "Is it going to snow?" Or any other nonsense that you might propose. Most likely, I was too stunned to say anything at all.

"I am one of you," she told me solemnly, and I thought that she meant one of the crew of our boat and tried to say something gracious about needing help without mentioning her missing arm. There is a saying among the fishermen, "One hand for yourself and one for the boat." It means that in a rough sea you are to hold on with one hand and do your work with the other, and as I spoke to Seawrack I could not rid my mind of the idiotic thought that she would be unable to do it.

"Do you like me?"

It was said so artlessly and with such childlike seriousness that I knew there could be only one answer. "Yes," I told her, "I like you very much."

She smiled. It was as if a child had smiled, and by smiling had rendered her face transparent, so that I could see the woman she would someday be and had always been, the woman who stands behind all women and stands behind even Kypris, Thelxiepeia, and Echidna. If that woman has a name I do not know it; "Seawrack" is as good a name as any.

Remaining where the smooth green shore dipped underwater, because it was plain that she was badly frightened, I asked where she had come from, and she pointed over the side. "Yes," I said, "I can see you've been swimming. Did you swim here from another boat?"

"Down there. Do you want me to show you?" This was said eagerly, so I said I did. She dove, not stepping up onto the gunwale as I would have, but diving across it with liquid ease.

I went aboard then, and Babbie with me, expecting to see her in the water. She was not there, although for ten minutes if not more I walked from one side to the other, and from bow to stern looking for her. She had vanished utterly.

At last I saw my own reflection (which I had been trying to look past before) and realized that I was covered with the batfish's blood, dry and cracking by this time, and remembered that I had planned to wash myself in the sea as soon as we got back to the sloop.

I had already begun to doubt my sanity. It occurred to me then that the batfish's blood had somehow poisoned me, or that I had eaten its flesh—I had actually cut some for Babbie—and so poisoned myself. I questioned him then, and from his answers knew that the young woman I had seen had been real. I had seen and spoken to a young woman with one arm who had worn rings and anklets set with gems, a young woman with a fine gold chain about her waist.

"Red earrings, too," I told him. "Or pink. I caught a glimpse of those through her hair. They may have been coral."

His look said very plainly, Well, *I* saw no such thing.

"A year or two older than Hoof and Hide, I'd say. Rounded and very graceful, but there was muscle there. We saw it when she dove. And she . . ."

The complete implausibility of what I was saying crashed down on me, and I pulled off my boots and stockings in silence, jumped out of the sloop, and washed myself and my clothes as well.

Returning, I spread everything in the foredeck to dry. "Do you remember the singing we heard? That was her. It had to be, and she's as beautiful as she is real." He regarded me sheepishly for a few seconds, then slunk off to the foredeck and his accustomed place in the bow.

I shaved and combed what remained of my hair, and put on fresh underclothes, another tunic, and my best trousers. The ones I had washed in seawater would be stiff and unpleasantly sticky, I knew, unless it rained so that I could rinse them in fresh. Because the air was sullen and still, I thought it might; and I made what small preparations I could, bailing the sloop dry and breaking out the few utensils I had that could be employed to catch rainwater.

After that, there was nothing more to do. Neither the vacant plain of green that seemed almost to roll like the sea, nor the oily sea itself, held anything of interest. I reviewed my brief conversation with Seawrack (whom I did not yet call that) trying to decide whether I might have kept her with me if I had spoken differently.

For I wanted her to remain with me. I wanted that very badly, as I was forced to admit to myself as I shaved. It was not only that I desired her. (What man can see a beautiful woman naked and not desire her?) Nor was it that I hoped to take her gold; I would have cut off my own arm rather than rob her. It was that I felt certain she needed my help, which I was very eager to provide, and that I had somehow frightened her back to the troubles she had fled.

The men who had commanded the black boat would certainly have robbed me if they could, and would very likely have killed me as well. They would not have killed an attractive young woman, however. Not if I knew anything of criminals and criminal ways. They would have forced her to join them, as they had no doubt forced the woman I had shot and the rest. They had (so I imagined) taken Seawrack's clothing so she would not escape; but she had escaped, and had first decked herself in their loot when she could find nothing else to wear—unless I was in sober fact a madman.

She had said, "I am one of you." I should have welcomed her then, and I wished desperately that I had. I had asked about the boat she had come from, and she had said it was "Down there."

Her boat had sunk after she got here, plainly; and while she had been waiting for us, she had swum underwater to inspect the wreck. When I had said that I wanted to see it, she had assumed that I would go with her, and so had dived into the sea—after which, something had prevented her from surfacing again.

I recalled the batfish with sick horror. It had been in the tarn, not in the sea; but the tarn must have been linked with the sea in some fashion, since its water had been too salt to drink and it could not have supported a creature as large as the devilish thing we found in it for long.

I baited several hooks, tied them to floats, and set them out around the sloop; and after an hour or so of inactivity which by that time I found very welcome, caught some good-sized fish that I gutted and filleted with the same knife that had killed the batfish. Using what little dry wood we had, I built a small fire in the sandbox, rolled my fillets in cornmeal and cooking oil, and fried the first in the little long-handled pan we always kept on the sloop.

"Are you going to eat that?"

I did not actually drop the pan, but I must have tilted it enough for the fillet to slide into the fire. "You're back!" I had practically broken my neck looking around at her; I stood up as I spoke, and that is when it must have happened.

"She made me."

Seawrack was not in the sloop with me, but she had pulled herself up to look over the gunwale. The music of her voice woke Babbie, and I saw again that she was terribly afraid of him. I assured her that he would not harm her, and told him emphatically that he was not to hurt her or do anything that might alarm her.

"Can I . . . ?"

"What is it?" I asked. "You can do anything you like—with me to help, if you'll let me."

"Can I have one of the others?"

"These?" I picked up one of the other fillets, and she nodded.

"Absolutely. I'll cook it for you, too, if you want." I glanced at the pan and realized that the one I had prepared for myself was burning on the coals. I added, "Not that I'm very good at it."

She was looking at the one I held and licking her lips, with something utterly wretched in her expression.

"Would you like it now?" I asked. "I know some people enjoy raw fish."

A new voice said, "Do not give it to her." It seemed that the words issued from the sea itself.

The top of the speaker's head broke the water, and she rose effortlessly until the oily swell reached no higher than her waist. I can never forget that gradual, facile ascension. Like the face of Kypris seen in the glass of General Saba's airship it remains vivid today, the streaming form of a cowled woman robed in pulsing red, a woman three times my own stature at least, with the setting sun behind her. I knelt and bowed my head.

"Help my daughter into your boat."

I did as she had commanded, although Seawrack needed scant help from me.

"Prepare that fish as you would for yourself. When it is ready, give it to her."

I said, "Yes, Great Goddess."

The goddess (for I was and am quite confident that she was one of the Vanished Gods of Blue) used Seawrack's name, saying, "You must go to your own people. Your time with me is ended."

Seawrack nodded meekly.

"Do not return. For my own sake I would have you stay. For yours I tell you go."

"I understand, Mother."

"This man may hurt you."

I swore that I would do nothing of the sort.

"If he does, you must bear it as women do. If you hurt him, it is the same." Then the goddess spoke to me. "Do not permit her to eat uncooked flesh, or to catch fish with her hands. Do not allow her to do anything that your own women do not do."

I promised I would not.

"Protect her from your beast, as you would one of your own women."

Her parting words were for Seawrack. "I have ceased to be for you. You are alone with him."

More swiftly than she had risen, she slid beneath the swell. For a moment I glimpsed through the water—or thought that I did—something huge and dark on which she stood.

Sometime after that, when I had recovered myself, Seawrack asked, "Are you going to hurt me?"

"No," I said. "I will never hurt you." I lied, and meant it with all my heart. As I spoke, Babbie grunted loudly from his place in the bow; I feel sure that he was pledging himself just as I had, but it frightened her.

I squatted and rolled her strip of raw fish in the oily cornmeal, put it in the pan, and held the pan over the fire. "Babbie won't hurt you," I said. "I'll make one of these for him next, and then cook another one for me, so that we can all eat together."

He was already off the foredeck and edging nearer to the fire.

"Babbie, you are not to hurt . . ." I tried to pronounce the name the goddess had used, and the young woman who bore it laughed nervously.

"I can't say that," I told her. "Is it all right if I call you Seawrack?"

She nodded.

"This is Babbie. He's a very brave little hus, and he'll protect you anytime that you need it. So will I. My name is Horn."

She nodded again.

Thinking of the silver jewelry Marrow had given me to trade with, I said, "You must like rings and necklaces. I have some, though they are not as fine as yours. Would you like to see them? You may have any that you like."

"No," she told me. "You do."

"I like them?" I flipped her fillet, catching it in the pan.

She laughed again. "I know you do. Mother says so, and she gave me these so you would like me." She took off her necklace and offered it to me, but I assured her that I liked her more than her jewelry. In the end we put her gold in the box with my silver, from which I gave her an ornamented comb. I contrived a sort of skirt for her as well, wrapping her in a scrap of old sailcloth which I fastened with a silver pin.

That evening, while we were watching the slender column of dark smoke rise and admiring the fashion in which the sparks flung up by our green firewood danced upon the air, she put Babbie's head in her lap, something I would never have thought of doing. As her left hand stroked it, I noticed the dried blood among the folds of skin on the stump that had been her right arm, and understood why she had been so afraid of Babbie, and whose blood had stained the deck at the bow. "It was not you who sang for us," I told her. "It was the goddess. I thought at first that it must have been you, but I've heard her speak now, and that was her voice."

"To make you like me."

"I understand. Like the gold. She wanted to find you a new home. Mothers are like that."

Seawrack shook her head, but I felt certain I had been right in principle.

So it was, I believe, in the case that the ambassadors from Skany described to me. The woman who had perished when their lander left the *Whorl* had been the bride's natural mother. The poor woman who called herself the bride's mother now had adopted her, or at least considered herself to have adopted her, and when she was old enough had found her a new home in the house of a man of wealth and position. Each was speaking what she believed to be the truth, and to settle the affair between them it would be necessary to determine the degree to which a real adoption had taken place. Had there been any attempt to record the adoption with someone in authority? Did the poor woman's natural children (if she had any) consider the bride their sister? Did the poor woman habitually speak of her as her daughter? And so on.

Seawrack's situation differed in that she considered the sea goddess her mother—much more so, I would guess, than the goddess considered Seawrack her daughter. Accepting the gold, I had accepted Seawrack; it was her dowry. The goddess's song, however, had not been payment but a species of charm (I am using the word very loosely) to soften our hearts and insure Seawrack a more friendly reception next time.

Did it work? I believe that I would have welcomed Seawrack without it, but would I? I was conscious that I was, at least in some sense, betraying Nettle; but what was I to do? Leave a maimed and friendless young woman alone in the middle of the sea?

She was frightened that night, and in pain from her amputation. I held her; and we slept, for the few hours that either of us slept, with my arms around her and her back to my chest.

★

★ ★

Too often I have merely glanced at the last sheet before I began to write, and taken up my narration, as I believed, from the point at which I left it the day before. Or as has sometimes happened, from the week before. Today I have read everything I have written already about Seawrack, growing sicker and sicker as I came to appreciate my own failure. I am going to start over.

Seawrack, as I have said, was waiting for us in the sloop. When I was a boy in Viron and I heard from her own lips how Chenille had wandered naked through the tunnels, I had longed to see her like that. She was, as I tried to make clear in the book Nettle wrote with me, a large and muscular woman, with big shoulders, a sharply defined waist, amply rounded hips, and large breasts. At that time, I had never seen a naked woman, not even Nettle, although I had caressed Nettle's breasts.

When I saw Seawrack in the sloop, it was as if I were a boy again, shaking in the grip of wonder. Perhaps it was the spell of the sea goddess's song, although I do not think so. If there was magic in it, the magic was in Seawrack's body, so tenderly and so sleekly curved, in her face, and most of all in her glance. She was a woman, but did not yet know that she was a woman. She had left childhood behind, but had taken all that is most attractive in children with her. Seeing her as the boy I had been would have, I would have given anything in the whorl to have her love. And I felt certain that I would never have it.

Soon I was to gaze upon the sea goddess of the Vanished People. Perhaps she was Scylla in another form, as Silk once confided to me that Kypris was becoming another form of the Outsider, whose many forms had spoken to Silk that unforgettable noon on the ball court as a crowd speaks, while one whispered to his right ear and another to his left.

Here I am reminded irresistibly of Quadrifons, Olivine's god, he of the four faces. Is it even possible that he is not a form of the Outsider as well? Considering Olivine, and the life she lived as a species of ghost in the Caldé's Palace, I do not think so. And if Quadrifons (whose sign of crossroads may well have become Pas's sign of addition) was in the final reckoning none other than the Outsider—which now seems certain to me—might not the Mother be Scylla as well?

Perhaps.

But I do not really believe it. In a town one cobbler, as the saying goes, and in another town another; but they are not the same cobbler, although they own similar tools, do similar work, and may even be similar in appearance.

This is what I think, not what I know:

Having the sea, as we in Old Viron did not, the Neighbors had also a goddess of the sea. She may have been their water goddess as well, as Scylla is at home; I cannot say.

Perhaps all gods and goddesses are very large; certainly Echidna was when I saw her in our Sacred Window. Our gods, the gods of Old Viron, dwelt in Mainframe. I saw Mainframe in company with Nettle and many others, and even what I saw was a very large place, although I was told that most of it was underground. It may be that our gods did not come among us except by enlightenment and possession because they were too large to do so; even the godlings that they send among the people now are, for the most part, immense. A man may like insects. Some men do. A man who likes them may make them gifts, giving a crumb soaked in honey or some such thing. But although that man may walk, he may not walk with his pets the insects. He is too big for it.

So it is, I believe, with the Mother. She dwells in the sea, and Seawrack spoke of hiding at times within her body as one might speak of taking shelter in the Grand Manteion, the Palace, or some other big building. Possibly the Mother's worshippers cast their sacrifices into the waves instead of burning them. (I do not know, and offer the suggestion as a mere guess.) What seems certain is that her worshippers were the Vanished People, whom I did not then call the Neighbors; and that they are gone, although not entirely gone.

She waits.

For what I do not know. It may be for her worshippers to return again. Or for us to become her new worshippers, as we well may.

Or perhaps merely for death. She shaped herself, I believe, a woman of the Vanished People so that they would love her. We are here now, and so she shaped for me a woman of my own race—a woman beside whom Chenille would stand like a child—who could sing and speak to me. Beneath it the old sea goddess waited, and was not of our human race, nor of the race of the Vanished People, whom I was to come to know.

I once had a toy, a little wooden man in a blue coat who was moved by strings. When I played with him, I made him walk and bow, and spoke for him. I practiced until I thought myself very clever. One day I saw my mother holding the two sticks that held his strings, and my little wooden man saluting my youngest sister much more cleverly than I could have made him do it, and laughing with his head thrown back, then mourning with his face in his hands. I never spoke of it to my mother, but I was angry and ashamed.

★

★ ★

It has been a long while since I wrote last. How long I am not sure. I went to Skany as its ambassadors asked, and remained there most of the summer. Now I have returned to this fine, airy house my people here have built for me, which they enlarged while I was gone. The west wing was torn to pieces by a storm, they tell me;

but they have rebuilt it and made it larger and stronger, so that I walk there among rooms that seem familiar and feel that I have shrunk.

The storms are worse. Green is great in the sky. Like the eye of a devil, people say; but the truth for me is that it is so large that I look up at it and think on other days, and fancy sometimes that I can smell the rot, and see the trees that are eating trees that are eating trees. I never hear the wild song of the wind without recalling other days still, and how we built our house and our mill, Nettle.

You were the dream of my boyhood. You shared my life, and I shared yours, and together we brought forth new lives. Who can say what the end of that may be? Only the Outsider. He is wise, Nettle. So wise. And because he is, he is just.

I hear the wind's song now at my window. I have opened the shutters. The flame of my lamp flickers and smokes. Through the open window I see Green, which will be gone in an hour as it passes beyond the windowframe. I want to call out to you that the tides are coming; but no doubt they have come already. It may be that the log walls of our house are turning and leaping in the waves as I write. Time is a sea greater than our sea. You knew that long before I went away. I have learned it here. Its tides batter down all walls, and what the tides of time batter down is never rebuilt.

Not larger.

Not smaller.

Never as it was.

★

★ ★

I see that before I left for Skany, that glorious, corrupt town, I wrote of how Seawrack and I slept in the cubby of the sloop, with Babbie sleeping too at our feet, or at least at times pretending to sleep so that he could be in our company; and I said that we did not sleep long.

Nor did we. I remember lying like that, then turning on my back so that both my ears might listen. I wrote about the song of the wind, too; but I am not certain that I had ever really heard it until that night, although I thought I had. To hear the song of the wind truly, as I heard it that night, I think that you must hear it as I did, lying on your back in a rocking, pitching boat upon the wide, wide sea, with a woman younger than yourself asleep beside you.

The wind was a woman, too. Sometimes it was a woman like General Mint, a small woman with a neat, pure, honest little face, a woman in flowing black astride the tallest white stallion anyone ever saw, singing as she rode like a flame before a thousand wild troopers who rode as she did or ran like wolves, firing and reloading as they came and halting only to die.

And sometimes the wind was a woman like the tall, proud women of Trivigaunte, galloping along Sun Street with their heads up and their lances leveled, women singing to their wonderful horses, horses that had always to be held back and never had to be urged forward. And sometimes the wind was a singing woman like the one beside me, a sea woman who sings like her Mother, a woman that no one ever completely understands, with silver-blue combers in her eyes.

As I listened, the wind seemed to me more and more to be all three women and a million more, spurred onward—faster, always faster—by the rumbling voice of Pas. Beneath me, the sloop was lifted by giant's hand, and rolled so far that Seawrack was tumbled onto me and clutching me in fear while Babbie squealed at the tiller.

Outside the shelter of the foredeck, I was drenched to the skin in an instant. It was pitch dark except when the lightning flashed, and the sloop was laid over on her beam ends and in danger of being dismasted. I meant to cut her moorings before they pulled her under, but there was no need. The stakes I had pushed into the damp softness of that mossy shore had pulled free, and we were being driven before the storm like a child's lost boat or a stick of driftwood, half foundering. I put out the little jib, hoping to steady her and keep her stern to the waves, but had hardly set it before it was carried away.

I will not write about everything that took place that night, because most of it would be of interest only to sailors, who are not apt to be found so far inland as this. I rigged a sea anchor that tamed the diabolical pandemonium of boat and storm to mere insanity; and Seawrack and I bailed and bailed until I thought my arms would fall off of my shoulders; but the sloop never foundered or sunk, or lost a stick. I have never been prouder of something that I myself have made, not even my mill.

What I want to tell whoever may read this is that in the flashes of lightning, which for whole hours were so frequent as to provide a hectic illumination that was nearly constant, I saw the green plain part for us, ripped in two by the fury of the waves, and seeing it so—lifted by great waves at one moment, then crashing down upon the sea again at the next—I knew it for what it was.

At that place in the middle of the sea, the bottom is not leagues removed from the surface; but is, as Seawrack confirmed for me, not more than two or three chains distant from it. Great herbs (I do not know what else to call them) grow there that are not trees, nor grasses, nor ferns, but share the natures of all three. Their tangled branches, lying upon the surface, are draped with the smooth green life over which Babbie and I wandered. It may be that it covers them as orchids cover our trees here in Gaon, or as strangling lianas cover the cannibal trees of Green. Or it may be that they cover themselves with it as the trees of land cover themselves with leaves and fruit. I do not know. But I know that it is so, because I saw it that night. I saw what I had once thought islands torn like banana leaves, and tossed like flotsam by the waves.

Something climbed into our sloop that night that was neither a beast nor a man, and was not a thing of the sea nor a thing of the land, nor even a thing of the air like the inhumi. I hesitated to write of it, because I know that it will not be believed; after thinking it over, I understand that I must. How many travelers' tales, although full of wise advice and the soundest information, have been cast aside because among their thousands of lines there were two or three that their readers could not be brought to believe?

If you do not believe this, believe at least that I believed that I saw it. And Seawrack also saw it. She confirmed for me that she had, although she did not like to speak of it. Babbie saw it, too, and rushed at it; it laid hold of him as a man might lay hold of a lady's lapdog, and would, I believe, have thrown him over the side and into the raging water if Seawrack had not prevented it. In appearance it was like a man of many arms and legs, long dead and covered over with crabs and little shellfish and other things; and yet it moved and possessed great strength, although I think it feared the storm as much or more than we. I do not know how such a monstrous thing came to be, but I have thought about it again and again, and at last settled on the explanation that I offer here. If you find a better one, I congratulate you.

Imagine that one of the Vanished People gained great favor with one of his people's gods, those gods who are said by us to have vanished too. Or who, at least, we think of as having vanished. This god, let us suppose, offered his worshipper a great gift—but only one. Silk, I believe, might say that this worshipper was in truth no favorite of the god's but merely thought he was. Many times our own gods, the gods of the Long Sun Whorl, punished those they hated with riches, power, and fame that destroyed them.

Offered such a gift, may not this man of the Vanished People have chosen a life without end? The immortal gods have it, or are said to. Given the gift that he had chosen, he may have lived for centuries enjoying food and women and fine days and, in short, everything that pleased him. Perhaps he tired of all of it at last. Or perhaps he merely discovered at length that though he himself could not die, the race that had given him birth was dwindling every year. Or perhaps he simply chose, in the end, to abide with the goddess who had favored him. In any event, he must have cast himself into the sea.

All of which is mere speculation. No doubt I have rendered myself ridiculous even to those who believe me. Remember, please, that those who believe me are not themselves ridiculous—I saw what I saw.

The storm had come out of the northeast, as well as I could judge. It left us out of sight of land, and some considerable distance south of the place at which it had found us, as well as I could judge from the stars on the following night. We had no way of knowing how far west it had driven us, but sailed west-northwest hoping each day to sight land.

Water was a constant concern, although Seawrack required very little. We caught such rain as the good gods provided, taking down the mainsail and rigging it in such a way as to catch a good deal and funnel it (once the sail had been wet enough to clean it of salt) into our bottles. In fair weather, when there was little wind or none, all three of us swam together beside the sloop. I found, not at all to my surprise, that Babbie was a better swimmer than I; but found too, very much to my surprise, that Seawrack was a far better swimmer than Babbie. She could remain under the water so long that it terrified me, although when she realized that I was both concerned and astonished, she pretended she could not. One night when I kissed her, my lips discovered her gill slits, three, closely spaced and nearer the nape of her neck than I would have imagined. I asked her no questions about them, then or later.

At first she said nothing about the goddess she called the Mother. After nearly a week had passed, I happened to mention Chenille, saying that although she had known nothing of boats, she had understood Dace's perfectly when Scylla possessed her. Seawrack seized upon the concept of divine possession at once and asked many questions about it, only a few of which I could answer. At length I said that she, whose mother was a goddess, should be instructing me.

"She never said she was," Seawrack told me with perfect seriousness.

"Still, you must have known it."

Seawrack shook her lovely head. "She was my mother."

At that point I very nearly asked her whether her mother had not demanded prayers and sacrifices. "We used to give our gods gifts, when I lived inside the *Whorl*," I said instead, "but that was not because they required such things of us. They were far richer than we were, but they had given us so much that we felt we ought to give them whatever we could in return."

"Oh, yes." Seawrack smiled. "I used to bring Mother all sorts of things. Shells, you know. Lots of shells and pretty stones, and sometimes colored sand. Then she would say that my face was the best gift."

"She loved you." At that moment, as at so many others, I felt I knew a great deal about love; my heart was melting within me.

Seawrack agreed. "She used to look like a woman for me and hold me in her arms, and I used to think the woman was the real her and make her bring the woman back. She looked like a woman for you too. Remember?"

"Yes," I said. "I'll never forget that."

"When I was older, she would just wrap herself around me, and that was nice, like when you hold me. But not the same. What do they ask gods for, in the *Whorl*?"

"Oh, food and peace. Sometimes for a son or daughter."

"For gold? She said you liked it."

"We do," I admitted. "Every human being wants gold—every human being except you. Because they do, gold is a good friend to those who have it. Often it brings them good things without going away itself."

"Has my gold brought you anything?"

I smiled. "Not yet."

"It's old. You say that old things are always tired."

"Old people." I had been trying to explain that she was much younger than I, and what that would mean to both of us when we found land, and people besides ourselves. "Not old gold. Gold never gets old in that way."

"Mine did. It wasn't bright anymore, and the little worms were building houses on it. Mother had to clean it, pulling it through the sand. I helped."

"She must have had them a long time. Possibly for as long as you lived with her." Privately I thought that it must have been a good deal longer than that.

"Can I see it again?"

I got the box out for her, and told her she could wear her gold if she wished, that it was hers, not mine.

She selected a simple bracelet, narrow and not at all heavy, and held it up so that it coruscated in the sunshine. "This is pretty. Do you know who made it?"

"I've been wondering about that," I said, and wondered as I spoke whether she would tell me. "It could have been brought from the Long Sun Whorl on a lander; but I would guess that it is the work of the Vanished People, the people who used to live here on Blue long before we humans came."

"You're afraid of them."

It had been said with such certainty that I knew it would be futile to argue. "Yes. I suppose I am."

"All of you, I mean. All of us." She turned the bracelet to and fro, admiring it, then held it in her teeth to slip over her wrist.

"The Long Sun Whorl was our whorl, our place," I told her. "It was made especially for us, and we were put into it by Pas. This was their whorl. Perhaps it was made for them, but we don't even know that. They're bound to resent us, if any of them are still alive; and so are their gods. Their gods must still exist, since gods do not die."

"I didn't know that."

"Where I used to live, the greatest of all goddesses tried to kill Pas. Wise people who knew about it thought that she had, although most of us didn't even know she'd tried. Then Pas came back. He had planted himself, in a way, and grew again. Do you know about seeds, Seawrack?"

"Planting corn. You told me."

"He re-grew himself from seed, so to speak. That's what a pure strain of corn does. It produces seed before it dies, and when that seed sprouts, the strain is back for another year, just as it was before."

"Do you think the Vanished People might have done that?" From her tone, it was a new idea to her.

"I don't know." I shrugged. "I have no way of knowing what they may or may not have done."

"You told me the seed waited for water."

"Yes, for rain, and warmer weather."

Babbie ambled over to see what Seawrack and I had in the box, snuffled its rings and chains and snorted in disgust, and returned to his place beside the butt of the bowsprit. I, too, looked away, if only mentally. My eyes saw bracelets and anklets of silver and gold, but I was thinking about Seawrack's implied question. Assuming that the Vanished People were capable of coming back in some fashion, as Pas had, what might constitute warmth and rain for them?

Would we know, if they returned? Would I? At that time I did not even know what they had looked like, and so far as I knew, no one did. Doubtless they had been capable of making pictures of themselves, since they had certainly been capable of constructing the great building whose ruins we had discovered when we arrived; but any such pictures—if they had ever existed—had been erased by time, on Lizard and in the region around Viron at least. Seawrack, who appeared so fully human, had gills beneath the golden hair that hung below her waist. Were those gills the gift of the goddess, or the badge of the original owners of this whorl we call ours? At that time, I had no way of knowing.

"I think I see another boat." She rose effortlessly, pointing at a distant sail.

"Then we'd better get these out of sight." I began to shut the lid.

"Wait." As swiftly as a bird, her hand dipped into the box. "Look at this, Horn." Between thumb and forefinger she held a slender silver ring, newly made in New Viron. "I like it. It's small and light. All that gold made it hard to swim, but this won't. Will you give it to me?"

"Certainly," I said. "It's a great pleasure." I took it from her and slipped it on her finger.

★

★ ★

In the light airs that were all we had that day, the other boat took hours to reach us. I had ample time to break out my slug gun and load it, and to put a few more cartridges in my pockets.

"Are you going to fight with that?" I had told her about the pirates.

"If I must. I hope I won't. Sailors are usually friendly. We trade information, and sometimes supplies. I may be able to get us more water." I hesitated. "If they're not friendly, I want you to dive into the sea at once. Don't worry about me, just swim away to—to someplace deep where they won't be able to find you."

She promised solemnly that she would, and I knew that she would not.

It was a much larger boat than mine, two-masted and blunt-bowed, with a crew of five. The owner (a stocky, middle-aged man who spoke in a way that recalled Wijzer) hailed us, asking where we were bound.

"Pajarocu!" I told him.

"Riding light you are," he said, clearly assuming that we were traders too.

Soon his big boat lay beside our small one. Lines from bow and stern united the two, we introduced ourselves, and he invited us aboard. "In these waters not so many boats I see." He chuckled. "But farther than this I would sail a woman so pretty to see. Whole towns even, not one woman like your wife they got." One of his crew set up a folding table for us, with four stools.

I asked how far we were from the western continent.

"So many leagues you want? That I cannot tell. On which way bound you are, too, it depends. North by northwest for Pajarocu you must sail."

"Have you been there?"

He shook his head. "Not, I think. To a place they said, yes, I have been. But to Pajarocu?" He shrugged.

I explained about the letter, and brought my copy from the sloop to show him.

"One it says." He tapped the paper. "Your wife they let you bring?"

Drawing upon Marrow's argument, I said, "One, if all the towns they have invited send somebody, and if all the people who are sent arrive in time. We don't believe either one is likely, and neither does anybody else in New Viron. If there are empty places, and we think there will be, Seawrack can come with me. If there aren't, she can wait in Pajarocu and take care of our boat." I tried to sound confident.

The sailor who had set up our table brought a bottle and four small drinking glasses, and sat down with us.

"My son," Strik announced proudly. "Number two on my boat he is."

Everyone smiled and shook hands.

"Captain Horn?" the owner's son asked. "From the town of New Viron you hail?"

I nodded.

So did Strik, who said, "To that not yet we come, Captain Horn. Looking for you somebody is?"

My face must have revealed my surprise.

"Just one fellow it is. Toter's age he is." (Toter was his son.)

"Us about Captain Horn he asked. Alone in a little boat he sails." The corners of Toter's mouth turned down, and his hands indicated the way in which the little boat was tossed about by the waves.

"When asked he did, Captain Horn we don't know." Strik pulled the cork with his teeth and poured out a little water-white liquor for each of us. "This to him we say, and in his little boat off he goes."

"You're from the mainland yourselves? The eastern one, I mean. From Main?" I was trying desperately to recall the name of the town from which Wijzer had hailed.

"Ya, from Dorp we come. New Viron we know. A good port it is. Word to you from somebody back there he brings, you think?"

I did not know, and told him so. If I had been compelled to guess, I would have said that Marrow had probably sent someone with a message.

Seawrack asked how long we would have to sail to find drinking water.

"Depends, it does, Merfrow Seawrack. Such weather it is." Strik spat over the side. "Five days it could be. Ten, also, it could be."

"It isn't bad for me." She gave me a defiant stare. "He makes me drink more than I want to, but the Babbie is always thirsty."

I explained that Babbie was our hus.

"You suffer too." She sniffed and tasted Strik's liquor and put it down. "You pour it into your glass, then back into the bottle when you think I'm not looking."

I declared that I saw no point in drinking precious water that I did not want.

"A little water I can let you have," Strik told us, and we both thanked him.

Toter told us, "If for two or three days you and your wife due west will sail, a big island where nobody lives you will find. Good water it has. There last we watered. Not so big as Main it is, but mountains it has. A lookout you should keep, but hard to miss it is."

"We'll go there," Seawrack declared to me, and her tone decided the matter.

★

★ ★

Two days have passed, and now I have re-read this whole section beginning with my encounter with the monstrous flatfish with disgust and incredulity. Nothing that I wanted to say in it was actually said. Seawrack's beauty and the golden days we spent aboard the sloop before Krait came, the water whorl that with her help I glimpsed, and a thousand things that I wished with all my heart to set down here, remain locked in memory.

No doubt such memories cannot really be expressed, and certainly they cannot be expressed by me. I have found that out.

Let me say this. Once when I was swimming underwater in imitation of her, I saw her swimming toward me, and she was swift and graceful beyond all telling. There are no words for that, as there are none for her beauty. She caught my hand, and we broke the surface, up from the divine radiance of the sea into the blinding glare of the Short Sun, and the droplets on her eyelashes were diamonds.

You that read of all this in a year that I will never see will think me wretched, perhaps—certainly I was wretched enough fighting the inhumi and their slaves on Green, fighting the settlers, and before the end even fighting my own son.

Or possibly you may envy me this big white house that we in Gaon are pleased to call a palace, my gems and gold and racks of arms, and my dozen-odd wives.

But know this: The best and happiest of my hours you know nothing about. I have seen days like gold.

Seawrack sings in my ears still, as she used to sing to me alone in the evenings on our sloop. Sometimes—often—I imagine that I am actually hearing her, her song and the lapping of the little waves. I would think that a memory so often repeated would lose its poignancy, but it is sharper at each return. When I first came here, I used to fall asleep listening to her; now her song keeps me from sleeping, calling to me.

Calling.

Seawrack, whom I abandoned exactly as I abandoned poor Babbie.

Seawrack.

7

The Island

As we cast off from Strik's boat, Seawrack said, "That was nice. I wish we saw more boats." The clear liquor had brought spots of color to her cheeks, and a dreamy smile I found enchanting to her lips. I explained (I can never forget it) that the sea was immense, and that there were only a handful of towns along the coast from which boats might come.

"If you and I were to take this sloop out on Lake Limna on a day as fine as this," I said, "we would rarely be out of sight of a dozen sails. Lake Limna is a very big lake, but it's only a lake just the same. It's the biggest thing near Viron, but it's not the biggest thing near Palustria, because it's not near Palustria at all. The sea is probably the biggest thing on this entire whorl. Besides, Lake Limna is close to Viron, which is a very large city. Half the towns that we talk about here would be called villages if they were near Viron. I would be astonished if we were to see anyone else before we sight land."

I was reminded of that little speech this afternoon, when someone told me I was minor god—by which he meant that I had insight into everything. It would be easy to let myself be misled by remarks of that kind, which both the speaker and his hearers must know perfectly well are untrue. They are made out of politeness, and no one would be more shocked than the people who make them to learn that they had been accepted like propositions in logic.

Up there I nearly wrote: "when I was in the schola." So accustomed have I become to talking in that fashion, as I must. If I were to speak of Nettle, and the building of our house and mill, or tell these good, happy, worshipful people how after failing as farmers we succeeded as papermakers, they would riot.

They would riot; and if I were not killed a second time, a good many others would die. I have so much on my conscience already; I do not believe I could bear that, too.

Nor would the people allow me to leave even if they knew who I really am. The poor people, I mean. Aside from Hari Mau and a few others, it is not the chief men who frequent my court who really need and value me, but the peasant farmers and their families, their women and their children especially. That, at least, seems the common perception.

It may not be true. The men are less noisy in their praise, less emotional, as one would expect. Still they are attached to me, as I have ample reason to believe. Women and children see me as a presiding councilor, as a chief man richer and more powerful than the chief men who oppress them, someone who will help them in time of trouble. Men see a just judge. Or if not a just judge, a judge who strives to be just. Silk (I mean the real Silk) valued love very highly. He was right, certainly. Love is a wonder, a magic potion, an act of theurgy or even a continuing theophany. No word is too strong, and in fact no word is really strong enough.

But love is the last need a group has, not the first. If it were the first, there could be no such groups. Justice is the first need, the mortar that binds together a village or a town, or even a city. Or the crew of a boat. No one would take part in any such thing if he did not believe that he would be treated fairly.

These people cheat one another at every opportunity—so it seems at times, at least. Under the Long Sun, they were ruled by force and the fear of force. Here on Blue there is no force and no fear sufficient to rule. There is nothing, really, except our book and me. In the Long Sun Whorl they believed that their rajan would take their lives for the least disobedience, and they were right. Here in their new town they must believe that every word and every action proceeds from my concern for them and for justice. And they must be right about that, too.

What will become of them when I leave? For a long time I was unable to think about it. Now that I have, the answer is obvious. Just as in New Viron, they will steal, cheat and tyrannize until one chief man rises above all the rest. Then he will not bully and cheat, but take whatever he wants and kill all who oppose him. He will be their new rajan, and their original city will have been transferred from the *Whorl* to this beautiful new whorl we call Blue, complete in every significant detail.

Meanwhile, here I am. They cannot help seeing that I am doing nothing that one of them could not do. Self-interest is necessary to every undertaking and to everyone—or that is how it seems to me, although I am quite sure Maytera Marble would argue passionately. They must be brought to understand that any action of theirs that makes their town worse is bound to be against their own interests.

It is better to have no cards in a town in which no one steals than to have a case of cards in a town full of thieves. I must remember that, and tell them so as soon as a suitable occasion arises. An honest person in an honest town can gain a case full of cards by honest means, and enjoy it when he has it. In a town of thieves, cards must be guarded night and day; and when the cards are gone, as they will be sooner or later, the thieves will remain.

★

★ ★

Looking over what I wrote last night, I see I strayed from my topic, as I too often do. I meant to say (I believe) that the man who called me a minor god meant that I am always right, when he ought to have meant that I always try to do what is right. What else can the distinction between a minor god and a major devil be?

The lesser gods (as Maytera Mint taught us before Maytera Rose displaced her, and long before she became General Mint) were

Pas's friends. He invited them to board the *Whorl* with his family and himself. The devils came aboard by stealth and trickery, like Krait, who came aboard our sloop that night, proving yet again to me (if not to Seawrack) that quite often I do not know what I am talking about.

The near calm that had succeeded the storm had endured throughout the remainder of the day. What woke me, I think, was the rattle of Babbie's feet on the planks, followed by a sudden stillness. I sat up.

The sea was so calm that the sloop seemed as steady as a bed on shore. Seawrack was sleeping on her side, as she frequently did, her mouth slightly open. The mainsail, which I had double-reefed and left set, found no breath of air to flutter in; nor did the mainsail halyards tap the mast, or move at all. Beyond the shadow of the little foredeck, the sloop was bathed in the baleful light of Green, which made it seem almost an illusion, a ghost vessel that would, when day at last returned, sink into the air.

Aft, I saw a dark mass that seemed too large as well as too splayed for Babbie, rather as if someone had thrown a cloak or a blanket over him. I crawled out from under the foredeck, got to my feet, and drew Sinew's hunting knife; and a cold, calm voice—the voice of a boy or young man—said, "You won't need that."

I went aft as far as the mast. To tell the truth, I was afraid that there might be more than one, and was as frightened as I have ever been in my life.

"Didn't you hear me? I haven't come for your blood." The inhumu must have looked up as he spoke; I saw his eyes gleam in the ghastly green light.

Seawrack called, "What is it? Oh!"

"If you do not stay where you are," the inhumu said, "I will kill your pet. I will have to, since I don't intend to fight all three of you together."

"That's nothing to me," I told him, lying consciously and deliberately. "If you haven't come for our blood, go away. I won't try to stop you, and neither will she." I had stowed my slug gun in one of the chests; it would not have been less available to me if it had been back on the Lizard.

"Where bound?"

I shook my head. "I won't tell you."

"I could find out."

"Then you don't have to learn it from me."

"Tell me at once," the inhumu demanded, "or I'll kill your hus."

"Go right ahead." I took a step toward him. "You said you didn't want to fight all three of us. The prospect of fighting you alone doesn't bother me. If I have to fight you, I will. And I'll kill you."

His wings spread in less than a second and he rose like a kite, leaving poor Babbie huddled and trembling in front of the steersman's seat.

"I had to take a little blood to quiet him." The inhumu had settled on our masthead, from which he grinned down at me like a very devil.

When I did not reply, he added, "You have a most attractive young woman."

Looking up at him, it struck me that he *was* a devil in sober fact, that all the legends of devils found their origins in him and in the vile race he represented. "Yes," I said, glancing at Seawrack, who had left the shelter of the foredeck. "You're right. She certainly is."

"A valuable possession."

"Not mine," I told him. "Not now and not ever."

Seawrack herself said, "But he belongs to me." She joined me at the foot of the mast, and linked her arm in mine. "The Mother gave him to me. What of it?"

"Nothing at all, if we're friends. I don't prey upon my friends, or pry into their affairs. It's not our way. Dare I ask where you two are going?"

I said, "No."

Seawrack's arm tightened. "You told that other boat."

"But I'm not going to tell him. I'm not even going to ask why he wants to know."

As I returned Sinew's knife to its sheath, I pointed to the chest. "There's a slug gun in there. I'm going to get it out. If you're still up there when I do, I'm going to kill you. You can fight or run. It's up to you."

I opened the chest without taking my eyes off him, and he flew as I reached into it. For a few seconds a great, silent bat fluttered against the stars before disappearing into the blackness between them.

"That was a . . ." Seawrack hesitated. "I don't remember the names, but you told me about them and I wasn't sure they were real."

"An inhumu. He was male, I believe, so inhumu. Females are inhuma. Their race is the inhumi. Those words come from another town, because we didn't know they existed in Viron and had no name for them but 'devil.' Anyway 'the inhumi' is what everybody here calls them."

She had dropped to her knees next to Babbie. "He's sick, isn't he?"

"He's lost blood. He needs rest and a great deal of water. That's a shame because we haven't got much, but if he doesn't get it he's likely to die. He may die anyway."

"They drink blood. You said that. We have—we had worms that did, too. But you could pull them off, and some fish liked them."

"We call those leeches." I was collecting Babbie's pan and a bottle of water.

"He wasn't like that."

"No," I agreed, "they're not. Do you know of anything they are like?"

She shook her head.

I knelt beside her and poured water into the pan, then held it so Babbie could drink from it, which he did slowly but thirstily, drinking and drinking, and snuffling into the water as if he would never stop.

"He's very strong," Seawrack said. "He was. I've—you know. Played with him. He was strong, and he has those big teeth. The inhumi must be strong too."

"I suppose they are. Certainly they'd have to be strong, very strong indeed, to fly. But they are light, too, and soft, which lets them reshape themselves the way they do. People say that a strong man can throw one to the ground and kill it in most cases. I'd guess that this one clung to Babbie's back where he couldn't reach it until it had weakened him—but I've never fought one myself."

"Will it come back?"

I shrugged, and went forward to fetch an old sail with which I hoped to keep Babbie warm. While I was tucking it around him, Seawrack said, "Couldn't another one come, too?"

"It's possible," I told her. "I've heard that they almost always return to houses where they have fed. I'm not sure it's true, however. Even if it is, an animal on a boat may not count. They generally leave animals alone."

"Your slug gun. Aren't you going to get it?"

I did, and loaded it. At home, I had grown accustomed to locking my needler away when the twins were small; plainly, I was not at home anymore. "We built our house on Lizard Island very solidly for fear of the inhumi," I told Seawrack. "Double-log walls and heavy, solid doors. Very small shuttered windows with iron bars across them. It's not possible for you and me to protect this sloop like that, but the better prepared we are for them, the less likely it will be that we'll have to put our preparations to use."

She nodded solemnly. "Show me how to use your gun."

"You can't. It takes two hands to control the recoil and cycle the action. A needler is what you need, but I gave mine to Sinew, so we haven't got one. I can give you his knife if you want it."

"Your son's?" She backed away. "I won't take it. You love it too much."

"Then get some sleep," I told her. "I'll stand guard, and in a couple of hours you can relieve me."

She edged past me to stroke Babbie's massive head. "He's still cold. He's shaking."

"There are a few other things," I said; I meant the blanket and another old sail with which we sometimes covered ourselves. "I can get them, but I don't know how much good they'll do."

"We could put him between us."

If Babbie had been even a trifle heavier, I doubt that the two of us could have moved him at all. As it was, we rolled him onto the cloth with which I had covered him and half lifted and half dragged him, after bailing the bilge until scarcely a drop remained.

When he lay feet-first under the foredeck, with Seawrack on his left and me on his right (and my slug gun between me and the sloop's side) and all of us almost too cramped to move, she said, "I've been trying to remember about the inhumi. You said they lived in the sky? In that green light? It doesn't seem like anyone could live in those things."

"Most people would tell you that everybody knows that people live in or on the lights in the sky, but that no human being could live in the sea. The inhumi are native to Green. That's what everyone says. Green is the big green light I showed you when we talked about them before. It's much larger and brighter than any of the stars."

"I know which one. We've got fish that shine like that down where it's always dark."

"They may look like Green," I said, "but they don't shine like Green. Not really. Green shines because the light from the Short Sun strikes it."

"It's a place, like this boat?"

"It's a whole whorl. When I was a boy, people talked about 'the whorl,' as though it were the only whorl there was—as if nothing could come in or go out. It wasn't true, even if it had been once. There are three whorls here, really, and I suppose you could say that as whorls go they're pretty close together. There's at least one other, too, now that I come to think of it—the old Short Sun Whorl, where my friend Maytera Marble was born."

"You have to tell me about the inhumi," Seawrack said urgently. Babbie's head and shoulders blocked my view of her face.

"I'm trying to. I don't think there were any where Maytera

Marble came from, because she didn't know about them. So the three whorls that we have to talk about when we consider the inhumi are the *Whorl*, which I'll call the Long Sun Whorl to keep things straight, Blue, which is where we are, and Green, the whorl that brewed the big storm."

"Go on."

"I'll try to point out the Long Sun Whorl to you as well sometime, because you'll never find it for yourself. All that you can see is a faint point of white light among the stars. I'm guessing now, but my guess is that it's a good deal farther from both Blue and Green than Green is from us—certainly it's much farther away than Green is from us right now."

"It's where you were born?"

"Yes." It rose like a ghost in my mind, and I added, "In Old Viron, the city I've sworn to go back to if I can," but I cannot be certain that I spoke aloud.

"Were there inhumus up there?"

"We didn't think so, but there was at least one. We thought that he was one of us."

"I don't understand."

"I wouldn't expect you to, because the inhumu you just saw didn't look like a human being. But he did, and I would guess that the one we saw could have looked like that too, if he chose. I surprised him when I woke up, and he didn't have time to disguise himself. If he'd had time and had wanted to deceive us, he'd have had a pretty good chance of succeeding. They frequently do."

Seawrack lay silent for a time. At length she said, "Babbie's more like people."

I suppose I was resenting Babbie's bristling back; in any event I said, "I'm the only person that you've ever seen. Me, and the sailors on Captain Strik's boat."

She said nothing.

"So you can't know how different people can be. I'm about the same age as—"

"Me. Since I've been up here I've seen me. My face, my legs and my arm, all in the water."

"Your reflection, you mean."

"And I'm like you and the ones on the boat. The inhumi wasn't. Babbie's really more like us. I told you that, and he is."

"The inhumi's bodies aren't like ours." I tried to think of an enlightening comparison. "We think of a crab as rigid—it's like a trooper in armor. A trooper in armor can move his arms and legs, and turn his head. But he can't change the shape of his body."

"I can't change the shape of mine either." Seawrack sounded puzzled.

"Yes, you can, a little. You can stand up straight or slump, draw in your stomach, throw out your chest, and so on. The inhumi can do much more. They can shape their faces, for instance, much more than we can by smiling or sucking in our cheeks. But I believe that a better comparison might be with the Mother, who—"

"I don't want to talk about Mother," Seawrack told me, and after enlarging upon that with some emphasis she slept, or at least pretended to sleep.

Whether she actually slept or not, I lay awake. I had been very tired when we had gone to bed that evening, and had dropped off to sleep almost at once. Now I had enjoyed three or four hours' sleep, and had been thoroughly awakened. I was still tired, but I was no longer sleepy. Perhaps I was afraid that the inhumu would return, although I did not admit that to myself. Whatever the reason, I relaxed, pillowed my head on my hands by dint of driving an elbow beneath Babbie's thick neck, and thought about all the things I would have told Seawrack if she had been willing to talk longer.

The inhumi can fly, as everybody knows. They can even fly through the airless vastness of the abyss, passing from Green to Blue, and back to Green, when they are at or near conjunction. I had never understood how that was possible, but as I lay under the foredeck that night with my head where my feet ought to have been, I recalled the batfish. Its wide fins had been a lot like wings, and I have no doubt that it swam with them in the same way that a bird flies. As a matter of fact, there are fishing birds that "fly" through the water, swimming with the same wings they fly with, and moving them in pretty much the same way.

From that it would seem possible for an ordinary fish to swim through the air like the glowing fish that accompanied us almost to Wichote, although it is not. If such a fish could, I decided, we could fly ourselves. We can swim, after all. Not as well as fish, certainly (here I found myself echoing Patera Quetzal, who had in sober fact been an inhumu); and I could not swim half as well as Seawrack, who shot through the water like an arrow. But although ordinary fish cannot swim in air, they can jump into the air, and sometimes jump quite far. I had seen fish jump many times, and had watched a fish jump from the water onto a flat stone when I was on the rock upon which Maytera Marble had built a hut for Mucor.

This, coupled with little need for breath, might explain how the inhumi could go from one whorl to another, or so it seemed to me. By an extreme effort, they could "jump" out of the great sea of air surrounding the whorl they wished to leave, taking aim at the whorl to which they wished to go. Their aim would not have to be precise, since they would begin to fall toward the whorl they were trying to reach as soon as they neared it. Landers, as I knew even then, must be built so that they will not overheat when they arrive at a new whorl. But landers are much larger than the largest boats, and being constructed almost entirely of metals, they must be much heavier. The inhumi are no bigger than small men, although they appear so large when their wings are spread; and even though they are strong, they are by no means heavy. Light objects fall much more slowly than heavy ones, something that anyone may see by dropping a feather as I have just dropped Oreb's here at my desk. The heat that troubles the landers must present no great problem to the inhumi.

The need to survive for some time without air, as a man does while swimming underwater, and the need to approach the target whorl closely enough to be drawn to it explained the observation that everyone who has looked into the matter has made, namely that the inhumi cross only when the whorls are at or near conjunction.

All this—as I would have told Seawrack that night—was not at all complex, and demanded only that we not think of the inhumi as men who could stretch their arms into wings. As soon as we accepted the fact that they differ from us at least as much as snakes do, it fell into place quite readily. The difficulty was explaining the presence of the inhumu I had known as Patera Quetzal in the *Whorl*. The *Whorl* is (or at least seems) far more remote from Blue and Green than they are from each other. As with so many other riddles, it is easy to speculate but impossible to know which speculation is correct—if any are.

My first, which I then believed the most probable, was that the *Whorl* conjoins with either Blue or Green, or both, but only at very infrequent intervals. We know that conjunctions with Green occur every sixth year. That interval is determined by the motion of both about the Short Sun. A third body, the *Whorl*, having a different motion, presumably conjoins with one or both at a different interval. Since we have observed no such conjunction during the twenty years or so that we have been here on Blue, the interval is presumably long. For convenience, I assumed an interval ten times as great, which is to say one of sixty years. We had been on Blue for about a third of that, and I was quite confident that Patera Quetzal had been Prolocutor of Viron for thirty-three years prior to his death, giving a total of fifty-three years and (under our assumption of sixty years between conjunctions) allowing him seven in which to reach the *Whorl*, become an augur, and rise to the highest office in the Chapter.

That seemed rather short to me—I would have imagined that such a rise would require fifteen years if not more. If the speculation I am recalling tonight had been correct, in other words if Patera Quetzal had in fact crossed the abyss to the *Whorl* in the same way that other inhumi go from Green to Blue, it followed that it had been at least sixty-eight years since the last conjunction. It appeared then, as it still does, that no conjunction is imminent; from which I concluded that the period between conjunctions had to be considerably longer, say one hundred years.

Even then, I realized that other explanations were possible and might be correct. The landers were intended to return to the *Whorl* for more colonists. Patera Quetzal could have boarded a much earlier lander that did so, a lander whose departure was unknown to the Crew, and perhaps even to Pas, as well as to us in Old Viron.

A third possibility (I thought) was that a group of inhumi had built a lander of their own, in which they had traveled to the *Whorl*, and that after arriving they had separated to hunt.

The fact of the matter, as I would have had to explain to Seawrack, was that we knew frighteningly little about them. They did not appear to make weapons for themselves, or to build houses or boats, or any such thing—but appearances may be deceiving. General Saba's pterotroopers had refused to fly wearing their packs, and in fact carried nothing beyond their slug guns and twenty rounds of ammunition. In the same way, the Fliers carried only their PMs (which actually helped them fly, rather than burdening them) and their instruments. It might be, as I thought that night, that the inhumi were even less willing to weight themselves with equipment. They flew much faster and much farther than Rani's pterotroopers had, after all.

Farther even than the fliers had.

★

★ ★

When I wrote last night I lacked the energy to say all that I had intended, which was a good deal. Regarding what I set down with detachment this morning, I can see that most of it was not worth the labor. My readers—should persons so singular ever exist—can speculate for themselves, and their speculations may be better than mine. What I came near to saying, and should have said because it is important and true, was that we on Blue had very little knowledge of the nature and abilities of the inhumi. Raided, we could not retaliate, and although they clearly knew a great deal about us, we knew next to nothing about them. They came from Green. They could fly, could speak as we did, and could counterfeit us. They were strong, swam well, drank our blood, and usually (but not always) fought without weapons, although they preferred stealth and deception to fighting. Few people on Blue knew more than that, and many did not know that much.

Even then I knew a bit more, having talked with Quetzal, and with Silk and the present Prolocutor, who had known Quetzal much better than I ever did. I knew that the inhumi were able to counterfeit the whole array of human emotions, and possibly even felt them just as we did; and that their deceptions were based on a comprehensive understanding of the myriad ways in which men and women think and act. I suspected that they were capable of deceiving the very gods, since Echidna knew the Prolocutor was present at her theophany, but did not appear to realize that he was an inhumi. (Of course, she may simply not have cared, or not seen any significant difference between them and ourselves.)

On the other hand, I felt quite certain that when Mucor had described Patera Remora as speaking to "the one who isn't there" when he was coadjutor, she did not mean that he prayed but rather that to her roving spirit Patera Quetzal did not exist.

Seawrack and I were soon to become much more familiar with the inhumi; but I am writing here of what I knew and guessed at the time, errors and all.

★

★ ★

My advisors, who are all good, well-intentioned men, are forever suggesting that I get down to business, although they never phrase it quite so baldly. If action must be taken, they want it taken now, immediately. Sinew was like that, too. When I decided that we ought to build a new boat, he wanted to lay the keel that very day, and would have been happy, I am sure, if he could have finished it that day as well. In Sinew this impatience was the effect of youth; it was something that he would get over, and indeed I believe that he has largely gotten over it already.

In Rajya Mantri, Hari Mau, and the rest, I think it must come from a tradition of warfare. Immediate action is the soul of war, as I learned many years ago by observing General Mint. It is not the soul of peace.

Last night Alubukhara (who is as round and sweet as the fruit of that name, and almost as dark) said, "If you wish to do a thing again, you must do it slowly." I do not believe that is a proverb here; if it were, I would have heard it before this. No doubt it was a saying of her mother's. But it ought to be a proverb for courts and for governments of every stripe, for sailors such as I once was, and for writers. Hard decisions, I have found, become easy ones when the judge understands the entire case. When a new burden must be laid upon the people, we should remove two, and look very carefully, first, at those we have chosen to remove. Those who sail fast do not sail for long, while what is written with great rapidity is rarely read—or worth reading.

I would like this read, and not by one woman or man alone (although I am very glad that you are reading it) but by so many that it reaches the eyes of the men and the woman for whom it is especially meant. My sons, I loved you so much! Am I really speaking to you now? Nettle, my heart's delight, do you recall our first night together in the Caldé's Palace? There has never been another night like that, and there can never be. I hope, and in my whole life I have never been more serious and sincere, that you have been unfaithful to me. That you have found a good and honest man to cast his lot with yours and help you bring up our sons. Nettle, can you hear my voice in this?

I wanted to write that the rest of the night on which Seawrack and I first encountered Krait passed uneventfully, and that I sat up for most of it stroking poor Babbie's head. There. It is written.

But I should have said first that Seawrack was quite right in thinking that I wanted to question her about the sea goddess she called the Mother. Having found Seawrack exceedingly reluctant to say much of anything about her, I had been trying to get at the truth indirectly. At some fraction of the truth, I ought to have written, and would have if I had not been hurrying ahead. (If Sinew's impatience was the result of youth, what is mine?)

A fraction of the truth, since even Seawrack, who had been cared for by the goddess since before she could swim, cannot have known everything.

Who, for that matter, could know the whole truth about Seawrack? Not Seawrack herself, and that is completely certain even if nothing else is. At the time about which I have been writing, the time before Krait, I had not yet grasped the real riddle; but I will give it here so that you who read may weigh things for yourself. I am not, after all, writing merely to entertain you.

The real riddle concerning Seawrack is this: If the Mother took care of Seawrack in order that Seawrack might lure others, as fowlers use a captive bird, did the Mother send her back among her own kind—among us—so that she might lure more or lure them better? To put it simply, did the Mother suffer a change of heart, or is she pursuing some deep plan that will culminate in our destruction? It is very important that we know this.

★

★ ★

The wind picked up before noon, and we cracked along in a way that had me plotting to spread more sail. I was ever a careful, cautious sailor, as I have implied. But the cautious sailor must avoid the sunken rock of overcaution, and it was apparent that additional sail would speed us on our way without endangering us.

After a great deal of squinting at the western horizon, spitting, and pulling my beard (all of which amused Seawrack in a way that gladdened my heart, although I did not say so), I contrived an extension to our mainsail from a stick that I lashed to the boom and a long, triangular strip of canvas whose top I tied to the gaff. It worked so well that I contrived another triangular sail, like a jib, that we set on the forestay in imitation of Gyrfalcon's boat, reassuring myself by assuring Seawrack that we would take both in the moment the breeze strengthened.

As a result of all this, we sighted the island before sundown. Or at any rate we sighted an island we assumed was the one at which Strik and his crew had watered. I have never been entirely confident that it was in fact the same, although it may have been. Certainly it fit their description, and we found it by following their directions, that is, by sailing close-hauled almost due west. Later I saw that there were many other islands of the same type all along that coast, mountains covered with lush greenery rising out of the sea. By favor of the southwest wind, we quickly discovered a small, sheltered bay on the north side of the island, and a swift, rocky stream at the end of it.

We anchored there and refilled our water bottles, and I sent Babbie ashore and let him trot around and explore the steep green wood. To tell the truth, I was feeling very guilty about having made him stay on the sloop so often when we were going up the coast, and was half minded to leave him there to recover his health as well as his freedom; I felt sure it would be a happier as well as a healthier place for him than my cramped little boat, and I recalled that Silk had tried more than once to free Oreb. Throughout my life I have done my best to imitate Silk (as I am doing here in Gaon), at times with some success.

Perhaps I am getting better at it. They seem to think so, at least. But I had better sleep.

★

★ ★

I should not have stopped last night before mentioning that we lay at anchor in the bay that night. Seawrack and I slept side by side under the foredeck, thankfully without Babbie; and that soon after we lay down she asked whether we would put out again in the morning. From her tone it was clear that she did not want to.

Neither did I; and so I said that I planned to stay another day to hunt, and that with luck we would have fresh meat for supper the next night. To the best of my memory, we had no meat left on board at that time except the shank of the very salty ham that Marrow had given me; and I was thoroughly tired of that, and still more tired of fish.

The following day began bright and clear, and presented me with what I then considered a serious problem, I having not the least presentiment of what the island held in store for me. Seawrack was anxious to go with me, and Babbie was even more anxious, if that were possible—it would have been sheer cruelty to leave him behind. Nonetheless, I was very conscious that if anything happened to the sloop all hope of bringing Silk to New Viron would be gone.

I considered leaving Babbie on board, as I had there; but how much protection could a young hus provide? A young hus, I should have said, who had by no means recovered all his strength? Against a sudden gale, very little. Against the crew of some other boat that put in to water as we had, just enough to get him killed.

I also considered asking Seawrack to stay. But if bad weather struck, the best thing she could possibly do would be to furl the sails (and they were furled already) and remain at anchor in the little cove we had found, which the sloop would do by herself. As for protecting it from the crew of another boat, how much could one young woman do, without a weapon or a right arm? Against honest men, the sloop would require no protection. By the other kind she would be raped, killed, or both.

For a second or two, I even considered remaining behind myself; but Seawrack could not use the slug gun, and might easily find herself in danger. In the end, we all went. No doubt it was inevitable.

It was a silent, peaceful, lonesome place whose thickly forested slopes seemed to be inhabited only by a few birds. Mighty trees clung to rocks upon which it seemed that no tree could live, or plunged deep roots into the black soil of little hidden dales. On

Green one finds trees without number, monstrous cannibals ten times the height of the tallest trees I saw on the island; but they are forever at war with their own kind, and are troubled all the while by the trailing, coiling, murderous lianas that have seemed to me the living embodiment of evil ever since I first beheld them.

There was nothing of Green here save the huge trunks, and bluffs and rocky outcrops resembling Green's distant, towering escarpments in about the same way that a housecat resembles a bale-tiger. In one, we discovered a deep cave with its feet in clear cold water, a dry cave with a ceiling high enough for a man to have ridden a tall horse into it without bowing his head or taking off his hat; and we spoke, Seawrack and I, of returning there after we had brought Silk to New Viron. We would build a wall of stout logs to close the entrance, and live there in peace and privacy all our days, plant a garden, trap birds and small animals, and fish. Was it really criminal of us to talk in that fashion? I knew that it could never be, that Nettle and my sons and the mill would be waiting when I came back to the Lizard.

And that even if I did not return, it could never be.

Seawrack, I feel sure, did not. So it was wrong of me, was cruel and cowardly, to share her snug dream and encourage her in it. I must be honest here. It was, as Silk would say, seriously evil. It was a crime, and I was (and am) a monster of cruelty. All that is true, but give me this—I have done worse, and for half an hour we were as happy as it is possible for two people to be. The Outsider may condemn me for it, but I cannot regret that half hour.

If it is true that in some sense Silk and Hyacinth remain forever beside the goldfish pond at Ermine's where I sought them, may not Seawrack and I live in the same sense in a certain dry cave among towering, moss-draped trees on the island that will always be "The Island" to me? I have said that I can be cruel because I know it for the truth; and I know too that the universe, the whorl of all whorls, can be much crueler. I hope it is not cruel enough to deprive even the smallest and most ghostly fragment of my being of the happiness that Seawrack and I know there.

There came a moment when I wanted to return to the sloop. We had seen no game and no sign of any; we were all tired, and Babbie, who had ranged ahead at first sniffing and snuffling here and there, lagged behind. What was worse (although I did not say it) was that I was not sure of the way back to the sloop; and I was afraid that we would have to strike the shore of the island wherever we could reach it, and try to follow it until we found the little bay to the north in which we had anchored. We were tired already, as I have said, and had not yet begun what might be a very long walk. It seemed more than possible that we would not be able to locate the sloop before shadelow.

Seawrack pointed to a ridge, not very distant but only just visible through the trees. "You wait here," she said, "and let me go up there and see what's on the other side. You and Babbie rest, and I'll come right back."

I told her that I would go with her, naturally, and took pains to lead the way.

"There's so much sunshine," she said as we climbed that final slope. "There can't be any trees there. Not big ones like these."

I told her it was probably a good-sized cliff, that we would see trees below it, and that we might have a fine view of the island and the sea around it. What we really saw when we topped the ridge was less dramatic but a great deal stranger.

8

The End

It was a circular valley entirely free of the mature trees that had formed the forest of the mountain slopes, and filled instead with the bushes, vines, and saplings that had been absent there, green, lush, and saturated with an atmosphere of *newness* that I really cannot describe but was immediately conscious of. After hours of climbing through the airless antiquity of the forest, it was as though we had been awakened from the deepest of sleeps with a bucket of cold water.

Seawrack cried, "Oh! Look! Look!" and pressed herself against me. From her voice, she felt wonder and even awe; but she shook with fear, and at that moment, I was ignorant of the cause of all three.

"The walls, Horn. Their walls. Don't you see them?"

I blinked and looked, then blinked again before I was able to make out one curving line of masonry practically submerged in the rising tide of leaves.

"I know places in the sea where there are walls like those," Seawrack told me. Her voice was hushed. " 'Underwater' is what you say."

I started down, followed reluctantly by Seawrack and even more reluctantly by Babbie. "Human beings, people like you and me, people from the *Whorl*, can't have built this. It's too old."

"No. . . ."

"It was the Vanished People. It had to be. There's a place near New Viron, but I don't think it's as old as this. And Sinew says he found an altar in the forest. I told you about that." Answered only by silence, I glanced over my shoulder at Seawrack and received a fear-filled nod.

"Sinew's altar was probably in a chapel of some kind originally, a shrine or something like that. This was a lot bigger, whatever it was." I stopped walking, having nearly tripped over a line of crumbling glass not much higher than my ankle.

"You wanted to go back." The fear had reached her voice. "So do I. Let's go back right now."

"In a minute." The glass was deep blue, but seemed more transparent than the clearest glass from Three Rivers. I picked up a piece, feeling absurdly that it would show me the place as it had been hundreds, and perhaps thousands, of years ago. It did not, but the valley I saw through that fragment of blue glass appeared more brightly sunlit than the one my naked eyes beheld.

"There's nothing left here," Seawrack murmured. "These are old, ruined, broken things nobody wants anymore, not even the trees."

"Something kept trees from growing here for a long while," I told her. "Some chemical they put in the ground, or maybe just a very solid, thick pavement underneath this soil. It can't have been many years since it gave out. Look at these young trees. I can't see even one that seems to be ten years old."

Silently, she shook her head.

"I've been trying to guess how this blue glass works. It's as if it sees more light from the Short Sun than we do and shows it to us. Here, look."

"I don't want to." Seawrack shook her lovely head again, stubbornly this time. "I don't want to look at their trees, and I don't want to look through their glass. Babbie and I and going back to your boat."

"If we could—" In my surprise, I dropped the glass, which shattered at my feet.

"What is it?"

I had been looking down into the valley as I spoke, and thanks to the blue glass I had seen motion. I pointed with my slug gun. "That bush shook. Not the big one, but the little one next to it. There's some kind of animal down there, a pretty big one."

"Don't!"

I had taken a step forward, but Seawrack caught my arm. "Let me tell you what I think. Please?"

I nodded.

"I don't think it was a—a medicine they poured on the ground, or stone underneath, or anything like that. I think they lasted longer here."

It was a new thought to me, and I suppose my face must have shown my surprise.

"Out on this little island, so far from all the other land people. For a long time they mended the walls and painted them, and dug up the trees and wild bushes. Ten years, is that what you said?"

"Yes." Another bush a little farther from us than the first had trembled ever so slightly, a ghost of motion that would have been easy to miss.

"Ten years ago, they gave up. There weren't enough left to do it anymore, or it was too much work that didn't make sense. I know you think I'm stupid—"

"I don't," I told her. "You're naive, but that's something else entirely."

"You think I'm stupid, but I can think of people, people like us? Two-legged people like you and me and all the people on that boat living here, and there wasn't anybody else anywhere. We'd mend our boats and the walls we'd built for a while, and then somebody would die, and there'd be more work for everybody who was left. And somebody else would die. And pretty soon we'd stop, but we wouldn't be dead, not all of us. The last of us wouldn't die for a long while."

"All right," I told her. "If it's one of the Vanished People, I won't shoot him. Or her, either. But I'd certainly like to see them." I did not believe that it was, and in that I was quite correct.

For a few minutes that seemed like an hour I scoured the

bushes with Babbie trotting at my heels; then a greenbuck broke cover and darted away, leaping and zigzagging as they do. Babbie was after it at once, squealing with excitement.

I threw my slug gun to my shoulder and was able to get off one quick shot. The greenbuck broke stride and stumbled to its knees, but in less than a breath it had bounded up again, cutting right and running hard. It vanished into brush, and I sprinted after it, all my fatigue forgotten, guided by Babbie's agitated *hunck-hunck-hunck!*

Very suddenly I was falling into darkness.

Here and thus baldly I had intended to end both tonight's labor and this whole section of my narrative. I wiped this new quill of Oreb's and put it away, shut up the scuffed little pen case I found where my father must have left it in the ashes of our old shop, and locked the drawer that holds this record, a thick sheaf of paper already.

But it cannot be. It cannot be a mere incident like Wijzer's drawing his map and the rest. Either that fall must be the end of the entire work (which might be wisest) or else it cannot close at all.

So let me say this to whoever may read. With that fall, the best part of my life was over. The pit was its grave.

It must be very late, but I cannot sleep. Somewhere very far away, Seawrack is singing to her waves.

9

Krait

When I regained consciousness it must have been almost shadelow. I lay on my back for a long while then, occasionally opening my eyes and shutting them again, seeing without thinking at all about anything I saw. The sky darkened, and the stars came out. I remember seeing Green directly above my upturned face, and later seeing it no longer, but only the innocent stars that had fled before it and returned when it had gone.

It was at about that time that I felt the cold. I knew I was cold and wished that I were not. I may have moved, rubbing myself with my hands or hugging myself and shivering; I cannot be sure. Glittering eyes and sharp faces came and went, but I appealed for no help and received none.

Sunlight warmed me. I kept my eyes closed, knowing that it would be painful to look at the sun. It vanished, and I opened them to see what had become of it, and saw Babbie's familiar, hairy mask peering at me over the edge of the pit. I closed them again, and the next time I opened them he had gone.

I think it was not long afterward that I came to myself. I sat up, cold, full of pain, and terribly thirsty. It was as if my spirit had gone and left my body unoccupied as it did on Green; but in this case it had returned, and my memories (such as they were) were those of the body and not those of the spirit. It was day again, perhaps midafternoon. I was sitting among earth and fallen leaves in a pit about twelve cubits deep.

(My own height, I should say, was three cubits and two hands at that time—a good deal less than it is now. Looking up at the walls of the pit while there was still light enough for me to do it, I estimated their height as three to four times my own.)

They had originally been of smooth stone of a kind that was not shiprock, or granite, or any other with which I was familiar. In places it had fallen away, and bare earth thick with gravel could be seen through the openings. These gave me hope of climbing out, but when I tried to stand up I found myself so weak and dizzy that I nearly fell, and quickly sat down again.

It is conceivable that the pit had been intended as a trap from its beginning, but I do not believe that it was. It seems to me instead that it was all that remained of some work of the Vanished People, possibly the cellar of a tower or some such thing. The tower (if there had ever been one) had collapsed centuries earlier, scattering its wreckage across the valley and leaving this pit to collect the leaves of autumn and unfortunates like me. Eventually treacherous vines had veiled its opening, weaving a sort of mat which I had torn to shreds when I fell. A few long strands hung over the edge still, and it seemed to me that I might be able to climb out with their help, if only I could reach them; but I was, as I have said, too weak even to stand.

Strangely, I did not sleep that night, although I had slept so long—three days at least—after my fall. I did not, but sat up shivering and tried to rake together a bed of leaves for myself that would keep me warm, or at least less cold, finding among them my slug gun and the clean bones and skulls of several small animals, instruments of divination in which I read my own fate. I prayed; and at intervals of an hour or so, I fired my slug gun into the air, hoping that Seawrack would hear the shots, wherever she was, and realize that I was still alive. When only two cartridges remained, I resolved to reserve them until there was some hope that someone was nearby.

(Until I heard her voice, I suppose; but in sober fact I hear her now although she is so far away.)

Then I would—this is what I promised myself—fire one shot more; and if that also failed, a last cartridge would remain.

Morning came, and with it warmth and a new face that looked at me over the edge of the pit. At the time I thought it the face of a boy or a small man. "There you are," the owner said. He stood, and I must have seen that he was naked. Possibly I realized that he was not human as well, but if I did it made little impression on my mind.

A moment more, and to my numb astonishment he leaped from the edge, down into the pit with me, saying, "I want to get you out."

No doubt it was said ironically, but I heard nothing of that. My rescuer had arrived.

"Shall I do it?"

Logically I should have said that he was trapped now just as I was; naturally I said nothing of the kind. "Please," I said, and I believe I must have nodded. "Please help me if you can."

"I can if you'll let me. Will you?"

No doubt I nodded again.

He strode over to my slug gun, a diminutive, sexless figure. Picked it up, cycled the action, and threw it to his shoulder, aiming at the sun, or perhaps only at the edge of the pit. "I can't use one of these, Horn," he said, "but you can."

"Be careful." My voice had become a weak croak, and seemed the voice of a stranger. "The safety's off, and you chambered a fresh round."

"I know." He grinned at me, and I saw the folding fangs that reached nearly to his chin. "You could kill me with this. All you've got to do is point it and pull the trigger. Isn't that right?"

"I won't."

"Your last chance would be gone." He grinned again, testing one slender fang against the ball of his thumb, as though making certain that it was sharp enough.

"I know," I said.

He laughed, a boy's cheerful, delighted chortle. "Do you know who I am, too?"

"I know what you are. Is that what you mean?"

"But not who?"

By that time I was sure he had come to kill me. I stared down at the leaves.

"I am your best friend, the only friend you have in all the whorl, Horn. Have you any others?" He sat down facing me, with my slug gun across his lap.

There was nothing to say, so I said nothing.

"You hate me and you hate our people. You made that clear when I visited your boat. Why do you hate us so?"

I thought of Sinew, livid and scarcely breathing in the little bed we had made for him; but I said, "I wouldn't hate you at all if you got me out of this. I would be very grateful to you."

"Why did you hate me so when you woke up and found me on your boat?"

It was a long time before I spoke, a minute at least; but he seemed prepared to wait all day, and at length I muttered, "You know."

"I don't." He shook his head. "I know why you Blue people dislike us, and it's regrettable though understandable. I don't know why you, the particular individual called Horn, hate me as you do."

I was silent.

"Me. Not my race in general but me; you do, and I can feel it. Why does Horn hate me? I won't name myself yet. I haven't quite decided on a name, and there's plenty of time. But why hate me?"

"I don't hate you," I insisted. "I was afraid of you on the sloop because I knew you had come for blood."

He waited expectantly.

"I know enough about you inhumi to frighten me ten times over. I know how strong you are, and that you can swim better than we can, and fly. I know how clever you are, too."

"Do you really know how clever we are? Tell me. I'd love to hear it."

"You speak my language as well as I do, and you could make me believe you were one of us if you wanted to. One of you was our Prolocutor in the Long Sun Whorl." I hesitated. "Do I have to explain what a Prolocutor is?"

He shook his head. "Go on."

"He pretended to be a doddering old man, but he saw through everybody and outwitted our Ayuntamiento over and over again. He outwitted the rest of us, too. We never doubted that he was human."

"I see. He was a cunning foe, who nearly destroyed you." At certain angles there was a light in the inhumu's eyes that seemed almost a yellow flame.

"No, he wasn't my enemy, he was my friend. Or at any rate he was Silk's friend, and I was Silk's friend, too." Exhausted as I was, and sick with pain, I did not consider how unlikely it was that the inhumu had ever heard of Silk.

"Are you saying you hated this man because he befriended your friend?"

"I've made it sound too simple."

"Most things are simple."

"Patera Quetzal wasn't a man at all, but we didn't know it. He was one of you, and he drank blood!"

"I wish that I could talk to him." The inhumu seemed to speak mostly to himself.

"He's dead."

"Oh. Really. You turned on your friend and killed him, when you found out he was one of us?"

I wanted to say that I wished I had, which would have been the plain truth; but I wanted much more—wanted desperately, in fact—to escape the pit. "We didn't. We didn't even know until he was dead. He was shot by the Trivigauntis we were fighting and died of his wound." That was the plain truth as well.

"So you hate him now because he drank your blood and deceived you, and that hatred has been carried over to me? Is that all there is?"

"You drank Babbie's blood."

"Your hus? Yes, I did. What else?"

I actually began to tell him, saying, "I have a wife and children—"

"I know. On the isle they call the Lizard, or Lizard Island."

I suppose I must have gaped.

"You've been answering questions for me, so I'll answer that one for you. When I was on your boat, the siren who was with you said you'd spoken to people on another one. Do you remember that?"

"A siren?" I was bewildered, and in no condition to think. "Do you mean Seawrack?"

"If we accept that name as hers."

"She's very good-looking." I tried to swallow, although my mouth was drier than the palms of my hands. "But she's not a—a seductress. She's still very young."

He smiled. Until then I had forgotten that they could. "Let's forget I used that word. The young lady with you said you had spoke to another boat."

"You can't have learned about us just from that."

"Certainly I could have. I did. I found the boat, which wasn't very far from yours, and talked to the men on it. They thought I was one of you, naturally, and I gave them valuable information, which I made up. In return, they told me your name and your wife's and where you were going, which was the chief thing I wanted to know. There aren't many towns where a man might be named Horn. I went to New Viron, which was the closest. We can fly, you know, a whole lot faster than your little boat can sail. I made more inquiries there, and I had no trouble at all."

If my face was not grim at that moment, it lied; I was very close to trying to snatch my slug gun from him and kill him. "Did you harm my family?"

"No. I flew over your island and had a look at your house and your paper mill. I'm curious at times, like anybody else. I saw a woman there, standing on the beach and looking out to sea, an older and somewhat plainer woman than the new wife on your boat. I didn't harm her, and I don't think she saw me. Is that sufficient?"

I nodded.

"Fine. Take this back, will you?" He passed me my slug gun. "I can't use it and you can, so you'd better have it."

Numbly, I accepted it and pushed up the safety.

"You aren't going to shoot me?" He raised his hands in a gesture of mock surrender.

"No. No, I'm not."

"You're remembering something. I sense it. Want to tell me what it is?"

"Nothing to the point." My head ached, and the hope that had given me new life for a minute or two had guttered out. Should I put the muzzle into my mouth? That might be the best way.

"Tell me, please."

Perhaps it was the shock of hearing one of these monsters say *please;* whatever the reason, I did. "I was recalling what a woman named Chenille once told Nettle about a man, a starving convict, named Gelada. He was in the tunnels. There are horrible tunnels running underground all through the Long Sun Whorl, where I used to live."

"Gelada was in them," the inhumu prompted me.

"He wanted to escape. Anybody would. He had a bow, but Auk, the man who was with Chenille, said he wouldn't shoot them, because they were Gelada's only chance. Without them, he would never get out."

"I said that. I said all that earlier, and you ought to have listened. If I were to get you out, it would be terribly dangerous for me, wouldn't it? Unless I disposed of that slug gun and your knife first." His face was that of a reptile, although his forehead was higher; his voice was a young man's—was my son's.

"No," I told him. I was almost too despondent to argue. "If you freed me, I would never hurt you. Never, not for any reason."

He stood up. "I'm going, but I'll leave you this to think about. We could kill you, all of you. We're stronger, as you said, and we can fly. Our race is older than yours, and has learned things that you can't even dream of. Since you hate us, and kill us when you can, why don't we do it?"

"You want our blood, I suppose."

"Exactly. You are our cattle."

I had expected him to fly, but he swarmed up the smooth stone side of the pit as a squirrel climbs a tree, making it look so easy that for a moment I almost imagined that I could do it myself. My thumb was on the safety; but without him I could not escape. Nor could I escape the memory of a time when Sinew was not yet born, and Hoof and Hide not even thought of, when Nettle and I had worked frantically to free someone else's cow from a quagmire in the vain hope that her owner would give her to us if we succeeded.

Then he was gone; and I, using the slug gun for a crutch, got to my feet and was so foolish as to try to climb out as he had, struggling in that way until I was utterly exhausted and never getting half as high as my own head.

★

★ ★

Last night I stopped writing because I could not bring myself to describe the rest of that day, or the night that followed it, or the day that followed that, the day on which I licked dew from the sides of the pit, lying on my belly at first, then kneeling, then standing—and at last, when the Short Sun peeped over the rim and the dew was almost gone, wiping the stone above my head with fingers that I thrust into my mouth the moment they felt damp. Altogether I got two mouthfuls of water, at most. No more than that, certainly, and very likely it was less.

Earlier I had prayed, then cursed every god in my heart when the rescuer they sent had proved to be Krait. On that day I did not pray, or curse, or any such thing.

This is what I least wished to write about last night, but I am going to try to write it down this evening. Once, as I lay there at the bottom of the pit, it seemed to me that a man with a long nose (a tall man or an immense spider) stood over me. I did not move or even open my eyes, knowing that if I did he would be gone. He touched my forehead with something he held, and the pit vanished.

I was standing in Nettle's kitchen. She was making soup, and I watched her add a whole plateful of chopped meat to her kettle and shake the fire. She turned and saw me, and we kissed and embraced. I explained to her that I was not really in her kitchen at all, that I lay at the bottom of a pit in a ruin of the Vanished People on an island far away, and that I was dying of thirst.

"Oh," Nettle said, "I'll get you some water."

She went to the millstream and brought back a dipper of clean, cool water for me; but I could not drink. "Come with me," I told her. "I'll show you where I am, and when you give me your water there I'll be able to drink it." I took her hand (yes, Nettle my darling, I took your hard, hardworking little hand in mine) and tried to lead her back to the pit in which I lay. She stared at me then as if I were some horror from the grave, and screamed. I can never forget that scream.

And I lay in the pit, as before. The Short Sun was burning gold.

It had crossed the pit and vanished on the other side an hour or two before, when the inhumu returned. He stood with his toes grasping the edge and looked down at me, and I saw that he was wearing one of my tunics and a pair of my old trousers, the trousers loose and rolled up to the knee, and the tunic even looser, so that it hung on him as his father's coat does on a child who plays at being grown. "Horn!" he called. And again, "Horn!"

I managed to sit up and to nod.

"Look, Horn, I've brought you a bottle of water." He held it up. "I carried an empty one, and filled it to the top at a spring I've discovered not far from here. Wasn't that clever of me?"

I tried to speak, to beg him for the water; but I could not. I nodded again.

"You'd promise me anything for this, wouldn't you?" He leaped into the pit with it. "I'll trade you this bottle for your slug gun. Will you trade?"

I must have nodded, because the bottle was in my hands, although he held it too. I put it to my lips and drank and drank; I would not have believed that I could drink an entire bottle of that size without ever taking it from my mouth, but that was how I drank that one.

"You feel better now," the inhumu said. It was a statement, not a question.

I found that I could speak again, although the voice did not seem mine. "Yes. Thank you. I do."

"I know. I've been in exactly the same position myself. I not only got you that bottle of water, Horn, but I brought you a coil of rope. It's small, but I think it may be strong enough. It's very hard to carry anything when you fly. It keeps pulling you down, and you've got to hold it with your feet." He held up one foot in a way that very few human beings could have imitated, and I saw that his toes were as long as my fingers, and tipped with claws.

"Thank you," I repeated. "Thank you very much."

"I'll get you out, or my rope and I will. But you'll have to help us, and I've got to get your promise first. Your solemn oath."

I nodded and tried to smile.

"A question." He leveled a forefinger longer than mine; it, too, was claw-tipped. "Are you a logical, unemotional sort of man, would you say? Are you willing to follow reason wherever it takes you?"

Halting and stammering, I tried to say that I made an effort to be, and thought that I was.

"Then let's go back. Not to the boat, we don't have to back up that far. The other day I wanted to know why you hated me, and you explained that it was because I wanted to drink your blood, and because one of us had deceived you into thinking he was one of you up there. Do you remember that?"

"Yes." I could not imagine what he was getting at.

"You drove me from your boat, despite the fact that I didn't try to deceive you. If I would not drink your blood—I will pledge myself not to—would you still drive me away?"

My thirst had been quenched, but I was weak and sick. "If I could."

"Why?"

"One of you nearly killed my son."

His head wagged. "That wasn't me. Haven't you any better reason?"

"Because you drank Babbie's blood, and would glut yourself on Seawrack's if you could."

"I pledge myself not to drink theirs either. I warn you, I won't go any further. I have to eat, just as you do. Now, if I get you out, will you let me remain on board?"

Quite certain that he would never rescue me, I said that I would.

"You have a good reputation in your town. Are you a man of your word? Is your word sacred to you, even when it's given to me?"

"Yes," I said.

"You lack conviction. Listen to me. You are going to Pajarocu."

My eyes must have opened a little wider at that.

"The men on the other boat told me. You're going to Pajarocu. Acknowledge it."

"We are trying to get to Pajarocu."

"That's better. You're going to board a lander there, and fly up to the great ship."

I nodded, and seeing that a nod would not be sufficient, said, "We're hoping to fly back up to the *Whorl*, as you say. I certainly am, and I'll take Seawrack if she wants to go and they'll allow me to."

The inhumu pointed to himself, his wrist backbent in a fashion that no human being could have managed. "I want to go with you. Will you help me, if I help you get out of this place?"

"Yes," I said again.

He smiled wryly, swaying as Patera Quetzal used to. "You don't mean it."

"Yes, I do."

"You'll have to give a better pledge than that. Listen to me, Horn. I'll do everything I can to help you get there before the lander takes off. You think I'll obstruct you. I won't. I'll help all I can. We're strong, you say. Won't I be a strong friend to you? You praised our cunning. It will be at your service. Don't say you don't trust me. You must trust me, or die."

"I trust you," I said, and I meant it; that is the measure of a man's desire to live—of mine, at least. An inhumu had demanded that I trust him if I wanted to live, and trust him I did.

"Better. Will you let me go with you and help you? Will you pledge yourself to reveal my nature to no one?"

"Yes, if you'll get me out."

"You still don't mean it. Do you believe in gods? Who are they?"

I rattled off the names of the Nine.

"Which means the most to you? Name him!"

"Great Pas."

"You're holding something back. Do you think you can trick me because I can trick you? You're wrong, and you'd better learn that from the beginning. Which means most to you?"

It was the end of my resistance. "The Outsider. And Pas."

The inhumu smiled. "I like you, Horn. I really do. I'm growing fond of you. Now listen to this. I swear to you by Pas, by the Outsider, and by my own god that I will not feed upon either you or Seawrack, as you call her. Neither will I take the blood of your pet hus, ever again. I further swear that there will be no trickery or double-dealing in the keeping of this oath I give, no sophistry. I will keep the spirit as well as the letter. Is that satisfactory?"

I nodded.

"Then I'll be wasting my time with the rest, but I'm going to waste it. I further swear that as long as I'm on your boat I'll never deceive you into thinking that I'm one of you, or try to. What more do you want me to say?"

"Nothing," I told him.

"I'll continue just the same. Listen to me, Horn. What does it matter to you whether I prey on your kind here or there? Is their blood more precious aboard the void ship?"

"No."

"Correct. It doesn't matter in the least. I'll have an easier time of it up there with less competition, that's all. And there'll be one fewer of us down here preying upon your friends and family." He was silent for a few seconds, gauging my reaction. "Suppose I leave you where you are. Who will prey upon your family then, Horn? That nice woman I saw, and whatever children the two of you have back home on Lizard Island? No doubt you've thought about it?"

I shook my head.

"Why, I will. I'll leave you in here, but I won't just leave you here and forget you. I'll go back there bringing word of you, and you won't be there to protect them. Do I have to speak more clearly than that? I will if I must."

I shook my head again. "I'll swear to whatever you want me to swear to, by Pas and the Outsider, and your god, too, if you'll let me."

"You'll have my friendship and assistance. Do I have to go through that again?"

"No," I said.

"Then swear you'll accept both. You're not to kill or injure me, or drive me away, or betray me to anyone else for any reason whatsoever. You're to do everything you can to see to it that I'm on the lander when it takes off. That we both are."

I swore, stumbling at times over the phrasing but corrected by him.

When I was finished, he turned away. "I'm sorry, Horn. I really am. That was close. You tried very hard. If I can, I'll be back tomorrow." Before I could say a word, he had begun to climb the wall of the pit.

I broke. I am a coward at heart, I suppose. Perhaps all men are, but I certainly am. I pleaded. I begged. I wept and shrieked aloud, and wept again.

And when I did, he turned back. Krait the inhumu turned at the edge of the pit, and looked down upon me in my misery. He may have been smiling or grinning or snarling. I do not know. "Horn?" he said.

"Yes!" I raised my arms, imploring him. Tears streamed down my face as they had when I was a child.

"Horn, your oath didn't convince me. I don't think any oath you could give would. Not today, and probably never. I can't trust you, and I don't know of anything that would . . ." He stopped, perhaps only to watch me weep.

"Wait!" My sobs were choking me. "Please wait. Will you let me talk?"

He nodded. "For a minute or two, as long as you don't talk nonsense."

"Hear me out—that's all I ask. My house is on the Lizard. You've seen it. You said you flew over it and saw Nettle on the beach."

"Go on."

"I built it, and we've lived there for years. I know how things are done in our house. Isn't that obvious? You've *got* to believe me."

He nodded again. "I do, so far."

"There are bars on the windows and inside the flue. There are good locks on both doors, and bars for them as well. Heavy wooden bars that you put up and lift down. When conjunction is near—"

"As it is. Go on."

"When conjunction's near, we always bar the doors. My wife bars them at shadelow, even if I'm still working in the mill. I have to knock and be let in."

"You're proposing that I knock and imitate your voice. I could do it."

"No," I said, and shook my head. "Let me finish, please. It—it's something better."

In his own voice, which might have been Sinew's, he said, "Let's hear it."

"When conjunction's past, she forgets. She never bars them then. I've spoken to her about it, but it didn't help. Unless I bar them, they aren't barred."

I reached into my pocket, got the key, and held it out. "You want to go to the *Whorl*. But if you don't go—if we don't—you'll be here. And you'll have the key."

He hesitated. Perhaps his hesitation was feigned; I do not know.

I said, "If we get to the *Whorl*, you and I both, I want you to promise me you'll give it back."

"You trust my promise?" His face was as expressionless as the face of a snake.

"Yes. Yes, I must."

"Then trust this one. I'll get you out at once, as soon as you throw me that key."

I did. I was too weak to throw it out of the pit the first time; it rang against the stone side a hand's breadth below the top, and fell back in. I tried to run and catch it in the air, and nearly fell myself.

"I'm waiting, Horn." He was kneeling at the edge, his hands ready.

I threw again, and watched those scaly hands close around it.

Without a word, he stood, dropped the key into his pocket, turned, and walked haltingly away.

There are times when time means nothing. That was one. My heart pounded like a hammer, and I tried to clean my face with my fingers.

When he came back, it might almost have been a theophany. I had wanted to see him so much that when I did I was horribly afraid that I was imagining it. "Get my slug gun," he said. "We may need it."

I did as I was told, slinging it across my back.

"I'm not heavy enough to pull you up. You'd pull me in." He tossed down a coil of rope. "I've tied the other end to one of these little bushes. If you can climb up, you'll be out. If you can't . . ." He shrugged.

I made use of every foothold, and tried to remember how Silk had climbed Blood's wall, and Blood's house, too; but nothing seemed to help. In the end Krait helped me, his hand grasping my own and his clawed feet braced against the side of a little depression he had made for them. His hand was small, smooth, cold, and strong; unpleasantly soft.

Then there came a moment when I stood at the rim of the pit I had come to know so well, staring down at its stones and bones, its fallen leaves and broken strands of vine.

"What about the rope?" he said. "Shall we take it with us?"

I shook my head.

"We may need it. I got it from your boat."

So the sloop was safe. Just knowing that made me feel a little bit stronger. "Leave it," I told him. "Somebody else may fall in."

Together we made the long walk back to the sloop. "You can fly," I said once when we stopped to rest. "Why don't you? I'll be there as soon as I can."

"You're afraid I don't trust you."

I denied it.

"You're right. It would be foolish of me to doubt you now that you're out of that hole and have my slug gun and your knife. You could kill me easily, and take the key from my pocket."

I nodded, although I was thinking that it would not be half so easy as he implied.

"I'm going to become one of you, and in fact I already have. I did it when I borrowed your clothes. So now I have to act like one of you and walk, even though walking's hard for me." He smiled bitterly. "Do I look like a real boy to you?"

I shook my head.

"You see, I'm keeping my promise. I'll look like a boy to the young woman you call Seawrack, however, and to everyone we meet, unless they're . . . Well, you know. So I can't fly. I can't because you can't. Do you enjoy paradoxes?"

I told him that Silk had liked them more than I did.

"He was wiser than you are, exactly as you say. I'll pester you with dozens before we part, Horn. Here's one. Those who cling to life lose it; those who fling their lives away save them. Do you like that?"

I said, "I might if I understood it."

"Paradoxes explain everything," he told me. "Since they do, they can't be explained."

★

★ ★

That was a second paradox, of course. Or rather, it was a great truth embodied in a paradox, the truth being that a thing cannot be employed to prove itself. We had a fortune-teller at court a few days ago. He had come partly, as he said, because he wanted permission to ply his trade in our town; and partly, or so I would guess, because he hoped to gain notoriety here.

He volunteered to read my future in the stars. I declined, pointing out that it was midday and that even if he went outside he would not be able to see them. He insisted that he knew their positions even when he could not, unrolling a score of big charts, and launching into a convoluted recitation that nobody understood.

I cut him off, ruling that he did not need my permission to tell fortunes, or anyone's, as long as he behaved himself. I added that he was free to take fees from anyone foolish enough to give him their money.

He retired to the back of the room, and I soon forgot about him; but after an hour or two he came forward again, announcing loudly that he had completed his prediction for me. (It was the usual mixture of flattery and menace—I would lead three towns not my own to victory, would be tried for my life, would return as a stranger to my sons' native place, find new love, and so on and so forth. I will not put myself to the trouble of recording the entire rigmarole.) When he had finished, I asked how I—or anyone whose future he foretold—might know that his prophecies were valid; and he solemnly declared that the stars themselves confirmed them.

Everybody laughed. But there is rarely a day on which I do not hear proofs of the same kind advanced with confidence. Somebody testifies, and his testimony being doubted, swears that it is true. A dozen heads nod sagely. Yes, since he declares it true, it must be.

That is easy enough; but what about Krait's first paradox? Now I think that he meant that I had doomed myself by my own anxiety to leave the pit. Given courage enough to refuse the help of an inhumu, I might have been rescued by someone else or freed myself by my own efforts, and so might have returned eventually to my home, which I feel certain that I shall never see again.

That I will never see more, even if the storms and waves have spared it.

★

★ ★

I had intended to continue my narrative tonight—or rather to resume it, telling how the inhumu and I made our way down the mountainside to the sloop, how we went in search of Seawrack, and so forth. I would then be very near the point at which she gave me the ring.

But I will not have much time tonight, and I am going to use it to write about something that happened today instead. In a way it bears upon everything that I had intended to write, and I will get to that soon enough.

A man came to court this morning to ask protection from the Vanished People. There was a good deal of laughter, and when I had restored order I pointed out to him that his fellow townsmen did not believe him—or even credit the present existence of the Vanished People—and suggested that he first put forward whatever evidence of their existence he possessed so that we would not be laughed to scorn.

This man, whose name is Barsat, admitted that he had no evidence beyond the testimony of his wife, whom he offered to bring to court tomorrow; but he swore that he had seen the Vanished

People on three occasions and felt sure they were by no means friendly.

I asked what he had done to offend them. He does not know, or at least says he does not. I then asked him to describe the circumstances under which he saw them the first time. He said he was going into the jungle to cut firewood when he saw several standing or sitting in thickets and regarding him in a less than friendly way, and turned back. I asked how many there were. He said he could not be sure, at which there was more laughter.

That and his obvious sincerity convince me that he is telling the truth. If he were lying, his testimony would have been both more circumstantial and more sensational. Besides, any number of Neighbors greater than two is difficult to count in my experience.

★

★ ★

It was already late when the inhumu and I started down the mountain, and neither of us was capable of swift or sustained walking. You are not to imagine from that, however, that I was downhearted or despondent. Health makes us cheerful, and illness and weakness leave us gloomy and sad—that, at least, is the common view. I can only say that I have seldom been weaker or nearer exhaustion, but my heart fairly leaped for joy. I was out of the pit. Free! Free even of the burning thirst that had at last become a torment worse even than hopelessness. The rocks and ancient, moss-sheathed trees were beautiful, and the very air was lovely. The inhumu assured me that he knew the shortest way back to the sloop; and I reflected that Patera Quetzal had been a good friend to Silk. Was it not at least possible that this inhumu would prove a good friend to Seawrack and me?

I quickly convinced myself that he already was.

Having satisfied my thirst from the water bottle he had brought, and again at the spring he showed me, I had become ravenously hungry. There was food on the sloop, I knew; and it was even possible that the inhumu and I might sight the game that had evaded Seawrack and me. If we did, I told myself, I would shoot it, butcher it, and eat it on the spot. I unslung the slug gun and carried it at the ready.

We had gone about two-thirds of the way when something rattled the branches of an immense flintwood that had fallen only a few days earlier. It was nearly dark by then; I heard the rustle of the dying leaves much more plainly than I saw them move.

I pushed off the safety and advanced cautiously, and when they rustled again, put the butt to my shoulder. Urgently the inhumu whispered, "Don't shoot until we see what it is."

I scarcely heard him. I was fairly sure I knew about where the animal was, and was resolved to cripple it if I could not kill it, telling myself that I would soon track it down.

The branches sounded a third time, I squeezed the trigger, and the inhumu slapped my slug gun to one side, all in far less time than it has taken me to write it.

Before the report had died away, Babbie broke from cover, charging straight at us with all the blinding speed of which hus are capable over short distances. If it had been five minutes later and thus a shade darker, he would have opened me from thigh to shoulder. As it was, he recognized me at the last possible moment, and recognizing the inhumu as well, diverted his charge to him.

Although I had written about Patera Quetzal's flying, and had heard him in flight when we were in the tunnels, I had never actually seen him fly. Here on Blue, I have seen inhumi in flight several times, but always at a distance, so that they might almost have been bats or even birds; in the shadow of those twilit trees, I saw one take flight when I stood so near that I might easily have touched him. He sprang into the air, and as Babbie passed beneath him his arms lengthened, widened, and *thinned*. His fingers spread a web of skin, each finger grown longer than my arms. That is something less than clear, I realize; but I do not know any other way to describe it. At once his arms beat, not slowly as one normally sees when the inhumi fly but with the most frantic haste, raising a sudden gale in complete and ghostly silence. Babbie turned back and leaped, his tusks slashing murderously at—

Nothing. The inhumu had vanished into the darkness of the boughs.

I called, "Babbie! Babbie! It's me!" and crouched as I used to on the sloop.

He came to me only slowly, clearly very conscious (as I was myself) that I had shot at him a moment before; and very conscious, too, that I still held the slug gun. I laid it aside and spoke to him, and although I no longer remember just what it was I said, it must have been effective; before long his head was between my hands, as it had sometimes been when we two were alone in the sloop upon the wide, wide sea. I talked to him until the day ended and the stars appeared, while stroking his muzzle and rubbing his ears; and no doubt a great deal of it was nonsense; one thing impressed me, however, and I should record it here. These, I believe, were my exact words: "You thought I was gone, didn't you, Babbie? Well, I just about was. Poor Babbie! Poor, poor Babbie! You thought I was dead."

At which he nodded.

★

★ ★

I went a-hunting today for the first time since Hari Mau brought me here. It might be more accurate to say that I watched the others hunt, since I killed nothing. But then, neither did they.

These people hold cattle sacred (as I may have mentioned before), seeing the embodiment of Great Pas in the bulls and that of Echidna in the cows. Out of regard for these deities, they will not eat beef or knowingly wear or possess any leather items made from the skins of cattle. When they sacrifice cattle, as they do almost daily, the entire carcass is consumed by the altar fire.

The result of all this is that cattle are raised here only for religious purposes, and although there was a good supply as long as there were frozen embryos from the landers to implant, their numbers have fallen so low of late that the priests are seriously concerned. Since the gods cannot be seen here as they used to be in the Sacred Windows of the Long Sun Whorl, the priests feel it absolutely necessary that their symbols be seen as often as possible. Thus no sooner had some farmers reported wild cattle than a party of eager volunteers was recruited to capture them. It was a delicate operation, since the sacred animals could not be harmed or even made to suffer any indignity.

We rode out about an hour after shadeup, located the herd without much trouble, and surrounded it, turning back the animals that tried to bolt by riding at their shoulders and flourishing yellow flags embroidered in scarlet thread with quotations from the Writings. Or rather, as I ought to have said, from what are called the Sacred Books here; these are rather different, I believe, from the Chrasmologic Writings we knew back in Old Viron.

They were generally effective, however, although we lost one heifer and a horse was gored. When we had tired the most rebellious and had the herd together, a holy man approached it on foot, hung every animal with garlands, put a noose of red and yellow rope over the head of each, and led them away, nine head plus three calves. They will be kept at the temple until they are tame enough to be permitted to wander at large. The priests say that will be very soon.

★

★ ★

Before I described our cattle hunt, I should have given some reason for including it; but to write the truth, I am not sure I had any at the time. It had occurred that day and my mind was full of it, and that is all; but when I think about the walk back to the sloop with Babbie, I can see that it fits in well enough. He had begun to revert to the wild state, as the cattle had. Like the holy man, I was able to retame him because I meant him no harm.

After chewing Oreb's quill for a minute or two, I have decided to take the analogy further. It should prove amusing, and may even be enlightening.

The inhumu had told me that we human beings were the cattle of his kind. They drink our blood in preference to the blood of animals merely because they prefer it (this is what he said), just as we prefer the milk of cattle to that of goats. Various other animals give milk too: pigs, dogs, and sheep, for example. Yet we do not even try to milk those.

The more intelligent an animal is, the more difficult it is to tame. I am not going to offer that as an opinion, because I am convinced that it is a fact. Let us consider a progression, beginning with the hus. Hus are more intelligent than nittimonks, nittimonks more intelligent than dogs, and dogs more intelligent than cattle. Adult cattle can be captured and tamed in a few weeks. Adult dogs, born in the wild, can scarcely be tamed at all; and unless they have been raised among humans they are almost untrainable. Young nittimonks can be tamed, but can be trained only with the greatest difficulty, and they are never reliable.

For hus to be tamed and trained, they must be captured very young, as Babbie no doubt was; and when I lived on Lizard I would probably have said that the surprising thing was that he could be trained at all. The truth, as I came slowly to realize during the time I had him, is that he was not. He did not obey me by rote, as my horse does. Instead, he tried to cooperate with me. I was inferior to him in strength and in many other ways, but I possessed powers that must have seemed wholly magical to him. What did he make of the slug gun? What *could* he make of it? Plainly it is in the best interest of a captive hus to cooperate with his captors, protecting their property, assisting them to hunt (he will share in the bag, after all) and the rest.

All that seems clear. Accepting it, how are the inhumi able to train human beings? How was Krait able to tame me like a hus, although I had not been taken young? In all honesty, I have no satisfactory answer. He offered himself as a valuable friend when he freed me from the pit, and afterward. And he liked me, I believe, in the same way that I liked poor Babbie. Before Krait died, he loved me, and I him. I had become the father of a brilliant, wayward, monstrous son.

It was dark when we reached the sloop. I had tied her to a tree before leaving with Seawrack and Babbie on our hunting expedition, and she seemed almost exactly as I had left her. There was no sign of Seawrack or the inhumu. I shared a good many apples and what remained of the ham with Babbie, and retired for the night.

It was still dark when I woke wet and shivering, or at least it seemed so. Fog had come in, chill and damp, and so thick that I literally could not see the bowsprit from my seat in the stern. I built a fire in our little box of sand, and Babbie and I sat before it, trying to keep as warm and dry as we could.

"I should have brought warmer clothes," I told him. "I knew perfectly well that I was going to a faraway place, but it never crossed my mind that the climate here was bound to be different."

He only sniffed the ashes, not quite convinced as yet that I was not cooking fish in them.

When I had gone to sleep, I had planned to search for Seawrack in the morning. This was the morning, presumably, but there was no looking for her in it, nor for anything else. For a while I considered ordering Babbie to find her for me; but I had no reason to think he knew where she was, and if he set off to search the entire island it seemed likely that I would lose him as well. At last I said, "This fog may last all day, Babbie, and I suppose it's possible it may be foggy tomorrow, too. But it's bound to lift eventually."

He glanced up at me, stirring the ashes tentatively with both forefeet.

Taking his silence for agreement, I continued, "As soon as it does, we'll sail all the way around the island. She probably got lost. Who wouldn't get lost in this? And the natural thing for her to do would be to walk downhill until she found the sea, and go along the beach."

A voice that seemed disembodied remarked, "You'll find her if you do it, but I can take you straight to her if you want me to." It was a boy's voice, and I had better make that plain at once; it might have been one of the twins speaking.

I looked around, seeing no one.

"Up here." With grace that reminded me vividly of a small green snake I had seen once, Krait slid down the backstay and dropped into the stern. Babbie was on his feet immediately, every bristle up.

"Do you want me to, Horn? You'll be surprised at what we find. Don't say I didn't warn you."

I had laid the slug gun beside me when I slept, and left it there under the foredeck when I woke up. My hands groped futilely for it, settling for Sinew's knife.

"What's this?" He took a quick step backward, but I could not be sure his alarm was real. "I'm offering to do you a favor."

"Have you killed her?"

He raised both hands, exactly the gesture of a boy trying to fend off a larger and stronger one. "I haven't! I don't remember exactly what I promised you when you were down in that hole—"

"You promised you wouldn't drink my blood, or hers, or Babbie's. It leaves you any amount of evil, though I didn't think of that at the time."

He would not meet my eyes. "It wouldn't be fair, would it? You'd call me a cheater."

I was so angry, and so frightened for Seawrack that I demanded he answer my question, although he already had.

"I haven't hurt here at all. She's alive, and from what I've seen of her, perfectly happy."

"Then take me to her!"

"This minute? Horn, listen. I promised not to feed on you, but I promised a great deal more. I promised to help you get to Pajarocu, and all that." He took the key to my house out of his pocket and held it up. "Remember this?"

I nodded.

"I haven't used it. Someday I may, but I haven't yet. You say you're reasonable. You said you tried to be, and you know that I want to find Pajarocu as much as you do. More, if you ask me. Would it make sense for me to hurt her, when I haven't hurt you or your family? Or your pet hus? I wouldn't guide you to her after I'd harmed her, would I?"

I was relaxing. The mere fact that he seemed afraid of me made me less fearful of him, although that is always a mistake. "I apologize. Why did you say I'd be surprised when we found her?"

He shook his head. "I won't tell you, because you wouldn't believe me. We'd fight again, and it would be bad for both of us. If you want to go now I'll show you, but we'll have to untie your boat."

We did, and got the anchor up; it was not until I had the sloop gliding like a ghost through the damp gray silence that I asked whether he could see to guide us in spite of the fog.

"Yes, I can. We all can, and now you know something that very few others do." He threw back his head, looking in the general direction of the block at the top of the mast. "What color is the sky, Horn?"

I told him that I could not see it, that I could not so much as see the masthead.

"No wonder you didn't spot me up there. Look anyway. What color is it?"

"Gray. Fog is always gray, unless there's sunshine on it. Then it's white."

"And when you look up at the sky on a sunny day? What color then?"

"Blue."

He said nothing, so I added, "It's a beautiful, clear blue, and the clouds are white, if there are any."

"The sky I see is always black."

I believe I must have explained that for us the night sky was black, too, and tried to describe it.

"It's always black," he repeated as he went forward and climbed onto the little foredeck, "and the stars are there all the time."

★

★ ★

No doubt my explanation will bore you, whoever you are, unless you are Nettle; but she is the reader I hope for, and so I will explain anyway for her sake. When I leave a break in my text like the one above, sketching the three whorls to separate one bit from the next, it is generally because I have decided to stop and get some sleep.

This was different. I wanted to think, and in a moment I will tell you what I was thinking about. I wiped my pen and laid it down, rose and clasped my hands behind my back. You know, dear wife, how I used to walk the beach deep in thought when we were planning the mill. In the same way I stalked silently around this big pink-and-blue house, which they have given me and expanded for me, and which we call my palace to overawe our neighbors.

All was silent, everyone else having gone to bed. In the stable-yard my elephant slept standing, as elephants do and as horses sometimes do also; but slept soundly nonetheless. From the stables I went out into the garden, and listened to the nightingales singing as I stared up at the night sky and at such stars as could sometimes be glimpsed between thick, dark clouds that would have been almost visible to Krait. Two nightingales in gold cages are kept there, as I should explain. (I ought to have written *were.*)

The weather has been sultry for a week at least, and I found the garden, with its jasmine, plashing fountains, ferns, and statues a very pleasant place. For half an hour or more I sat upon a white stone bench, looking up at the stars through torn and racing clouds, stars (each a whorl like Blue or Green) that must seem to the inhumi like fruit glimpsed over the high wall of a garden.

Trampin' outwards from the city,
No more lookin' than was she,
'Twas there I spied a garden pretty

A fountain an' a apple tree.
These fair young girls live to deceive you,
Sad experience teaches me.

That is not singing as Seawrack understands it, nor as she has made me understand it either; but she has been silent since shadelow, and the old rollicking song marches through my head again. How young we were, Nettle!

Oh, how very young we were!

When I went back inside, I heard Chandi weeping in the women's quarters. Because I was afraid she would wake the others I made her come out with me, and we sat together on the white stone bench while I did my unskillful best to comfort her. She was homesick, poor child, and I made her tell me her real name and describe her parents and brothers and sisters, the town she comes from, and even her mother's cook and her father's workmen. She was born in the *Whorl*, just as you and I were; but she can remember nothing about it, having left as an infant. I got her to tell me everything she had learned about it from her parents, but there was very little beyond self-glorification: they had lived in a much bigger house there, and everyone had deferred to them. That sort of thing. She knew that the sun had been a line across the sky, but imagined that it rose and set as the Short Sun does here.

As for me, I did not weep; but I was at least as homesick as she, and when she was calmer I told her about you, Nettle, calling you Hyacinth. She understood very little but sympathized very much. She is a good-hearted girl, and cannot be much over fifteen.

When I had talked her out, and myself as well, I promised that I would send her back to her father and mother. She was horrified, and explained that no matter what she or I said they would believe that I had rejected her, as would all the people of her town; she would be shunned by everyone, and might even be stoned to death. She is mine, it seems—but not mine to set free. I could not help thinking that she and I, who are so different in appearance, age, and gender, are in fact two of a kind.

Together, we released one of the nightingales and watched it fly away, a symbol for both of us of what we wished for ourselves. She wanted me to open the cage of the other, but I told her that I would not, that another night would come on which she would be as she had been tonight; and I said that when that night came we would talk again and set the second bird free.

It is not well to spend one's symbols improvidently.

As for what I left this lovely table to think about, it was Krait's remark. He had said the stars were always there, and I (that so much younger I aboard the sloop) had thought he meant merely that they did not vanish in fact when they vanished to sight. It seemed a trivial observation, since I had never supposed they did—everyone has seen the flame of a candle disappear in sunlight and knows that the invisible flame will burn a finger.

Now I think differently, and I feel certain I am right. The black sky that Krait saw was not the night sky, or the day sky either. It was *the sky*, the only sky there is, without clouds and without any change save for the slow circling of the Short Sun and the other, more distant, stars, and the somewhat quicker rising and setting of Green. The whorl to him and to all the inhumi is the airless starlit plain we saw when poor Mamelta led us to the belly of the *Whorl*. Small wonder then that the inhumi are so wretched, so cruel, and so hungry for warmth.

When Chandi and I glimpsed Green from our seat in the garden, she told me that her mother had told her once that it was the eye of the Great Inhumu, whose children he sends here. I nodded, and was careful not to mention that I had lived and fought there.

★

★ ★

Dreamt that Oreb was back. Very strange. I was in the Sun Street Quarter again, made inexpressibly sad by its devastation. I sent Pig away as I actually did there, with Oreb for a guide; but at the last moment I could not bear to be parted from him and called him back. He returned and lit upon my shoulder, wrapping a slimy tentacle around my neck, he having become Scylla. In Oreb's voice, she demanded that I take her to the Blue Mainframe. I explained that I could not, that there was no such place, only the Short Sun. While I spoke I watched Pig's disappearing back and heard the faint tapping of his sword.

I "woke" heartbroken, and found that I had fallen asleep in the jungle, lying beside Krait. I picked up his hand and rubbed the back, feeling that rubbing would somehow restore him to life, but his body was dissolving into fetid liquid already, a liquid that became the filthy water of the sewer I opened there.

10

Seawrack's Ring

I have been hunting again. Some of the men who captured the wild cattle invited me to go with them, and being curious I made time for it. It was very different from the cattle hunt, a butchery bloody enough to satisfy any number of augurs.

We were after wallowers, the most prized game hereabout, and the most difficult to hunt. A silence of eight or ten had been located not much more than a league from the town, but we had to ride a long way out of the direct route and through difficult country in order to approach them upwind. All the men said that wallowers never remain in a place where they have been hunted, and may move forty leagues or more before they stop again.

I had a slug gun like the rest, and although I had not the least intention of using it when we set out, I realized before long that I would have to if the opportunity arose; otherwise Kilhari, Hari Mau, and the others in our party would feel I had betrayed them.

Kilhari posted us in a wide semicircle well out of sight of the silence (as the herd is called), telling us that when we saw the stalkers approaching it we might edge in a little. I asked him to put me in the worst place, explaining that I had borrowed my gun, was half blind and badly out of practice, and so forth. He posted me last, at one of the tips of the crescent, saying that those were the worst places. They are actually the best, as I suspected at the time and verified this evening.

After about an hour at my post, I caught sight of the decoys. These were two men in the wickerwork figure of a young wallower covered with hide. They advanced slowly and cautiously through the open, swampy forest, often turning away from the denser growth where the silence was thought to be, so as to give the stalkers hidden behind them better cover. Their part of the hunt is the most dangerous as well as the least glorious, because a real wallower will often charge their false one, and they have no slug guns and would have no chance of firing them if they did. For protection they must depend upon the stalkers behind them.

Their gradual advance must have taken the better part of another hour. Because I was eager to catch a glimpse of the great beasts about which I had heard so much on the ride out, I advanced, too, pushing my way through the high, rough grass, although not nearly as far as the decoy and the stalkers, and standing on tiptoe from time to time in order to see better over it. The suspense was almost unbearable.

Quite suddenly, both stalkers rose and fired over the back of the wickerwork figure. Up until that time, I had been unable to see the wallowers, but as soon as the crash of the slug guns sounded, a dense patch of saplings and brush seemed almost to explode as twenty or more enormous dark-gray beasts with towering horns dashed from it.

And vanished. It was one of the most amazing things that I have ever seen. At one moment these huge animals, twice the size of an ordinary horse and six times its weight, were charging madly in every direction. At the next they were gone. Several hunters were firing some distance from me, but I saw nothing to shoot at.

I do not remember seeing the young bull rise from the scythe grass, although I suppose I must have—only slamming my slug gun to my shoulder and pulling the trigger, then flying through the air without fear and without pain, and then one of the other hunters (it was Ram, whose name, I fear, makes him sound as though he comes from my own Viron) helping me up. In retrospect it was rather like my hunt in the Land of Fires, but of course I did not think of that until tonight.

Wishing very much that Babbie were with us, I told Ram that we had to track the wallower that had charged me, that I had fired at him from very close range and felt certain I had wounded him. He laughed and pointed, and in a few seconds half a dozen men were gathered around the dead wallower, which had not run ten strides before collapsing. Since two or three hunters often empty their guns to bring one of these animals down, it was an extraordinary shot. As for me, I had torn trousers and have some big bruises here and there, but I am well otherwise.

These hunts are only occasionally successful, and a single kill is considered an achievement. We had two, one killed by the stalkers (who are generally the most experienced hunters and the best shots) and this one by me, so we returned to town as heroes. I will have to refrain from all hunting in the future if I want to keep the reputation I have won.

At any rate, we are having a great feast tonight, with everyone who took part sharing in the meat. I excused myself as soon as the serious drinking began, which is how I have this opportunity to write. The hide, the Y-shaped horn, the bones, and especially the big canine teeth, all of which are valuable, will be sold. I will receive the money from my animal, and since I do not need it I hope to use some of it to benefit the poor.

And some, dear Nettle, I hope to use to rejoin you. They have almost ceased to watch me, and I am careful to do nothing to arouse their suspicions.

No doubt I have written too much about our hunt, which can be of little interest to you; but I wanted to set down this account while the facts were still fresh in my mind. I had another purpose, too, which I hope to make clear if I have time for a good session tomorrow.

★

★ ★

I meant to tell you how Krait deceived Seawrack tonight. I will, but there is something else I ought to describe first, although it will be hard to represent exactly, and I may fail to make it clear. Put simply, it is that I saw the sea (and afterward the land as well) from that time forward as I do today. If I say that I believe I am seeing these things, and houses, too, and occasionally faces, as a good painter must, will you understand me?

Probably not, because I am not sure I understand it myself. You told me about the beautiful pictures upstairs in the cenoby, and I put them in our book because Maytera Marble had posed for Molpe. Describe that picture again to yourself, and imagine me looking at the sea as the sea would have appeared in it.

As for the rest of you who may read this, whether you are our sons or strangers or both, there is a sharpness of detail born of a consciousness of detail. When we untied the sloop, I saw the unnatural calm of the little bay beneath the fog that veiled it, and when I had steered us out (guided by Krait, who stood upon the mainsail gaff to advise me), every coiling, foaming wave that slapped our hull was as clearly drawn as any of my brothers.

I heard Seawrack long before I saw her. She was singing just as she is singing now, singing as the Mother had, her sweet, clear voice at one with the fog and the waters, so that I knew the sea had been incomplete without her song, that it was fully created, a finished object, only while she sang. Fog muffles sound, so we must have been near her then; I would have taken the sloop nearer still to hear her, although Krait warned me against it; but he slid down the forestay and loosed the jib, so that we swung into the wind with the main flapping like a flag. He told me to call to Seawrack, but I could not. How I wish you could have heard her, Nettle! You have never heard such singing.

We quarreled at that point, the inhumu and I. We were to quarrel almost daily afterward, but that was the first and one of the worst. I was angry at him for untying the jib, and he was angry at me for steering too near the rocks. The upshot of our quarrel was that the sloop was free to sail herself, and the course she chose took her a good league into open water. By the time we had made peace, Krait could no longer see the island or anything else, or so he said.

"I'll have to fly," he told me, "and I may have to fly high. Then I'll come down again and give you an approximate direction."

I asked whether he could find the sloop again in the fog, and suggested that I might build a fire in the sandbox to guide him, although the truth was that I was hoping to crowd on sail and evade him. He laughed and asked me to turn my back; I did, and when I turned around again he was gone.

Babbie snorted with relief, and I felt as he did. Much more, I felt—I *knew*—the sea and the cold gray sea-fog that wrapped us both. I have said that I saw it as a painter would, and I may even have said that I saw it as a picture; but it was a picture that surrounded and saturated me, and mixed with my spirit. The sea whose spray wet my beard, and the fog I inhaled at every breath, were no longer things apart from myself. If they were pictured, I was pictured, too; and it was the same picture. We lived in and through each other then, in a picture without a frame.

Something had happened to change my perception, and that change remains in force to this moment. How I wish I could make you see our hunt for the wild cattle as I did! The milling herd with rolling eyes, and we riders with our embroidered flags! You will want me to explain, but I have no explanation, although at that time and for a long time after it I felt that it was the inhumu's presence. I taxed him with it when he returned to the sloop, landing softly behind me and announcing his arrival with a boyish laugh. He denied it, and we quarreled again, although not as bitterly as before. Even then, I knew that his denials were without value.

Since Krait is not present to speak for himself, let me speak for him. I will try to do it with more logic than either of us displayed when I argued with him on the sloop.

First, he did not have that effect on others, as well as I could judge.

Second, it did not benefit him, and in fact he lost by it.

Third, it persisted even in his absence, as I have tried to show.

And fourth and last, I had experienced nothing of the sort when we were with Quetzal in the tunnels.

Yet he was capable of affecting our perception of him, for Seawrack and others saw him as a human being, as the boy he claimed to be, whereas I would sooner have called poor Babbie a child.

Seawrack, as I should explain, swam out to the sloop once she understood that I was on it and that I still wanted her. The inhumu had made me promise I would call to her as loudly as I could the moment I heard her voice; but I did not call then or for some minutes afterward, only telling him to be quiet when he spoke and once striking him with Marrow's stick.

A time came when she sang no longer, and I recalled my promise and pleaded with her; but by then she was already in the water and swimming toward us. This happened hours after we had sailed out to sea with no one at the helm, because we had first found the mainland (which Krait had mistaken for the island) and only after we had discovered our mistake returned to the island—and we had to sail some distance around it to reach Seawrack again, I still blinded by the fog and in terror of submerged rocks, which the inhumu could no more have seen than I could.

By the time we had relocated her it was probably about midafternoon, and the fog had lifted somewhat. It parted, and I glimpsed her sitting upon a rock thrust up from the sea like the horn of some drowned monster. She was naked (more so than when she had first come on board, since she no longer had her gold) and her legs, which were very long, as I may have said, seemed almost to coil about her.

"She is going back to what she was," the inhumu told me when I would listen to him again. "While she was with you, she was becoming one of you. That was why the Mother gave her to you, I think." While we sailed out of the bay, I had told him how Seawrack came to be with me.

I echoed him. "You think?"

"Yes, I do, which is more than I can say for you. Do you imagine that now that she's coming back to you she'll sing for you the way she did out there?"

I had not considered that, and it must have showed in my stricken expression.

"You're right. She probably won't sing a note, even if you beg."

Having seen her small, white hand upon the gunwale, I put a finger to my lips—at which he smiled.

We helped her aboard and she stared at the inhumu (whose name I had never learned, thinking of him up until then only as "the inhumu"). I told her (as he and I had agreed I should) that he was a boy who had been left behind on the island by some boat's crew, and that he had helped me out of the pit. It was difficult for me to lie like that, because as I spoke I could see very plainly that he was not a boy or a human being of any kind. Looking at her instead should have helped but did not, only making me that much more conscious of the purity and innocence of her face.

"Don't you want to see me?" she asked.

I told her that I could not look into her eyes without falling in love with her. Forgive me, Nettle!

The inhumu offered her his hand, and I felt certain she would feel his claws, but they had vanished. "I'm Krait," he said. It was the first time I heard the name.

She had turned from him before he had finished speaking, stroking my cheek with her fingers. "You were dead."

I shook my head.

"Yes, you were. I saw you down there." She trembled ever so slightly. "Dead things are food."

"Sometimes," Krait amended.

She ignored him. "Where are my clothes?"

They were not on the sloop, and I had no more tunics to spare, but we contrived a sailcloth skirt for her, as I had before, while she stared vacantly out at the broken fog and the tossing water. "You must hold on to her now if you want to keep her," Krait told me.

"Can you sail?"

"No. But you must do what I tell you, or she'll be over the side in half an hour." He pointed to the little space under the foredeck where she and I had slept. "Lie with her. Talk to her, embrace her, and try to get her to sing for you. I won't watch, I promise."

I trimmed the sails and tied the tiller, warning him that if he did not want to see us drowned he would have to call me at any change in wind or weather, and persuaded Seawrack to rest with me for an hour or so.

She agreed, I believe, mostly so that we could talk in private. "I don't like that boy," she told me.

"He got me out of the pit after you and Babbie had abandoned me." Now that she was back with me and safe, I had discovered that I was angry with her.

"You were dead," she said again. "I saw you. Dead people are to eat."

Anxious to change the subject, I asked her to sing, as Krait had suggested.

"The boy would come in then. I don't want him in here with us."

"Neither do I. Sing only to me, very softly, but not like you used to when we were alone. The way you sang out there."

"He would still hear me." She shuddered. "His feet are twisted."

"You think he's a boy?" (I was incredulous, feeling very much as I did a few days ago when I realized that the wallowers had in fact been deceived by the wicker figure.)

She giggled. "I don't think he's a boy that way. He's old enough. You couldn't keep him out."

"He would come to you in here, if you sang?"

"Oh, yes!" The only hand that she possessed slipped into mine.

Aching for her, I asked, "What would I do, Seawrack? I'm in here with you already."

"Mother told me to stay with you."

I nodded. I could hear Babbie rattling up and down on the foredeck above our heads like a whole squad of troopers, half mad with nervousness and suppressed aggression; and now I wonder whether he saw Krait as an inhumu or a boy, and whether he made any distinction between the two. "Out there," I told Seawrack, "you thought I no longer liked to look at you. The truth is that I don't like to look at him."

"At the boy?"

"At Krait," I said. "I'm afraid I'll stare, and that wouldn't be polite."

"Stare at his feet?"

"That's right. That must be why he walks so badly. But what does he look like, the rest of him?"

"You know."

"Men and women often see the same people very differently," I explained, thinking that it had never been truer than it was for the two of us that afternoon. "I'd like to know how he seems to you."

"You're jealous!" She laughed, delighted.

At that time I still hoped that Seawrack would see Krait for what he was without prompting from me. As seriously as I could, I said, "You don't belong to me, and I belong to Nettle, my wife. If you want to give yourself to another man, I may advise against it. I will, if I don't think he's suitable for you. But don't ever give yourself to that boy—to Krait, as he's calling himself."

"Well, he's very good-looking." She was steering my hand to her left breast.

I pulled my hand away. "No doubt he is."

"Don't be angry with me."

I told her I was not angry, that I was only worried about her, which was not entirely true. Up on the foredeck I heard the chatter of Babbie's tusks; Babbie was angry, at least, and angrier still because he had to behave as though he were not.

"I came as soon as I heard your voice. I should have let you come to me. Then this would be wrecked. Do you remember how you kissed me the first time?"

★

★ ★

It has been a week since I wrote the words that you have just read, a week of heat and terrible, violent storms, and reports of the inhumi from many outlying farms. Not far from town, a woman and her two children were found bloodless by a neighbor child.

So I have been busy, although not too busy to continue the account I began last year and have labored over for so long. The question is not whether I should tell the truth—I know well enough that I should. The question is how much of it must I tell?

("A close mouth catches nae flies," Pig would advise me. I wish he were here to do it.)

If Silk were to have intercourse with another woman, he would confess it to Hyacinth, I feel sure; but that is small guidance, because she would not care—or at least, would not care much. How much would he tell her? That is the true question, and a question to which I can give no satisfactory answer. The mere fact? Will the mere fact not make things look worse, much worse, than they really were?

When I began, these were things I planned to omit. I see now that if I omit them, nothing I say should be believed. No doubt I should burn every scrap of this.

★

★ ★

I will not be believed in any case. I know it. Hari Mau and the rest will not even believe that I am who I am, and I have known that I would not be believed ever since I wrote about the leatherskin. I am going to tell the whole truth, as I would at shriving. I will hide nothing and embroider nothing, from this point forward. It will give my poor dear Nettle pain in the unlikely event that she—or anyone—reads what I write; but she will at least have the satisfaction of knowing that she knows the worst.

I had asked Seawrack to sing for me, as you have already read. The truth is that I implored her to, and at last threatened her, and she sang. She sang only a note or two, just a word or two in some tongue never spoken by human beings, and I was upon her. I tore off the clumsy sailcloth skirt and bit and clawed and pummeled her, doing things no man ought ever to do to any woman.

Perverse acts that I would like to believe no other man has performed.

When it was over at last I slept, exhausted; and when I woke we were sailing briskly north-northeast, with a cold coast of deep green foliage to port. I stared at it, then at the inhumu seated at the tiller.

He grinned at me. "You thought I couldn't do this."

My jaw hurt, and in fact there was precious little of me anywhere that did not; but I managed to say, "You told me that you couldn't."

"Because I don't know how. I can pull a rope, though, if I'm told which one, and my mother told me that."

"Is your mother here?" The thought of sharing the sloop with two inhumi made me physically ill. I sat down on one of the chests, my head in my hands.

"She's dead, I think. I was referring to your second wife, Father. That's what we'll have to tell people, you know. She's not old enough to be my mother, not even as old as I am." I looked at him sharply, and he put his finger to his lips as I had earlier, grinning still.

"I don't like your pretending to be my son," I said, "and I like your pretending to be Seawrack's even less. Where is she?"

"Her stepson, and I can't tell you where she is, Father dear, because I promised her I wouldn't." The ugly, lipless slit that was Krait's mouth was no longer grinning. "You promised me something, too. Several things. Don't forget any of them."

I got up, went to his seat at the tiller, and sat on the gunwale, so close that our elbows touched. "Can she hear us now, if we keep our voices down?"

"I'm quite sure she can't hear me, Father. But I'm equally sure that you won't keep your voice low for more than a minute or two. You never do. It might be better if we didn't talk at all."

"You told me to lie down with her, to . . ."

"Do what you did," he supplied.

"You said all that while she was standing there with us, while I was wrapping the canvas around her. You didn't worry about her overhearing us then."

"I didn't worry about her overhearing *me*. Anyway, she wasn't thinking about either of us right then. Not even about her skirt. Couldn't you see that?"

"Just the same—"

"Her thoughts were very far away. You'd say her spirit. We were less to her then than your hus is to you."

I looked around for Babbie, and found that he was lying at my feet.

"You see? He makes a noise when he walks. He can't help it. Tappa-taptap behind you. But you don't even know he's there."

"She's in the water, isn't she? She went over the side, and now she's holding on to some part of the boat." I looked along the waterline as far as I could without rising, but saw only waves.

"No. . . ." Krait's expression told me nothing about his thoughts; but I sensed that he was troubled, and it made him seem oddly human. "I'd better say it so you understand, and this is as good a chance as I'll get to do it. Do I look like a boy to you?"

I shook my head.

By a gesture, he indicated his face. "This looks just like a boy's, though, doesn't it?"

"If you want me to say so, I will."

"I don't. I want you to tell the truth. We always do." (I feel sure he did not mean that the inhumi always tell the truth, which would itself have been a monstrous lie.)

"All right. You look a lot more human now than you used to, a lot more human than you did when we talked in the pit. But you don't really look like a boy up close, or like one of us at all."

His nose and chin receded into his face as I watched, and the ridge over his eyes melted away. All semblance of humanity vanished. "One of the things I promised you then was that I wouldn't deceive you. The man you hated—"

"Patera Quetzal?"

Krait nodded. "You said you thought he was an old man, and

you were angry because he had tricked you. You told me some trooper shot and killed him."

I nodded.

"Did you see his corpse?"

"Yes." Something of the revulsion I had felt must have shown on my face. "What difference does that make?"

"Being dead makes a great deal of difference to some of us. Did he look like an old man then?"

I hedged. "We don't like to look at corpses. I didn't look for long."

"Did he, Horn?"

There was something indescribably eerie about sitting there in the stern of the sloop talking to the inhumu about the death of Patera Quetzal twenty years ago. Wisps of fog blew past us like ghosts, and the gossiping tongues of small waves kept up an incessant murmur in which it seemed that I could catch a word or two. "I suppose not," I told Krait, and heard a wave whisper, *Moorgrass.* "Nettle—that's my wife, you saw her—and some other women were going to wash his body. They screamed, and that was how we knew."

"You looked for yourself after that, didn't you, Horn? You must have."

I nodded again.

"He didn't look like an old man anymore, did he? He couldn't have."

I shook my head.

"What did he look like?"

"He looked like you."

When Krait said nothing, only transfixing me with his hypnotic stare, I added, "He powdered his face, and painted it. Like a woman. We found the powder and rouge in a pocket of his robe."

"So would I if I had those things, just as I wear this shirt and these pants, which I took from you. The eyes see what the mind expects, Horn. Babbie there, lying still with a green twig in his mouth, could make you think he was a bush, if you were expecting to see a bush."

"That's right. It's why we use tame hus, or dogs, to hunt wild hus."

Krait grinned; his jaw dropped, and his fangs sprang out. "The young siren you call Seawrack doesn't see me the way you do. She doesn't see what you saw when you looked at that dead man."

I agreed.

"Knowing that, is it so hard for you to believe that at times she doesn't hear me *at all*?"

More shaken than I would have liked to admit, I went to the bow, looking down into the water for her on both sides of the boat but seeing nothing. After a time, Krait motioned to me, and reluctantly I went aft again. His voice in my ear was less than a whisper. "If she's listening, she hears you alone, Father. Only the murmur of your voice. She probably thinks you're talking to yourself, or to your hus."

"I hurt her."

He nodded solemnly. "You intended to, as we both know. As all three of us know, in fact. You intended to, and you succeeded admirably. Given time, she may find some excuse for you. Would you like that?" His fangs had vanished, and his face had resumed its boyish outline.

"How badly?"

"Very badly. She bled quite a lot from—oh, various places. It was difficult for me."

Unable to think of anything else to say, I asked whether he had found the bandages and salves.

"She knew where they were. I helped her tie the knots, where rags could be of use. Stopping the bleeding was hard. I doubt that you have any idea just how much trouble we had." He paused, tense; I knew that he was expecting me to attack him. "Do you understand everything I'm telling you?"

"Certainly. You're speaking the Common Tongue, and you speak it at least as well as I do."

He dismissed the Common Tongue with a gesture. "Well, you don't understand her at all."

"Men never understand women."

He laughed, and although I had not been angry with him a moment before there was something in that laugh that made me yearn to kill him.

★

★ ★

I searched the waterline for Seawrack, and failing to find her probed the sea for her with the boat hook, which was absurd. After that, I wanted to return to the rocks where we had found her before, but Krait dissuaded me, giving me his word that she was still on the sloop, but telling me quite frankly that I would be a complete fool to search it for her, since finding her would be far worse than not finding her. Soon after that, he left.

To the best of my memory, it was already dark when she came out. I had long ago concluded that she was in one of the cargo chests, and was not at all surprised to see the lid of the one in which I kept rope and the like (the one on which I had sat) opened from within. I held up the little pan in which I had been cooking a fish and invited her to join me.

She sat down on the other side of the fire. I thanked her for it, since I could see her better there; and she looked surprised.

"Because I've been so worried about you," I told her. "I didn't know how badly you were hurt, and I thought you had to be getting hungry and thirsty." I passed her the water bottle.

She drank and said, "Weren't you hurt, too?"

It touched me as few things ever have. "No. I'm fine. I was exhausted, that's all."

She nodded, and drank again.

"You could have killed me while I slept, Seawrack. You could have found my knife and stabbed me to death with it."

"I wouldn't do that."

"I would have, in your place." I put our last strip of fish on a plate and handed it to her across the fire. "Do you want a fork?"

She said nothing, staring down at her small portion of fried fish, so I got her a fork as well. "That fish is just about all we have left," I told her. "I should have brought more food."

"You didn't know about me." She looked away from the fillet I had given her with something akin to horror. "I don't want this. Can I give it to Babbie?"

He rose at the sound of his name and trotted around the box to her.

"Certainly, if you wish." I watched Babbie devour the morsel of fish.

"I feel a little sick."

"So do I. Do I have to tell you that I'm terribly, horribly, sorry for what I did to you? That I'll never do anything like that again?"

"I sang for you," she said, as if it explained everything.

Somewhere she is singing for me at this moment, singing as she used to before Krait came. I hear her, as I do almost every day, although she must surely be many hundreds of leagues away. I hear her—and when I do not I dream of my home beside the sea. Of it and of you, Nettle my darling, my only dearest, the sweetheart of my youth. But if ever I find my way back to it (as Seawrack has beyond any question found her way back to the waves and the spume, the secret currents, and her black, wave-washed rocks) there will come a stormy midnight when I throw off the blankets, although you and the twins are soundly sleeping. I will put out then in whatever boat I can find, and you will not see me more. Do not mourn me, Nettle. Every man must die, and I know what death I long for.

★

★ ★

We buried alive an inhumu and two inhumas today, taking up three of the big flat paving stones in the marketplace—all that cruel business. One smiled at me, and I thought I saw human teeth. All three looked so human that I felt we were about to consign to the grave a living man and two living women. I insisted that they open their mouths so I could inspect them. The woman who had smiled would not, so hers was pried open with the blades of daggers; there were only blood-drinking fangs, folded against the roof of her mouth.

Inhumi are burned alive in Skany—I am very glad that I had to watch that only once. I have heard of the same thing being done in New Viron, and I admit that I would cheerfully have burned or buried the inhuma that bit Sinew when we were living in the tent. They are vile creatures, exactly as Hari Mau says; but how can they help it, when we are as we are? I wish sometimes that Krait had not told me.

★

★ ★

So little, the last time I wrote. Nothing at all about Seawrack and Krait, the sloop, or the western mainland I call Shadelow; and it has been two days. If I continue at this rate, I will be the rest of my life in telling the tale of my failure, simple though it is.

On the evening I wrote about before the inhumation, we sat before the fire and said very little. The apple barrel, which had once seemed inexhaustible, was empty at last, and the flour gone. I had used the last of our cornmeal that night. I had two fishing lines out, and from time to time I got up to look at them; but they caught nothing.

Seawrack asked where the boy was, and I told her that he had gone ashore to hunt, which tasted like a lie in my mouth although it was true. My slug gun was still under the foredeck in the place where we slept, and I was afraid she had seen it there and would want to know how he could hunt at night without Babbie and without the gun. Perhaps she thought it, but she never said anything of that sort. What she actually said was "We could sail away without him."

I shook my head.

"All right."

"Will you forgive me?" I asked her.

"Because you won't leave him?" She shrugged, her shoulders (thin shoulders now) rising and slumping again. "I hope we will, sometime, no matter what you say now."

"To get out of the pit, I had to promise him that we'd take him to Pajarocu with us, and try to get a place for him on the lander."

"I haven't promised him anything, and I won't. Is there any more corn flour?"

"No."

She got up to look at my fishing lines. "Do women catch fish?"

"Sometimes," I told her. It had been a very long time since Nettle and I had gone fishing.

"How? Like this?"

"Yes," I said. "Or with a pole, or a net. Sometimes they spear them, too, just as men do. Men fish more, but there's nothing wrong with women fishing."

"If you would tie your knife to your stick for me, I might be able to spear some for us."

"In the water?" I shook my head. "You'd start to bleed again."

She made no reply, and she was a step too far from the firelight for me to judge her expression.

"I'll hunt tomorrow myself," I promised her. "This time I'll get something, or Babbie and I will."

"What are those?"

I had to rise to be certain that she was pointing toward shore.

She said, "Those little lights?" and I went up onto the foredeck for a better view. The weather was calm, although not threateningly so; and we were anchored some distance from the naked coast of the mainland, Krait and I having been unable to find a protected anchorage before shadelow. North along the coast so far that they were practically out of sight were two or three, possibly four, scattered points of reddish light. As I stood there shivering, one vanished—then reappeared.

Behind me Seawrack said, "I thought the boy might have decided to stay there, but there are too many."

I nodded, and returned to our own fire. To my very great surprise and delight, she sat down beside me. "Are you afraid of them?"

"Of the people who built those fires? Not as much as I ought to be, perhaps. Seawrack, it would be easier for me, a great deal easier, if you were angry with me. If you hated me now."

She shook her head. "I'd like it if you hated me, Horn. Don't you understand why I hid?"

"Because I'd attacked you, and you were afraid I would hurt you again, or even kill you."

She nodded solemnly.

"I'm sorrier than I can say. I've been trying and trying to think of some way I can—can at least show you how sorry I really am."

She touched my hand and fixed me with her extraordinary eyes. "Never leave me."

I wanted to explain that I was a friend, not a lover. I wanted to, I say, but how could I (or anybody) say that to a woman I had forced that very day? I wanted to tell her, as I had several times before, that I was married, and I wanted to explain all over again what marriage means. I wanted to remind her that I was probably twice her age. I wanted to say all those things, but I knew that I loved her, and all the fine words stuck in my throat.

Later, when we lay side by side under the foredeck, she asked me again, "Don't you understand why I had to hide from you today?"

I thought that I did, but I had given my answer already; so I asked, "Why?"

"Because I made you and wouldn't let you."

"You didn't make me," I told her.

"Yes, I did, by singing. The song does that. I'm trying to forget it."

"Your singing made me want you more than ever, but it didn't make me do what I did. I surrendered to my own desire when I should have resisted."

She was quiet so long that I had nearly fallen asleep when she said, "The underwater woman taught me to sing like that. I wish I could forget her, too."

"Your Mother?" I asked.

"She wasn't my mother."

" 'The Mother.' You called her that."

"She wanted me to. I was on a big boat, and I remember a woman who talked to me, and carried me sometimes. I think that was my mother."

I nodded; then realizing that Seawrack could not see me said, "So do I."

"After that, there was only the underwater woman. She doesn't look like a woman unless she makes part of herself a woman."

"I understand."

"She's another shape, very big. But she is one. She told me to call her Mother, and I did. My real mother drowned, I think, and the underwater woman ate her."

"The sea goddess. Do you know her name?"

"No. If I ever did, I've forgotten it, and I'm glad. I don't want to remember her anymore, and she doesn't want me to. I do remember that much about her. Would you like me to sing for you again?"

"No," I said, and meant it.

"Then I'm going to try to forget the song."

As I drifted into sleep, I heard (or believed I heard) her say, ". . . and forget the water and the underwater woman, and the boats underwater with people in them. That was why I wouldn't eat your fish. I don't want to eat fish or drowned meat, never any more. Will the boy bring us back something to eat?"

Perhaps I mumbled in reply. At this remove I cannot be sure.

"I don't think so. He'll eat, and come back here with nothing."

Which was precisely correct.

I recall thinking, as I declined from consciousness into the first deep sleep of the night, that Seawrack was forgetting the goddess she had called the Mother because Krait (whom she herself called "the boy") intended to call her "mother." That there was a place for only one mother on my sloop, and it was to be Seawrack.

There was a place for only one wife, as well. With the eyes of sleep I saw you, my poor Nettle, fading and fading, sinking into the clear blue water like the hammer I used to keep on board until I lost it over the side and watched it sink, weighed by its iron head but buoyed by its wooden handle, smaller and smaller and dimmer and dimmer as the waters closed around it forever. My love was like a line tied to you then, a cord so thin as to be invisible, playing out cubit after cubit and fathom after fathom until the time arrived when I would haul you up again.

Have I insulted you? I do not blame you. You may blame me, and the more you do the happier I will be. Let me say now, once and for all, that I was not compelled by the song the sea goddess had taught Seawrack. Was I inflamed? Yes, certainly. But not compelled. I could have left. The inhumu would have seen my manhood raised, and witnessed my agony, and would have derided me for both whenever he thought his taunts would tell. But that would have been nothing.

Or I might have clapped my hand over Seawrack's mouth and forced her to be silent. I would have been ashamed then, since I had threatened to beat her if she would not sing for me; but I have been ashamed many times of many things, and been no worse for it afterward.

For this I was worse, as I am.

I should tell you this too: Chandi has come in pretending to believe I sent for her, and I will have to stop writing this rambling account that has become a letter to you while I persuade her to leave.

★

★ ★

I am not sure when I wrote last. Before the big storm, but when? I ought to date my entries, but what would such dates mean to those who may read them? Every town on this whorl, every city in the old *Whorl*, uses a different system; even the lengths of our years are different. This Great Pas did, to prevent our leaguing against Mainframe; and it divides us still. I will give the day and the month as we reckon them here in Gaon: Dusra Agast. That may mean something to you; but if it does not, not much has been lost.

Conjunction is past. It was as bad as I feared, and worse. (It is still very bad.) Many of the inhumi came, and many have remained. My servants close the shutters at sundown, and when they are asleep I inspect every window in this palace myself to make sure they have done it.

My bedroom has five windows north, six west, and five south. I double-check every one of them before I get into bed, and lock and bolt the only door, for fear of the inhumi and for fear of assassins, too.

An inhumu drinks blood until his veins are full and his flesh is nourished again; thus satisfied, he goes his way, like a tick that falls off when it has drunk its fill; but there are men here where land is free for the working who want land, and more and better land, and others to work it for them, and they always believe that someone else's land is better. They would crush the small farmers if I let them.

I will not.

A lean young man with a long curved dagger was shot to death in my garden last night. Awakened by the booming of the slug guns, I went to view his body, and could not help thinking of Silk climbing Blood's wall with the hatchet in his waistband. Had this young man thought me as bad as Blood? If so, was he right? We have the inhumi to prey on us, yet we prey upon one another.

When I ended my last session with this old quill of Oreb's, Seawrack and I were on the sloop on the night of the fires. I dreamed that night about shadowy figures creeping from those fires to swim toward us, and climbing aboard bent upon murder. I sat up and found my slug gun, and nearly fired it, too; but there was no one there.

I lay down again and muttered an apology to Seawrack for having awakened her.

"I wasn't sleeping."

I knew why she had not slept, or thought I did. "You're frightened and upset, and that's only natural. I don't suppose you want to tell me about it; but if you do, I'll listen to whatever you have to say without getting angry."

"I'm angry at myself," she muttered.

"Then your anger is misdirected. You should be angry at me. I am." For an instant (only an instant) I had heard Silk's voice issuing from my own mouth. I tried to prolong it, but could not. "What would you like to tell me?"

"Nothing."

"Then let me say a few things, and after that you'll have a few things of your own, I feel sure." I waited for her to object.

When she did not, I continued, "First, the fault was mine, and mine alone. It wasn't yours or anybody else's. There was no reason for me to act as I did, and you resisted as fiercely as you could. You have—"

"I shouldn't have." It might have been a child, a small girl, speaking. "I hurt you. I know I did."

"I hurt you a great deal more." It was so overwhelmingly true that I found it impossible to go on.

"I deserved it."

"You did not. You never will. You are entitled to be furiously angry with me. That was the second thing I was going to say, although I said it already this afternoon. If you had killed me while I slept, no one could have blamed you."

"I would have blamed myself."

"It occurred to me that you might before I fell asleep, and to tell the truth I was hoping you would."

"No!" She shook her head violently enough for her hair to brush my cheek.

"Here is a third thing. I am a fool on a fool's errand. I've been struggling to hide that from myself ever since I set out. To go to the Long Sun Whorl and bring back the strains of corn we need, and an eye for Maytera Marble, and so forth, is reasonable; but it's a task for a bold and able man of twenty, not for me. Ten or fifteen years ago, I might have been adequate. Tonight I'm worse than inadequate. I'm thoroughly ridiculous."

"You went because you were afraid they'd want your wife to go if you wouldn't," Seawrack reminded me. "You told me about that."

"She might have done it, to. She's brave and practical, with a good level head in a crisis. I won't list my shortcomings—you know them already. I'll simply point out that that's not a description of me."

"But—"

I raised my voice. "As for bringing Silk here, it's less than a dream; and I very much doubt that Marrow and the rest even want me to do it. A trader named Wijzer told Marrow that to his face in my hearing, and Wijzer was right. All their talk about bringing Silk to New Viron was nothing more than a trick to get me to go. Or to get Nettle to, if I wouldn't. A cheap and obvious trick that even Hoof and Hide should have seen through."

Seawrack turned her head to whisper into my ear, so that I felt the warm caress of her breath. "You were right. I have things to say too. Is that all right?"

"Go ahead."

"When you're through. You're going, in spite of all you've said. I know you are."

I sighed; I could not help it. "I've told you I'm a fool, and I promised I would. That doesn't mean you have to come with me. The lander in Pajarocu will probably explode as soon as they try to get it to go fly. Everybody on it will be killed, and it would be better if you weren't one of us."

"Is there more you want to say before we both go to sleep, or is it my turn?"

"I'm practically finished. Fourth and last, you're not a prisoner on this sloop." I recalled Sciathan the Flier then, and what Silk had said about him after Auk got him out of the Juzgado, and how Nettle and I had re-created that speech in our book. "You are my guest, a guest who's been treated very badly. You're free to leave any time—right now, if you like. Or when we reach Pajarocu or any other town."

I fell silent, and after a time she murmured, "Are you waiting for me to jump into the sea again, Horn?"

"Yes," I said.

"I'm not going to yet, and it's my turn to talk. While you were sleeping I was trying to forget."

"I don't blame you."

"Not what you think. I was trying to forget the water, and everything I did in it. Every time I remembered something that happened there, I would think of something that's happened since I've been with you, some little thing or something you said, and put it there instead."

"Can you do that?" I was incredulous, as I still am.

"Yes!" she said fiercely. "So could you."

It was not the time to express my doubts.

"That's the first thing *I* had to say, what I've been doing. I wasn't angry or afraid, the way that you think I was. I was remembering and forgetting."

For half a dozen gentle rockings of the sloop, she said nothing more.

"The second thing is that I'm one of you. Like you and the boy, but I don't like him."

"A human being."

"Yes. I am a human woman. Aren't there women who aren't? What does the Babbie have?"

"A female hus. Not a woman."

"Well, a woman is what I am. Like your Nettle, or the Tamarind you talk about sometimes. I am a woman, but I don't know how to."

I tried to say that I would help her all I could, but it would be much better if she had an actual woman to emulate. If Nettle were with us, for example.

"I'm learning how from you."

Possibly there is something adequate that could be said in response to that; but I could not think of it, nor can I now.

"You said you were a fool on a foolish errand." (This was an accusation.)

"It's the truth."

"You're not a fool, and I can prove it. Then I'm going to swim. You said the people who sent you to bring this good man Silk don't even want him. Didn't you just tell me that?"

"Yes. I said it because I know it to be true. I believe I've known it ever since I set out, but I couldn't bring myself to admit it to anyone, not even to myself."

"All right. They really don't want him. I think they'd say something else if they were here, but I won't argue about it. They don't want him."

Thinking wistfully of Patera Silk, I nodded and grunted my assent.

"But I'm going to ask you just one thing, and you have to answer me. Do you promise?"

I nodded in the dark. "I will if I can. Did you say a moment ago that you were going to swim? Did you mean tonight, Seawrack?"

She ignored my questions. "Here's how I prove. You have to tell me honestly. Do they need him?"

I opened my mouth to say no, but closed it again without speaking.

"Do they? You promised."

"I know I did." I was recalling our dreams for this fair new whorl, and contrasting them with the realities of the past twenty years. "Yes. Yes, I'm sure they do. But Seawrack, you mustn't swim. Certainly not at night, and not even during the day until you've had time to heal."

She rolled on her side, her back to me. I lay upon my own, feeling the easy motion of the sloop and, whenever I opened my eyes, seeing a scatting of bright, cold stars along the horizon. If she needed to forget a great deal, I needed to remember even more, and to think about it all as honestly as I could. And I did, or tried to at least.

An hour later, perhaps, she murmured, "I'm hungry, Horn.

Will you get us something to eat tomorrow? Not fish."

"Yes," I promised. "Certainly. I will if I can."

I had not realized that Babbie was near us, but he gave a little snuffle of contentment as I spoke, and lay down at my feet.

When I woke at shadeup, he was still there; but Seawrack had gone.

★

★ ★

Rain and more rain, all day long. I held court and heard three cases. It is hard to be fair in such foul weather; there is that in me that wants to punish everyone; but I try hard to be fair, and to point out to everyone who appears before me that if only they themselves had been fair, they would not have to come to me for justice. This I say in one fashion to one, and in another to another. Still, I thank the Outsider, and all the lesser gods, that I had no criminal cases today. The impressions of his fingers are on all these quarreling, handsome, mud-colored people; but the light is bad on such days as this, and it can be terribly hard to see them.

Back to the events I have resolved to record.

As well as I can remember I had planned, as I lay there in the dark next to Seawrack, to sail north along the coast the next day until I found a good spot to anchor in, then go ashore and hunt, leaving her to watch the boat. When I woke and found her gone, I realized that I could do no such thing. She had said that she was going for a swim, not that she was leaving me forever. What if she returned, and could not find the sloop?

Krait returned, although Seawrack did not. After a long and no doubt somewhat dishonest account of his adventures ashore (he was full of blood and full of himself as well) I explained the situation. The acrimonious quarrel I had expected followed, and he left again. That was midmorning, perhaps, or a little earlier.

It would be easy—and pleasant as well—to pass over the day

that followed in silence. It was not nearly as easy or pleasant to pass it as I did. I had plenty of water, but no food at all. My conscience urged me to pull up the anchor and proceed to Pajarocu—or at least to proceed to search for it; but I could not bring myself to do it. Babbie swam ashore to forage for food, I think finding little or nothing. I remained on the sloop, cold and hungry. My fishing lines caught nothing, and indeed I had no proper bait. (One hook was baited with a knotted scrap of sailcloth, I remember.) I spent hours looking over the side with my new harpoon in my hand. I believe that in the whole time I glimpsed one small fish, which vanished before I could throw.

About shadelow, a fat bluebilly leaped on board. Seawrack was back, and I knew it. I put a line through its gills and put it back into the water, built a fire in my box of sand in record time, pulled the bluebilly back up and cleaned it, and soon had it sizzling in our largest pan.

She climbed in about then, and I thanked her.

"You got nothing with your hunting." I knew she was tired from the sound of her voice.

I shook my head and ventured to ask how she knew that, though no doubt a glance at my face would have made it plain to anyone.

"If you had shot something you wouldn't watch the sea with the spear for fish. Where is the Babbie?"

I explained that I had not gone ashore to hunt in spite of my promise, that Krait had declined to remain with the sloop, and that I had not dared leave it in a completely unprotected anchorage with no one on board. "I'll hunt tomorrow," I told her, "but you must remain here, and put out to sea if there's even the slightest chance of bad weather."

She shrugged, and I knew there would be an argument next day. "I'll eat a piece of that. Can I? I know I said I wouldn't, but I will."

When we had finished our meal, she asked me to hold out my hand. I did, and she slipped a ring on it. The mounting was white gold, I believe—some silvery metal that did not tarnish as plain silver would have. The stone was white and dull, scratched and very old.

"You have given me a ring," Seawrack said, "and now I am giving you one." Her little hand—the only one she had—had slipped into mine. "You must wear it, because you might fall in the pit again."

She kissed me, but would not explain. At the time, I had no idea what that ring was (although I would soon find out), and certainly would never have guessed that it would someday save my life in a ruined lander on Green, as it did.

It was left behind, of course, with everything else. I wish that I had it back, if only to help me with Barsat and to remind me of her.

11

The Land of Fires

With the block and tackle, and Krait and Seawrack to pull the rope with me, and Babbie pushing and lifting the stern with his shoulders, we were able to get the sloop well up onto the beach. When there was no moving it any farther, I stowed the block, fetched my slug gun and some of the silver jewelry, and moored the sloop to dwarfish but sturdy-looking trees at both the bow and the stern.

After that, I climbed the biggest dune I could find to study the wide, flat expanse of sand and dark green, tangled brush. It did not look promising; but I reminded myself that the majestic trees of the island had produced no game at all, while we had shot at a green-buck in the ruins, which had not appeared any more promising than this.

Some minutes passed before it struck me that I was actually standing on what I myself had named Shadelow—that for the first time ever my feet were solidly planted on the unknown western continent upon which Pajarocu and its working lander waited. Behind me to the south lay the sea, and to eastward I could see the sea as well. Far to the north, too, I could just make out the gleam of it, or thought I could. But to the west the land widened, rising so much that I was reminded of home, where the distant lands to north and south bend up around the sun and at last close over one's head to become the majestic skylands.

At my elbow Krait drawled, "It's a big country."

With more conviction than I felt, I told him that we would find Pajarocu in it, and soon.

He shrugged. "I'll help as much as I can."

"Then I feel sure you must have found out something of value last night."

"No." The wind whipped his loose clothing and he trembled, looking at least as cold as I felt.

"But you fed again. You said so at some length when you came back, and marveled that a place with so few people could provide such good hunting. Didn't you have a chance to talk to anybody?"

"You'd like it better if I starved."

I would not be diverted into a quarrel. "You found someone here. Human beings from whom you fed."

"Not here I didn't. Up there, farther in." He pointed westward.

"Didn't you ask them about Pajarocu? You must have. What did they say?"

He shook his head. "I had no opportunity to ask anybody anything. They were all asleep."

"Good," I said.

"Yes, she was." He grinned, though without displaying his fangs.

Behind us, from the foot of the dune on which we stood, Seawrack called, *"Aren't you going to hunt?"*

"In a moment!" I told her. "I'm going to go down the other side!"

"We'll meet you there!"

I turned back to Krait. "I want you to stay here and protect the sloop. Will you do that?"

"Gladly, if you'll tell me why you were happy that I hadn't asked for directions."

"Because I was warned that people friendly to the town would mislead us if we asked where it was. These people don't like strangers, even when they're human."

Krait grinned again, stroking the chin he had shaped for himself that morning. "And one of us isn't."

It was my turn to shrug. "A detail."

"I agree, Father. We're every bit as human as you are, whatever that means. Don't you want to know where the humans I found are?"

"I want to know a good deal more." I tried to study his face, and turned away from its glittering eyes. If he chose to deceive me, there was nothing I could do about it. "But that will do to start with. Where are they?"

He pointed west again. "See that notch in the mountains?"

I nodded. It was ten leagues at least.

"A little river runs through there, coming pretty well straight toward us. If you look carefully, you can see the sun on it through the trees here and there."

I tried, but my eyes were not as sharp as his.

"They have a lean-to on the bank, down where the land flattens out and the water slows down."

"Thank you," I said. "Can you tell me where the river goes after that?"

He shook his head. "Sinks into the ground, maybe. It's pretty sandy all around here. But I don't know, and it might reach the sea. I didn't follow it."

"We're going to hunt here, for greenbucks or whatever we can find that can be shot and eaten. What do you think of our chances?"

He hesitated, scanning the monotonous expanse of thickly spaced bushes and scrubby trees just as I had earlier. "Not much, but I could be wrong."

"Did you see any game?"

He shook his head again.

"What did you see? I mean here, where we are now."

"Trees, mostly." Before I could stop him, he had started down the dune toward the sloop. I watched him for a moment or two, then clambered and slid down the other side, reaching the bottom just in time to meet Seawrack and Babbie, who had walked around the end.

"I was going to climb up there after you," she said, "but it hurt my feet, and our Babbie sank down in it. Sand that's full of sharp little rocks belongs under the water. Could you see much from up there?"

"All sorts of things," I told her, meaning more than the mere geography I had observed. "Some of which I don't want to talk about. Not yet, at least."

I scratched my beard. "Seawrack, I plan to hunt due west, which will mean we'll be walking almost parallel to the shore for a long way, but tend gradually inland. The nearer to the mountains we get, the better the hunting is likely to be. Do you still want to come?"

She nodded, and we set out.

I tried more than once to show her the mountains, but in every place we stopped our view was obstructed by leaves and branches. "It's going to be horribly easy to lose our way," I told her. "We'll have to stop and look at the sun wherever it can be seen. The boy says there's a river, though, and we can follow that—if we can find it."

"Did he kill something?"

That called for a flat lie, and I supplied it, saying that in spite of his boasts I thought that he had really eaten raw shellfish.

We started off again, but had not walked far when Seawrack asked whether Krait had met any of the people who had built the fires we had seen the first night. I replied that I believed he had, but that he had been unwilling to tell me anything about them.

"Aren't you willing to tell me either?" She was following me as we made our way through the tangled trees, but apparently my voice had been all the clue she needed.

"I'm willing, because I'm very worried about you as well as worried about us both. I don't quite know how to go about it, however, because I don't actually know anything about this part of the whorl and its people. Everything I might confide is guesswork."

"Then tell me your guesses." It was a demand; and Babbie,

who had been ranging ahead of us, stopped and looked back at us, ears spread.

I took a deep breath, more than half certain that Seawrack knew more about the fires and their builders than I did. "To start with, I don't believe they were human beings."

"But you're not sure."

"No, I'm not. Krait said he met some people along this river I'd like to find, a good long way from here. According to his account, he must have gotten pretty far inland. Whoever built the fires would have been much nearer."

"Didn't he see them?"

"I don't know," I told Seawrack. "He didn't want to say. If you'd like my guess, I think he knew who or what they were and avoided them." She would have questioned me further if I had allowed it, but I told her that our noise would frighten the game, if there was any, and that she would have to be quiet or wait on the sloop with Krait.

About noon (squinting up at the sun every chance I got kept me very conscious of the passage of time) we struck the little river and stopped to drink. Its water was clean and cold and good. Seawrack asked, "Are we going to follow this now?" and I told her we were.

"You want to find the people the boy found?"

"If I can." I had stopped drinking and was taking off my boots. "For me the easiest way will probably be to wade through the shallows."

I waited for her to speak, but she did not.

"Are you going to do that too, instead of swimming?"

She nodded.

"There'll be less brush for me to deal with." I had been forced to cut our way with Sinew's knife in half a dozen places. "And if I try to hike through the brush next to it, I'm liable to lose it every chain or two. The people that Krait met lived alongside it, he said. If I lose it and find it again upstream of their camp, I'll miss them completely."

She nodded again. "Maybe they'll give us something to eat."

"Exactly. We need food, more clothing and blankets, or even hides. Something to keep us warm. Boots or shoes for you, if we can get them."

I stood up, and stepped into the river, finding the water that had been so refreshing unpleasantly cold, and pulled off my tunic. "This is something I should have done as soon as you swam out to the sloop," I said. "Here, take it. Put it on, and please don't argue with me."

She began to protest, but fell silent when she saw that she was only making me angry. "Women in New Viron never let strangers look at their breasts," I explained. "Allowing it would be like singing that song you're trying to forget. Do you understand?"

In a whisper so soft I could scarcely hear her, she said, "You're not a stranger."

"I know, and there are exceptions. This is best, just the same. Put it on."

"You'll be cold. I was."

I told her that I had been getting chilled anyway when I was wearing my tunic, which was not particularly warm. After that, we waded upstream for two or three leagues before the water became so frigid that we had to get out and try to trace the river from one side after all.

Shadelow (I still have no other name by which to call it) is a colder continent than ours, from what I saw of it. Even places we would consider southern are colder than New Viron, and much colder than this town of Gaon. I would think that it must be due to the western winds, or to unfavorable currents in the sea.

★

★ ★

It was nearly dark by the time we reached the lean-to Krait had visited. It belonged to a family of four—a husband and wife, a boy of twelve or thirteen, and a plump little girl whom I judged to be eight or nine. The man was away hunting when we arrived, and the boy was spearing fish in the river. His mother called out to him when she saw us, and he came at a run, brandishing his barbed spear. Seawrack and I smiled and tried to show by signs (since the woman seemed not to understand the Common Tongue) that we were friendly.

The girl had been Krait's victim. She lay on her back beside their fire, deathly pale beneath her deep tan and only occasionally opening her eyes; I do not believe she spoke the whole time we were there. Remembering what Silk had told me about Teasel, and what Teasel herself had told Nettle and me later, I tried to show her mother by signs that she should be kept very warm and given a great deal of water, at last fetching a soft greenbuck skin myself and covering her with it. The boy was—or rather, seemed to be—more intelligent, bringing water in a gourd as soon as I pointed to his sister and pretended to drink from my hand.

Soon the father returned carrying two big gray-and-red birds he had killed with arrows. He proved to speak the Common Tongue fairly well, and asked us many questions about Babbie, having never seen a hus before. When I told him that Babbie could understand what we were saying, he explained (with some difficulty, but very earnestly) that it was true of every animal. "He listen. No talk. Sometimes talk. Long time the shearbear, he talk me."

It was an animal I had never heard of; I asked him what the shearbear had said.

He shook his head. "No tell."

"Change blood," his wife explained, making Seawrack blink with surprise.

That sounded as if it might be significant, so I asked her about it.

"He-pen-sheep cut arm, shearbear cut same." She crossed her arms to illustrate the mingling of their blood, then pointed upward. Her husband and son pointed upward as well, he with his bow and the boy with his fishing spear. I pointed upward with my slug gun, and they nodded approval, at which Seawrack too pointed upward as the woman had.

They invited us to join their meal, and we accepted eagerly. After we ate, I traded two silver pins for a soft skin smaller than the one with which I had covered their daughter, saying that I was cold.

He-pen-sheep (who was naked to the waist himself) cut a slit in the middle of it for my head and cut away a long, thin strip that he tied around my waist as one would tie a trouser cord, making a rough but warm leather tunic with half sleeves of the skin. "You stay," he urged me. "She-pick-berry make together for you."

Neither Seawrack nor I understood "make together," so he brought out a pair of beautifully made hide boots and pointed out the stitching. Too eagerly, perhaps, I offered them a silver necklace if She-pick-berry would make a pair for Seawrack, since the pair that he had shown us would have been much too large for her. After some discussion we agreed that the boots could be undecorated, and I offered another pin in addition to the necklace.

She-pick-berry then made the boots in something less than an hour, folding and cutting soft leather around Seawrack's feet, punching holes in it with one of the pins she had gotten from me already, and sewing it quickly with a big bone needle. They were very simple in construction, one piece forming the sides and the sole, another the front and top, and a third the back.

Pretending ignorance, I asked He-pen-sheep what had happened to his daughter.

"Inhumu bite." He indicated the inner part of his own thigh.

Seawrack told him that an inhumu had bitten Babbie some days ago, although it had not attacked us.

He nodded solemnly. "Afraid Neighbor-man." When I asked what a Neighbor-man was, he laughed and pointed to the ring Seawrack had given me. "You Neighbor-man."

"Many Neighbor here," his wife told Seawrack. She paused to moisten the sinew with which she sewed, running it through her mouth. "Build many fire. Neighbor-man," she pointed to me, "come, talk Neighbor."

I indicated the wilderness of sand and scrub through which we had walked for most of the day. "Are there many Neighbors down there?"

Without looking up from her sewing, she nodded emphatically. "Many Neighbor. Many fire."

Her son displayed both palms. "No kill Neighbor."

His father laughed again. "He no kill. Change blood Neighbor," to which he added what seemed to be several sentences in a tongue that I had never heard before.

"Neighbor kill you?" I suggested.

He shook his head. "Kill inhumu."

By that time the Short Sun had set; She-pick-berry was finishing her sewing by firelight. The ground had begun to rise here; the soil was darker and not so sandy, and the trees much taller. I climbed a likely-looking one, gaining enough height to see that the fires Seawrack and I had watched two nights before had been re-kindled, and were more numerous if anything. It seemed strange that we had not come across the ashes of one at least during our long hike through the scrub. For some time I stood upon a convenient limb, surveying them and speculating, before I climbed down again.

★

★ ★

We stretched ourselves upon the ground to sleep in daisy-petal fashion, our feet toward the fire and our heads outward. If I had been warm and comfortable, I might very well have nodded off quickly, and slept the night away in spite of the resolution I had formed while I had stood in the tree. As things were, I shivered, huddled with Seawrack, and reviled myself through chattering teeth for not trading for the greenbuck hide and letting the exsanguinated child freeze for me.

Seawrack, as I ought to mention here, went to sleep at once; but hers was a troubled slumber, in which she trembled and twitched without waking, and sometimes spoke. I could not understand most of what she said, which seemed to me to be in several rather different languages. Once I thought she was cajoling someone or something; and once I overheard her say quite distinctly:

"Yes, Mother! I'm coming, Mother!" After a time, it occurred to me that she might begin to sing in her sleep, crooning the song I had heard when she sat naked on the wave-swept rocks; when it did, I got to my feet without waking her, as I had intended all along.

The night was silent, cold, and clear. I made sure of Sinew's hunting knife and picked up my slug gun, then scanned the sky for Krait—as everyone knows, inhumi are prone to return to places in which they have been successful. He was not to be seen, only the bright stars, very cold and far, and baleful Green low upon the eastern horizon.

The scrub trees of the peninsula had been troublesome by day; now they were nightmarish, raking my face with spiky limbs the moment I ceased to guard it with my hand or the slug gun. Every so often I was obliged to stop and chop my way through some tangle by touch alone; it must have taken me a full two hours to travel half a league.

At one point I stopped and looked behind me, footsore, exhausted, and sorely tempted to return to the fire and lie down again, and was irrationally cheered to find that it was still in sight, although it looked as remote as the stars. Save for Pig, Patera Silk and you, Nettle, I have seldom found a lot to love about my fellow human beings, even when I liked them; but at that moment I must have felt the way that Silk himself habitually did. The chill wind, the twisted, useless little trees, and the impoverished soil I trod were hostile, foreign things scarcely better than Krait and possibly worse. We six had faced them in the day now past and would face them again in the day to come; and it was our glory that we faced them together.

The feeling faded as soon as I turned my eyes away, but it has never disappeared completely. It is good to live as I do here: in a palace, with important work to do and plenty to eat. It is good—but those who live as I do here cannot ever know the feeling I experienced that night in the scrub when I looked back up the slope and saw the lonely scarlet glow that was She-pick-berry's humble fire. There are worse things for the spirit, Nettle, than fatigue and sore feet, a little hunger and a little cold.

★

★ ★

Yesterday Barsat reported finding a house of the Vanished People, as the Neighbors seem to be called on this eastern side of the sea wherever the Common Tongue is spoken. Today he and I rode out to see it, escorted by Hari Mau, Mota, Ram, and Roti. It was a dismal place, roofless, and empty of everything except twigs and dead leaves; but Barsat informed me that it was happy now. Naturally I asked what he meant.

"It didn't like me," he said. "As soon as I came in, I had to go back out."

The others laughed at that, and I asked Barsat why he had gone inside at all, which may not have been an altogether fair question since we had gone in as a matter of course.

"I was hoping to find something I could sell," he told me frankly. "Was that wrong, Rajan?"

I shook my head.

"They can afford to laugh." He shot Hari Mau and his three friends a glance compounded of envy and admiration. "We poor men like to laugh too, but we don't have much to laugh about."

I began to explain that I was almost as poor as he, that my palace belonged to the town, which could tell me to leave whenever it wished, and so on; but before I could finish, we heard a single clear note sounded in another room. It was as though a bell had been struck.

Going to investigate, I discovered this chalice (at any rate, it is an object that seems more or less like a cup), which appears to be of silver or some shining alloy. It was standing on the only section of clear floor that I saw in the whole place, looking for all the whorl as if it had been set down there a moment before. I picked it up and tried to give it to Barsat. He reached for it but would not take it, although he hunted very industriously through the litter of leaves and twigs for something else.

My point, such as it is, is that I could not feel the happiness of the house, assuming it existed—as I believe it did. Nor could I feel any such emotion in the ruins on the island, the place where I fell into the pit through my eagerness to run down the greenbuck. Nor did I receive any gift at all there, save Krait's rescue.

★

★ ★

I must have spent three or four hours, if not longer, laboriously picking my way through the scrub. At last I hung my slug gun on the stub of a broken branch and sat down under one of the little trees with my back to the trunk, weary to the bone. Soon I let my eyes close (which they were only too willing to do) and abandoned myself to disappointment. I had hoped to reach the closest of the fires I had seen from my perch in the tree and catch a glimpse of the mysterious "Neighbors" about whom I had thought so much. I had also hoped to kill some animal that would furnish us with food. As I slumped there, I knew that both my hopes had been without foundation; I had exhausted myself and abandoned the comfort of the fire for nothing. I believe that I slept then, for a few minutes at least, and very likely for an hour or more.

A tap on my shoulder woke me. The face that looked into my own was invisible in the darkness, but I took no note of that, thinking that mine must be equally impossible to see. In much of the account I have written, I have set down my own words or the words others spoke to me. It a few cases I have been quite certain (at the time I wrote, if not subsequently) that I recalled them precisely. In most others, I have merely re-created them as you and I re-created so many of the verbal exchanges we put into our book, relying upon my knowledge of the speakers, and of the gist of what they had said. But we have come to a very different matter.

The tall, shadowed figure before me said, "Get up." To which I replied, "I'm sorry. I didn't mean any harm." Those are the exact words that he spoke, and the exact words with which I answered him. Everything the Neighbors said to me, and every reply I made, has remained in my memory from that night to this, as fresh as though it had been said only a few seconds ago. I do not know why this should be true, but I know that it is.

As for the reason I answered as I did, I can only say that upon awakening (if I had in fact been sleeping as sleep is generally accounted) I felt in a confused fashion that I had been trespassing, that this flat land with its covering of scrub was his, and that he might be understandably angry at finding I had ventured on it.

"Come with me," he said, and he helped me to stand up, grasping both my hands while lifting me under the arms. I ought to remember how his hands felt, I am sure—but I do not. My mind was on other things, perhaps.

He strode off through the trees, then turned to me and took my hand again to make certain that I was following him. I trotted after him, and in that way we walked some considerable distance, he always a stride in advance. I am what is ordinarily called a tall man now, and I believe that I must be about as tall as Silk was when you and I were young; but the Neighbor was a good deal taller, and a great deal taller than I was then, taller even than Hammerstone, though far more slender.

I trotted, as I have already written, because I could not keep pace with the Neighbor's four long legs by walking. But the branches of the twisted trees no longer raked my face, and I am quite certain that there was no place where I was forced to get out Sinew's knife and cut my way through. If there were anything in the whorl that could have convinced me that the entire episode was a dream, it would be that. It was not a dream however. I knew even then (exactly as I know now) that it was nothing of the kind.

I had hurried after the tall figure of the Neighbor so promptly that I had left my slug gun dangling from the low limb on which I had hung it, but I do not believe I was conscious of that at the time. I would not have been greatly disturbed, I think, if I had been.

By the time we reached their fire, I was panting and sweating despite the cold. There were more shadowy figures seated around it; they wore dark cloaks (or so it seemed to me at the time) and soft-looking hats with wide brims and low crowns. Most were sitting upright, but one lay at full length. He may have been dead; I do not believe he spoke or moved while I was there, and it is conceivable that he was not one of them at all but a fallen log or something of the sort, and that I only imagined that there was a sixth or a seventh who was lying down. If this sounds impossibly vague, you must understand that the fire did not illuminate him, or them, in the way I would have expected.

"Do you know who we are?" the shadowed figure who had come for me asked.

I replied, "My friend He-pen-sheep calls you his Neighbors."

One of the seated Neighbors inquired, "Who and what do you yourself think we are?"

I said, "I'm from New Viron, a town on the eastern shore of the sea, and I believe that you're the Vanished People. I mean, I believe that you're some of the people we call the Vanished People in New Viron."

Another said, "Then you must tell us who the Vanished People are." All this was in the Common Tongue.

"You are the people whose whorl this was before our landers came to it," I said. No one replied, so I continued, fumbling now and then as I tried to find the right words. "The *Whorl* up there," I pointed, "that was our whorl. This whorl, which we call Blue now, was your whorl. But we thought something had—had happened to you, because we never see you. Sometimes we find things you made, like that place on the island to the south, though I never did until I found that one. My son Sinew says that he and some other young men found an altar of yours in the forest, a stone table on which you used to sacrifice to the gods of this whorl."

I waited for one of them to speak.

"Since you haven't really vanished at all, we're—I'm very glad that you've let me live here with my family. Thank you. Thank you very much."

They said nothing, and after a while the one who had brought me to their fire indicated by a gesture, a motion of his fingers as if he were drawing words from my mouth, that I should go on talking.

I said, "I'm seeing you here tonight, I realize that, and I'm happy that you gave me this chance to express my gratitude. But I've never seen any of you before in twenty years, and most of us think that you're all dead. I'll try to tell them that's a mistake when I get back home."

As I spoke, I was reminded of Patera Remora's long, foolish face, and the dark and dusty little sellaria in which we had conversed, and I said, "I think perhaps our Prolocutor has seen you. He seems to know something, anyway. I hadn't realized it until now."

They remained silent.

I said, "We think your gods are still here. To tell the truth, we're afraid that they are. I've encountered one myself, your sea goddess. I don't know what you call her." As I spoke I looked from shadowy face to shadowy face. That was when I realized that they were not made even slightly more visible by the fire. The fire was there. I could see its light on my hands and feel its heat on my cheeks. I do not doubt that its light was shining on my face, as firelight always does; but it did not light them.

Lamely I finished, "Seawrack calls her the Mother. I mean the girl—the young lady that I call Seawrack. I mean, she used to."

The Neighbor to my left said, "That is one of her names." He had not spoken before.

"We're here now," I said, "we human men and women and children who came out of the *Whorl.*"

All of them nodded.

"And we're taking your whorl, or trying to. I don't blame you for being angry with us for that, but our gods are driving us out, and we have no place else to go. Except for me, I mean. I'm trying to get back to the *Whorl,* but not to stay. To bring back Patera Silk. Would you like me to tell you who Patera Silk is?"

The Neighbor who had awakened me said, "No. Someone you care about."

I nodded.

"Most of what you have said, we might say. This whorl of yours was ours. We, the remnant of our race, have abandoned it, giving it to no one and making no provision to keep it for ourselves. We found a way to leave and we left, seeking a new and a better home."

He turned from me, his face lifted to the western stars. "Some of you call the place where we are the Neighbor Whorl. It does not matter what we call it, or what we once called this one. This whorl is yours now. It is called Blue. It belongs to your race."

I stammered my thanks. I could set down everything I said, but there is really no way to describe how clumsily and haltingly I said it.

"We have brought you here as the representative of your race," he told me when I had finished. "You, here tonight, must speak for all of you. We have a question to ask. We cannot make you answer it, and if we could we would not. You will oblige us greatly by answering, even so. You say that you are grateful to us."

"For a whorl? For Blue? It's a godlike gift, like Pas giving us the *Whorl*. In a hundred years we couldn't repay you. Or a thousand. Never."

"You can. You yourself can repay us tonight, simply by answering. Will you?"

I said, "I'll try. I will if I can. What is the question?"

He looked around at the others. All those sitting upright nodded, I believe, although I cannot be sure. "Let me remind you again," the Neighbor who had brought me to their fire said, "that you will speak for your entire race. Every man of your blood. Every woman, and every child."

"I understand."

"I chose you, and I did so because I hoped to incline your race's judgment in our favor by choosing someone apt to be well disposed toward us." By a trifling gesture he indicated the ring that Seawrack had given me before we left the sloop. "If you wish to hold my choosing such a person against us, there is nothing to prevent you."

I said, "Certainly not."

"Thank you. Here is our question. Nearly all of us have abandoned this whorl, as I told you. Tonight we give it to you who call yourselves human, as I have also told you. Do you humans, the new possessors, object to our visiting it from time to time, as we are doing tonight?"

"Absolutely not," I said. Realizing that the words I had used could be understood in a sense opposite to the one that I intended, I added, "We have no objection whatsoever."

"From this whorl we sprang. You spoke of a hundred years, and of a thousand. There are rocks and rivers, trees and islands here that have been famous among us for many thousands of years. This is one such place. I ask you again, may we visit it, and the others?"

Trying to sound formal, I responded, "Come whenever you wish to, and stay for as long as you wish. Our whorl is your whorl."

"I ask a third time, and I will not ask again. You must answer for all your human kind. Guests are frequently awkward, embarrassing, and inconvenient. Your ways are not ours, and ours are not yours. They must often seem foreign, barbaric, and irrational to you. May we come?"

I hesitated, suddenly fearful. "Will you come as the inhumi do, to do us harm?"

There was stir among those seated around the fire. I could not be certain whether it was of amusement or disgust. "No," the Neighbor who had brought me said, "We will not come to do you harm, and we will help you against the inhumi when it lies in our power." The rest nodded.

I swallowed, although my mouth was as dry as my knees. "You are welcome. I know I've said it already, but I don't know how else to—all I can do is repeat it. You may visit this whorl you have given us whenever you want to, and go back to your own whorl whenever you want to, freely. I say that for every human man and every human woman, and even for our children, as humanity's representative."

They relaxed. I know how strange it will be for you to read this, Nettle darling, but they did. It was not anything I saw or heard; I could feel the tension drain away. They seemed a little smaller then, and perhaps they were. I still could not see their faces clearly, but they were not so deeply shadowed as they had been; it was as though they had been wearing veils I could not see, and they had drawn them back.

The Neighbor who had brought me stood up, and I did, too. "You spoke of a companion," he said, and he sounded almost casual. "Seawrack, you named her. You did not give us your own name, you who have been every being of your kind."

"My name is Horn." I offered him my hand.

He took it, and this time I felt his hand and remembered it. It was hard, and seemed to be covered with short, stiff hairs. Beyond that I will not say. "My name is Horn also," he told me. I felt that I was being paid an immense compliment, and did not know how to reply.

He pointed. He was tall, as I have said, but all his arms were too long even for someone as tall as he was. "Are you going back to your companion? To the fire where she and others lie sleeping?" She-pick-berry's little fire seemed very near when he pointed it out.

"I was hunting," I told him, "and I left my slug gun hanging on a tree. I'll have to get it first."

"There it is."

Looking where he pointed, I glimpsed it through the trees, and saw the red reflection of the flames in its polished and oiled steel. It seemed much too near to be mine, but I went to get it anyway, took it down from the broken limb upon which I had hung it, and slung it behind my right shoulder as I usually did. When I turned to wave to him and the others, they were not there.

Nettle, I know that you are going to think it was a dream, not so very different from the dream of you I had when I was in the pit, the dream in which you brought me a dipper of water. It was not. It seemed dreamlike at times, I admit; but I have had a great many dreams, as everyone has, and this was not one of them.

★

★ ★

I was lost when I could no longer see the Neighbors' fire. I knew that to return to He-pen-sheep's camp all that I had to do was walk uphill. It should have been easy; but again and again I found myself walking across level ground or down a gentle slope, and so toward the sea, when I felt certain that I had set out in the correct direction.

After two or three hours of this mazed wandering I realized that I ought to have been exhausted, but I was not even slightly tired. I was thirsty and ravenously hungry, so hungry that my teeth seemed as sharp as knives; but I was not fatigued, or footsore in the least.

Just about then I heard a twig snap, and the rattling and rustling of a big animal in the scrub. I had just warning enough to unsling my slug gun and push down the safety when Babbie snuffled, and I felt the familiar, waist-high probing of his soft snout. It was the second time I had nearly shot him, and it struck me as very funny, like one of those stories the men who sell us wood tell, in which some ridiculous situation occurs and recurs. I dropped to one knee, still laughing, rubbed Babbie's ears, and told him that I was very glad indeed to see him, as I was.

When I looked up, there was something looming above us so enormous and so dark that in that moment it seemed larger than a thunderhead. I remember (I shall never forget) seeing its long curved horns among the massed stars, and feeling that they were actually there, that when the beast moved they would extinguish stars as they might have poked out eyes. In another moment they vanished as it lowered its head to charge. I fired over Babbie's back, and pumped the action faster than I would have thought possible, the opening and shutting of the bolt a single sound like the slamming of a door, fired again without bringing the butt to my shoulder properly, and was knocked over in literal earnest, knocked sprawling amid the sand and roots. I remember the angry rattle of Babbie's tusks, and picking up the slug gun again and jerking the trigger without any idea whether it was pointed at the beast, at Babbie, or at my own foot, and wondering why it did not fire, too dazed to realize that I had not chambered a fresh round.

All that lasted only a second or two, I believe. I climbed to my feet and pumped the action again; and then, seeing nothing and hearing nothing except Babbie, pushed on the safety. You will accuse me of exaggeration, dearest Nettle, I know. But I actually tripped over one of the immense horns before I knew that the huge beast lay there. I nearly fell again, and would perhaps have fallen myself if I had not caught myself upon its fallen shoulder.

I had to explore it then with my hands, because it was black and lay in pitch blackness under those closely packed trees, none of which were much above five cubits high but all of which were still in full leaf in spite of the cold. I do not know what they are called, but their leaves are hard, thick, pointed, and deep green, not much longer than the second joint of my forefinger.

It was enormous, that beast, and I was still trying to grasp just how enormous it was when He-pen-sheep and his son burst out of the scrub, howling like a couple of hounds in their exultation. "Breakbull," they said over and over. "You kill breakbull, Horn." The son cut off the tail and tied it to my thong belt; it made me feel a complete fool, but that is their custom and I could not have taken it off or even implied that it was unwelcome without offending them. I thought then about what that other Horn had said concerning the customs of his race, and wondered what I had let us in for. Our own differ greatly from one town to the next, as everyone knows. Those of another race (I thought) must be very peculiar indeed. As they are.

At this point I have told you everything of interest. I am going to make the rest very short and so finish writing about all this before I go to bed.

He-pen-sheep and his son skinned the breakbull in the dark with a little not very valuable help from me. I cut off a haunch, and tried to shoulder it without getting too much blood on the slug gun (which I had hung across my back with the butt up), at which I was not very successful. The two of them carried the skin back to their lean-to, and it was so heavy that the son fell once under its weight and was deeply shamed by it. As for me, I brought back ten times more meat than was needed to feed all seven of us. I say seven because Babbie ate at least as much as the hungriest, who was without a doubt your loving husband.

I have been tempted to omit this next observation, and have already pushed my account past it; but whether it fits here or not, I am going to tell you something very strange. On the way back to He-pen-sheep's camp, he and his son often had a good deal of difficulty working their huge roll of hide through the tangle of scrub that had obstructed me so often. I, who stood taller than either of them and had the massive haunch (it must have weighed as much as the twins) over my shoulder, should have been at least as inconvenienced by the angular, wind-twisted trees.

But I was not. My face and arms, which were already a mass of scratches from their limbs, were never scratched again. Although the haunch I carried was brushed now and again by leaves, it was never caught, not even momentarily. I cannot explain this. The limbs certainly did not move aside for me. The sky was gray by the time we were finished skinning the breakbull, and I would certainly have seen them if they had, and heard them, too. I can only say that it seemed to me that no matter in which direction I looked, I could see a clear path for me and my burden. And when I went forward, that was what it proved to be.

We reached camp about sunrise. She-pick-berry leaped up shouting and woke her sick daughter and Seawrack, which neither appeared to mind. We ate, and although all of us ate a great deal I am sure I ate the most of all, so much that He-pen-sheep was open in his astonishment and admiration. Even the daughter, who had been so ill the evening before, ate as much as would make a good big serving on one of our big dinner plates back on Lizard.

Afterward, She-pick-berry showed us how she would smoke the rest, making a sort of rack for thin strips of meat out of green twigs. We agreed that He-pen-sheep and his son would help Seawrack and me by bringing as much meat as they could carry to the sloop. In return, they would receive the hide (which She-pick-berry was already scraping by the time we left their camp) and the remainder of the breakbull.

Escorted by Babbie, we four returned to the carcass, cut loads of meat, and made our way through the scrub to the sea, striking the beach only a short walk from the sloop. Krait was aboard and greeted our arrival with ill-natured sarcasm, twitting Seawrack and me for being as bloody as inhumi and laughing inordinately at his own witticisms. Before we realized that Patera Quetzal had been an inhumu, Nettle, I would have thought that a sense of humor was an exclusively human possession. Associating with Krait made me wish more than once that it were so; he had an overdeveloped sense of humor, and as ugly a one as I have ever met with in all my travels. Since then I have learned that the Neighbors, who treated me with so much solemnity that night, are notorious for theirs.

When He-pen-sheep and his son had helped us get the sloop back into the water, and had waded out to her with the loads of meat that they had brought and washed themselves in the sea, he drew me aside. Indicating Krait with a jerk of his head, he told me, "No like," and I acknowledged that I did not like him either.

"You beat, Horn?"

I shook my head.

"Big beat," he advised me. Then, "You talk Neighbor?"

I nodded.

"What say?"

I considered. At no time had the other Horn or any other Neighbor asked me to keep our conversation confidential, or put me under any sort of oath. "We changed blood," I told He-pen-sheep. "I," I touched my chest, "for you and all the other men, and for all the women and all the children, too. The Neighbor for all the Neighbors."

He-pen-sheep stared at me intently.

"Because I spoke for you, I can tell you what we said. We agreed that where men are, Neighbors can come as well." I waved my arm at the horizon, indicating (I hope) that I intended the whole whorl. "They can visit us in peace and friendship."

"Big good!" He nodded enthusiastically.

"I think so too," I told him. "I really do."

As we hauled up the sails, he and his son waved farewell to us from the beach, and when we had so much sea-room that I could no longer distinguish one from the other, I could still hear them calling, *"You kill breakbull, Horn!"*

★

★ ★

I had thought to end this part of my account with the words you just read, Nettle darling, the final words that I wrote last night; but there is more to tell, and it will fit in here better than anywhere else.

When we left He-pen-sheep and his son on the beach, I supposed that we would never see them again. That was not the case. In justice to them I ought to tell you here, since I neglected to do it last night, that when we had gone back to the breakbull's carcass I had been much taken with its horns, all four longer than the blades of swords, sharp, black-tipped, elaborately grooved, and cruelly curved. After examining and admiring them, I had asked He-pen-sheep what he was going to do with them, and he had explained to me all of the many uses to which horn can be put, things that I ought to have learned long ago, since I am named for that substance.

Krait, Babbie, and I were more than sufficient to work the sloop under the light airs that were all we were granted even when we were well out to sea, so Seawrack set out to smoke as much of the meat as she could. She had prepared for the task by cutting a good supply of green shoots before we put out, and she trimmed them and fitted them together with her one hand as cleverly as She-pick-berry had with two; but our firewood was soon exhausted. As a result, Krait and I went ashore again before we rounded the point of the big sandspit I have called the Land of Fires and collected more.

(It was then, I believe, when I found myself yet again trying to cut wood with Sinew's knife, that I resolved once and for all that I would acquire an axe or a hatchet at the first opportunity, or at least a bigger, heavier knife, if no axe or hatchet was available.)

By the time we had gathered as much dry wood as we could find without ranging far inland and loaded it into the sloop, wading out with bundles of it held clear of the water, the Short Sun was slipping away behind the distant peaks, and even Krait (who had done next to nothing) said that he was tired. Seawrack and I were close to exhaustion.

There was no good anchorage along that very exposed stretch of the coast, and no place suited to beaching, but I decided to remain where we were until morning. Since the weather had been good and was not actually threatening even then, I judged the danger to be less than that of sailing an unknown shore by night. I took Krait aside and warned him that He-pen-sheep and his son had been suspicious of him, which I believe he knew already, and suggested that he go elsewhere if he intended to hunt. He pointed out that he could scarcely use hunting to justify his absence to Seawrack as he had before—we had far more meat than we needed. I know how you feel about the inhumi, Nettle; and why you feel as you do. If you were looking over my shoulder as I write this, you would declare in the strongest possible terms that no one ought to crack jokes with such creatures; and certainly the bond that was to grow between Krait and me in the lander had not even begun to form. But I still felt grateful to him for rescuing me, and so I proposed that I tell Seawrack that he was hunting for napkins. He laughed and we separated, leaving me under the impression that he would remain with us on the sloop that night.

I took the first watch, and Seawrack the second. Krait was to take the third; he was to awaken me, of course, for the fourth and last watch of the night.

Here for art's sake I should insert some account of dreams in which the Vanished People figured, I suppose; or perhaps reveal whispered confidences exchanged with Seawrack. In fact there were no dreams of any kind and no whispers. I roused her with considerable difficulty when it was her watch, and when she returned to lie beside me, leaving Krait on watch, she did not disturb me in the least.

It was Babbie who actually woke us both, squealing with alarm and nuzzling our faces. One of the gusty northwest winds that are so common in that region had set in, and the sloop had dragged her anchor until it found a solid hold in deep water and was about to pull her under. I was able to cut the cable just in time to keep her from swamping.

We had rounded the point of the spit at sunrise, and were heeling sharply under a reefed mainsail and making excellent time when Krait found us. I saw him, lit by the rising sun and carried swiftly along by the wind, at a height that few birds ever reach. Seawrack, I believe, did not.

He was in a quandary, as I realized immediately. If he landed on the sloop, Seawrack would know that he was no ordinary boy at the very least, and would in all likelihood see through his disguise. If he landed on shore and tried to signal us to pick him up, we might not see him—or might, as he would certainly have imagined, pretend not to.

He solved his problem by landing on shore well in advance of us and swimming out to the sloop. I saw him, threw him a rope and hauled him on board, shook him, gave him as violent a tongue-lashing as I am capable of, and followed it by grabbing him by the back of his tunic (which had been one of mine), peeling it off him, and beating him with the rope's end until my arm ached. When the wind had moderated and we could talk privately, he reproached me for it, reminding me that he had rescued me from the pit and insisting, erroneously in my view, that we had sworn eternal friendship.

"I have been your friend ever since you got me out," I told him. "Have you been mine?"

He managed to meet my eyes with a defiant stare that I found more familiar than it should have been, but could find nothing to say.

"You very nearly sunk this boat. We saved it, but if Babbie hadn't roused us it would have gone down. I don't suppose that Seawrack could drown, but I can."

He said, "The weather was fine when I left and I would have come back before the end of my watch."

"I would have died before the end of your watch. I would have been dead, and the sloop sunk, and my mission to the *Whorl* a total failure. I would be completely justified if I put my knife in you this minute."

My hand was on it as I spoke, and he took a step backward. There was fear in his eyes. "You've hurt me as much as you could already."

"Not half as much," I told him, "and I've kept my promise even though you've broken yours. I threw you that rope; and if I hadn't punished you severely for what you did, Seawrack would have known that you couldn't possibly be what you pretend to be."

He hissed at me. The hiss of an inhumu is at once a more sinister sound and an uglier one than the hissing of any serpent that I have ever heard.

"If one of my own sons had done what you did, I'd treat him exactly the way I treated you," I told him. "If that isn't what you want, what is it?" I did not say that at least one of my sons would have exhibited the same poisonous hatred; but I could not suppress the thought.

I put him to work in good earnest after that, something I had not done before, bailing, trimming sail and snugging up the standing rigging, tidying the sail locker, coiling and stowing the rope I had thrown him, and bailing again. I watched him every moment and shouted at him whenever he showed signs of slacking; and when he begged for mercy I started him scraping paint.

It was not long afterward that Seawrack spotted He-pen-sheep and his son standing on the beach with the head of the breakbull held upright between them. We were already some distance past them, but I put up the helm and ran down the wind until we were within hailing distance. He-pen-sheep cupped his hands around his mouth. *"You take! You kill breakbull, Horn!"*

Seawrack glanced at me, her lovely eyes wide. "They want to give you that head." Standing upon its muzzle, it was nearly as tall as the son, and the spread of its horns exceeded that of my outstretched arms, as I had found out when we had returned to the carcass.

"You'll have to take it," Krait told me, looking up from his scraping; and of course he was right.

Besides, I wanted it. You will not understand, Nettle my dearest darling, although perhaps some others who read this will. It had seemed a grim irony when He-pen-sheep's son had tied the breakbull's tail to the belt of the crude leather garment his father had made for me. I had wanted the head—yes, even then—if only to prove to myself that I had actually done what I remembered doing—and the tail seemed only a sort of mockery of that desire, some god's cruel jest to punish me for my dawning self-satisfaction. You will ask now, and very reasonably, whether I did not want the head of the wallower I shot a few weeks ago as well. I did, but not nearly so acutely; and since no one talked of retaining the heads as trophies, I kept my peace.

When after considerable labor we had the breakbull's head on board and had waved good-bye once again, Krait took great pleasure in enunciating the obvious. "You can glory in it for a day or three, if the flies don't get at it. But after that, it will have to go over the side, or we will."

I muttered something about sawing off the horns, if I could trade for a saw.

"You could have shot them off back there." He pointed with the scraper. "It would have saved a lot of work."

Seawrack asked indignantly, "How much work do you think they did, cutting it off and carrying it to the other side, when they couldn't even be sure that we'd be going this way?" (I had questioned He-pen-sheep about a big river to the north the evening before, but that was surely not the time to mention it.) She turned to me. "Would you settle for the skull with the horns still on it, and no smell?"

I assured her that I would, and gladly.

"Then all we have to do is tow it behind the boat. Not too long a rope, because you don't want it to go too deep. I'll show you."

She did, and I surprised myself and them by lifting the huge thing and carrying it to the stern for her. We balanced it on the gunwale, tied a noose in the rope that Krait had coiled and stowed a couple of hours earlier, tightened it over the horns, and pushed the head overboard. Although we were still making respectable time, it seemed to sink like a stone, and Seawrack had me shorten the rope.

By evening, we were accompanied by a flock (I cannot bring myself to call them a school) of the strangest and most beautiful fish that I have ever seen, each a little bit longer than my hand. They are luminous, as so many fish here are, although I cannot recall any luminous fish in the market in Old Viron. Their heads are scarlet, their bellies an icy white, and their backs, dorsal fins, and tails are blue. All four of their cubit-long pectoral fins (with which they not only glide but fly like birds or insects) are gauzy, and invisible at night. When they flitted around the sloop after shadelow like so many oversized and multicolored fireflies, it really seemed that we were sailing far beneath the waves, with some convenient current swelling our mainsail. Seawrack assured me that they would strip the skull of the last scrape of flesh in a few days, and they did.

And now good night, Nettle my own darling. My night thoughts circle your bed, glowing but invisible, to observe and to protect you. Never doubt that I love you very dearly.

12

War

I am not sure how long it has been since I wrote all this about the breakbull's head. I might guess, so many days or so many weeks, but what does it matter? A week of war is a year, a month of war a lifetime.

I have been wounded. That is why I am back here now, and why I have had the leisure to read so much of this tissue of half-truths. (Of lies I have told to myself.) And it is why I have the leisure to write.

My wound throbs. A physician has given me a pretty little pot containing some dirty, sticky stuff I am to chew, the dried sap of some plant or other. When I chew it my wound is a drum beaten softly very far away, but I cannot think. Everything flows together, dancing with Seawrack in the swirling waves of my thought and taking on unimaginable colors—the play of candlelight on Pig's blind face as he ate soup, Babbie rushing upon the devil-fish, Nettle screaming with pain and relief as Hide followed Hoof. If I were to take a pinch from the pink porcelain pot now, the wall of this room would blush for my self-pity.

I do not believe I have written this by daylight before. Why not say that was why I had not noticed how much falsehood is in it.

Where to begin?

Nothing about my travels with Seawrack and Krait today. I have too much to recount that is recent. Let us begin with the war.

No, let me spit my bile. Then I will begin with the river. With the Nadi, the town of Han upriver, Han's invasion, and the first fighting.

Bile: I finished reading this one hour ago, appalled by my own hypocrisy. Particularly sickened by the last few words I wrote before the outbreak of the war. Did I really think that I could lie like that to myself, and make myself believe it? While all the time I was imagining myself Silk, forever thinking of what Silk would do or say? Silk would have been ruthlessly honest with himself, and worse.

No more. My hand was shaking so badly that I laid down the quill just now, raging against myself. I wanted to get up and retrieve my azoth, to press it against my own breastbone and feel the demon beneath my thumb. Wanted to, I say, but I am too weak to leave my chair. Moti came in with a little brass kettle and mint tea, and I could have killed her, not because I have anything against the sweet child, but as a substitute for myself. I handed her my dagger and told her to stab me between the shoulder blades, because I lacked the courage to drive in the point. Bent my head and shut my eyes. What would I have done if she had obeyed?

Died.

My dagger lies on the carpet now not two cubits from this chair, long, straight, and strong. Thick at the back so that it will not bend when I stab someone.

Someone, I say, and mean someone else.

Not stab myself. I will not do that. If I need more courage than I have to live, I will pretend to have it and live anyway. I did that on the battlefield. How frightened I was afterward, and how ridiculous I feel now!

My hands shook. It was all that I could do to keep my voice steady, and perhaps it was not, or not always. I acted the part of a hero. That is to say, I acted as it seemed to me I would have if I had actually possessed dauntless courage. They believed me. What fools we were, all of us, losing battle after battle!

But O you gods of the Short Sun, what a thing it is! What a thing it is to see frightened men stop and reload, and fight again!

They were too many for us. All you had to do was listen to the shooting, three and four shots from them for each one of ours.

Choora. That is the word they use here for this kind of a dagger. I have been trying to think of it. *Choora.* It sounds like one of my wives, and no doubt it could be a woman's name as well, a woman slim and straight, with brown cheeks and golden bangles in her ears and nose. Loyally, Choora remained at my side when we charged and when we broke; and if she never drew a single drop of blood, it was my fault and not hers. All hail Princess Choora!

I traded for the big chopping knives in Pajarocu. Maybe I should have given each a name, but I never did. If Choora is a princess, they were a washerwoman and a maid of all work; but there are times when a sturdy girl who will turn her hand to whatever may be needed is better than a princess with a coral pommel.

A strange expression—"turn her hand." Did somebody travel once with a woman who had only one arm? Yes, and it was I. And did he sleep with her, and make gentle love to her as I did in our cozy corner under the little foredeck? Were neither of them ever quite able to forget that he had raped her once?

I have tried hard to punish myself for that, and certain other things. No more. Let the Outsider punish me; we deceive ourselves when we think that we can measure out justice to ourselves. I wanted to end my guilt. What was just about that? I should feel guilty. I deserve it.

I should feel a lot more guilty about having had other women while I was (as I still am) wed to poor Nettle. When I read that business about my thoughts flying around her bed, I was sickened.

Sickened!

For all our lives I have been a false lover and a false friend. I would beg her to forgive me if I could. If only I could. I do not dream about her anymore.

Is that bile enough? No, but there will be more later as the occasion demands. As the mood strikes. Let us move on to the river.

That is what I would have called this half-baked book of mine, if only I had thought of it in time: *The River.* The title would stand equally for the great river on Shadelow—the river on whose bank we found Pajarocu—and for our own much smaller Nadi. (Another wife, a temptress in a swirling skirt, with flashing eyes and hurrying feet, sensuous and tempestuous, suddenly languid and lazily thrilling; a woman like gold at evening, full of blood and crocodiles.)

Anyway, it was my fault. No doubt it always is.

I had set some men to work to tame Nadi's Lesser Cataracts. First, because I knew we would become richer if we could trade more with the towns nearer the sea, and second because we had men who needed work and could find none except at harvest. To raise the money, I made every foreign merchant who came to our market pay a tax, so much for each man and so much for each beast.

I also lopped the heads of two men who had collected the tax for me and kept part of the money for themselves. I was proud then, and talked to myself about "iron justice." Yes, iron justice, and I killed two men who had been boys in the *Whorl* when I myself was a boy there. I do not mean I killed them with my own hands; I did not, but they died at my order, and would have lived without it. What else can you call it? Steely justice from the big, curved blade of my executioner's sword. How does he feel, that hulking, hard-faced man, slaying men who have done him no harm? Chopping off hands? No worse than I, I hope. Better. I would not want an innocent man to feel the way I do.

I have been away a long time. Will my wives expect me to sleep with them tonight? What will I say to them?

The work went far faster than I had imagined. Our men dug, they blew rock to rubble with powder from the armory, and soon there was a second Nadi, slower, longer, and narrower, looping around the rapids, a Nadi only just deep enough for small boats; but Nadi herself is taking care of that, and quickly, cutting into the red clay and bearing it off. She is still swift in both her divided selves, but not so swift in her new one that boats cannot be hauled around the rapids with bullocks. The Man of Han asked us to cut another such channel around the Cataracts upriver so that boats that reached Gaon could reach Han also. Our merchants were against it, as was only to be expected.

So was I. Hari Mau and I made a trip with the surveyors to look at possible routes, and everything was much worse—steeper slopes, and a lot more rock. All of us agreed it would take a long time and might never be suitable for boats of any size, which would have to be hauled along a lengthy ladder of sharp bends. I told the Man of Han that he would have to pay our workers, and that the work would take years. He offered to send men of his own, which we refused.

★

★ ★

As you see, I have made the old design. Does it mean that I am going to continue this folly? No doubt. Nettle will never read it, I know. Neither will my sons. Or I should say, neither will the sons I left behind on Lizard Island. [Nettle has read it. So have Hoof and I.—Hide]

Neither will my sons, except, perhaps, for Sinew. It was very strange—I must remember to write more about this—to come to Pajarocu knowing that Sinew had been there before us. Can he have followed me from Green to the *Whorl*, and from the *Whorl* back here? Surely not. Yet stranger things have happened. I almost hope he has.

Bahar came in to tell me we have been pushed back again, nearly to the town. It was an interruption, but not enough of an interruption for me to draw the three whorls again. Or so I judge.

He is a thin and nervous man, is Bahar. How did he get such a name, which should mean that he is fat? He combed his scraggly beard with his fingers, rolling his eyes to let me know that all is lost, the town will fall within a day or two, we men will be slaughtered like goats, our children enslaved, our women made off with. I chirped at him like a cricket, and heartened him a little, I think. Poor Bahar! What can it be like to be a good man, yet always expect bad luck, and a whorl of thieves and murderers?

I have a wife from Han, if the others haven't killed her already. We call her Chota. The name (it is "small") fits her.

Too cruel, maybe.

Just talking to Bahar has made me hungry. He always looks so thin and starved. I cannot remember the last time I was hungry.

★

★ ★

Chandi was slow when I rang the bell. To punish her I told her I wanted someone else to bring my food. If only I had thought, I would have realized that she was afraid I was going to ask her to kill me. Moti will have told her, as I should have realized; they tell each other everything. At any rate, inspiration struck. Everyone has a good idea now and then, I suppose, even me. Nettle had most of ours, except for the paper.

(And yet, the paper was our one *great* idea.)

She wrote a clearer hand than I did, too, but hated thinking everything out in sentences and paragraphs; left to her, our book would have been nothing but summary.

Like this one. I can hear her say it.

So Chota brought in my wine and fish and fruit, the fresh and the pickled vegetables, the pilav, and the thin panbread that everyone eats here at every meal, as round and flat and sallow as her face. She remained to serve, and I soon realized that she was hungrier than I was. They have not let her eat, or kept her too upset to eat.

I made her sit beside me and scooped up some pilav for her, little balls of boiled dough mixed with chopped nuts and raisins, and made her eat it. Soon she was talking of home and begging me to keep her here with me. She told me her real name, which I have forgotten already. It means music played at shadelow.

I talked to her about the war, and said I hoped that Han would welcome her back if Gaon fell. She insists that her sister-wives would surely kill her the moment they heard I was dead, and that if they did not her own people would cut off her breasts.

What is the matter with us? How can we do such things to each other?

She is asleep now. Poor, poor child! I hope the gods send her peaceful dreams.

Bahar wanted me to sacrifice to Sphigx. Maybe I will. That might hearten our people, too.

It is a weary work, to write about everything. Briefly then, and I will sleep beside Chota.

She begged me to take her with me, so I did. She had never ridden on an elephant. Our troopers were overjoyed to see me, or at any rate they were polite enough to pretend that they were. I think they thought I was dead and that nobody would tell them. I left Chota in the long tent on the elephant's back and borrowed a horse, and rode up and down our line, smiling and blessing them. Poor, poor spirits! Most had never handled anything more dangerous than a pitchfork. They are brave, but few have any idea what they are about. Their officers have read about Silk, just as Hari Mau and Bahar have, and that is why I am here. These poor troopers have only heard tales—fantastic tales for the most part. Yet they cheered for the one-eyed man with white hair.

We have elephants, but they will not trample our enemies. The booming of the guns frightens them, just as it does me. The elephants frighten our horses, who are not afraid of guns. What a whorl!

Elephants frighten our prisoners as well, as I soon saw. We have twenty-two, everything from grandfathers with wrinkled faces to boys who cannot yet have reached puberty. When I saw that they were afraid of my elephant, I had three of them sent up the ladder one by one, so that I could question them upon its back. Chota helped me greatly at times, explaining the customs and idioms of Han. She had brought along the pickled parsnips, pilav, and some other food; our prisoners' mouths watered as they watched her eat. They are as hungry as she was, I think. Food is scarce, so Hari Mau has allowed them very little.

Now that I come to think of it, I was told that one had been captured only an hour or so before we got there.

★

★ ★

I have been busy all day, trying to catch up on matters that should have been attended to while I was with our troopers. (What would I not give for Hammerstone now! Olivine, lend us your father, please.) Most important: I have sent Bahar and Namak downriver in a boat, each with his little case of cards. Bahar is to buy rice and beans—whatever is cheap and filling—and he is just the man for it.

Namak will try to hire men who will fight alongside us. They will have to be men who have their own slug guns, since guns are in very short supply. (I wonder how they are coming in New Viron, making their own? Certainly the one that Marrow gave me was serviceable enough.) It is probably for the best—we must have men who can shoot. Hunting can be a cruel amusement and it often is; but it is the best training in the whorl for a trooper.

I hope Bahar sends something back for us soon. Food is very scarce, and of course everything north along the Nadi is gone, all those rich farms.

Hari Mau came from the front to confer. It is an hour's ride now. He had made sketch maps. Our left flank is quite secure, he says, an impenetrable marshy forest. (What can a man who has not been on Green know about that?) Our right is on the river, and in spite of all that he says I am worried about both.

He was worried about Chota, so much so that I made her go back to the women's quarters for a while. Nobody trusts her, poor child.

Nobody but me.

Prisoners in despair, he says.

★

★ ★

Even war has benefits, even being wounded and more than half expected to die. Maybe nothing real is wholly good or bad. (But *real* is not the word. *Tangible*?) I still long for home and Nettle's pardon, should she be so moved as to give it; but the pain in my side kills the pain of that, and I have been mercifully busy. Which is the god of busyness? Scylla, perhaps, if there is one. Scylla tossing up waves to dance in sunlight and starlight. I have written so much about our life on the sloop, and nothing about that, yet aside from Seawrack of the golden hair it is what I recall the best from all those days—the ceaseless, restless waves gleaming with reflected stars and dyed by Green. What blessings mere busyness brings us!

I have hatched a plan and have been seeing that it is carried out for half the day. We have been driven back again and again. Several of our river workers were injured by flying rock, and one died. Both those are facts. We are trying to combine them.

A note reports that four of our prisoners have killed themselves. This must be stopped. I have ordered the remaining prisoners brought here to me by noon tomorrow. I want another look at them.

*

* *

Talked to the prisoners with Chota present as before. At first we learned nothing new. I ordered a good hot meal prepared for them and spoke to them again afterward, and was lucky enough to get to the bottom of it.

First, food is scarce on their side. It must be brought from Han on pack animals, horses and mules, because of the Cataracts. They think that we have plenty, and that they have been starved on Hari Mau's orders.

Second, they think the whole war is a plot to make them lose their land. They are small farmers for the most part, just like our own troopers, and one of them accused Evensong (Chota) to her face, calling her the Man's woman and making her furiously angry. She tried to get me to have him killed. I told her he is precious to me, and have asked for a truce instead.

*

* *

Truce agreed to. I sent Rajya Mantri to tell the Hannese we wanted to exchange prisoners, all that we have for all they have. They would not agree, but we got eighteen of ours for eighteen of theirs. The important thing is that those men are back where they can talk to their fellow troopers. The retreat is all arranged, and should be just far enough to get them over the buried kegs.

At every odd moment I find myself thinking about that "impenetrable" forest, and remembering the forest at the mouth of the big river, the jungles on Green, and so forth—the tangled trees on the big sandspit I was writing about before Han invaded us.

When we found the mouth of the river, all three of us thought that the search was almost over. I got out the map Wijzer had drawn for me and showed it to Krait, and he agreed to search for Pajarocu whenever he went hunting. Supposing that we would be there in another week at most, Seawrack and I agreed that she would remain behind to look after the sloop. I explained at some length that a great deal might still go wrong even if the lander flew into the sky without crashing and told her to assume me dead if I had not returned within a month.

It has been nearly two years now, I believe. More, perhaps. How is it that her song reaches me?

The river was broad and slow, but after three days' sailing it became obvious that the stretch before the first fork was a good deal longer than Wijzer had indicated. When I saw a town (a cluster of huts, really) on the south bank, I put in there, intending to barter for blankets and a few other things we needed, and sail on that day. We ended by staying four. Once you stop, you and your journey are at the mercy of the god of the place. I have learned that, at least, from all my traveling. Nevertheless, I must stop this writing right now and get a little sleep.

Wound healing, I believe. I feel better (less feverish) and there is certainly less inflammation. Less drainage, too. Phaea be thanked. Or whomever.

★

★ ★

All the temple bells are ringing. A great day! We have driven them back.

The retreat did not go quite as planned, but it was good enough. I stood upon the head of my elephant and watched the whole battle, although everyone said that was too dangerous, even Mahawat, who drives him for me and stood beside me dancing with excitement.

The Hannese rushed forward as we had hoped, waving knives and swords, yelling and shooting. Our men ran, then turned and fired when they reached their new positions. That was the point that had worried me. I had been afraid they would keep on running, but only a handful did. There was a hot fight then for about an hour before the buried powder went off.

They were very big charges, much bigger than we had ever used in blasting rock, and we had packed jagged flints around the kegs. The plan was to have our men rush the enemy after the explosions, and send in the horsemen only if the enemy broke; but Hari Mau sent them in at once, seeing that the enemy would break at once. It was very strange for me, standing high up there in front of the long platform that holds my silk tent, because I could see that the horsemen should go immediately. I had no way to give the order, but trumpets blew as if I had, with the final notes lost in the thunder of the hooves, and after that it was lances and swords and needlers and dust, the flag dipping and leaning and always seeming about to fall, but advancing! Advancing! Advancing!

And blood, always blood, although there was great deal of that already.

But the important point is that I must not let myself get caught like that again. I must always have some means of relaying my orders immediately, or if not immediately as fast as possible.

I have sent for the armorer. He is to bring me a needler and several short swords, so that I can choose the one I like. We need slug guns and ammunition badly, but we have plenty of knives and swords at least.

As I penned that last, it struck me that I ought to send for the head gardener as well. I have been wondering how I could get a spade, and a bar of some kind to pry up the stones. He can supply them both, and it should be safer than having Evensong buy them for me in the market. I have seen him at work often, a silent old man with a faded blue headcloth and a big white mustache. Both the younger gardeners are away fighting, and he will be having a difficult time of it, poor old fellow. He should be eager to get on my good side.

This may be the most dangerous thing I have ever done. But I am going to do it. Not tonight, however, because the weather is clear and Green will light up everything. On the first dark night, I shall see how effectual Krait's secret is. I will be confiding it to someone who knows it already, after all. That cannot be betrayal.

The town on the river consisted of twenty or thirty rough wooden houses and a hundred or so crude little huts covered with bark and hides. Nobody there would sell anything except on market day. I had never heard of such a custom, and went around complaining, and demanding things that I did not get. Eventually Krait and Seawrack persuaded me that it was better to be patient, to get to know the people and find out all we could. We ate Seawrack's smoked meat, mostly, chopped and stewed with pepper and some local wild garlic I found, and drank river water before we found the little stream from which the people of the town got their own drinking water. I felt sure that the muddy river water would make us sick, but it did not.

The people looked like He-pen-sheep and She-pick-berry for the most part, lean and muscular with bandy legs, big shoulders, and noses like hawks. They all have long, straight hair, glossy black and really quite beautiful. All the women braid it; so do some of the men. Their complexions are dark yet translucent, so that the brown is touched with pink and red from the blood beneath; it can be very attractive, particularly in the children and the young women.

They are silent and suspicious in the presence of strangers, although the women seem to chatter incessantly when they are by themselves. Like She-pick-berry, they frequently pretended not to understand the Common Tongue. I was angry already (no doubt they saw it) and that made me angrier still.

Another traveler, also bound for Pajarocu he said, told me that the town (it was called Wichote) was the last outpost of civilization. I asked how he could be sure of that if he had gone no farther, and he claimed that he had gone much farther, together with a young man older than my son (by which he meant Krait) whom he had rescued at sea.

"He looked like you." The traveler grinned. "But with more hair."

Here I would like very much to be able to say that I knew at once, but it would not be true. I asked whether the young man he had rescued had known the way to Pajarocu.

"He thought he did," the traveler said, "and got us lost a couple of thousand times."

Thinking that the young man's information might be of value, I asked to speak with him.

"He wouldn't come back with me." The traveler grinned again. "I wouldn't worry about him, if I were you."

"I won't, if he's not in Wichote; but I'd like to have a talk with him. You and he separated, up the river? How far was it?"

The traveler shrugged. "Two weeks' travel, or about that."

"You left him alone?"

"Sure. He'll be all right. He's a little raw at the edges, but you can't break him. Or bend him very much, either. And he's got a needler. He can take care of himself."

We parted, and he must have gone back to his boat and put out, afraid that I would reach Pajarocu before him and take the last seat. (He was not on the lander, however.) After it occurred to me—very late—that the young man he had traveled with had certainly been Sinew, I was never able to find the traveler again, although I walked up and down those muddy little streets for hours and looked in at every open door, questioning everyone who would talk to me. When at last I accepted the fact that he had gone, I went back to the sloop, half minded to leave Seawrack ashore for the time being and go after him. But if I had caught up with him, and he had told me that the young man's name had indeed been Sinew, what would I have learned? And what could I do when I had confirmed it, except continue searching for Pajarocu, which Sinew was searching for as well? We would meet in Pajarocu, wherever that was—or we would not meet at all.

Seawrack was ashore then, as I have said; we had not yet come to terms with the intractable necessity of waiting until market day, and she had taken a few of my silver trinkets in the hope of trading them for warmer and more durable clothing. I sat with Babbie in the stern of the sloop, thinking back upon the days when Sinew was small and looking at the big, slow river until shadelow. Now, if I shut my eyes, I see it still, a far larger and more sluggish river than our Nadi, with wide stretches of mud visible in many places. The setting of the Short Sun on Shadelow is never as dramatic as it is here.

I ought to have said the setting of the Short Sun as seen in and around New Viron—on the coast, in other words. Here the sun comes up out of the mountains late in the morning, and sets among mountains, too, briefly painting their snowy peaks with purple and flame (or is that the brush of Wijzer's Maker?) and giving us a long twilight.

In New Viron, the Short Sun sinks into the sea, a wonderful sight when the weather is calm. Nettle used to make me go out onto the beach to watch it with her, and I was impatient much too often. I would give a great deal to stand beside her once more and hold her hand while we wait for the momentary flash of limpid emerald that appears as if by sorcery as the last fragment of the Short Sun vanishes behind the swelling waves, a green so pure that it cannot possibly have anything to do with the evil, festering whorl of that name. I, who never saw the sea until I was almost grown, did not come to love it until I left it. So, too, with Seawrack, or so I have reason to believe. The sea did not call to her while she lived in it as the—

I do not know what word to use.

The pet? The adopted daughter? The hook-studded lure of the old sea goddess? Very likely she was all three. Why should the sea call to her then? It had her. Only after she had left it, only when she was trying to put it behind her in that crude and dirty little village on the bank of the great river, did the sea sing to Seawrack as Seawrack herself sings to me tonight.

Up there I wrote that I could close my eyes and see the great river again. I can, and hear it again, too: the nearly stagnant water whispering as it slips past, the narrow little boat that holds only a single paddler, the mournful cries of the snake-necked seabirds (for there were still seabirds aplenty, although we were leagues from the sea), the rising mist, and the distant howl of a felwolf. The vast and empty flatness of it, so lonely and so desolate.

All that has vanished now. When I try to summon it again as I sit here between the lampstands, I see only Seawrack, the long, supple line of her legs, hips, and back.

Only the thrust of her pink-tipped breasts and the whiteness of her flesh, when first she left the sea.

★

★ ★

The head gardener came yesterday after I had stopped writing. He was tired and so was I, yet we talked for over an hour. I believe I can trust him if I can trust anybody; and I have already resolved to trust Chota, so as to have somebody to keep watch. I might not be able to move the stone by myself, and might reopen the wound in my side if I try. Two of us should be able to move it pretty easily.

If I am any judge, Mehman is not one to flinch, but I wish that Krait and Sinew were here with me.

The armorer came this morning with a dozen swords, most far too long, and no needler. He had given all the needlers out to our officers, he said. I told him that he had kept one for himself and ordered him to give it to me, but he wept and groveled, swearing that he had not. One of my guards may have one. I hope so. If not, the short sword and Choora, with Hyacinth's azoth hidden under my tunic, *to be used only in the gravest extreme.*

Tonight I called a meeting: wives, guards, and servants. I told them that I was going out tomorrow and taking Mahawat and the remaining guards with me. (There are only half a dozen.) Pehla will be in charge, as she was when I was upriver before I was wounded. Mehman and his assistants are to guard the palace. (I solemnly handed out the rest of the swords to the old men and boys he has found to help him.) We leave at shadeup, so I had better get some sleep.

★

★ ★

What a day! What a night, for that matter. I have never been so tired.

I had just gotten into bed and closed my eyes, when here was Evensong slipping under the bedclothes beside me, quite naked except for a good deal of the sandlewood scent I gave her the other day. I thought that she must have hidden in my room when I believed she had gone out, and told her sternly that she must not do it; but she says she climbed in through a window. She wanted to go too, and since I had already told her something about the other matter I said she could. Her gratitude knew no bounds.

We rose before the sun, dressed, got a little fruit to eat on the way, and were off. I had asked Hari Mau to find me a trooper who knew the forest, and he had—but Merciful Molpe, he was only a boy. He had a slug gun and swore that he was fifteen, but I would guess him thirteen at most. It was crowded on the elephant with my six guards (all big men) and their weapons, Evensong, "Trooper" Darjan, and me. I was glad to get off.

Darjan made a little speech when we reached the forest, inspired by Hari Mau I feel quite sure. How thick the growth, how low and wet the ground, how many thorns—no one could go through. When he had finished, I asked whether he had ever gone through it.

"Not through, Rajan."

"Well, did you ever go in there?"

"Yes, Rajan, I used to play in there when I was smaller." (By which he must have meant before he learned to walk.)

I told him to start in, and I would follow him. We would go two leagues north, then turn east and see what we could. He nodded and began to pick his way through the tangle. I told Mahawat to follow me, but to keep some distance.

In the beginning I kept my eyes on Darjan and walked where he had, snagging my tough cotton military tunic at every step and mightily tempted to use the azoth—but also determined not to reveal to anyone, including him, that I had it. After about an hour of that the Neighbors' gift came back to me, as it had on Green. Perhaps I had never really lost it, but only lost sight of it.

Whether or not that last is true, it became apparent to me that Darjan was not choosing the best way. I took it, and was soon so far ahead that I was forced to stop and wait for him. After that, we both had to wait for my elephant.

I had been of two minds about that elephant. To begin with, on Green I had seen that even the largest animals can penetrate thick cover, as the wallowers we hunted here had. (If elephants can be domesticated, why not wallowers? We must try it.) Their size and strength let them force the heaviest growth, while their leathery skins protect them from all but the worst scratches.

On the other hand you have warts, as my father used to say, the wart in this case being that these large animals are too big to pass between big, solid trunks growing close together. Fortunately this forest has only a few large trees, and a great many bushes and saplings.

It seemed that the elephant had little experience of such places, but he learned his business quickly. After the first hour or so, he was going faster than Darjan, so that Darjan, whom we had brought along to guide us, was in danger of being trodden flat. I had told Mahawat to watch me and go where I did, but the elephant learned how to do that before Mahawat did, keeping the tip of one trunk touching my headcloth and padding along behind me with surprisingly little noise. We had struck the tent before setting out; but Evensong and my guards had a rough time of it just the same, having to lie flat on the platform and fend off the limbs and twigs any way they could.

I had intended to stop at the edge of the forest and wait for one of the Hannese trains of mules and pack horses to pass, then attack it from behind; but in that I had not counted on the elephant. He was so happy to see an open space that he ran past us and out onto the road before Mahawat could get him stopped.

I got back up then, very glad of a chance to sit down after all the walking I had done, and told Mahawat he would have to get us back under the trees where we could not be seen. Mahawat agreed, but the elephant did not. When he realized that we wanted him to go back into the forest, he rebelled, charging up the road like an eight-legged talus while trumpeting with both trunks in a way that I found frightening myself and that absolutely terrified poor Evensong. I suppose I have heard as many women scream as most men have, and I may even have heard more than most men, having heard a good many wounded Trivigaunti troopers when Nettle and I fought for General Mint; but Evensong's scream is in a class by itself. It is louder and shriller than the scream of any other woman I have ever met with, and it lasts two or three times longer.

Nettle, I know that you will never read this, nor would I wish you to; but I am going to pretend you will. Try to imagine us, my six guards, Evensong, Mahawat, and me (with Darjan lost in the dust behind us), holding on to anything and everything in reach and every one of us about to fall off, as we rounded a turn in the road and found ourselves among three or four hundred Hannese lancers.

A few days ago I wrote that our elephants could not be induced to charge the enemy. I was wrong. This one did, and you have never seen so many shaggy little ponies thrown into such a state of abject panic. Perhaps no one has.

When I think back on it, it seems miraculous that even one of us escaped alive. Riders were being thrown left and right, and few of those who stayed in their saddles seemed to have slug guns or needlers. The road turned again, but my elephant kept running in a straight line, into a sort of cleft between two masses of rock. Before long his sides were scraping and Mahawat got him back under control. A handful of horsemen tried to follow us in, but a few shots from my guards quickly put an end to that. Eventually we found our way onto a gentle slope dotted with brambles. It became lower and wetter, trees took the place of the brambles, and we were back in the familiar "impassable" forest.

By that time all of us were very glad to be there, even my elephant.

★

★ ★

Morning, but dark as night with pounding rain. No one came to awaken me—or what is more likely, Pehla did but the guard at my door would not admit her. Very late morning, I ought to have said. I have slept twelve hours at least.

I would like some tea and something to eat, but I wanted to read over what I wrote last night first, and make a few corrections. (I seldom correct anything, as you will have seen, but in this case there were far too many simple errors in spelling and the like. I have recopied one whole sheet, and thrown the old one away.)

But before I tell the guard I am awake and send him for some breakfast, I cannot resist speculating a little. Was what we did of any real value? If it simply shows the enemy that the "impassable" forest is indeed passable, it may have been worse than useless. If it teaches us (and compels them) to watch that flank, it will have been well worth doing. I must see that it does, and that further raids are organized and carried out.

What, you will ask, became of Trooper Darjan? The truth is that I do not know. By the time we had gotten clear of the enemy horsemen, I had forgotten him utterly; and I seem to have been too fatigued last night to spare him a thought, although I was stupidly determined to write down everything before I slept.

Silk would have remembered him for the rest of his life.

I stopped writing this long enough to scribble a note to Hari Mau asking about Darjan. I called him "my guide." Hari Mau should be able to tell me whether he returned safely.

I also asked about the men's comfort. We knew the rainy season would begin soon and tried to make provision for it. Now that it has begun, I must see that the waterproof cloaks are actually handed out to the men who need them, that they get the meals and hot tea and so on. I will set out for the front this afternoon, assuming I am well enough.

The winter wheat should have been planted before this; now it is too late. Not much was. The shortages will only get worse, although three boatloads of food from Bahar arrived yesterday. Two to the troopers, one sold in the market to help raise money for more.

We must have an animal of some sort tonight. I meant to take our milch cow, but with the gardener there I cannot risk it. I should have thought of this sooner. I will have to find something else today if we are to do it tonight. Not my horse, because I cannot spare him. Not the elephant, either. We could not control him, and Mahawat sleeps in his stall with him in any case.

No, someone else will have to find a suitable animal for me. I will be too busy, and everything I do is noticed.

Breakfast.

Chandi brought in my breakfast tray, solicitous of my health while trying very hard to keep a scratched cheek turned away from me. I asked her how it happened, expecting her to say she fell. (How long has it been since I thought about old Generalissmo Oosik? Not since Nettle and I wrote, I am sure.) She surprised me by saying she had bent to pick a rose in the garden and the bush scratched her. There is a variety there that blooms almost constantly, so her story was not as absurd as one might think. It was original and imaginative, too.

But not true. She has been fighting with a sister-wife, and I can guess which. I told her to send Pehla in to me, and she went, pale and silent. Chandi thinks she used to be my favorite, so it is easy to see what happened.

★

★ ★

Back again. (I almost wrote *home.*) Two days of rain, wet and mud. My wound throbs and my right ankle hurts, but dry and comfortable otherwise. Evening—nearly eight by the big clock.

Saw the men. It is not as good as I had hoped. I sent a third of them home. Hari Mau objected so violently that I was afraid I was going to have to put him under arrest. He says that if the enemy attacks we are done. I told him the truth, that the enemy will not attack again until the rains end, that in this weather two boys and a dog could hold off a hundred men.

The men I sent home are to come back in a week. (I imagine that at least half will have to be dragged back.) When they return, we will send home another third. I told the men, or at least I told as many as I could reach.

Spoke to the head gardener again before I left. I tried to give him money and asked him to buy a goat. He said a cow would be better, and he would find one. You never know with these people.

Chicken for my supper, chopped up and mixed with fruit and pepper in the usual way. Since I see it like that twice a week at least, it should not have reminded me of anything, but it made me think of the meat pudding we got in the market at Wichote, and I should be writing about that anyway instead of all this day-to-day stuff. Just imagine what this record would be like if I had written about everything in the same way that I have been setting down these daily doings of mine. "I got a splinter in my finger today—left, index—while scraping the third cargo chest on the starboard side, and Seawrack kissed it for me."

No, it really could not be like that, because we would still be a hundred pages at least from Seawrack, the bat-fish, and the floating isles. Back with Mucor and Maytera, in all likelihood.

At any rate, we—I—bought a species of pudding there on market day. I had never seen one like it before, and the woman selling them said they were good (naturally) so I took a chance and traded a silver earring for one. It was dried meat pounded to powder and mixed with fat and dried berries of several kinds (two black, one red and deliciously tart, and one green and fruity as I remember). Not bad-tasting, but a moderate slice of it left me feeling overfull for two days, and it was too much like what we had been eating, the breakbull meat Seawrack had smoked.

That night—I shall never forget it—Krait woke me. Or it might be better to say that by trying to approach me while I slept he stirred up Babbie enough to wake me. "I've found it," he told me. "Pajarocu."

I started to reply, but he laid a finger to his lips and motioned toward the stern.

"It's a long way. It will take ten days or more."

My heart sank. I had been thinking that Seawrack and I would have another month of travel at least. "The lander's still there?"

"Yes." He looked around cautiously at the other boats as he spoke, his reptilian eyes gleaming in the Greenlight; and I wondered why he should be afraid that the people on them might hear him, when I knew that Seawrack could not. "They still have quite a few empty places, too. About half, a woman told me, even though their town is full of men who have come to make the trip."

"What sort of a town is it? A real town like New Viron? Or is it more like this?" By a gesture I indicated the huts at the water's edge.

He grinned. "It's more like one of ours, Father dear. You won't like it."

"What's that supposed to mean?"

"Why should I tell you and have you call me a liar to my face?"

"You are a liar, Krait. You know that much better than I do."

He shrugged and looked angry.

"Did you talk to He-hold-fire?"

"No. Just to whoever was still awake and willing to trade a bit of gossip with me." He watched me silently, weighing me in scales that I could not even imagine. "Are we going to take Seawrack with us?"

I hedged. "Let's hear what she has to say. I don't think she wants to go."

"She wants to do what you want her to do. Why force her to guess what it is you want?"

"Then I won't. I won't take Babbie, either. This whole continent seems to be covered with trees." I was thinking of Babbie living the natural life of his kind in the forest. I did not know whether there were wild hus on Shadelow, but it certainly seemed like a place where he could live happily.

"Was it like this around Pajarocu?"

"More so. The trees are bigger up the river. Bigger and older, and not so sleepy."

"Then I'll let him go. Free him. Why shouldn't he be happy?"

"I should've told you we can't take him anyway. No animals. You could sell him to somebody there, perhaps."

I shook my head. Babbie was my friend.

"Seawrack's going to be the problem. I don't think you realize it yet, Horn, but she is."

I wanted to say that she had not been a problem until he came, that she had helped me in all sorts of ways, but it would have been such an obvious opening for him that at the last moment I did not speak.

"An aid and a comfort." He grinned again, fangs out. "Don't jump like that. I can't read your mind. I read your face."

"You saw the truth there," I told him. "How do we get to Pajarocu?"

"I know something about human ways, as you've seen. But you, being human, not only know them but understand them. Or so I assume."

"Sometimes," I said.

"Sometimes. I like that. Have I ever told you how much I like you, Horn?"

I nodded. "More often than I've believed it."

"I do. The thing that I like is that I can never tell when you're being truthful. Most of you lie constantly, as Seawrack does. A few of you are practically always truthful, this Silk you like to talk about would seem to have been one of those. Both are boring, but you aren't. You make me guess over and over."

I asked what his own practice was, although I knew.

"The same as yours. That's another reason to like you. Seriously now, you need to think about your woman, not as I would but as you would. She's a human being, exactly as you are. Don't settle for an easy answer and put it out of your mind."

"I do that too much."

"I'm glad you know it."

I sat on the gunwale. "What is it you're trying to get me to say? That I need your advice?"

"I doubt that you do. I merely think that you haven't thought as much as you should about the situation she'll face, left alone in Pajarocu."

"She'll have Babbie to protect her."

"So much for a life of woodsy freedom. You wanted to know how to get there. Up the river, right at the first fork and left at the second. I know that's not what your map shows, but I followed the rivers to get back here. That's it, and a long fly it was."

"Do you think they'll let three of us, all supposedly from New Viron, have places on the lander?"

Krait nodded. "It's barely half full, I told you that, and they'll want to go before winter, since nobody's likely to come after the bad weather sets in. The ones who are there already are getting impatient, too. If they wait much longer, they'll be losing more than they gain."

Evensong came. This time I watched her slip through my window. When peace returns (if it does) I'm going to have another sentry in the garden. Or bars on these windows. Bars would be more practical, I suppose, but I cannot forget how I hated the bars on the windows of my manse.

I told her that it would be hours yet, and I wanted to get a few hours sleep before we went out. She said she did, too, but her sister-wives would not let her. She asked who would wake us when it was time, and I told her I would wake myself.

As I now have. We will go soon. I will wake Evensong and give her the note I have prepared, a blank piece of paper with a seal. She will leave by the window, bring her note to the sentry at my door, and demand to be admitted. He will refuse. I will open my door (pretending that their voices have awakened me), look at her paper, get dressed, and leave with her. We will meet the head gardener at the lower gate.

Just writing those words made me think of the garden at my manteion at home. We sprats said Patera Pike's garden, and then almost without a pause to catch breath, Patera Silk's. With barely another pause, we are old, the garden a ruin (I sat there for a while just the same), and that spot, in which some nameless much earlier augur had made his garden, a hundred thousand leagues away or some such ridiculous number. "Do you imagine that a man of your age will find another woman as young as she is?" Krait asked me. He wanted her on the lander, of course; I know that now. "Or one as beautiful?" Trying to be gallant, I told him there were no other women as beautiful as Seawrack.

Nor are there.

Evensong is as young—I would not be surprised if she were a year or two younger. Nettle was never beautiful or even pretty, but my heart melted each time she smiled. It would melt again if I could see her smile tonight.

I must have a needler, and get it without taking it from someone who will use it against the enemy.

We cannot surrender. I cannot. Because I could not leave Pig blind, these people were able to bring me here, and so ended any chance of success I might have had. You could argue that I owe them nothing, and in a sense I believe that it is true; but to say that

I owe them nothing is one thing, and to say that they deserve to be despoiled, raped, and enslaved is another and a very different thing.

All this time I have tried to be Silk for them. I have thought of Silk day and night—what would he do? What would he say under these circumstances? On what principles would he make his decision? Yet to every such question there is just the one answer: he would do what was right and good, and in doubt, he would side against his own interests. That is what I must do.

What I will do. I will try to be what he tried to be. He succeeded, after all.

I have been pacing up and down this big bedroom. This palatial bedroom my oppressors built for me. Pacing in my slippers, so as not to wake Evensong or let the guard at my door know I am awake. When I came here I was a prisoner—a prisoner who was respected, true. I was treated with great kindness and even reverence by Hari Mau and his friends, but I was a prisoner just the same. I knew it, and so did they.

Let me be honest with myself, tonight and always. With myself most of all. That has changed, had changed even before the war. I am their ruler, their caldé. I could leave here at any time, simply by putting a few things into saddlebags, mounting, and riding away. No one would lift a finger to stop me. Who would dare?

I said I could; but I cannot. A prisoner is free to get away if he can. I am no prisoner, and so I cannot. I said I owed them nothing; let that stand. Better—I owe this town and its collective population nothing, because I was taken from the *Whorl* against my will. But what about the individuals who make up the town? Do I owe Hari Mau and my troopers nothing? Men I have bled with?

What about Bahar? (I take one example where I might have a hundred.) He was one of those who forced me to come here. At my order he bought a boat, boarded it, and left his native place, reminding me forcefully of a man named Horn I used to know. I have not the slightest doubt that he has been working at his task, and doing it as well as it can be done. Three boatloads of good, simple, cheap food so far, and it would not surprise me if three more docked tomorrow. At my order he went without a word of protest, leaving his shop to his apprentices. Do I owe Bahar nothing?

Say I do. It is wrong, but say it.

What about my wives? Pehla and Alubukhara are with child. I have lain beside every one of them, and whispered words of love that to many men mean nothing at all. Am I, their husband, to be numbered among those men?

I say that I am not.

Neither were the teachings I tried to pass along to my sons things that I myself did not believe. I am a bad man, granted. Sinew always thought so, and Sinew was right. I am no Silk, but am I as bad as that? I left Nettle, but I did not leave her to be raped and murdered.

Lastly, Evensong and all the people of Han. Say that she counts only as a wife, that she means no more to me than Chandi. Does she mean less? She has a mother and a father, brothers and sisters, two uncles and three aunts, all of whom she loves. They are at the mercy of a tyrant, and if Gaon loses or surrenders they will remain at his mercy.

If we win, there will be no difficulty about getting a needler, or anything.

I have been writing here, I see, about that town on the river. It seems so very long ago.

Where did I put Maytera's eye? In the top drawer at the back, to be sure. Should I put it in a saddlebag now? How happy she will be!

And my robe. I must have my robe and the corn. Where is that?

Found it—back of wardrobe. I put Olivine's eye in the pocket.

On Green I learned the secret the inhumi wish nobody to

know. I promised not to reveal it, but who will ever read this, besides me? Although I swore, I did not swear not to reveal my oath. I can threaten them as well as save them, and I will do both.

We must win this war.

Then I will go home.

13

Brothers

After writing those words, "Then I will go home," I threw away the last of Oreb's quills. I am writing with the gray feather of a goose now, like other men. And there is so much to write about before the great day comes—the day when I can leave this place—that I hardly know how to begin.

That small boy, the gardener's grandson, said I was the Decider. One of the things I must decide (one of the smallest and least important) is how much I should set down before I go. Since I fully intend to carry this account away with me, you may say that it makes very little difference what I decide; but I enjoy a certain rounding out in such things, a sense of completion. Clearly I cannot set down everything, but I hope to carry it to the point at which the lander left Blue. There were many days on the lander that I would far rather forget. Surely the best way is to end before I reach those; and after that I will write no more.

Before I begin, however, I ought to write about what the three of us did last night. That, at least, will not take long. Everything went as planned—Evensong bringing the note, and so on. The head gardener was there to meet us, leading a scrawny, docile old cow. Off we splashed through the warm rain. Prying up the stone was a good deal more difficult than I had anticipated, I having seen four workmen handle those stones without much trouble. I do not think the gardener and I could have managed without Evensong's help.

With it, we scarcely got it up. He dug. He has been digging all his life, and he knows his business.

I had half expected to find no more than the corpse, a thing like a dried jellystar, of someone like Krait. It was an inhuma, and seemed more nearly the mummified remains of a child. Possibly she tried to make me think she was human, as they commonly do, even as I lifted her from her grave. If she did, she succeeded horribly.

Evensong and I tried to talk to her. (I had meant for Evensong to keep watch, but it was raining so hard that I could scarcely see the cow. She could not have seen someone coming until he bumped into her.) It was hopeless; the inhuma was too weak to speak a word. I put her on the cow's back and pressed her mouth to the unlucky cow's neck. I have washed my hands a dozen times since.

She fed for what seemed to us, soaked and steaming as all three of us were, a very long time. She became somewhat larger, and perhaps somewhat lighter in color, although it was not easy to tell by the light of Mehman's sputtering lantern; but that was all.

Then . . .

I doubt that I can set it down in ink in any meaningful way—I wish I could make you see it as we did. Two things happened at once, but I cannot write about them both at once; one must be first and the other second. Nettle, will you ever read this? What will you think of me?

The rain stopped in an instant, the way rain often does here. At one moment it was pouring. At the next the only drops that fell were those that trickled from the roofs of the shops around the market square. At that instant the inhuma slipped off the old cow's back, and when her feet touched stone there was no inhuma. In her place stood a woman a little taller than Evensong, an emaciated woman with burning eyes whose hairless skull somehow conveyed the impression of lank reddish hair. I put my chain around her neck and snapped the lock, and for an instant felt something quite different.

I said, "You must be wondering why we released you."

"No." She looked down into the grave in which she had been

imprisoned. "Don't you want to fill that up before someone sees it?"

We did, and before the work was complete Evensong and I were ready to jump out of our skins when Mehman dropped his spade. I had intended to talk to the inhuma there, but had assumed that the rain would continue; it would have been madness to do it when the rain had stopped. After a little discussion we decided to go to Mehman's cottage, at the farther end of my garden.

The cow made everything much more difficult; she was almost too weak to stand. Mehman would have left her where she was, but I would not hear of it, wanting nothing left behind that would draw attention to the spot. Our prisoner offered to return a little of the blood she had taken; but however deceived by her appearance I may have been, her eyes told me what she intended, and I would not permit it.

Eventually we got the cow into my garden, shut the gate, and let her lie down. This morning Mehman was to take her to the stables and tell the stableman that I have decided to take her in and care for her. It is a thing that pious people here do occasionally.

He and Evensong waited outside while I explained what I had learned from Krait on Green. I tapped the window when I had finished, and they came in again. "Will you do whatever we tell you, if I release you?" I asked the inhuma. "Or shall I make good on my threat?"

She said nothing in reply, her face buried in her hands—a naked, hairless, reptilian thing in woman's shape, stripped for the moment of all her pride. Mehman and Evensong positioned their chairs a half step behind mine and sat in silence, watching her.

"I warn you, if you will not I am going to spread my knowledge everywhere. I will be believed, because I am ruler here."

The face she lifted was a woman's once more, beautiful and depraved. "What do you want from me?" Her eyes were green, or if they were not, they appeared so.

"You are quick." I sat too, drew my sword, and laid it across my lap.

"I used to be. Tolerably so." Her bony shoulders rose and fell, much narrower shoulders than Seawrack's, and thinner than hers had ever been. Skeletal.

Mehman stood, having remembered his duties as host. "You will honor me by drinking tea, Rajan?"

Seeing that it would please him, I nodded and asked him to bring me a bowl of warm water, soap, and a clean towel as well.

"Tea for the rani?" He bowed to Evensong; when I was newly come it never occurred to me that my wives would be awarded the title of the ruler of Trivigaunte.

Evensong nodded and smiled, and Mehman bowed again and bustled away.

"I'd ask you how long you were in the ground under that stone, if I thought you knew," I told our prisoner, "but I don't see how you could."

She shook her head. "Years, I think."

"So do I. Is your word good?"

"Freely given to you? Yes."

"Then give me your word that you will do exactly as I order you."

She shook her head more vigorously, so much so that the chain clanked and rattled. "It would be worth nothing at all as long as I have to wear this. Take it away, and my oath will bind me."

I got out the key, but Evensong caught my hand.

The inhuma began, "You were surprised that I didn't want to know why you had—had . . ."

Her emotion may have been feigned, although I doubt it.

"I wasn't free. You had locked this thing around my neck. Take it away."

Motioning for Evensong to remain where she was, I did.

"I will obey you in all things, Rajan," the inhuma declared. She rubbed her neck as if the chain had chafed it, and although they were faint I could see scales where pores should have been. I glanced at the window, and found that it was gray now instead of black.

I said, "You give me your word for that?"

"Yes." Even knowing that her empty jade eyes and hollow cheeks were more than half illusion, I pitied the face I saw. "You have my word, unless you command me to go back into that place of living death."

"I won't. And when you have completed the task I'll give you, I'm going to let you go."

Evensong made a little sound of displeasure.

"I don't like it either," I said, "but what else can I do? Kill her after she's fought for us?"

The inhuma made me a seated bow that may or may not have been mockery.

Because I thought it would be better to wait for Mehman to return, I said, "It's just occurred to me that you inhumi are rather like a kind of lizard I've noticed in my garden. It can change colors, and because of its size and shape, and because it remains so still, it is easy to take one for a piece of brown bark, or a green leaf, or even the flesh-colored petal of a rose. While I acknowledge that you inhumi are a much higher form of life, it seems to me that the principle is about the same."

I expected her to say that we three were merely large monkeys without tails (as Krait would have), which would have been at least as just; but she only nodded. "You are correct, Rajan."

Evensong said, "Pehla showed me one of those. They catch insects with their tongues."

The inhuma nodded as before. "We do the same, rani. You haven't asked my name, or given me yours."

Evensong introduced herself. I explained to her that I had not inquired about the inhuma's name because I knew that any name she gave us would be false, at which the inhuma said, "Then my name in this town of yours shall be False. Is that how you say it?"

Mehman came in just then with my water, soap, and towel. "I have no tray, Rajan. I am shamed."

"I am shamed, not you," I told him. "I ought to have paid you better, and I will. I'll give you a tray, too. This inhuma would like us to call her by a name that means *false* or *lying*. Something like that. What would it be?"

"Jahlee."

"Thank you. Jahlee, this man is Mehman. Mehman, we will call this evil woman Jahlee, as you suggest."

He bowed to her.

"Jahlee," I said, "you are not to harm Mehman or any of his people."

"I am your slave."

"Look at him carefully. Neither Evensong nor I are typical of the mass of people here, but he is. He is a typical citizen of our town, tall and dark, with a nose, eyes, mouth, and so on quite a bit like mine."

"I have seen others, Rajan."

"Good. These are my people. Under no circumstances whatsoever are you to harm any of them. If you do, you know what I will do."

"I do, Rajan. But I must live."

"You must do more, as we both understand. I'm about to get to that."

Evensong said, "Suppose another inhuma comes here and hurts someone. We might think it was her."

"We might indeed. Because we might she will warn the other inhumi to keep away, if she is wise. Jahlee, Evensong is from a different town, a foreign town called Han, with which our own town is at war. She is a young woman of Han, more attractive than most."

The starved and empty eyes fastened upon Evensong's face. "I understand, Rajan."

"You are not to attack the common people of Han, or of any other town. You may attack any and all of the troopers fighting against us, however. They are fair game for you."

Jahlee started to object, but fell silent.

"There are more than enough for you. You may also attack their animals, if you wish."

She shook her head. "That is most gracious, Rajan. But I will not."

"Sarcasm will win you no friends here."

"Is it possible for me to win friends, Rajan?"

"Not like that. Will you attack the troopers from Han, as I have suggested?"

"I am your slave. But it would be better if I had clothes." With both hands, she smoothed her starved body, a body that appeared wholly human. "A wig or headdress of some sort, too. Powder, rouge, and scent."

I glanced at Evensong, who nodded and hurried out.

"A few gauds, Rajan, if it's not asking too much."

"She will think of that, I'm sure. She's an intelligent young woman."

Mehman re-entered with a steaming teapot and two cups, and I assured him that Evensong would be back soon.

"There is more," I told Jahlee. Rinsing my fingers for the third time, I sipped tea and nodded my appreciation to Mehman.

"More duties, Rajan? For me?" Her voice had become breathlessly feminine.

"You might say so. Are you aware that there are other inhumi entombed here as you were?"

"No." For a moment the empty eyes flashed fire. "You torture us as we never torture you."

"There are, and I know where they are buried. Han's our enemy, but only Han's troops. You understand that."

Mehman brought in a fragrant cup for himself and another for Jahlee, and I motioned for him to sit down.

Jahlee asked, "Do you intend to dig them up to fight for us, Most Merciful Rajan?"

"I may. In addition to preying upon those troops, I want you to do whatever may occur to you to weaken and discomfort them. Knowing the cunning of your race, I leave the nature of those things entirely to you. You may do whatever seems good to you, as long as it doesn't harm us."

"I understand, Rajan."

"When you have done something sufficiently impressive that you feel that word of it is bound to reach me, return here. My palace is in the same garden as this cottage. If it's a court day, come to court. If it isn't, ask for Evensong, who is also called Chota."

"Your servants may detect me, Rajan."

"See that they do not. If what you have done really is a major stroke, you and I, with Mehman here and Evensong, will rescue a second member of your race just as the three of us rescued you, and on the same conditions. He or she will be sent against the Horde of Han exactly as you are being sent. When either of you achieves a major success, a third will be rescued. And so on."

"If you win your war, you will release me from my promise?" Her expression was guarded.

"Exactly."

"Will you rescue the rest of us who are still in the living graves then?"

"No." I shook my head. "But I will tell you—and the others who have been freed—where they are. You may free them yourselves, if you wish."

Slowly, she nodded.

Soon after that, Evensong returned. She had a crimson silk gown over one arm and was carrying two elaborately inlaid boxes. "There are shoes in here," she told Jahlee, handing her one, "and a good ivory bracelet and my second-best ivory ring. Women in Han don't wear a lot of brass bangles the way women do here."

"Scent," Jahlee whispered. "I must have scent." She opened the box and took out a fanciful bottle.

"That's not the good perfume you gave me," Evensong told me. "It's what they gave me in Han when they sent me here." As she spoke, a heavy, spicy fragrance filled the room. "You don't need that much," she cautioned Jahlee.

Jahlee laughed then, laughter so dark and exulting that I wondered whether I had not made a serious mistake when I had decided to undertake this experiment after weeks of worry and indecision.

"Here's a woman's traveling hat." Evensong opened the other box and took it out. It was wide and flat, rather like an oversized saucer or a wide soup bowl of tightly plaited white straw turned upside down.

There was a knock at the door; Mehman looked to me for guidance, and I asked whether he was expecting company.

"My daughter and her little boy."

"Put on that gown and go," I told Jahlee. "You know what you are to do."

Stepping swiftly into the shoes, she pulled it over her head. "Night would be better."

"Most people are still asleep." I turned to Evensong. "Will you give her that box to keep the cosmetics in?"

She nodded.

Mehman's daughter knocked again, and I told Mehman to admit them, adding to Jahlee, "When they come in, you are to leave immediately."

She did, favoring the humble woman and her little son with a flashing smile in which no actual teeth were to be seen, and running across the soft green grass with one hand clapped to the traveling hat and Evensong's gown flowing and floating around her.

Mehman made obeisance. "My daughter Zeehra, Rajan. My grandson Lal."

His daughter looked askance at Evensong and me, plainly dressed and soaked to the skin, before bowing almost to the ground.

"The rani and I were discussing an expansion of the herb beds with your father when we were caught in the rain," I explained.

Little Lal started to speak, but was hushed at once by his mother.

"We are about to return to the palace," I continued, "but there is something of importance I must tell you first. Your father will confirm what I say after I leave, I feel certain. The woman whom I dismissed as you came in is not to be trusted. I would not wish you to think, because you saw her with my wife and me, that she is someone I trust, someone to whom you ought to defer."

Evensong surprised me by saying, "She is a thief and worse than a thief."

"Exactly." I stood. "The two-hands spider kills our rats, but it remains a spider."

"You're the Decider," little Lal burst out. "The other people talk and talk, then you decide."

"I am," I told him, "but I can't decide everything. You must decide whether to obey your mother, for example—and accept the consequences if you don't. What would you do, Lal, if that woman in the red gown came to your door?"

"I wouldn't let her in," he declared stoutly.

"Very good," I said. "In time you may be an important and respected man like your grandfather."

★

★ ★

That was four days ago. Jahlee may have been active. I hope so, but I have heard nothing.

My wound seems worse, Evensong says from the rain but I think it is actually from the strain of lifting that big flagstone in the market. Maybe it is for the best that we have no news about Jahlee.

This rain makes my ankle ache.

If I were to give every detail of the painfully slow voyage that Seawrack, Krait, Babbie, and I made up the river, I would use up as much again of this thin rice paper as I have consumed already.

Which is too much. Paper is dear here, and I have several times come close to proposing that we build our own mill. The Cataracts (upper or lower) would supply far more water power than our little stream on Lizard Island. But it is out of the question as long as the fighting continues, and as soon as it ends I will go.

A lot of paper, and to confess the truth it would have a good deal of interest written on it. On the lower reaches around Wichote, the lack of winds was the chief problem. The river was very wide there; even so, the center of its stream offered few such winds as one hopes for, and often gets, at sea; and when we tried to tack, whatever wind there was generally died away altogether as we approached the thickly wooded banks. The current was slow, however, and what progress we made was often made with Babbie and me at the sweeps. Earlier I recorded my dismay when Krait said we might be in Pajarocu in ten days. I need not have worried, and after a good long session with the sweeps I would gladly have arrived that very instant if it had been possible. There were many days on which we could see the point at which we had dropped anchor the day before when we stopped for the evening meal.

Somewhere I should say that we were attacked only once. Half a dozen men, perhaps, swam out to our boat while Krait was away and Seawrack and I were sleeping. Babbie and a couple of shots from the slug gun routed them, and one left behind a long knife that became Seawrack's tool and weapon thereafter. Basically, no harm was done; but it taught me to anchor well away from shore on those rivers, as I invariably did from that time forward. As an added precaution, I made it a set rule to travel some little distance after we had finished our evening meal and put out the fire in the sandbox, and not to drop anchor until full darkness had arrived and the place could not easily be observed.

Having found Pajarocu, Krait visited it almost every night; and I assumed that he was feeding there as well. He asked for and received my permission to leave us if it appeared that the lander was about to fly. In return, he assured me repeatedly that he would continue to guide us, faithful to the promise he had made when he rescued me from the pit, so long as it did not mean that he himself would miss the lander.

Food was a continuing difficulty. Much of the meat Seawrack had smoked had spoiled, either because it had not been dried enough, or because it had gotten wet. We had brought a little food from Wichote as well, most notably the famous pudding I have already mentioned and a sack of cornmeal; but after the first week on the river the cornmeal was gone and the pudding (which had once seemed as permanent as a stone) showed signs of unwelcome shrinkage. Seawrack took fish in the river for Babbie and me, fish which she caught with her hands and at first refused to eat. She also went in search of wild berries—these were very welcome indeed when they could be found—while Babbie and I hunted with the slug gun.

To the very few of you who read this who may venture upon the western sea, I say this. Hunger and cold will be the chief dangers you face, and they will be far worse than the hostility of the people of Shadelow, and a thousand times worse than its most dangerous beasts.

(It was not so on Green; perhaps someday I will write about that after all, even though Green's monstrous beasts would never be credited. If I do it I will have to represent them as slower, as well as smaller, than they actually are.)

Hunger and cold tormented us, as I have said, and each made the other far worse. In cold weather a starved person is scarcely ever warm, even with a blanket and a fire; and a healthy person exposed to cold soon becomes ravenously hungry. When I sailed from Lizard Island, I took a few changes of clothing, a warm wool blanket, and bales of paper to trade for more supplies at New Viron—paper that was stolen from me almost at once. For my needler Sinew threw me his knife, and Marrow very generously provided me with food, the slug gun and ammunition, and the silver jewelry I have occasionally mentioned. I bought more food (with vinegar, cooking oil, black and red pepper, and dried basil), the sweeps, a new harpoon, and a few other odds and ends, after which I considered myself adequately equipped.

I—we—were not. I am tempted here to write at great length about gloves, stockings, and boots. There were times when I would have traded the sloop for a warm wool cap and a stout pair of warm leather gloves; but to dwell on this item or that would be to obscure the real point.

One cannot stock a boat with sufficient food for such a voyage as I so lightly undertook. If its entire cargo consisted of food, that would not be sufficient. All that one can do is to load up with as much as the boat can reasonably carry, choosing foods (vegetable foods, particularly) that will keep for weeks or months. We fished and hunted, as I have indicated; but an exclusive diet of fish and meat is not healthy and quickly becomes maddeningly monotonous. The best gift that Marrow gave me was not my slug gun, but the barrel of apples. Before we reached Pajarocu, I wished heartily that it had been a half dozen. I must add that each day spent hunting and gathering wild fruits or nuts was a day lost, and that we often got little or nothing.

Possibly I should also say here that when the barrel was empty I broke it up and used its staves for firewood. If I had kept it and stored Seawrack's smoked breakbull in it, much that was spoiled by wetting would have been saved.

There was little cloth in the market at Wichote, although furs and hides were plentiful. Seawrack and I got fur caps that came down well past our necks and ears, butter-soft leather tunics of greenbuck hide (I wore mine under the stiffer garment that Hepen-sheep had made for me), big fur robes, and clumsy fur mittens, as well as blankets much thicker and warmer than the one I brought from Lizard. These purchases will show the sort of clothing that will be essential on the voyage. Add to them sturdy trousers—several pairs—at least two pairs of seaboots, and a dozen pairs of wool stockings.

One should also bring needles and thread with which to repair one's clothing. I was fortunate in that I had several of the large needles I used to sew sails and a big ball of coarse linen thread. Finer needles and finer thread would be advisable, to—as well as a pair of scissors.

With boat's stores I was tolerably well provided. The second anchor I had bought in New Viron, particularly, proved invaluable. I had also laid in a bolt of sailcloth, tar, varnish, and paint, and came to regret that there was not more of all four. There cannot be too much rope on a boat bound on a trip of great duration.

After the first fork, the current became our chief obstacle, and one about which we could do very little. Even on the lower reaches, where it was almost undetectable, it would slowly bear the sloop backward toward Wichote, although the water appeared quite motionless. After the first fork, we had to creep along very near one bank or the other, which meant we could not tack. We had to wait for a good, strong wind not worse than quartering, or crawl forward with the sweeps. On more than one occasion, and more than two, we thus waited and crawled and waited again for days at a time. There were even times when I walked three hundred strides upriver (that being the greatest distance that we had rope for) and hitched a block to a tree, after which we hauled the sloop forward—"we" being Babbie and I, very largely. I do not recall a good, strong, favoring wind that lasted a full day during the entire trip.

In the long hours of idleness Seawrack and I became more intimate than we had ever been before, more intimate even than we had been during those first idyllic days when her poor stump of arm had not yet healed and she used to confide to me that the fingers she no longer possessed touched something hard or soft, smooth or rough.

There was none of that now; if those soft and graceful phantom fingers groped or stroked anything, I was not apprised of it; but she talked about her life beneath the sea, of people she had known and liked or known and feared there (not all or even most of them actual, I believe), the freshwater springs on the seafloor at which she had drunk, the pranks she had played upon unsuspecting men in boats, and the pets she had adopted but eventually discarded, lost, or eaten.

"It seemed completely normal to me then," she said, and I knew in my heart that it still did—that it was her life aboard the sloop with me that seemed the aberration. "I knew most people lived on the land, and I think I knew, somewhere behind my ears, that I had too, a long time ago. It wasn't something I thought a lot about."

She was silent for a moment, staring out at the last gleams of sunshine on the water.

"There were certain places around Mother where I slept, and I would go into them when it got dark. The sea is more dangerous after dark. So often you don't see hungry things until you bump into them, or they bump into you, and a lot of those hungry things have ways of seeing in the dark with noises that I can't do."

She seemed to catch her breath, scanning the forest shadows. "So when it got dark I would go into one of my sleeping places. The water was always warm and still in them, with Mother's smell in it. I'd curl up and go to sleep, knowing that Mother was so big that nothing frightened her, and that most of the dangerous things and people were afraid of her. You probably think it was awful. But it wasn't awful, not then. It was really very, very nice."

Babbie stretched out beside her, resting his chin on her thigh and looking up at her with eyes like two dark red beads that tried terribly hard to melt, although they had been made for maniacal ferocity.

"The land was like that for me, when I thought about it at all. Like the dark, I mean. I felt that it was always dark up there, and the people there weren't really people at all, that they weren't really people. Mother wasn't human, though. Isn't that what you say?"

Feeling very much like Babbie, I nodded.

"She always seemed human to me. She still does, and I think it's because in the sea being people means something different. In the sea, it's talking. If you talk, you are a person, so she was and so was I, because in the sea there's a lot of noise but not very many talking voices. In a place like that town where we stayed waiting for market day, there are so many people talking all the time that nobody wants to hear any more talk. After that, being human becomes something else, like walking on your hind feet."

I smiled. "Human chickens?"

"And having two arms and two hands instead of wings. So I'm almost human. Isn't that right?" She began to comb her long, golden hair, holding the comb in her mouth when she needed her hand for other matters.

"Your hair changes color," I told her.

"When it's wet. It looks black then."

"No, it doesn't. When it's wet it's a tawny gold, like the beautiful old gold you wore for me when you first came on board."

She laughed, pleased. "But when I go down deep, it's black."

"If you go down deep enough, I suppose it must be. But now it's changing color, and every color is more beautiful than the last, and makes me forget the last and wish that it would stay the new color always."

I watched the comb, and the shimmering highlights it left behind. "There's gold so pale that it's almost like silver, like this ring you gave me, and pure yellow gold, and red gold, and even the tawny color your hair has when it's wet—the color I thought it was for the first few days."

"I was still spending a lot of time in the water then," she said pensively.

"I know. And now you're afraid of it, even when you catch fish for us. I see you nerving yourself to go in, to take the plunge as people say."

"I'm not afraid I'll drown, Horn. I never, ever will. Sometimes I wish I could."

Obtuse though I was, I knew what she meant. "You'd die." I tried to make my voice gentle. "Isn't that worse than going back to your old life in the sea?"

We watched Krait haul on the painter to bring the sloop nearer shore, then walk out onto the bowsprit, jump down, and vanish among the crowding trees. The sun was sinking behind the mountains already, wrapping the river that had become our whorl in silent purple shadows.

"He's one, isn't he?" Seawrack sighed, put away her comb.

"One what?"

"One of the things that hunt through the night, the things I was so frightened of when I slept in Mother."

Not knowing what to say, I did not reply.

"There was a cave in the rocks that I used to play in. I've probably told you."

I nodded.

"I used to say I was going to sleep in there." She laughed again, softly. "I was always really brave in the daytime. But when the dark started coming up out of the deep places, I would swim back to Mother as fast as I could and sleep in one of the places where I'd been sleeping ever since I was little. I knew what a lot of the things out there in the dark were, even if I didn't have names for them, and just this moment it came into my head that Krait is one of those, even if I don't have any name except Krait."

I said, "I see," although I was not sure I did.

"He sleeps all day, more than Babbie, even, and he hardly ever eats anything. Then at night he hunts, and he must eat everything he catches, because he never brings us back anything."

"Sometimes he does," I objected.

"That little crabbit." Contemptuously, she waved the crabbit aside. "He seems like a human person to me, but he doesn't to you."

It caught me completely off guard. I did not know what to say.

"He has two hands and two arms, and he walks standing up. He talks more than both of us together when he's awake. So why don't you think he's people?"

I tried to say that I considered Krait fully human, and that he was in fact a human being just as we were—but tried to do it without telling a direct lie, stuttering and stammering and backing away from assertions I had just made.

"No, you don't," Seawrack told me.

"Perhaps it's only that he's so young. He's actually quite a bit younger than my son Sinew, and quite frankly, Seawrack, my son Sinew and I have been at each other's throats more often than I like to remember." I swallowed, steeling myself to force out all the lies the situation might require. "He looks like Sinew, too—"

A new voice—Sinew's own—inquired, "Like me? Who does?"

I turned my head so fast that I nearly broke my neck. Sinew was almost alongside, standing perilously erect in one of the little boats made by hollowing out logs that the local people used.

"Krait does," Seawrack told him. It was as though she had known him all her life.

Sinew looked at her, gulped helplessly, and looked at me, plainly not yet up to speaking to a woman whose eyes, lips, and chin had rocked him like a gale.

I asked whether he wanted to come on board.

"She's—is it all right?"

"Certainly," I told him; and I caught the rope of braided hide he threw me and made it fast.

If you had asked me an hour earlier, I would have said that I would be delighted to see any face or hear any voice from Lizard, even his. Now I had both seen and heard him, and my heart sank. Here in this strange and wondrous town of Gaon, I tell myself (and I believe that it is true) that I would be overjoyed to see Sinew again as I saw him that evening on the great cold river that rushes through the hills of the eastern face of Shadelow; but I know that if my feelings were to take me off guard here as they did there, I would call my guards and tell them to take him into the garden and cut off his head in any spot they liked, as long as it was out of sight of my window. If, somehow, he had appeared when Seawrack was ashore looking for the seedy orange fruits she had twice found growing in the clearings left by old fires, I really believe that I might simply have shot him and let the torpid waters carry his corpse out of my sight. What might have happened subsequently on Green, I can scarcely imagine.

As it was, he sprang over the gunwale as I never could and sat down with us, looking at Seawrack with embarrassed admiration.

"This young man is Sinew, my oldest son," I told her. "He followed me from Lizard Island, apparently, and now he has caught up with me. With us, I ought to have said."

She smiled at him and nodded; and I added, "Sinew, this is Seawrack."

Shier than ever, he nodded in return.

"You did follow me, didn't you? I had asked you—in fact, I had begged you—to stay there and look after your mother."

"Yeah, I know."

Gently, Seawrack asked, "How was she when you left, and how were your brothers?"

"It wasn't that long after you," he told me. For a few seconds he paused to gawk at the mossy leather stretched tight by Seawrack's breasts. "Mother was fine then, and the sprats were fine too."

Seawrack smiled. "Did you take good care of her while you were there, Sinew?"

"No." He had summoned up the courage to speak to her directly. "She took care of me, like she always does. See, my father—hey! What are you doing?"

I was taking his hunting knife from the belt of my hide overtunic, sheath and all. "Returning this to you." I held it out; and when he did not accept it, I tossed it into his lap.

"I can't give your needler back." He eyed me, clearly expecting me to explode.

"That's all right."

"I had it. I should have left it at home with Mother, only I didn't. I took it with me in the old boat, and it was a really good thing to have, too. I used it a lot before I lost it."

He turned to Seawrack. "Father wanted me to take care of the family, and for a couple of days I tried, only there wasn't anything to do. He thought I'd take the paper to town in the little boat, our old one that wasn't much bigger than my old skin boat. Only it leaked and wouldn't hold near enough, and as soon as everybody found out he'd gone away and left my mother there, Daisy's mother came over and said they'd take Mother and our paper in their fishing boat anytime she wanted to go. This new boat here is like a fishing boat, that's what we copied it from when me and Father built it, only we put in these big boxes, too, to keep the paper dry. He keeps rope and stuff in one, though."

"I know," Seawrack said.

"Real fishermen keep theirs up front under that little deck that they stand on when they've got to fool with the forestay or the jib."

"That's where we sleep now, Sinew, your father and I." Seawrack's tone thrilled me as much as it must have pained him; even tonight I thrill to the memory of it.

He stared, his mouth gaping. His hands fumbled with his knife, and for a moment I believed that he might actually try to stab me with it.

As if she spoke to a child, she asked, "Do you want to come with us? Where will you sleep tonight?"

"Yeah. In my boat, I guess. That's where I've been sleeping. I'll get in it and tie it on in back." He looked to me. "Is that all right?"

I nodded.

"Only if you've got a blanket or anything that would be great. I brought some, but I lost them."

I was about to say that we had brought only one, and had slept for most of the voyage under sailcloth and our clothing, but Seawrack explained that we had bought blankets in Wichote and rose to get him one. I suggested that he might want some sailcloth as well, in case of rain.

"All right." For a second or two he fingered his reclaimed hunting knife. "We could trade for some furs with people around here, if you've got anything to trade."

I nodded and said that I should have thought of that when we put in at Wichote.

"They'd skin you there."

(My irony had been wasted.)

"Only out here and farther west you can get good furs cheap because they don't want to have to load them in their boats and take them down the river to sell."

He accepted the blanket that would be his from that moment forward. "After we bring back Silk I'm going to build a real big boat and just go back and forth trading. I'll buy slug guns and stuff like that back home and sell them for furs all up and down the river, and then go back for more."

It recalled what the traveler had said, and I asked him whether he had been farther west than we were now.

"Oh, sure. I've been to Pajarocu. I hung around there about a week waiting for you, then I started back down looking for you."

Seawrack said admiringly, "You're very brave to travel alone here in that little boat."

"Thanks." He smiled, and for a moment I actually liked him. "See, a little boat like mine is what you need out here, so you can get way over to one side and paddle. My father's probably hanging on to this big one 'cause we're going to have to have it to bring

Silk back to New Viron in. We'll have to have something that can make it across. That's right, isn't it, Father?"

Back to Seawrack before I had a chance to reply. "This one will do it. It'll be fast, too, when we're going back down, bringing Silk back. We'll need it because the lander's coming right straight back to Pajarocu, when it comes back." He waited for one of us to challenge him.

"You bet it is. They're not going to let a thing like that get away from them. Would you? There's quite a few towns over on the other side that've got landers that work. That's what I heard. Only they won't let anybody but their own people get anywhere around them. Just try it and you'll get shot. Some won't even own up that they've got them."

I cleared my throat. "I've been thinking. I want to propose a plan to both of you."

Sinew held up his knife, inspecting its blade by the last light of the day that was now past. "You nicked the edge," he said, and inspected the place with a thumbnail.

"I know. I've been cutting wood with it. I had to." I expected him to enlarge upon his complaint; but he did not.

Seawrack had been studying his face. "You don't look very much like your father."

"Everybody says I do."

She shook her head, and he smiled.

I asked them, "May I tell you what I propose? The plan I mentioned?"

"Sure." Sinew sheathed his knife.

"As you said, we'll need this boat when the lander returns. As you also said, it's not well suited to river travel. Seawrack and I have seen that for ourselves. So has Krait."

I waited for his agreement, and got it.

"Seawrack and I haven't talked very much about the hazards involved in flying back to the *Whorl* on a lander jury-rigged by somebody in Pajarocu. Neither did you and I before I left, and I don't like to talk about it even now. I don't enjoy sounding as if I were boasting about the dangers I'll face. I don't even like to think about them, and I'd gladly make them less—if I could."

"It looks pretty good, that lander," Sinew assured me. "I've seen it."

I nodded. "I'm very glad to hear that. But before I continue, I ought to ask you something. What happened to our old boat, the one you set out in?"

He shrugged. "I traded it for the one I've got now and some other stuff."

"May I ask what the other stuff was?"

"It doesn't matter. It's gone now."

"What was it?"

"I said it doesn't matter!"

"He's hungry," Seawrack interposed. "Would you like a piece of smoked meat, Sinew?"

"Sure. Thanks."

This time I waited until he was chewing it. "I have to go on that lander. I promised I would, and I intend to. Krait wants to go, too. He's told me why, and he has an excellent reason; but he made me promise not to reveal it. Neither of you have any reason at all."

They objected, but I silenced them. "As I said, it will be very dangerous. It's quite possible that the lander will explode, or catch fire, or crash when it tries to take off. Even if it flies away safely and crosses the abyss between the whorls, landing in the *Whorl* is liable to be very difficult. Krait's been concerned about you, Seawrack. I doubt that he's told you, but he has been."

She shook her head.

"He'd been assuming that you'd come with us if there was a place for you on it. He mentioned it to me not long ago, and I said just what I'm saying now, that it's too dangerous to subject you to. I told him that I intended to leave you in Pajarocu until I came back."

Seawrack shook her head again, this time violently, and Sinew said, "Me, too? I won't."

"Krait had objections as well. He pointed out that she would be an attractive young woman alone and friendless in a strange town. I had to admit that he was right." I filled my lungs with air, conscious of what failure to persuade them now would mean.

"So here's the new plan I would like to propose. When Krait returns in the morning, we'll go back to Wichote. We'll be sailing with the current then, and it shouldn't take more than two or three days."

Sinew's nod was guarded.

"When we get there, Krait and I will trade for another little boat like the one you have. He and I will take those two boats to Pajarocu. You and Seawrack will wait for us in Wichote, on this one."

"No." Seawrack sounded as firm as I was ever to hear her, and that was very firm indeed.

"You won't be alone there, either of you. Furthermore, you'll have this boat to live on, together. And if I'm not back within a month or so . . ." I shrugged.

In so low a tone that I scarcely heard him, Sinew said, "I knew you didn't want me as soon as I saw you. Only I didn't think you'd give her up to get rid of me."

"I'm not trying to get rid of you. Can't you get it through your head that I may never come back? That I may die? I'd like to arrange things so that neither of you dies with me." It was so dark by that time that it was difficult for me to see their faces; I looked from one to the other, hoping for support.

Seawrack said, "Sinew's been to Pajarocu. He can take us to it."

Sinew nodded.

I said, "If you found it, so can Krait and I."

There was a long silence after that. Sinew took advantage of it to get himself another strip of smoked meat, and I am going to take advantage of it now to get a little sleep before Jahlee and Evensong come.

★

★ ★

Heavy rain from midnight on, which gave us good cover. I did not go out or even get up this morning, although my wound seems better—breakfast in bed from a tray, and so forth. Hari Mau talked with me as I lay in bed, stamping up and down the room and more than ready to fall upon the Hannese that very moment. He had ridden half the morning with a rain-soaked, bloodstained bandage where his white headcloth ought to be, and is planning a major attack as soon as the rainy season ends. Our enemies are weaker than they look, he says, and I pray to the Outsider and any other god who may read this that he is correct. He swears that if I could talk with his new prisoners I would agree.

He has gone now, and I have gotten up to write this in my nightclothes, more than half ashamed.

We could have built a fire in the box or lit the lantern that night on the sloop, but we did not. The darkness and the overpowering presences of the forest and the swiftly sinister river created an atmosphere that I cannot possibly convey with ink on paper. The people of Shadelow believe that each of their rivers has a minor god of its own who lives in and under it and governs it, a god whose essence it is. Also that the forests hold minor gods and goddesses as numerous as their animals, gods and goddesses for the most part malign and unappeasable. When Seawrack spoke to Sinew and me that night in the dark, it almost seemed to me that we had one with us on the sloop. What it must have seemed to Sinew, who did not know her as I did, is far beyond my ability to express.

"You said it was good that I can't drown," she began. "Do you remember that?"

I did.

"I said I wished I could." There was an odd, rough sound, loud in the silence; after a moment I realized that she was scratching Babbie's ears. "You thought it was foolish of me, wanting to drown. But I don't want to drown. I've seen a lot more drowned people than you have, probably. I've seen what the sea does to them, and watched Mother eat them, and eaten them myself."

For the space of a score of breaths no voices were heard but the wind's and the river's.

"What I'd like is to be able to, because you can. You think I can wait for you in that town where the river comes to the sea. Do you think Babbie will wait, too? Do you think he can live in the forest until you come back, and then come back to you?"

"No, I don't," I said, "although Babbie has surprised me before."

"You don't think he's a real person. To you he's just like Krait, and Krait's not a real person either."

I tried to say that I did not think Babbie a person at all, that Babbie was not a human being like Krait and the three of us. I cannot be certain now precisely how I may have put it, although I am quite sure I put it badly. Whatever lies I may have told, and however I phrased them, I made Seawrack angry.

"That's not what I said! That's not what I said at all! You're twisting all the words around. You do it once or twice every day, and I'd do anything, if only I could make you stop it."

"I apologize," I told her. "I didn't intend to. If that isn't what you meant, what did you mean?"

Sinew began, "Did she really—?"

She cut him off. "What I'm trying to say is, there are two people on this boat you don't think are people at all, Babbie and Krait. You don't think they are, but you're wrong. You're wrong about both of them."

Sinew muttered, "He doesn't think I'm anybody either."

"Yes, he does!" In the chill starlight, I could see her turn to face him. "You've got it exactly backwards. No wonder you're his son."

While Sinew was wrestling with that, she added, "It's the other part he doesn't like, the thingness. You try to be less of a person and more of a thing because you think that's what he wants, but it's really the other way." Her voice softened. "Horn?"

"Yes. What is it?"

"Tell me. Tell us both. What does it take to make a person for you?"

I shrugged, although she may not have seen it. "I'm not sure; maybe I've never thought enough about it. Maytera Marble is a person, even if she's a machine. An infant is a person, even if it can't talk."

I waited for Seawrack to reply, but she did not.

"A while ago you said that it was talking for you. The sea goddess spoke to you. So she was a person no matter how large she was or how she looked, and I have to agree. Then you said that Babbie is a person. But Babbie can't talk. I don't know what to tell you."

Sinew asked, "Babbie's the hus?"

"Yes. Mucor gave him to me. I don't believe you've ever seen Mucor, but you must have heard your mother and me mention her many times."

"She could just sort of be there. Look out of mirrors and things."

"That's correct."

Seawrack said, "She sounds like me. Is she very much like me, Horn?"

"No."

Sinew asked, "Can she do that stuff?"

I was not quite certain that he was addressing me, but I said, "Do you mean Seawrack? I'm no expert on what Seawrack can do. If she says she can, she can."

"I can't," Seawrack told me, "but Mucor reminds me of me, just the same."

"In one way, I agree. Both of you have been very good friends to me."

Again almost whispering, Sinew said, "I've been hearing about Mucor ever since I was a sprat, only I thought she was just a story. You know? Way out here, she's real. When I was in town," (he meant New Viron) "somebody said you'd been to see the witch.

That was her, wasn't it? You went to see her like you'd go to see Tamarind."

"Yes."

"Babbie can talk," Seawrack insisted. "He talks to me and to you all the time, it's just that you hardly ever pay attention."

Babbie stood and shook himself, then lay down again with his broad, bristle-covered back against my legs and his head in my lap. I said, "Can you really speak, Babbie?" and felt his head move in reply.

"You think Krait is a—a monster, like an inhumi. I don't like him either, he's not nice, but he's a person."

Sinew asked her, "Is Krait the boy that looks like me?"

"Yes, our son."

I should have made some attempt to straighten that out, but I did not. The hisses and whisperings of water and wind closed around us once more while I sat silent and tense, waiting for Sinew to fly into one of his rages. The back of my neck prickled, and the left side of my face cringed under the regard of his unseen eyes.

"Father?"

"Yes. What is it?"

"About Mucor. Is she listening to us now?"

"I have no way of knowing. I suppose it's possible, but I doubt it."

"In your book—"

Confident that he had never read it, I remained silent; and eventually he began to explain what we had been talking about to Seawrack. "In the book, every so often Patera Silk would wonder if Mucor was around, so he'd call her. He'd say her name, and if she was there she'd answer some way. Ask him to do it now."

I was stroking Babbie's head; Seawrack's hand found mine there, and its lightest touch thrilled me. "Will you Horn? Do you want to?"

"No," I said. "If Sinew wants Mucor called, let him call for her himself."

Sinew was silent.

Seawrack told me, "Babbie's a person. Whether you know it or not, he is. So am I."

"I never doubted it."

"When you go away and leave us, Babbie will go into the trees looking for things to eat." Her fingers left mine as she pointed. "He talks now, and he picks up things to look at. You said "hind legs," and he does. He stands up when you tell him to, like to row."

I nodded. He had been invaluable at the sweeps.

"And he does anyway sometimes when he thinks we're not paying attention, so he can use his hands. When he goes into the trees, it will be a real person going in there. But he won't be a real person in there for very long."

I muttered, "If you and Sinew will wait for me in Wichote as I suggested, he could stay there with you. That would solve everything."

"With the sea singing down at the end of the water? I never have told you how it was for me when you died."

I heard Sinew's indrawn breath.

"I thought he was dead," she told him. "I was absolutely sure he was, so sure that I didn't dare to go near his body. I watched for a long, long time, and he lay so still and never moved once. When it got dark I went down to the beach and took off my clothes and threw them into the water, and talked to the little waves. And they came up the beach, up and up, washing my feet and legs. My knees. Pretty soon they were laughing over my head, and I couldn't drown."

Sinew choked and coughed.

"Do you like that meat?"

"It's good," he assured her politely, "but it takes a lot of chewing."

"Just bite it off and swallow. That's the best way."

None of us spoke much after that, or if we did, I have forgotten what was said.

When we had gone a little farther up the river and anchored in midstream for the night, Sinew called softly, "Mucor? Mucor?" I had never realized until then how much his voice resembled Krait's. (Perhaps I should have written, how very near Krait's it came in certain moods.)

Seawrack touched my knee and whispered, "He sounds just like you."

14

PAJAROCU!

I have been away from this untidy stack of manuscript a long while, and tonight I would like to make up for all of my neglect before I pack it away. In another week the rains should end, and they may end even sooner; I have been questioning the farmers in court, and all say they recall years in which the rainy season ended a week early. It is not completely inconceivable that it will end tonight, although the rain beats against my shutters at this moment with such violence that tiny droplets find their way through, a coarse mist that dribbles from the windowsill and wets the carpet. I have had to move my writing table to escape it.

I must be brief. There really is very little time left for all this.

When the rains end, Hari Mau will fall upon the enemy, a general advance by all our troops after a flanking action by the mercenaries. If he wins, we will win the war—and in fact the war will be effectively over. Hari Mau will be a hero, and I have seen enough of the whorl to know that everyone in Gaon will demand he rule. To give him his due, I do not think that he would kill me. I know him well; and there is nothing sneaking or ungrateful, and certainly nothing murderous, in his character. But I will be murdered by his friends, and everyone will be his friend.

(I remember how it was in Viron when we won.)

His friends will expect him to pardon them, and I would guess that they will not be disappointed. If we win, I will die.

If we lose, I will die equally; and in all probability by torture. In Han people die like that often. Why should the Man show me more mercy than he shows his own citizens? Thus I am doomed whether Hari Mau succeeds or fails. Nor is that all.

Our inhumi do as I ask because I have continued to free others, eighteen so far. When the war ends, I will have no use for them, and they will have no reason to wish me alive. With me dead, their precious secret will be safe. (Krait, who loved me and wanted so desperately for me to love him, can never have imagined that he was dooming me.) I have promised over and over to give them the locations of the remaining interments, which are concealed now by booths and the like. When I have done so, I will be as good as dead.

I have sent Evensong to buy a boat for me, telling her that it will be used by a spy whose identity I cannot reveal. When she has come back and the palace is asleep, I will go. I am still too ill to ride far, I fear; but I will be able to manage a small boat, or hope I will.

I will have to. How strange it will seem to be alone on a boat again. As though Green and the whole *Whorl* had never happened. Back on board a boat, and sailing down Nadi to the sea!

There is not time enough for me to re-read the earlier pages properly, but I believe I promised myself (and you, Nettle darling, if the Outsider someday grants my prayer) that I would not end this account before Sinew, Krait, and I went aboard the lander. That I would not end it, in fact, until we flew away from Pajarocu. I may not have time, however, if I continue to trace our way up the rivers.

No, I most certainly will not. Evensong may return from her errand at any minute. She can tell me where it is docked, and I will give her an hour to get to sleep. An hour at most, then I will leave Gaon forever.

So the lander first, and I will work my way backward from that as well as I can.

Krait, Sinew, and I had places on it. So did Seawrack, but Sinew and I had seen to it that she was not on board. We knew by then and had hidden weapons, he his hunting knife and I the two big, broad-bladed knives I had traded two silver pins for there in Pajarocu.

I should say, perhaps, that I had not bought them because I expected a fight on the lander at that time. (I assumed then that we would not board it.) I had gotten them, one for myself and one for Sinew, I thought, because I had resolved to get a knife of that type when I had found the floating tree and had been forced to chop it up with Sinew's hunting knife. At that time I had not seen the lander, and had only just recovered from the shock of my first sight of Pajarocu, which I had, in my pitiful ignorance, imagined would be a town like New Viron or Three Rivers. They had no guards, and plain, somewhat roughly fitted handles of dark brown wood; their blades were broad, but thin enough to be flexible. I had tied them together, one hanging down my chest and the other down my back, and the rough leather overtunic that He-pens-sheep had made for me hid them very well.

They were taken from me, and I got instead the ancient black-bladed sword with which I cleared the sewer of corpses—but all that is outside the scope of this account, unless I am permitted to continue it on my own paper, in my own mill, on Lizard.

May the Outsider grant it!

Tonight that seems too much to ask even of a god.

How the rain thunders against the roof and walls! Who would have believed that there could be so much water in the whorl?

Sinew had tied his hunting knife to his thigh under his trousers. To tell the truth, I believed that he had my old needler as well. I may as well admit that, which is the truth. I believed he had lied to me about it, as he had lied to me so often about so many other things; but the traveler who had taken our old boat and abandoned him far up the rivers had taken my needler as well. Neither Sinew nor I ever set eyes on him again, but we soon united in wishing that he had boarded the lander with us, and that he had retained his weapon—my needler—as we had urged all the men boarding the lander to do. He was a bad man without a doubt, an opportunistic adventurer more than ready to exploit those he called friends, and to leave them in the lurch the moment it appeared to his advantage; but most of the men on the lander were as bad or worse, and more than a few were much worse.

I must make that clear. Were the inhumi who controlled it monsters? Yes. But so were we.

The rain has stopped. After so many days of rain it seems uncanny, although it does not actually rain without cease during the rainy season. If the season has not ended, it will rain again in an hour or two; if it has, this may be the last rain we will see for months. I have thrown open all the windows, determined to enjoy the respite.

Oreb is back! I got up just now to have another look at the sky, and he landed on my shoulder, scaring me silly. "Bird back!" he said, as if he had been gone for an hour. "Bird back! Good Silk!" and "Home good!"

And, oh, but it *is* good. It is so very good to see him again, and to know that when I go I will not go alone.

After writing that last I got out my old black robe, the robe that Olivine stole for me and that His Cognizance Patera Incus persuaded me to wear when I sacrificed in the Grand Manteion. Will I be wearing it still when I arrive at New Viron to report my failure? It seems likely I will. I have my jeweled vest under it, and am going to keep my rings. They owe me those, at least.

Good luck, Hari Mau!

Good luck, all you good folk of Gaon! You are better than most peoples I have met, hardworking, cheerful, and brave. May Quadrifons of the Crossroads, and all other gods both new and old, smile on you. No doubt they do.

Having written that, I cannot help adding that the very same things might be said with equal justice about the people of Han.

They are argumentative and love to shout their displeasure at others (I have seen something of it in Evensong) but that does not mean they are vindictive, and in fact they are the exact reverse, quick to laugh and forgive everything and be friends again. They deserve a far better government than the Man's.

Will Hari Mau's be better? Beyond all question. But if Hari Mau is wise, he will appoint one of them the new Man, some leader whom everyone there respects, a kind and steady man, or even a woman, who has seen life and learned moderation and compassion. I should put that in the letter I am leaving for him, and I will.

Listen to Rajya Mantri, Hari Mau, but make your own decisions. Let him *think* that you confide in him.

Still no Evensong. I have been talking with Oreb, who has flown over this entire whorl—or says he has. When we fall silent I can hear Seawrack, faint and far, her voice keeping time with the beating of the waves.

Pajarocu is a portable town, as Wijzer said. I should say, rather, that it is a portable city, the shadow of the real City of Pajarocu, which must be somewhere in the *Whorl.* There are a few huts and a few tents; but they are not Pajarocu, and are in fact frowned upon. Let me explain what I mean, Nettle.

When you and I, with Marrow, Scleroderma and her husband, and all the rest came here, we looted the lander that had brought us and named the new town we hoped to build after the old city in which we had been born, and thereafter, for the most part, forgot it. (I remember very well how you and I had to rack our brains to recall the names of certain streets while we were writing our book; no doubt you do too.) We spoke of "Our Holy City of Viron," or at least our augurs did when they blessed us; but save for the fact that it was the center of the Vironese Faith, there was nothing particularly holy about it.

Things are very different with Pajarocu and its people. In the Long Sun Whorl, their city seems to have been not so much a city like Viron as a ceremonial center, the place where they assembled on holy days and feast days. Each of the Nine had his or her lofty manteion of stone, there was a processional road like our own Alameda, a vast public square or plaza for open-air ceremonies, and so on.

So attached to it were and are they that they have refused to duplicate it here on any lesser scale, although duplicating it on its original scale is still far beyond their reach. What they have done instead is to duplicate its *plan* to perfection—without duplicating, or attempting to duplicate, its substance at all.

There are "streets" paved with grass and fern between "buildings" and "manteions" that are no more than clearings in the forest marked in ways that are, to our eyes, almost undetectable. When the adult citizens we sought to question were willing to talk to us, they talked of gateways, walls and statues that did not in fact exist—or at least, that did not exist here on Blue—and described them in as much detail as if they loomed before us, together with colossal images of Hierax, Tartaros, and the rest, called by outlandish sobriquets and the objects of strange, cruel veneration.

But when the streets are too badly fouled or the river rises, this phantom Pajarocu goes elsewhere, which I think an excellent idea. Our own Viron was built on the southern shore of Lake Limna; when the lake retreated, our people clung to the shiprock buildings that Pas had provided when they ought to have clung to the idea that he had provided instead, the idea of a city by the lake. Many (although certainly not all) of Viron's troubles may ultimately have been due to this single mistaken choice.

Listen to me, Horn and Hide. Listen all you phantom readers. Buildings are temporary, ideas permanent. Rude as they are in so many ways, the people of Pajarocu understand it thoroughly, and in that respect they are wiser than we.

Since I have taken the time to characterize the people of Gaon and Han, let me do the same for the people of Pajarocu. You have seen them already in my words, since you have met He-pen-sheep and She-pick-berry. They are short for the most part and frequently bowlegged, dark and hard-featured, with piercing eyes and long coarse hair that is always black unless the years have done their work or they have shaved their heads, as many young men and boys do.

Seawrack complained that people in Pajarocu were forever talking, but compared with us they are actually rather silent. The adults never laugh unless they are talking to children, which made me think them humorless for a time—the exact reverse of the truth. They are muscular and agile, both the men and the women; and many are extremely thin, so that one sees their muscles as though the skin had been peeled away. There is a disease among them that causes the throat to swell. At first I believed it a disease of women only, because the first few sufferers I saw were all women; but He-hold-fire had it, as did various other men.

No doubt that is enough, and it may be too much; but I am going to add a few more items as they occur to me. In Viron, Nettle, we men wear trousers and you women gowns. In Pajarocu, women often wear trousers like men, and I was told that in the winter they never wear gowns. In good weather—and even in weather that you and I would think quite cool—a man may wear no more than a strip of soft greenbuck skin suspended from a thong, or nothing. Men and women bathe together in the river. I saw this on a day when the weather was warmer than it had been and the Short Sun shone brightly. Seawrack and I joined them, which only one little boy and the many strangers who thronged the town thought odd at all.

Oreb wanted something to eat, which gave me a fine chance to roam through this palace and make certain everyone is asleep. The only person I saw who was not was the sentry before my door. He was surprised at my black robe, I believe, but he showed it only by a slight widening of his eyes. If it were not for my wound, I would climb out the window when I take my departure, although it is hard to imagine that my own sentry will try to stop me.

If Evensong can climb up, I can climb down, surely, weak though I feel. I will leave my door locked, and they will think I am sleeping late. Very likely no one will venture to knock before noon, and by then I will be far away. When this account halts in the middle of a word, you are to understand that Evensong has returned with news of the boat that I sent her to buy.

No, I will have to wait a bit to give her time to get into bed and get to sleep.

"Bad thing!" says Oreb. "Thing fly!" So there are inhumi about, just as in Pajarocu. I do not believe they will attack Evensong, whom they all know. But what a thought! If only we protected one another, they would all be idiots or worse. As it is, they always get enough to keep them going.

I put my head out the window and tried to see them, although I would have been horrified if I had. The azoth is in my sash, next to Princess Choora. (I wonder how she likes her company?) No needler, but that should be more than enough. I am inclined to take my sword as well. I cannot cut firewood on a boat with the azoth—it would sink her at the first attempt. When I'm not using my sword, I can stow it on the boat, provided Evensong finds one for me. How I wish that I had the black-bladed sword the Neighbor gave me now!

I wish that I had been able to choose the boat for myself, too. Evensong's choice will be too large, almost certainly. Sinew crossed the western sea in a boat that would scarcely carry Nettle and me, with a few bales of paper.

If Evensong does not buy one at all, I will send somebody else tomorrow night. Jahlee? Old Mehman would surely be better. The inhumi do not understand such things, even when they make use of them.

My inhumi have done some good things for us. Cutting loose the barges to break that bridge on the upper river was masterly. The Man saw no risk in moving gravel for his new road by water; but his troopers, who were very hungry already, went hungrier still.

Starting rumors and sending false messages, too. We dug up two of them for that. It was only just.

They are cunning, but like all cunning people they put too much faith in cunning. That was how it was in Pajarocu, when they allowed me to inspect their lander, never dreaming that I was the one man in thousands who would recognize it as Auk's.

That is just how it has been here, at times. Three dead so far, Jahlee says, but she cannot know of all those whose lives have been lost.

In Pajarocu, I got my first warning from Seawrack. I woke and found her clinging to me and trembling. Whispering, I asked her what was wrong. "They're hunting the night." Her teeth were chattering so that she could scarcely speak. A bad dream, I thought, and many times the inhumi had seemed no more than a bad dream to me, so that I half expected Krait to vanish at sunrise. I tried to tell Seawrack that she had spent too many years under the sea, and that the creatures she had feared there could not reach her here.

Then I sat up, crawled out from under the foredeck, and looked around, hoping that she would join me and look too. I saw a man on one of the other boats some distance away; I thought I recognized him as one of those who had shown Seawrack, Sinew, Krait, and me through the lander the day before, and would have hailed him if I had not been afraid of waking others who were sleeping in their boats just as Seawrack and I had been sleeping in ours. He stooped and I heard a scuffle that quickly subsided; I supposed that it had been no more than the noise he had made taking off his boots, and told Seawrack there was nothing to fear.

The next day was the warm and sunny one I mentioned, and was a market day besides. She and I went out to have another look at the invisible town, and bargained for food and a few other things. Returning to the sloop we saw twenty or thirty men, and what appeared to be every woman and child in the town, swimming in the river. After stowing our purchases we joined them. Seawrack's missing arm and yellow hair attracted a great deal of attention, and the children (who were all good swimmers) were amazed to find that she, with only one arm, could swim much faster than the fastest of them.

One bright-eyed little boy of eight or nine asked whether I were her father. I declared that I was, and he informed me very firmly that foreign women were not permitted to take off their clothes. "Here lady yes." By pantomime he became a young woman, mincing along with hands on swaying hips, then pulled a nonexistent gown over his head. "You lady, no, no!" Arms folded, scowling.

It reminded me first of Maytera Marble, who had pulled off her habit to put it on Mucor, and afterward of Chenille, who had scandalized Patera Incus by going naked in the tunnels after she had been sunburned during Scylla's possession. I told the boy that some of our women did, and a little about both of them. He wanted to know where Maytera Marble and Mucor lived, and I did my best to explain that their rock was on the other side of the sea, which he had never seen.

"Big lady too?"

"Chenille? No, she and Auk went to Green. Or at least that's what we think must have happened, since no one in New Viron—that is my own town here—has gotten word of them. Do you understand what I mean by Green? It's that big light in the sky at night, and it's another—"

He had run away.

That was when I knew, the moment at which it came to me. I had recognized the lander earlier, as I have said. It had been one of the Crew's, and had differed in certain respects from those provided for Cargo, landers like the one in which we had come, being somewhat smaller and much better adapted to carrying large, nonliving loads. When we had been in Mainframe I had visited it twice with Silk and Auk, and there was no mistaking it. I had recognized it without understanding what its presence here signified.

But when the boy ran, I knew. I understood everything after that.

We went back to the market, which was smaller and less well organized than the one in Wichote, as well as substantially cheaper. A leather worker there was making a sheath for one of the knives I have described; I offered him a silver pin for the knife and its sheath when he had finished sewing it, and he suggested that I take another quite similar knife, whose sheath he had completed already.

In the end I bought them both, as you have read, intending to give one to our son.

A fellow foreigner approached us. "Meeting tonight at the Bush." I asked what and where the Bush was, and learned that it was an oversized hut near the river in which the local beer was sold and drunk. A man from one of the Northern towns had brought his wife so that she could sail his boat home, and compelled her to keep him company while he waited, as we were all waiting, for Auk's lander to fly. She had been asleep on her husband's boat last night while he sat drinking in the Bush, and had been bitten by an inhumu. Tonight we would decide his punishment.

I went that night, bringing Sinew; we stayed only long enough to have a look at the woman, who was indeed pale and weak (as well as bruised), and displayed the marks of an inhumu's fangs on her arm, and to ask her where her boat had been moored. As we returned to our own, Sinew said, "I thought that didn't happen here."

It puzzled me; I knew that as we had come nearer Pajarocu, Krait had flown there nearly every night, and I had certainly assumed that he was feeding there. I asked Sinew who had told him so.

"One of these people, when I was hanging around here before. I told him how I got bitten when I was just a baby, and he said they never did it here. His name is He-bring-skin."

I had already told Sinew how He-pen-sheep and his son had cut off the breakbull's head for me. Now I said, "It can't be true. When Seawrack and I visited He-pen-sheep's camp, his daughter had been bitten the preceding night. I don't recall her name, but she was extremely weak. Weaker than that woman back there."

"Only here in Pajarocu," Sinew explained impatiently. "They never get bitten here. That's what he said."

"But foreigners do."

"I guess. She did."

We had reached the sloop by then, and were greeted with a snort of pleasure by Babbie. Seawrack came out with her knife in her hand. I had told her to remain aboard and get some sleep if she could, although I do not believe she had actually slept. She asked whether I had seen the woman.

"Yes, and spoken to her, though not for long. She'll recover, or at least I believe she will."

"But you are not happy. Neither is Sinew, I think."

"You're right, I'm discouraged." Like old Patera Remora, I groped for a better word. "Humbled. Silk old me once that we should be particularly grateful for experiences that humble us, that humiliation is absolutely necessary if we're not to be consumed by pride. He was subjected to a shower of rancid meat scraps shortly after he came to Sun Street. Maybe I've told you."

She shook her head; Sinew said, "Sure, Scleroderma did it. You and Mother talked about it a lot."

"No doubt. Well, I can report that I'm in the gods' good books, since they've provided an unmistakable sign of their favor. I ought to be ecstatic, but I don't feel particularly ecstatic at the moment."

Seawrack kissed me. When we parted, I gasped for breath and said, "Thank you. That's much better." (I can feel her lips on mine as I write. Seawrack kissed me many times, but in retrospect all her kisses have merged into that one. It may have been the last—I cannot be sure.)

"I don't see why you're so down," Sinew muttered. "We're here, aren't we? Pajarocu? This is it. They kept stalling around when I was here before, but now they say they'll take off any day now."

"Providential," I told him bitterly. "It's almost as if they'd been waiting for us, isn't it?"

"You think so?" He grunted skeptically, or perhaps I should say thoughtfully. "Why should they?"

"Because there are three of us."

"Four, with Krait."

"Exactly. Four, if you count Krait, and three if you don't. Three of us risking our lives to bring back Silk, when only one of us was sent to do it. That's bad enough, and I haven't even begun to deal with that. What depresses me tonight is the quality of the rest, the nature of our companions-to-be. You saw them in there, and you must have seen a good deal of them when you spent a week here earlier. Tell me honestly—what do you think of them?"

Seawrack murmured, "They are not kind. Not like you."

"You're wrong about that," I told her. "I'm one of them, and that's the most depressing fact of all." (At that moment, I nearly confessed what I had once done to her in Sinew's hearing. Whoever has read this knows.)

He said, "What's the matter with them?" He was challenging me, as he had so often on Lizard.

"They're drinkers, brawlers, and troublemakers. That man you were with—he said he'd rescued you—the one who took our old boat. What was his name?"

"Yksin. When he was mad at me, he told me it meant *alone*. He was fixing to go off and leave me then, only I didn't know it."

"It's a good name for him, and it would be a good name for all of them. They're outcasts who believe that it's some failing in their fellow townsmen that has made them cast them out."

A moment later I smiled, and Seawrack said, "You've thought of something, what is it?"

It was that forty such men would be quick to seize control of the lander as soon as they suspected that it was not bound for the *Whorl*. But I did not tell her, then or ever.

Oreb has been pulling my hair. "Go now? Go Silk?" (Or perhaps it is "Go, Silk!" I cannot be sure.) I feel exactly as he does, but Evensong still has not returned. I am going to try to snatch an hour's sleep.

★

★ ★

The clock just struck. The hour is two, to the minute.

It has always been like this for me. Once I have decided to leave a place (as I decided, for example, to leave the hopeless little farm that had fallen our lot) I cannot wait to be away. No doubt I felt just the same way that night, as I sat before our fire in the sloop with Seawrack and Sinew, trying to put my thoughts in order.

Seawrack asked Sinew whether he was a drinker, a brawler, and a troublemaker, too; I doubt that she had any very clear idea of what those words represented. He grinned and said no to the first and yes to the others, adding, "Ask my father. He knows me." I did indeed, and that was when I decided not to give him the second knife, although I had gotten it for him, until he had need of it.

Seawrack wanted to know more about the woman who had been bitten; and I, needing desperately to speak to Sinew in private, suggested that he and I might be able to bring her back to our sloop so that Seawrack could talk with her in person, adding that she and Sinew might be able to help her in some way after the lander flew.

"No! We will be on it with you." She turned to Sinew. "Or will you stay?"

He shook his head. "I didn't come all this way to get left behind. When I was waiting here, I thought that if they were going to go and Father didn't come I'd go by myself and bring back Silk if I could. Only they didn't fly and didn't fly, and so I went looking for you."

I stood up. "We'll argue about this later. Meanwhile, Sinew and I are going back to the Bush and get her. We'll come back as soon as we can."

Sinew said, "She'll be looking after her husband. They're going to whip him or something."

I said, "It will be difficult, I know. That's why I'll need your help."

When we were some distance from the sloop, I halted in the shadow of a towering tree. "I can't make you obey me. I know that."

He nodded and glanced around suspiciously. "What are you whispering for?"

"Because it's just possible that Seawrack may have followed us. I doubt it, but I can't be sure, and it's very important that she not overhear us—that no one does, especially the inhumi; I have reason to think there may be inhumi about. Do you remember how He-hold-fire told us in the lander than nobody would be permitted to bring slug guns, needlers, or even knives? That no one was to bring so much as a stick?"

"Sure, but I'm hanging on to my knife just the same."

I hoped that he would not be going at all, but that was not the time to say it. "When he said that, I thought it a prudent precaution. I reminded myself that we would be a week or more on the lander. Clearly it wouldn't be unreasonable to suppose we might fight among ourselves. Now I know that what they have in mind is something much worse. Listen to me, Sinew. If you're ever going to listen to anyone in your life, listen now. That lander's not going back to the *Whorl.* It's going to Green."

I had expected him to ask what led me to think so, but he did not.

"It is controlled by inhumi, and it will go to Green unless I can redirect it with the help of the other men who'll be on it with me."

I waited for him to speak; when he remained silent I added, "You know that the inhumi fly here from Green. Maybe you also know that the passage is a very difficult one, and that many of those who try it are killed."

"Good."

"No doubt it is, but not for us. Not now. They like human blood; and because they do, they do their best to steer human beings to Green to supply it. Your mother and I have told you many times how Patera Quetzal deceived us. He was an inhumu, and he would have directed our lander to Green if he could, even though he himself was dying."

"It's in your book."

"As I said, the inhumi—other inhumi—control this lander. It must bring them from Green, and it must carry hundreds at a time. Then—"

"They trick us into getting on it and bring back a bunch of us." Slowly Sinew nodded. "Pretty clever."

Knowing his skepticism and stubbornness, I had thought that it would be practically impossible to convince him. I was weak with relief.

"There's a whole lot of inhumi around here, that's what I think. Maybe I should have said something sooner. I saw a bunch together one time when I was here before."

"You did?"

"Yeah, three. They didn't know I was there, so they weren't bothering to look like people. I watched for a while until one flew away. Then I got away myself and went looking for somebody, and I found He-bring-skin and said there's two inhumi over there, and if you'll give me a knife I'll help kill them. That's when he told me they didn't bite anybody—that was what he said—in Pajarocu."

"I see."

"He said they had a deal. They don't bother them here, and they don't bite. Father . . . ?"

"What is it?"

"You're going on their lander just the same?"

"Yes, I am. Krait and I will board it, as we have planned from the beginning."

I had promised that I would not betray Krait's secret and I did not, although I knew by then that Krait was betraying all of us. The memory of the pit, or perhaps only my twisted sense of honor, remained too strong.

"To me this is a high and holy mission," I told Sinew. "That hasn't changed. New Viron needs the things I've been sent to bring back very badly. Most of all, it needs someone like Silk."

"You'll get killed."

"Not if I can seize control of the lander—and I think I can." I paused, collecting my thoughts. "If I can, I'll have it in which to bring Silk back. When we return, I can order it to land at New Viron. What is even more important, the inhumi will no longer be able to use it to come here in relative safety, or to transport human beings to Green."

He shook his head and repeated that I would be killed.

"Perhaps, but I hope not. I said I couldn't make you obey me, and I can't. I know that. All that I can do is beg you to help me keep Seawrack off the lander. Will you do it?"

He swore that he would, and we shook hands; and after that I hugged him as I had when he was a child.

Evensong has returned!

Just a moment ago I heard the sentries at the main entrance challenge her, and her reply. Time presses.

Next day, Sinew and I circulated among the other travelers, telling them that we suspected that the lander might actually be bound for Green, and urging them to bring weapons they could conceal when they boarded. That night, he and I decided that the best plan would be for him to sail some distance down the river with her after telling us about a good place to gather wild berries. I would excuse myself at the last moment, saying (quite truthfully) that I had to bargain in the market for the food we would need on the lander.

Evensong has bought me a boat that sounds like it is exactly the sort I need. She smiled proudly as she described it, and even borrowed this quill and a sheet of paper so that she could sketch it for me, small enough for me to handle alone and even row if need be, with a little shelter like a hut at the waist, and a mast that can be taken down, or put up by one man to spread a small sail. It is newly painted, she says; crimson and black, which in Han are thought to be the luckiest colors.

Best of all, she said that she was very tired and asked if I would mind terribly if she slept in the women's quarters, offering to send Chandi or Moti to me if I wished. I said that I was half asleep already after having waited up for her. When Oreb croaked loudly, "Silk go!" I explained that he wanted me to go to bed.

A line or two more, but only a few.

They collected our weapons, promising to return them to us as soon as we reached the *Whorl*. I gave up the slug gun Marrow had given me, ignorant of the fact that the inhumi were arming their slaves to subdue the human settlers on Green and supposing that I had seen the last of it. Ironically, everything we had surrendered was loaded into one of the freight bays—exactly as promised.

I should have anticipated that some of us would believe the inhumi, and side with them. They were proud and stupid men, too proud and too stupid to believe that they could have been so badly deceived. Many, I would guess, had believed that the lander could not fly, and had hoped to loot its cards when it failed. When it took off, crushing us into our rough wooden cradles with a speed that seemed liable to persist long after we were dead, they were ripe to believe anything that He-hold-fire told them. The monitor, too, said we were bound for the *Whorl.*

The inhumi would not let us into the cockpit, as it was called on the Trivigaunti airship. I do not know what it should be called on a lander.

Yes, I do. Silk said Mamelta had called it the nose, and that is what you and I called it when we wrote, Nettle. We on the lander simply said "the front" or "up front."

There were three inhumi among us, besides Krait. They called themselves the first three travelers to reach Pajarocu, and said that He-hold-fire had put them in charge of us. One was the one I had seen on the other boat, I believe. I demanded to know why they would not let us into the nose one at a time. I should have killed him (it was he I was arguing with) but I hesitated until it was too late. He looked like a man, and I was still not certain I was correct. Krait pretended to side with me, which made me doubt my conclusions. I reproach myself now, as I should.

All this took longer than I have indicated—a day, at least.

Except for Sinew, the others thought I was insane, or most did. They offered to tie my hands, but those who had believed Sinew and me would not allow it.

But I am far past our leaving Blue already, and that was as much as I intended to write. Before I leave Gaon as well, I should explain that Sinew had cut the halyards while Seawrack was ashore picking berries, and returned to Pajarocu in his hollow-log boat, arriving in the nick of time to be taken on the lander, the final passenger to board it. My heart leaped for joy when I saw him and heard the airlock slam shut behind him. I am ashamed of that even now—I thought that he was going to his death and that we all were—but how glad, how very glad, I was to see him!

I feel sure that Seawrack made what repairs she could and that she and Babbie tried to sail the sloop back up the river. They must have arrived much too late, if indeed they arrived at all. She has returned to the sea now, for which I would be the last to blame her.

That is enough. The inhumi struck me, tearing my cheek with claws. Everyone knew after that, and Sinew stabbed him for it. I had forgotten how it was when Patera Quetzal died, although I would have sworn that I remembered everything. He appeared to be a human man still, for some time after his death agony.

The illusion is the last to die. I must bundle up this paper and put it into my bag at once. Good-bye, Nettle. Good-bye to all of you.

15

The Last Sheets

After what I wrote last night, what right do I have to take up the quill again? None, to be honest; but it will be two or three pages at most. I am going to write as long as we are in quiet water, but no longer. Evensong wants to trim the little sail and steer, and this is an opportunity for her to learn. (I am pretending not to watch her.)

Yes, she is with me, having deceived me most thoroughly and hidden herself in our little hut until we were well away from Gaon. "Good girl!" proclaims Oreb. "Clever girl," I tell him.

She knew what I planned when I sent her to buy this boat. I asked how she knew, and she said that if I had really intended it for a spy I would have had the spy buy it. I had no answer for that. She was right.

She bought it after a long search for the owner and a great deal of haggling, then stocked it with a variety of things she felt we might need: blankets and even pillows, wine, a lot of simple food, and cookware. We have no box of sand in which to build a fire, but as long as we remain on the Nadi we should be able to land somewhere.

"Good boat," proclaims Oreb every few minutes. It is, small and slender (almost too slender) and quick to answer the helm, a boat for fast travel, not for freight; but we have no need to carry fifty or a hundred thick bales of paper. Babbie, Seawrack, Krait,

Sinew, and I would sink it; but we are but three, and Oreb takes up very little room.

What Nettle will make of Evensong—or make of me for bringing her home with me—I cannot conceive; and yet I am very glad that she is here. I have told her several times (too many, she says) that I am not the ruler of New Viron. She said she always wanted to be a farmer's wife. I explained that I am no farmer, that I tried farming and failed at it, that my wife and I have built a mill where we make paper. And she told me that was even nicer.

What more can I do or say?

All this reminds me of what Seawrack told Sinew—that she was my travel wife. It shocked him as nothing else did; so I was glad that she had said it, even though I was terrified that he would repeat it to Nettle. Outsider, you great and mysterious god behind all the gods, grant that he does someday. It will mean that he has come home.

Are the gods merely farther from us here? Or is it the Vanished Gods—those of the Vanished People—who rule here, as Sinew theorized?

Or are there no gods here on Blue at all, as so many of us are beginning to assume? Sinew may merely have been trying to discomfit me; it was something he did almost as much as Krait, and rather more skillfully. Even so, he may have been correct. Silk once said that the Outsider was so far from us that he was always both behind and beyond us.

Or at least, that is the sort of thing Silk would have said; I cannot remember his actually saying it, although he may have.

In Gaon, they love racing their horses above all other amusements, and I watched them race whenever it seemed to be expected I would. The harrowed course they gallop along is shaped like an egg, so that we distinguished spectators who had the best view of the start had the best view of the finish, as well. For a short race they gallop around the egg once, but for a longer race, it may be two, three, four, or even five times. Imagine then an eternal race, in which we run on such a track, observed by gods. The god we see before us is not the god nearest us. The god nearest us is the one we have only just left behind.

And whether we realize it or not, it is he to whom we run.

Perhaps Silk would mean something like that.

I have been looking at the sky. I don't think I have ever seen a clearer, brighter blue since I came to Gaon. By the favor of the Outsider, Green and the stars (and the *Whorl*, too) are covered by this lovely cerulean impalpability during the day, so that we cannot see outside.

So that we can go about our daily business and not be afraid.

Where Pas used rock, the Outsider uses this and lets us look out on clear nights; and that is the difference between them.

We have lines, hooks, long cane poles, sinkers and bobbers, and even a landing net. It appears that the previous owner used this boat for fishing, mostly. I have baited my hook with a scrap I pulled from the meat Evensong bought, and we shall see.

"May Scintillating Scylla and all the gods smile upon you, my daughter," I told Evensong a moment ago. It is Scylsday; and I am an augur of Viron once more, at least in appearance, having left off my headcloth and shortened my hair with Choora. I never went to the schola, but I heard so much about it as a boy that at times I feel I did, for a year or three at least, long, long ago.

My father wanted me to help him in his shop, and to keep it when he died. I intended to do anything in the whorl except that—yet something very much like it came to pass, just as he wished. Some god favored him.

I made Sinew help me in the mill as my father made me help him, and Sinew resisted and resented me in exactly the same way. The time will come, Sinew, when it will all come back to you, the gears and shafts and hammers, and the paddles churning in the big tank of slurry, and you will be very glad indeed that you knew them once.

My father stayed behind to fight for General Mint. I would

never have believed that he had a drop of courage, going to his little shop on Sun Street day after day, always hoping to clear enough to feed his family and to keep his resentful eldest son in the palaestra.

His ungrateful, purblind oldest son. What my father did required no courage at all. So I believed.

Yet he went off to war, balder than I have ever been but smiling, with his new slug gun and his stiff canvas bandoleer of cartridges; war must have seemed very easy after all he had been through. When our roads crossed again before Hari Mau and his friends carried me off to Gaon, I did not even recognize him. Then Quadrifons whispered, "Those are the years you see. Look past them."

And I knew him at once. I wanted to say, "Where you were, I have been, Father," but I knew he would reply, "Where I am, you will quickly be, Son," whether his lips uttered those words or not. Knowing it, I lacked the courage to speak.

Wijzer warned me.

Work hard, Sinew. Work well and wisely. Live free if you can, and live so that you will not be ashamed, as I am at times, to look back on what you have done.

Your grandfather was no hero. He was the kind of man who slept in the rain with Hari Mau and me on the marches of Han, too wet, too tired, and too hungry for heroics. No hero, but when our trumpets rang and the Hannese kettledrums thundered I saw men like him firing and chambering a fresh round and firing again, out in front of the flag.

He has married a second time, and begun a new family. I have small half brothers I have never seen.

Caught one! A good one, I believe. I have run a long string through its gills and put it back into the water just as we do on Lizard.

Just as I did on the sloop with the bluebilly Seawrack chivvied until it jumped aboard.

We have passed beyond the tilled fields of Gaon, which means that I can stop worrying about being recognized; I saw the last cart drawn by the last carabao some time back. Nadi is gentler here, although not yet stagnant or sullen. She is like a woman who sings at her work.

Evensong keeps us to the middle, or wherever the current is strongest, leaning her slight weight this way or that against the steering oar. "Good boat," Oreb repeats; and then "Fish heads?" The banks are lined with trees so tall that I cannot catch sight of the summits of the mountains, trees that might almost be the savage trees of Green, although it may be only that the summits are lost in mist. Just before the fish bit, I saw something better, a felwolf that had come to the river to drink.

This is such a beautiful whorl that my poor gray quill falls silent from shame when I try to write about it.

This quill is exactly like the ones I used to tie in bundles of thirteen for my father, binding each bundle tightly but not too tightly and knotting the soft blue twine. I wish I had seen the bundle before Evensong cut it for me and put the quills into the old pen case I brought here.

We sold pen cases like this one, too, of course. I remember going into the little shed of a manufactory where they were made with my father and watching two women there smearing the leather and the pressboard cases with glue, and the waxed wooden forms they were put into until the glue dried. We could have brown or black, the man who employed those women told us, or any other color that we wanted, even white. But we had better keep in mind that the pen case would soon be stained with ink. It was best, he said, to choose a dark color, so that the ink stains would not show.

My father ordered black (like the one I am writing on), yellow, and pink. I thought he was being very foolish, but the yellow and pink ones sold first, bought by the mothers of little girls at our palaestra.

Why do we wage war, when this whorl is so wide? I believe it is because rulers such as I was in Gaon live in towns. There are so many people: a great number. So many farms: a smaller number, but still very great. People and houses, and animals that are in fact slaves, although we do not call them slaves.

(Marrow did not call his clerk a slave either; nor were the men who carried his apples and flour to my sloop called slaves.)

Buying and selling. Selling and buying, and never looking at the trees of the forest, or the side of the mountains. If we were wise, we would give the rulers of all the towns a stick and a knife apiece, and tell them we will be happy to take them back when they have traveled around this whorl, as Oreb did.

I can describe a tree or a felwolf, but not Blue. A poet might describe it perhaps. I cannot.

With nothing better to do than fish and catalogue the slow changes of the river, I have been thinking about my sons—about Krait on the lander, particularly. They caught him and forced open his mouth. I saved him, and thought that I had lost him forever when he joined the other inhumi barricaded in the cockpit. I wish that he were here now, here in this little boat with Evensong and me.

Evensong asks if it will be all right to stop when she sees a clearing. She wants to prepare my fish for us and cook some rice, she says. If I am any judge of women, she really wants to try the pots and pans she bought for us, enough to cook for all the men on Strik's big boat. In any case, I said she might; it will be hours before she sights the perfect spot, I feel sure, and we will both be hungry.

Babbie was my slave, no doubt. I could have led him to the market and sold him. But he did not object in the least to his slavery, and in that way freed himself by freeing his spirit. He was my slave, but he could have escaped any time when we were on the river, simply by jumping into the water and swimming to shore. For that matter he could have escaped even more easily on any of the many occasions when I left him to guard the sloop. He never liked being left alone, but he protected the sloop as instructed just the same.

He was my slave, but in his heart we were companions who shared our food and helped each other when we could. I could see farther and better, although he may not have realized that; he could run and swim much faster, and hear better, too. He possessed a more acute nose. I could talk; and despite what Seawrack said, Babbie could only communicate. It did not matter. He was stronger than I, and a great deal braver; and we were there to support each other, not to boast of our superiorities. What would he think of Oreb, I wonder?

And what would Oreb think of him? Good thing? Good hus?

Is this, my Oreb whom I love, my Oreb who has returned to me after more than a year, the true Oreb? Is this really the tame night chough I played with as a boy, waiting in Silk's sellaria for well-deserved punishment that never came?

"Oreb, why did you come back to me?" I asked him.

"Find Silk."

"I'm not Patera Silk, Oreb. I've told you—and everybody—that over and over." I ought to have asked him to find Silk for me, but I feel sure he could not unless he discovered some way to return to the *Whorl*, and I do not want to lose him again. "Where did you go, Oreb?"

"Find god."

"I see. Passilk? I think that's what the surgeon called him. Did you find him, and is that why you returned to me?"

"Find Silk."

"You are free, you know. Patera Silk wouldn't cage you, and I won't either. All you have to do is fly off into these trees."

"Fly good!" He flew from my shoulder to Evensong's and back, a graphic demonstration.

"That's right," I told him, "you can fly, and it's a wonderful accomplishment. You can soar above the clouds on your own, exactly like we did on the Trivigaunti airship. I envy you."

"Good boat!"

I offered to take over the steering and give Evensong a chance to rest, if she would tend my pole; but she refused. "You won't stop no matter how pretty the place is, and I'm hungry."

"You're never hungry," I told her. She must be hungry at times, surely, and she was very hungry the first time we spoke with Hari Mau's Hannese prisoners; but she never talks about how hungry she is, or admits it when I ask. Set a roast fowl before her, and she will accept a wing, clean the bones until they shine, and announce herself satisfied.

How green everything is after the rains!

We have stopped here to cook our fish and rice, and have decided to travel no farther today. We left Gaon before shadeup, and are not likely to find another place as pleasant as this if we travel on. It is a tiny island now, an isle I will call it, although I feel sure it must have been part of the riverbank before the rains. The river must cover it from time to time and drown any trees that try to take root on it; there is only this soft green grass, spangled with little flowers of every imaginable color that bloom the moment the rainy season ends and set seed in a wink.

I have been studying them, my nose four fingers from the soft, rich soil that nourishes them. To say that they are simply purple and blue would be quite false; they are every shade of both and more besides, some as blue as the sky, and some as purple as evening flowing over the sea. And red as well (various tinctures of red, I ought to say), yellow, orange, white, off-white, and even a dusky russet. Pink and yellow are the most attractive of all colors; the women who bought those pen cases were right.

I look at Evensong sleeping, and think again: yellow and pink are the most beautiful of colors. We cooked and ate, and made love among the flowers. I will catch another fish or two for her while she sleeps. We will eat a second time under the stars, and sleep. Rise early and travel on. I wish I could be certain that New Viron is on the coast of the sea to which this Nadi of ours runs. I believe it must be, but I cannot be sure.

16

NORTHWEST

Oreb has rejoined me. Somehow that has made it possible for me to sit down here and rub my feet, and write as long as these few sheets last. I will not begin this entry by telling you where I am or how things stand with me. I do not know where I am—or how anything stands with me.

The sun had scarcely set when I felt their wings. I write "felt" because one cannot really hear them. They make no more noise when they fly than owls. Looking up, I saw two, so high that they were in sunlight although the Short Sun's light had vanished from our isle. "Bad things," Oreb solemnly declared them. "Things fly."

"You're right," I told him, "they are indeed evil beings. But they're bringing good news. Hari Mau has fallen upon the enemy." The inhumi came looking for me, pretty clearly, as soon as the Hannese broke.

"This is very bad." Evensong shook her head; she may have been frightened—no doubt she was—but her impassive face showed nothing.

"This is very good," I told her. "It means you can go back home to your parents in Han."

"No!"

Trying to sound gentle I said, "I married Nettle before you were born, and married half a dozen other women before you were given to me by the Man. You owe me nothing at all. In fact, it is

I who owe you, and I owe you a great deal." I began pulling off my rings.

"I am your only wife!" She shook her little fist.

"You know that isn't true."

"Where are the others, Rajan? You cannot show them to me!"

I dropped my rings into her lap, and refused them when she tried to give them back.

After a great deal of shouting, she put them into a pocket in the sleeve of her gown, saying, "Maybe it's a long way to New Viron and we will need these."

I agreed, but thought to myself that it was an even longer way from New Viron to her family in Han. When she decided to go back there, as I felt certain she would before long, she might have to buy passage on a dozen boats.

Aloud I said, "Good. Thank you for accepting them. I want you to take these too." I gave her Choora and my short sword. "We may have to fight before the night is over, and you can fight better than I with those. I have my azoth." I may have tapped its jewel-studded hilt confidently—the Outsider, at least, knows how hard I tried to—but I felt very weak and ill at that moment.

"I have seen that sword. It has no blade."

I told her she might see its blade, too, before shadeup; and that she would not enjoy the sight.

"Bad fight," Oreb croaked.

I knew that he was right; they would wait until they were so many they felt confident of victory and rush us when we least expected it. Since it was not blood but my death they wanted, some might well have needlers and other weapons.

As we embraced beside the fire, Evensong whispered, "You know their secret. You could destroy them."

"Yes. I couldn't kill them here and now, if that's what you mean; but I know how they might be returned to the mere vermin that they once were—mindless, hideous, blood-drinking animals seeking their prey in Green's jungles."

I stared into the embers of the fire that we felt we could not let die, remembering the time that Krait had crept out of the nose, how we had embraced and wept (his tears of pale green slime that stained my tunic) while the other passengers slept.

"Father . . . ? Horn . . . ?" His breath still smelled of blood, Tuz's, as I learned a few minutes later.

I sat up, thinking in confused way that Sinew had become Krait, or Krait Sinew.

"They sleep. I wanted to warn you."

"Krait? Is that you?"

"Your sentries. I bit one." Krait's voice betrayed his uncertainty.

"I understand, and if it was one of the sentries, he deserved it, and worse. But Krait—"

"Ours too. We—we can't do it, Father. We don't have the discipline."

"And you're ashamed of that, as you should be. Well, neither do we, apparently."

"He-hold-fire, He-take-bow, and He-sing-spell stand guard for us because we make them. But when it's quiet and everyone else sleeps—"

One of my sleeping men had stirred. For a while neither Krait nor I dared speak.

"If you could break in suddenly . . ."

"We'll try—but Krait, you're risking your life just to tell me. I'm not sure I could get them to turn you loose again."

I believe he shrugged; the Short Sun was nearly dead ahead then, and in the near darkness of Number One Freight Bay it was difficult to be sure. "There are only two needlers, and I've bent some needles in one."

Evensong shook my shoulder. "You must tell me."

"I won't break my oath. My son confided it to me as he lay dying. If I were to betray him now, I would have to die, too, because I couldn't live with myself."

"Then say as much as you can." She had never asked that before.

"About him? He was an inhumu. We called him Krait, and Seawrack and I called—"

"That is the woman who sings?"

"Yes, though she is not singing now." I tried to collect my thoughts.

"It was a mere lie at first, Evensong. Something to tell people in Wichote and Pajarocu who wanted to know why Krait was with us. It remained a lie as long as there was no danger to Krait but me, and none to me but Krait. Once the lander took off everything changed, and Krait and I discovered that we merely supposed we had been lying."

"Hold me."

I was already, but I held her more tightly. "We were in the freight compartments. They had never been intended for passengers; but they could be pressurized, I suppose because the Crew might have to transport animals at times, and of course the inhumi had to keep us alive or we were of no value. They controlled the forward part of the lander, with three human slaves from Pajarocu who were supposed to be operating it. The slaves had slug guns, and the inhumus had needlers, some of them."

I waited for her to ask me about Pajarocu, but she did not.

"Krait tried to divert the lander to the *Whorl*, but he couldn't—it was already too late. He promised me that Sinew and I would not be drained. On Green they have thousands of human slaves whose blood they take only rarely, as long as the slaves can work and fight for them."

Evensong trembled in my arms.

"Krait told me why they have to have it as he lay dying. He didn't intend to give me power over them, you understand. I'm certain he wasn't thinking of that in his final moments. He was thinking of the thing that linked him to me, and me to him—of the bond of blood between us."

She said nothing.

"For a long, long time I didn't realize what he had done either. If I'd understood the power of Krait's secret while Sinew and I were on Green, things might have gone differently."

"No cry," Oreb urged me from my knee.

"I'm sorry, I can't help it. Perhaps . . . Perhaps I did realize it. But Krait's death was so recent then, and I felt that I'd be betraying him. Before I knew it, it was too late." Under my breath I added, "I still feel I'm betraying him, in a way."

Evensong murmured, "Tell me. You must tell me, my husband. My only ever lover. You must tell me tonight."

"Once I watched some men who had a wicker figure of the wallowers they were hunting. Two walked inside it, while two others hid behind it. That's the kind of thing the inhumi must have done before the Vanished People reached Green—reshaped themselves to look like the animals they hunted, disguised their odor by smearing themselves with the excrement of their prey, and uttered the same cries, moving as their prey did until they were close enough to strike."

They were uttering our own human cries at that moment, or something like them, talking among themselves in the air, their voices faint, pitched high, and floating. I wondered whether they could hear me.

"If only we cared about each other sufficiently. If only all of us loved all the others enough, they would go back to that. We would still think them horrible creatures, and they would still be dangerous, as the crocodiles in this lower river water are. But they would be no worse."

"That is the secret, what you said?"

"No. Of course not."

They were circling above us, I knew, and sometimes they flew so low that I could actually feel the wind from their wings upon my face. I decided that they might well overhear anything we said, and I counseled myself to keep that in mind each time I spoke.

"You must tell me!" Evensong demanded.

"I must not—that is the truth, the fact of our situation. They know that I know; I've proved it to them. They also know that you don't, that you know where the others are buried but do not know the secret they would die to protect. They have to kill me, or feel that they do, even though I've sworn never to reveal it."

She started to protest and I silenced her with a kiss.

When we parted, I said, "They don't have to kill you, not as things stand. In fact, if they killed you like that, without reason, I would consider myself free to speak out about them." It was a lie, and may have been the last that I will ever tell, the final lie of so many thousands. I hope so.

For a while we tried to sleep; but I, at least, could only stare up at the flying inhumi I glimpsed at almost every breath between Green's shining disk and ourselves. After an hour or more I stood up and called out to them (addressing them as Jahlee, Juganu, and so forth) in the hope that we could come to some agreement under which they would spare us. They neither replied nor came to our fire, although I invited them to. There seemed to be about twenty at that time.

Eventually we went back to the boat and lay down in its little hut of plaited straw, leaving our fire to die. Evensong fell asleep almost at once. I prayed, not on my knees as I felt I should (the hut was too low for that) but lying on my back next to her. Every so often I crawled outside with my azoth, looked up the sky, fingered the demon, and crawled back into the hut as before. Tired as I was (and I was very tired, having slept for only an hour that afternoon), I was striving to convince myself that I was protecting us—protecting her—in some unclear way.

That I was not, I was well aware. By not returning to Gaon the moment I discovered she was on board, I had put her into deadly danger; and my presence kept her there.

After a time that seemed long to me, three or four hours I would guess, when I was practically asleep, too, I heard myself calling Babbie.

Certain that I had been dreaming and had spoken aloud in a dream that I could no longer remember, I rubbed my eyes and rolled onto my hands and knees. The inhumi had gone. I had no idea how I knew that, but I knew it with as much certainty as I have ever known anything.

I crawled out of the hut. Our little fire had sunk to a glow so faint that I would not have seen it if I had not known where to look. Oreb was gone, too, and I was afraid that the inhumi had killed him.

Someone on shore called again for Babbie, and I understood that he meant me; it never so much as occurred to me then that I had sometimes been called "Silk" or "Horn." He who called me seemed quite near, and he called me with more urgency than Seawrack ever has. I searched the shadows under the closest trees for him without result.

I had on my trousers, with Hyacinth's azoth in the waistband, and I got my tunic as well and the augur's black robe that Olivine had found in some forgotten closet for me; I left behind stockings, boots, sash, and the jeweled vest. For a moment I considered taking back my dagger and the sword that I am still too weak to use, but the voice from the forest was calling to me and there was no more time to waste upon inessentials. I waded ashore and set off through the forest at a trot. I have the pen case on which I am writing and this rambling account of my failure, with a few other possessions, because they were in the pockets of my robe.

Oreb has been urging me to rise and walk, and in a moment I will. It may be that we are lost. I do not know. I have been trying to go northwest, that being the direction in which I think New Viron must lie, and I believe that I have succeeded pretty well.

★

★ ★

Another halt, and this one must be for the night—a hollow among the roots of (what I will say is) just such a tree as we had on Green. It is what we call a very big tree here, in other words. I will write, I suppose, as long as the light lasts; I have three (no, four) more sheets of paper. The light will not last long, however, and I have no way to start a fire and nothing to cook if I did. The last time I ate was at about this time two days ago with Chota. I am not hungry, but am afraid I may become weaker.

If the inhumi find me here and kill me here, then they find me here and kill me. That is all there is to it.

Good-bye again, Nettle. I have always loved you. Good-bye, Sinew, my son. May the Outsider bless you, as I do. In the years to come, remember your father and forget our last quarrel. Good-bye, Hoof. Good-bye, Hide. Be good boys. Obey your mother until you are grown, and cherish her always.

I found him in the forest, sitting in the dark under the trees. I could not see him. It was too dark to see anything. But I knelt beside him and laid my head upon his knee, and he comforted me.

★

★ ★

It has been four days, I believe, and could be five. I stumbled upon a hovel (I do not know what else to call it) in the forest. Two children are living alone there: they call each other Brother and Sister, and if they have ever had other names they do not know them. They showed me where they had buried their mother.

They took us in and shared what food they had, which was very little. They collect berries and fruits, as Seawrack used to, and Brother hunts with a throwing stick. At first they wanted to kill Oreb; afterward he entertained them.

With their knife—a sharp flint—I cut a likely stick and made a fishing spear like the one that He-pen-sheep's son had used. Brother took me to the stream from which they got their water, and I was able to spear fish for them. "You must stand very still," I cautioned him. "Make no noise at all until the fish come near enough, and don't move a muscle. Then strike like lightning."

My own lightning days are past, I suppose, if they ever came at all. I missed, and Brother laughed (I was laughing too) and ran away. Sister came and watched wide-eyed, and I speared a fish for her that we both called big, although it was not. A little farther down there was a good big pool, and there I speared another. I let her try after that, and she got two, one of them the largest of the four we caught. Brother had taken a bird almost as big as Oreb, so we had a feast.

In that way whole days flew past. I cut Sister's long, dark hair and wove a little cord of it, and set a snare along a game trail the boy showed me, recalling the demonstration snare that Sinew made years ago to show Nettle, in which he had caught our cat.

When I left yesterday they followed me, but this morning they are gone. I hope they get home safely, and to tell the truth I was afraid I would draw the inhumi to them, although I have seen none since that terrible night on the Nadi.

Very little paper remains.

★

★ ★

Last night I dreamed that Pig, Hound, and I ran into an abandoned house to get out of the rain. It seemed familiar, and I set off to explore it. I saw a clock—I think the very large one that stood in the corner of my bedroom in Gaon—and the hands were on twelve. I knew that it was noon, not midnight, although the windows were as black as pitch. I turned away, the clock opened, and Olivine stepped out of it. "This is where you lived with . . . This is where you lived with Hyacinth," she told me. Then Hyacinth herself was beside me in sunshine. Together we were chopping nettles from around the hollyhocks. Hyacinth was fourteen or fifteen, and already breathtakingly lovely; but in some fashion I knew that she was terribly ill and would soon die. She smiled at me and I woke. For a long time the only thing I could think of was that Hyacinth was dead.

It has faded now, somewhat; and I am writing this by the first light coming through the leaves.

*

* *

I have re-read most of this. Not all, but most. There are many things I ought to have written less about, and a few about which I should have written more. Hari Mau's smile, how it lights his face, how cheerful he is when everything is bad and getting worse.

Nothing about the first days of the war, before I was wounded. Or not nearly enough.

Nothing about my dream of an angry and vindictive Scylla who talked like Oreb, the dream that woke me screaming and so terrified Brother and Sister: "Window! Window! Window!"

Nothing about the fight on the lander, and how horrible it was. The inhumi had barricaded themselves in the nose, Krait and the rest. We had to fight the ones who still believed—half a dozen. Eight or nine, I think, really. (Some wavered, coming and going.) We tried to reason with them, but won over only two. In the end we had to rush them to prevent them from joining the inhumi, and I led the rush. They were as human as we, and they may have been the best of us.

Brave, certainly. They were extremely brave, and fought with as much courage and determination as any men I have ever seen. They died thinking they were on their way back to the *Whorl*, and to this moment I envy them that.

If only Sinew had stayed with Seawrack as I had told him, I would have let the others fight, taking no part. He was there and would know, so I played General Mint for an audience of one, kicking off and hurtling toward them, yelling for him and the others to follow me, a big knife in each hand. I was so frightened afterward that I could not sleep, and by the time we broke into the nose it was too late anyway and we were bound for Green irrevocably.

Brother and Sister should have made me feel younger, as the girl did. I felt old instead. So much older! They see the Vanished

People sometimes, they told me. Sometimes the Vanished People even help them. That is good to know.

I asked them about the Vanished Gods. They said there was one in the forest, so I told them about him. And a lot more, things that I should keep to myself. I tried to teach them how to pray, and found that they already knew although they did not have the word.

This is the last sheet.

Saw my own reflection standing in the water holding up my spear, wild white hair and empty socket, lined and worried old face. My wives in Gaon cannot have loved me, although they said they did. Chandi—it means "silver." Chandi was playing politics, I know, yet it is no small thing to have a woman as beautiful as Chandi say she loves you.

"I'm old now, and soon must leave you, But a fairer maid I ne'er did see. Curse me not that I bereave you, I cannot stay, no more would she. These fair young girls live to deceive you, Sad experience teaches me." I hope the Hannese girl gets home safely, and is welcomed by her family.

Little space left. I am ashamed of many things I have done, but not of how I have lived my lives. I snatched the ball and won the game. I should have been more careful, but what if I had been? What then?

Printed in the USA
CPSIA information can be obtained
at www.ICGtesting.com
LVHW041432140724
785451LV00019B/62

9 780312 872571